Delta Blues

EDITED BY
Carolyn Haines

TYRUS
BOOKS

Published by
Tyrus Books
1213 N. Sherman Ave. Unit 306
Madison, WI 53704
www.tyrusbooks.com

Printed in the United States of America
14 13 12 11 10   1 2 3 4 5 6 7 8 9 10

9781935562061 (paperback)
9781935562078 (hardcover)

For David Thompson
and McKenna Jordan,
whose love of books and mysteries
has touched the lives of writers
all over the world

Acknowledgments

This is my first effort at editing an anthology, and it's been both rewarding and surprising. First, I want to thank the most generous contributors to this collection. These authors wedged time to "do a story" into an already over-loaded schedule, and they did it with ultimate professionalism. Every time a story came in, I had the delight of reading something wonderful and fresh about a musical form and a place that I love. I met characters who are unforgettable, and I took journeys that are forever now a part of who I am.

Bill and Francine Luckett, the Luckett Tyner Law Firm staff, the management of Ground Zero Blues Club, and Morgan Freeman are also owed a huge debt of thanks. "Above and beyond" is the only way to describe their help with this book.

Tyrus Books is a rare gem in the realm of publishing. Benjamin LeRoy and Alison Janssen, the publishers, are an amazing duo. It's been an honor to work with them.

As always, my agent Marian Young has been a source of support and encouragement. She's patiently listened to me sing the blues for years—thank goodness I now have something to show for it.

And special thanks go to the booksellers and readers who make this kind of collection possible.

Foreword

Delta soil is deep and rich. Down here *things grow.* When the alluvial soil washes over the land by the Mississippi River, cotton, corn, and soybeans take root and jump up. You see, as the water runs slow the heavy particles settle, and only the finest elements are deposited along the banks at the mouth of the river. This loam contains not just minerals, but the blood, sweat and pain of countless souls. While a few acquired great wealth, many broke their backs for little pay, or none at all.

And because of that, other things grow here too. The seed of imagination spouts powerful story tellers who, like their *griot* forebearers, use both words and music to create tales rooted in the old traditions, yet completely their own. Stories of lust, betrayal, loss, bad choices, revenge, heartache and heartbreak, but also grand hyperbole and dark humor. In this land a unique American form of music was born, a rootstock strong enough to spawn many derivatives. The Mississippi Delta is ground zero of the blues, meaning it was here where it all began.

This collection of short fiction captures both the art of the tale and the power of the blues, and is a nod at the human condition that often inspires musicians to write and sing the blues. These stories tell about bad men and bad women who sometimes do good—or sometimes follow their true nature. Some of these characters know all about the dangers of making a bargain with the devil. And some know the power of redemption. These are characters who would not be out of place in a Honeyboy Edwards tune, and would be right at home alongside the desolate wail of Clarksdale, Mississippi, native Son House—

Looked like 10,000 were standin' 'round the buryin'
   ground
You know I didn't know 1 loved her til they damn laid
   her down

Lord, have mercy on my wicked soul
I wouldn't mistreat you baby, for my weight in gold.

In the preface of his book *The Land Where the Blues Began,* Alan Lomax notes that "the blues has always been a state of being as well as a way of singing." He goes on to quote Leadbelly as saying, "When you lie down at night, turning from side to side, and you can't be satisfied no way you do, Old Man Blues got you." And as Leadbelly himself knew all too well, those dark moments can lead to very dark thoughts, and even darker acts. As Howlin' Wolf said of that same feeling, "That's evil. Evil is goin' on."

This music is the rootstock for all forms of American music from jazz to rock, not to mention the gritty (and often violent) narrative tradition it shares with the best of contemporary rap. Off this hardy, adapting Delta vine grew Chuck Berry, Led Zeppelin and the Rolling Stones. This land, which has seen so much wealth and so much poverty, is where it all began, in the heat and humidity of the Mississippi Delta cotton fields.

The story told by the blues is one of loss and suffering, bad luck and trouble, and joy and excitement as well. My grandmother kept me out of the juke joints during my youth calling them "buckets of blood." Hard times, yes. But also hard rhythms, hard liquor, and "doin' the mess-around." Howlin' Wolf sang about fire, death, crime, and of course evil, but he also said, "We gonna pitch a wang dang doodle all night long." *That's* the blues.

Those same elements, both contradictory and complementary, illustrate many of the stories in this volume.

Like the blues, these tales move and shift over the character of human nature. They combine an element of crime or noir with the world of the blues. A partnership that is easy to understand. Both are messy, and they both tell about pain.

The South, and Mississippi in particular, has a long tradition of nurturing talented writers. But a writer doesn't have to be born or live in the Pine Barrens or the Delta to feel this particular love of character and story. Writers, just like blues players—and blues lovers—come from all over the world. These stories, written by some of the finest authors working today, exemplify a natural talent for crafting a tale. Whether these are native born or adopted Southerners, each person in this collection shares a love of story that would make William Faulkner, Eudora Welty or Tennessee Williams proud. So lay your burden down a spell, have yourself a cool drink and hitch a ride down that dark and lonesome highway with these masters of the literary craft, and watch as their characters, their tales, and their take on the blues come to life.

—MORGAN FREEMAN

Preface

I've been a lot of things in my life, but one thing I'd never anticipated was being the editor of an anthology. As most good blues players will tell you, sometimes fate steps across a person's path, and there's no point fighting destiny.

I experienced the Mississippi Delta and the blues at roughly the same time. My first lengthy visit to the Delta involved a photojournalist assignment in the Mississippi State Penitentiary at Parchman. If there's any place where the blues linger, it's certainly there. Once I had a taste of that flat, rich land that comprises the Delta and the music of the jukes that made me want to dance with abandon and wish for a voice where I could wail out my woes and joy, I had to go back. Again and again. Like my home state of Mississippi, the blues and the soil that birthed them crept into my blood.

I met Benjamin LeRoy, now publisher of Tyrus Books, at a writers' conference in Ft. Walton Beach, Florida, where we were both speakers. I had been impressed with the anthology *Chicago Blues* that Bleak House had published. He proposed the *Delta Blues* collection to me and asked me to edit it. By this time I had an inkling of who Ben was and the reputation that Bleak House was rapidly building in the world of literary crime fiction. Of course, I said yes. (And I said it so fast I didn't even stretch the word into two syllables.)

And here, a little over another year later, is the effort of our labor—a collection that contains stories by some of the finest writers working today. While you can plainly see the abilities of these writers as you read the stories, I want to also mention their generosity. Writing short fiction is some of the hardest work around, and many of these contributors took time out from writing novels to do a story for *Delta Blues*. Their take on crime and the blues fills a wide road, but each twist and turn is executed with skill.

John Grisham takes us down to Parchman where we travel with a family cut from the whole cloth of bad decisions as they make a visit to that infamous prison farm, a place they are far too familiar with.

Sometimes music can lift a man out of the worst of circumstances, if only momentarily. Sometimes that isn't enough. Sometimes the price is much higher, as James Lee Burke tells us in his masterful tale.

Charlaine Harris gives us her unique vision of a bargain with the dark side—a world that comes to life when the moon is high and also in dimly lit bars.

Nathan Singer, Les Standiford and Daniel Martine also explore supernatural forces, which are a vital element in the history and mythology of the blues. Legend is a powerful force at work in our lives, and these writers dig in and take a hefty bite.

David Sheffield offers us a very different take on the death of the legendary bluesman who met the Devil at the crossroads and made a bargain that left him dead at twenty-seven.

Dean James, Michael Lister, Suzann Ellingsworth and I have stories centered by women who take the necessary action—for survival, or maybe for revenge. Toni L. P. Kelner, Ace Atkins and Mary Saums give us a more traditional detective/lawman as protagonist, but these stories pack a special twist, while Suzanne Hudson takes us on a trip to Memphis with a young female blues singer . . . and a murderess . . . or maybe not.

Bill Fitzhugh uses the blues as the basis for deception in a tale about human greed. And Alice Jackson finds political intrigue woven with murder and the blues.

Lynne Barrett's story is a blues lament, an exploration of a murdered woman from two different points of view, one black and one white, one who loved her and one who loved her murderer.

Writing as a team, Tom Franklin and Beth Ann Fennelly give us a strange and brutal story about a single act that leads to redemption.

The collection is diverse, and that is part of the joy. Short stories are meant to be read at a sitting, but I'll lay odds that one story won't be enough. So make time to read several when you pick up this volume.

—CAROLYN HAINES

Contents

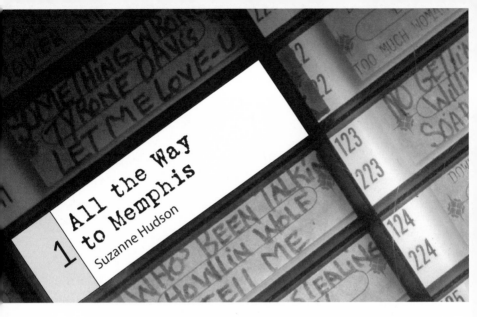

CLISTA JUNIPER WAS A METICULOUS WOMAN, from her immaculate housekeeping to her perfectly enunciated sentences to the way she presided over the Tender County High School library in southern Mississippi. It even extended to her daily wardrobe, which consisted of tailored suits in every shade of beige —so that the coral lips and nails, her trademark, would stand out all the more—her platinum-dyed hair double-French twisted in a tight, inwardly curling labial sheen, a la Tippi Hedren. Indeed, her colleagues—for she had no real intimates—often teased her about her early sixties look, whereupon Clista might express her practiced, breathy giggle and respond, "It is me, the look. Always has been."

"Right down to the girdle?" a teacher might ask.

"Absolutely."

"With the clips and all?" another might chime in.

"Certainly."

"They still make those?"

"I have always believed in stocking up."

"What's a girdle?" a neophyte, a young woman poorly read who took no note of puns, might ask.

So Clista, though she was senior staff at sixty-something, would leave it to another woman, a fifty-something, to explain, getting back to her shelves and her silence and her computerized Dewey decimal system (although she maintained a card catalogue as well), shushing students with a coral pucker against her coral-nailed index finger.

The automobile she drove on this day, her champagne-colored Cadillac, was as meticulously kept as she, although, on this particular day, she was thinking of taking up a former bad habit and filling the car's ash tray with coral-printed filters on the butts of fags she had smoked. She was on edge, shaky, the twists of her coif slightly wispy, like the frayed nerves she so tightly held inside the emotions she rarely let loose. She had let loose this morning, though, before performing her usual ablutions and applying her makeup, to step into the Cadillac and drive not to the high school, where she would be expected after the weekend, but north, to some indeterminate place, she knew not where.

When she saw the figure in the distance, on the side of the highway, she knew immediately what she would do. And, even though Clista was nothing like the sort to pick up a hitchhiker, she would certainly make an exception on this day, as she put her life, her profession, her town behind her, making a sure-to-be futile attempt to run away. This was a day of making all kinds of breaks, the shattering of facades, the clattering of realities, a day to step out of character and try to locate her self, if there ever was such a thing. It made a crazy kind of ironic sense to pick up a hitcher, who, as she drew closer, looked more and more like a teenage girl, finally becoming one, sturdy but slight of frame, like a gymnast. Certainly not threatening, like the haggard and tattooed serial killer stereotype that had forever lived in her wagons-circled mind. She pulled to the shoulder of the road and watched in the rearview mirror as the girl gathered up her things and bounded toward the waiting vehicle, then, catching her own eyes in the reflecting oval of silvered glass, saw a shadow of the emotion and primal fear that had captured her in the pre-dawn hours this morning, when she shot and killed her husband of forty-something years.

It was only an oddity to her now that she had done such a thing; it seemed distant and sketchily surreal. Strange how rapidly those tautly-bound emotions came undone, ramping into the kind of sight-blotted rage that would allow a person to do murder, settling afterwards into a numbness of spirit and mind that allowed her to believe in the possibility of, simply, running away—to almost believe it never happened in the first place. The numbness vibrated in an ear-humming buzz, as if her entire skull were swaddled in layer upon layer of cotton sheeting, but there were fuzzy sounds of car doors and heavy canvas bags thudding into the leather seats. Then a voice, a face, something like words.

"What?" Clista managed.

"It's just that you've saved my life, that's all. If I had to be in this nothing place just one more day, just one more day, I would go nut case. See, my family is an insane asylum. My dope fiend mother especially. And so I just now packed up my shit, marched my butt down that dirt lane, and sat myself on the side of the highway. And here you come right off the bat. Shit, what's your name?"

It was a jarring question, and inside of Clista's hesitation, her guest continued.

"I'm Savannah. But I don't think I'll keep that name. It's just not the blues. Savannah. It's a city in Georgia, not a bluesy person. Oh, what about Georgia? For a name, I mean. Do you have any chips or something? I'm always hungry. I'm definitely set on a different speed than most other people. Are you going to put it in drive?"

Again the out-of-left-field questions caught Clista off guard. "I—yes," she said, pulling back onto the pavement. Ever prepared for emergencies, she gestured at the glove box, where Savannah found a pack of cheese crackers.

The girl tore into the package with her teeth, orange crumbs scattering, then, "I love states for names—Bama, Carolina. Cities, not so much. Missouri is nice. What's yours?"

"My—"

"Name."

"It's Clista," she said, thinking, *and I murdered my husband this morning, because he did the unimaginable and betrayed our decades of sameness and safety and "understoods," and "inasmuchases" and such immaculate respectability as most couples never achieve. He took all that was invested in our public presentation as a couple and crumbled every iota of trust into talcum powder and the fairy dust that magically transformed me into a cold, cold killer.*

"—so of course you know that," Savannah was saying.

"Know what?"

"What I was saying. Are you alright? I was saying how your name sounds something like a female part, but I guess you caught a lot of teasing at a certain age, so of course you know that. Junior high is hell for everybody." She sucked in a breath. "I'm sorry if I offended you. Sometimes I go over the top. My mind goes faster than I can talk and I try to keep up and so words get blurted out before I know it. You know?"

Clista was not accustomed to such talk, talk of female parts with sexual references, cursing, and just plain chattiness of a distasteful bent, as she had no good best girlfriend, having kept the world at a polite, respectable distance. This girl, however, felt unthreatening in spite of her verbiage. "How old are you?" the driver attempted to divert.

"Twenty-six," was the reply. "I know, I know. I look sixteen. I get it all the time. It's because I'm so small-boned. And flat-chested. I've thought about store-bought tits, implants, but I just don't believe in doing that shit to your body." She sighed with a flourish. "It's a blessing and a curse, being my size. I mean, when I tell people I'm a blues singer, they laugh. 'Ain't no big, bluesy voice gonna come out of that little thing.' Plus I'm white, obviously. 'Little bitty white chicks can't sing the blues.' Folks just don't take me seriously. But when you've lived through the low-down dirty shit I've lived through, you can damn sure feel the hurt. Like, what do you do when it takes your crack-head mother two years to get rid of a man who's pushing his hands in your panties and you're nine years old? Two years!"

"Oh, my!" Clista drew away from her, an instinct, and was immediately embarrassed.

"Well, it wasn't my fault, you know."

"Of course not. Absolutely not. I'm so sorry. I'm just not accustomed—"

"My point is, that's just one of the crappy things I've experienced. And it wasn't even the worst. But I keep it upbeat, you know? Keep it in the sunlight. Positive thoughts. Let it out in the lyrics. So do you believe I can sing?"

"I would imagine so," she said, thinking, *betrayal feels like the big, silver blade of a very sharp knife slicing cleanly through the jugular. He betrayed me and I was unleashed in an unthinkable way, into utter insanity. I was not responsible, nor do I regret. The lioness kills to protect her vulnerable offspring, after all. Is there an analogy to be had? Does it even matter?*

"—and my boyfriend—he's a tattoo artist—he did all of mine, see?" She turned her leg to reveal the serpent-like lizard inked around her calf, winding toward its own tail; turned a shoulder bearing a crucifix, Jesus and his blood upon an elaborately detailed cross, the eyes of the holy martyr cast up in surrender to the Father. "His name—my boyfriend's—is Dakota. A state, right? It fits with my world view. He's amazingly talented.

I mean, isn't this gorgeous?" She pulled down the front of her t-shirt to reveal, just above her heart, a small but beautifully intricate insect of some kind—something like one might find in a fly fisherman's tackle box. "I have others, but they're in hard to find places, if you know what I mean."

Clista's husband was a fly fisherman with a vast, three-tiered tackle box loaded with treasured lures, some even from his navy days, the days of their courtship. He took regular and frequent fishing trips to Colorado at solitary resorts, to the Rocky Mountain streams where he danced his line in the rhythmic ballet of a cast. She did not accompany him as she had no interest in his hobbies other than as fodder for those sometimes necessary social conversations.

"Paul loves his lures as much as he loves me," she might joke, "but at least he finds me more alluring." Not that she alluded to any sort of physical sensuality between the two of them. Clista had always found that particular expression of human instinct to be distasteful at best, more of the time disgusting. There were unartful fumblings early in their union, a marriage that followed a courteous courtship, but they soon settled into a life of platonic rhythms, ebbing away into their separate daytimes then flowing into their dining room and den of an evening, watching the woods at night from their isolated split-level home, tucking into the twin beds connected by a night stand bearing an antique Princess telephone, pink, with a nine millimeter loaded and at the ready in its French Provincial drawer.

"—so why don't you just take a look," Savannah had opened a cell phone and was scrolling through some photographs. "Here you go," and she turned the screen to Clista.

"Oh!" It came almost as a shriek paired with another recoiling of her whole body. The wheels left the blacktop for a few seconds.

"Holy Christ—what was that?" Savannah looked at her as if she had two heads and then studied the screen of her phone, a close-up of her pubic area and the peace lily engraved above the curls. Her face fell. "Oh. I thought you wanted to see my other tattoos. Sorry."

"No, it's alright. I—I'm just not accustomed to such images."

"No shit. Well, I didn't mean to scare you. I mean, it's just skin, basically. I've never seen what the big deal is. Skin is skin. It holds in our organs. Sex is something else, but it really amounts to just rubbing. But you're the driver so I sure as hell won't fuck with you. But you have to know up front that I was born without a filter."

"Filter?"

"You know, I tend to blurt out whatever's in my head. I'm ADHD, so it kind of goes with the territory. I'll try to watch my mouth, though. I mean, you could easily just dump me on the side of the road again. And there I'd be with my thumb out. Again."

"I won't do that." Then, for no real reason she could fathom, she added, "I'm going all the way to Memphis."

"For real? Holy shit, that's awesome. How lucky is it you picked me up, And don't worry—no more tattoo pictures," and she laughed a trilling, lively laugh.

Paul had a tattoo, from the time he served in the navy during the Vietnam Conflict. It was of two intertwining snakes encircling a cross, the word "Bound" crowning the top of the cross like a bent halo. He said it represented his love of country, how bound up in it he was. And he believed in what he was doing in fighting the Red Menace off the shores of Southeast Asia, even if he never had to dodge any bullets.

"Your husband?"

"What?" Clista had not realized she had spoken.

"With the serpents. So symbolic. I mean, my uncle Jessie actually fought over there—lost a leg and an eye. He has a cool glass eye he entertained us with—my cousins and me—when we were kids. He'd take it out and toss it up in the air and catch it in his mouth like popcorn."

Clista shuddered.

"I know, pretty gross. But not if you're a little kid and not really at all if you think. I mean, look what he's been through. He deserves to do whatever the hell he wants, huh? He doesn't have a fake leg anymore. He used to. And he could make it do fart noises, another thing little kids love."

"Goodness!" Paul was not allowed—had not been allowed—to fart in her presence. Clista insisted that he step into the bathroom or outside if that urge was upon him. On those occasions when it happened serendipitously, he apologized with abject humiliation to her stony disdain.

Black earth was turned in the fields bordering Highway 61. Planting was done, and within months the rich soil would nourish the snowy crop of bolls, and cotton puffs would litter the roadside after picking time. Picking. To pick off. She had killed him, shot him in the head right there in his study, where she had found him before dawn, crept up to the door, borne witness to the sounds of lecherous, staccato-rhythmed motions and gritty, profane talk. He was preoccupied enough not to notice the slight click as she eased the door open, just a crack, just enough that she could see the man facing him on the computer screen, knew immediately who he was—the man in the photographs holding stringers heavy-laden with fish—the best friend from the navy, Spencer Kraus, also married. She fetched the gun and returned to wait it out. He didn't notice, even when the screen had gone dark and he'd lain his head down on his arms, exhausted, as she padded across lush pile in one dreamlike motion, squeezed two bullets into his skull, turned and left just that quickly, with the stealth of a jungle cat.

"So tell me more." Savannah's words, again jarring.

"What do you mean?"

"You just said you were a cat."

"What?"

"Yeah, a jungle cat. And I'm thinking, what the hell?"

"I'm sorry," Clista stammered. "I'm just upset." She had to watch her words, slipping out unintended and quick, like minnows darting across currents.

"Well, then tell it, sister. What did the son of a bitch do?" She pulled out a pack of American Spirit cigarettes. "Okay if I smoke?"

"Yes." Her surrender felt like the beginning of some kind of relief. "But only if you light one for me."

THE SOUND OF CLATTERING DISHES and running water came from a kitchen in the back of the diner. Savannah was putting heart and soul into devouring her sandwich, dousing it mid-chew, and frequently, with Dr. Pepper. "Thank you so much for buying," she gulped. "My money situation is pretty busy, but that'll change when I hook up with Dakota."

Clista had attempted to force down a salad, but nausea made that impossible so she nibbled a couple of Saltines. She had bought her very own pack of cigarettes, Virginia Slim menthols, the brand of her younger years. *You've come a long way, Baby*, the old advertising jingle rattled around in her head. She exhaled a mushroom cloud of smoke. "I can't think, can't know what to do."

"Sure you can." Savannah leaned across the table, speaking in a hushed but animated tone. "You can absolutely know what to do. You just have to connect all the dots. That's what my uncle Jessie used to say, anyway. But he was pretty PTSD. You're probably kind of PTSD about now, too."

"The dots are scattered all across the floor." And she thought of throwing jacks as a child, the scattering stars, the ball bouncing. "That's the way the ball bounces," she murmured, smiling.

"Okay, okay, you're not going all mental on me, right?"

"No. I've already been mental. Can I go sane on you?"

"That would be good, but dude, your life is going to go end over end either way. I mean, you've got to either get a new identity and disappear—and that's really hard—or go back and come clean—and that's really hard, too. Man!" Her eyes widened at the enormity of it all.

"Are my eyes still red and puffy?"

"Yeah, but that's good. I think it keeps the waitress from coming over too often."

Clista took out her compact and applied a fresh coat of coral to her lips. *I am a coral snake.* She blotted with a napkin pulled from the stainless steel holder.

They were in a desolate part of the state where the crook of the Mississippi separated Arkansas, Tennessee and Mississippi, at Buck's Diner, where time had stopped decades earlier, an eatery with worn red plastic seats, dull chrome, and a hanging musk of aged bacon grease. It was just past the lunch hour, so the two women had the place to themselves while a sour-faced teenager bused a few tables. A grizzled-looking cook sat at a booth near the kitchen door, smoking, chatting in a low, gravelly voice with the one waitress, who sauntered over to the travelers once in a while, called them "honey" and "sugar" and "baby" as she offered more tea.

"Man, you're in some serious shit. I've known all kinds of people slogging through all kinds of shit. Hell, my own mother only had me because she couldn't afford another abortion. She was a drug addict. Cocaine. Sometimes she did men to get money for it. Now she's killing herself with meth. I was trying to help her get straight, but that stuff is insane. In-fucking-sane. You really saved my life by picking me up."

A hopeful little ripple went through Clista. "Do you think maybe that cancels out the other?"

"Maybe so," Savannah grinned. "Maybe the karma is right now. Maybe that's a reason to keep running. Or to go back."

"I can't believe I actually told you everything. It's not like me at all."

"But it is me. Seriously. It's something about me," Savannah said. "People tell me stuff all the time. Strangers. I mean, I'll be in the checkout line and somebody will just unload their whole entire bizarre life story. It happens all the freaking time."

But I don't confide in anyone, Clista thought, still marveling at how Savannah had coaxed the darkness out of her.

"What did the son of a bitch do?" she had asked.

"How do you know it's about a man?"

"Always is. Your husband?"

"Yes."

"So come on with it."

"No."

"Come on. Tell it."

"I can't."

"Just say the words."

And Clista's fingers had tightened on the steering wheel of the smoke-filled champagne-colored Cadillac. "My husband betrayed me."

"You know it."

"He lied and cheated and did it from the start."

"Uh-huh."

"And it's worse than that."

"How?"

"My husband betrayed me."

"Tell."

"With a man."

"Holy Christ."

"A double life."

"You're right. That is worse. Way fucking worse."

"I was faithful to that man forever and he was faithful to his man forever and I caught him in a despicable act and I killed him."

"Killed?"

"Shot."

"The fuck you say!" And Savannah had turned her body fully facing her in the car. "You are so not the type!"

"Apparently I am." And she had pulled onto the shoulder of the road, rested her head on the steering wheel and howled like a wounded animal as Savannah, effervescence disarmed by the rawness of it all, tried impotently to console her.

THE WAITRESS SAUNTERED OVER. "Here, sweetie, let me get this out of your way," she said, and began collecting plates and utensils, blood red fingernails clicking against heavy white glass.

Savannah picked up the last of her BLT and pushed the plate. "Are you still taking me to Memphis?" she asked as the waitress sauntered away.

"Of course."

"You're not, like, dangerous or anything, right?" It was almost a whisper.

"I have no weapons or designs upon your possessions."

"I know that. It just felt like a question I had to ask, you know? I mean, how dumb would I feel if something really happened—and I know it isn't—but something happened and I never even asked the question in the first place. Man, would I feel dumb."

"Certainly."

"Plus, I just got to get to Memphis."

"What will you do when you get there? Where will you live?"

"With Dakota, of course. He'll come pick me up wherever you and I land. He has a place off Beale Street, right in the thick of things. Man, I can't wait to go out to some of those clubs. Not the touristy ones on the main drag. The real ones. The ones you have to just happen into. But the first thing I'm going to do—and I know this is stupid and touristy and all—but I'm going to get me some barbecue."

"Can I join you?"

"Sure. Are you like, buying?"

"Of course. It'll be my Last Supper."

"Holy shit. You're not going all suicidal or anything, are you? Because that's even more messed up than what's gone down. Seriously."

"You're right. Besides, I don't know. Could I actually go home to that—mess, and put the gun to my own head? I just don't see it."

"Well, you know they say it's a permanent solution to a temporary problem, right?"

"It would certainly be a problem for both my permanent and my temple," Clista said, but her puny, half-hearted attempt at punning fell on deaf ears.

MEMPHIS WAS A PRESENCE she could feel well before hitting the outskirts. It was in the whispery thrum of potential stories in song—a spiritual imprint that webbed out and out to the rising hills and farms, cascading down the Mississippi River to rich Delta dirt.

Savannah must have felt it, too. She threw her head back and let fly several bars of melodic anguish, big and rich, at odds with the tiny vessel making the music. "You might think you're living large, baby, but you'll be dying when you get home. You might think you're hitting the mark, baby, but you'll just be trying when you get home." She turned to Clista. "What do you think? It's something I've been working on."

"You're very talented. I don't know a lot about the blues, but you have a unique sound."

"Unique good or unique I-can't-think-of anything-good-to-say-so-I'll-say-unique?"

"Definitely good. Raspy good."

Savannah beamed. "Thank you. And you're wrong about the other."

"What other?"

"The blues. You know a hell of a lot about the blues."

"I do? Well, yes, now."

"No, always. Can you talk about your life? Your self? I mean, okay, you spent a very long marriage being some guy's beard, but that doesn't happen in a vacuum, you know?"

"A beard?"

"You know—the wife of a gay man who lives in a really deep closet."

"There's actually slang for it?"

"Sure. You don't know a lot about sex, do you?"

"I know it's messy."

"Okay, see, this is what I mean. You don't like sex. That's how you and your husband connected, on a really basic level. So if you think about it, it was not a bad arrangement. You each got what you needed. You just couldn't handle knowing it, right?"

"I'm not sure. What I've done is so much worse than knowing anything."

"Who really knows anything?"

"What do you mean?"

"Well, my boyfriend Dakota, right? He believes that there is nothing but thought and that we've thought all this up. Like, you thought me up on the side of the road and poof, there I was. You thought up a husband who used you as his beard so you killed him."

"This is all a lot of pseudo-philosophical malarkey."

"Oh my god, you said 'malarkey.' You are so not the type to kill a person. But anyway, here's the thing."

"I suppose I could just think him back alive, correct?"

"Well?"

"You must be crazy."

"Yeah, I am, but so is everybody—including you."

Clista's muscle memory sprang into a mode of defense that immediately fizzled. Crazy? With such a buffed and polished image? With a picture perfect life? With the dead husband laid out across his computer desk? "Maybe I can think him back alive?"

"Damn right. It's got to be worth a freaking try."

They ate just outside the city limits at Uncle Stumpy's Bodacious Barbecue Bin, thick brown sauce crawling across their fingers, down their chins, sticky napkins piled on the tabletop. Clista found herself laughing at the mess of it all. "This is real barbecue. I've never had the real thing," and she sucked on her fingers just like Savannah did. And when Savannah flipped open her cell phone to call her boyfriend Dakota to come and pick her up, Clista studied the way the young woman cocked her head, trilled her voice up and down, like a delightful little bird, as she spoke. Twenty-six, yet so much like a young girl—enthusiastic, forward-looking, hopeful, on the verge of a dream.

They embraced in the parking lot. "I never knew," Clista said. "How could I not know?"

"But didn't you, really? Come on, didn't you? Way down deep? In your guts?"

Clista opened her purse and withdrew the compact and tube of coral lipstick. "I guess that's a thing to consider." She reapplied her signature color, pulled out a Kleenex and blotted a kiss onto it. She folded the Kleenex and handed it to Savannah. "If you're ever really low, give yourself a kiss from me."

"Oh, I've already been plenty low. I'm aiming for up now. But, just in case, thanks."

"You'll be okay here?" Clista glanced around the parking lot. It was not the best neighborhood, judging by the buildings in various stages of disrepair, and day had fallen into dusk.

"Oh, hell yeah. Dakota won't be too long."

"But it's getting dark and you're unfamiliar with the area." There was a pharmacy across the street that was well-lit. "You should go to the bench by that drug store."

Savannah giggled. "Are you kidding? Nothing's going to happen to me. You should know this about me by now. No point in letting worry rule your world, huh?"

"I guess."

"So have you decided what you're going to do?"

"Yes, I have."

"And it feels right?"

"Yes."

"Good."

The champagne-colored Cadillac was warm from the sunlight trapped inside just a short time ago—invisible but there, the traces of a star. Clista rolled down the windows and waved as she waited to pull out of the parking lot. She looked back for a few seconds longer to see Savannah arrange her possessions and plop down on her duffel bag next to the front of the rib joint, a snapshot of a reality Clista had enjoyed for a day. She wasn't sure if the woman— no, the girl—was a chance that fell out of the sky or a providential event sent by some spiritual presence in an effort to set things right. Maybe the girl really would fade from existence once Clista turned away, so she hesitated for a moment, not wanting that vibrancy to dissipate, like the rays of the sun were.

"Just go!" Savannah shouted, waving her off, laughing.

Clista giggled, a genuine sound, pressed the gas, and pulled away. She started to roll up the windows but caught herself, even told herself "No," right out loud. Then, at a glimpse of her eyes in the rearview mirror, she even whispered, "You crazy fucker."

And she left the windows down into the evening, rolling south through the farm country, past the scrubby towns and lives of folks left behind. The push of air blew a rhythm of comfort into her soul, disengaging strands of platinum blonde that whipped about her face, growing into a small hurricane of color-treated hair spiraling around the eye of coral lips. She would drive well into the night, until she made it all the way home, consuming every millisecond with the fierce energy of thinking, thinking hard, thinking him back alive.

2 Love in Vain
David Sheffield

TO PUT IT REAL DELICATE, Miss Odessa Hervey was a woman of what you would call very ample girth, and so it was with some considerable difficulty that I rolled her over to complete the process of washing her down with germicidal solution. I had such fond memories of Miss Hervey from when she taught us fifth grade at Nichols Colored Elementary. Sadly, she had succumbed to the sugar diabetes, which no doubt contributed to her largeness.

I placed a modesty cloth over her privates before I called in Elnora to help me set the features. Sure enough, she was still acting all sulky with me.

All I said was, "Please go easy on the lip rouge this time."

"Why you want to criticize me and I haven't even started?" Elnora said with her eyes all snappy.

"All I'm saying is Miss Hervey was a Christian lady and I'm pretty sure her family wouldn't like to see her done up too strumpish."

"You just set her jaw and let me worry about the life picture," Elnora said.

We went on about our separate business without saying a word, me bending and flexing Miss Hervey's flabby arms to ease the rigor mortis while Elnora began the process of setting the poor lady's hair in pin curls.

About that time a call come in from the Leflore County Coroner, Mister Ernest Hemplewhite, saying there was a colored man for pickup at an address in Baptist Town.

Maurice and me headed over there in the older hearse, the '34 Buick. We have a new '38 Packard-Henney at the Pruitt Funeral Home, but Maurice said it was in the shop to get the name painted on it. It's always something with Maurice. He took to picking on me before we was even out of the drive, asking why was Elnora so touchy lately and cutting his eyes real sly.

"Me and Miss Elnora are colleagues," I said. "That's all."

"I hear she colleagues with Lonnie Earl now," Maurice said, checking me out to see how I would react.

This cut me but I decided to let it slide, looking out the window while Maurice drove down Fulton Street toward Baptist Town. It was one of those miserable days in August, so hot the tar was popping up out of the pavement in little bubbles that crunched under the tires of the hearse.

When we arrived at the location, a big old rambly yellow house at 109 Young Street, Mister Hemplewhite was waiting outside in the yard with a clipboard in his hand, acting all fidgety like he ready to get this over with. I been knowing him since he was elected coroner last November and I get the feeling he don't much care about colored people. I'm not saying he hates. I'm just saying he regards people of color as some kind of bother to him.

We had to climb up some narrow outside stairs to get to the room where the body was at, and it was sweaty work hauling the gurney up there.

The room was dark and close where he was laying, with all the curtains shut and no electric light. It was two women in there, an older lady that owned the house, and her daughter, a very plain girl, no more than eighteen or nineteen, holding the hand of the deceased, waving a cardboard fan over his face like she was tranced. When we told her it was time to go, the girl commence to wail and moan from deep inside her chest with such a sound of grief and misery that it give me chills. The girl's mama, the landlady, almost had to carry her out, with the girl still clutching that fan and wailing so hard her body shook. Then I heard some more women from another room take up the wail in that old Africa way they have that don't hold nothing back.

Mister Hemplewhite carry out his examination of the decedent, checking for a pulse, palpating the chest and so forth. It was a tall, thin, fine-featured young colored man laying there, wearing his underwear shirt and just the pants of a pinstripe suit. His skin was chalky and his lips was parched but you could see he was what the ladies call a pretty boy. The thing I remember most was his hands, his uncommon long and slender fingers, froze like they was reaching for something.

The landlady come back in and Mister Hemplewhite asked her what did she know about the dead man.

"Some peoples calls him R.J. and some calls him Bobby," she said. "His last name could be Spencer but he go by Johnson. I know for sure his mama married a Dodds from down around Robinsonville."

Mister Hemplewhite was writing all this down. "Age?" he asked.

"I believe twenty-seven."

"This his regular address?"

"No, sir. He stay here with my daughter while he play music at the juke in Three Forks."

"What'd he die of?"

"He come in the other evening with a terrible colic which he had for the last three days." The landlady stop and give a shiver.

"Right up to he died he was trembling and struggling for every breath he took."

"Prob'bly pneumonia," Hemplewhite said. "Y'all should a called a doctor."

"Yes, sir, I know," she said, "but ain't nobody have the money."

Under "Cause of Death" on the coroner's report, Mister Hemplewhite wrote down, "No doctor."

Just about then we heard somebody thumping up the stairs and in come a young colored man in a rumply suit, all out of breath, looking a little crazy eyed, like a man that hasn't had no sleep.

"My name is Honeyboy Edwards," he said. "If y'all fixing to signify how my friend R.J. died, then I'm here to tell you—the boy was poisoned."

Honeyboy asked the landlady could he have a glass of water and when she left the room, he lower his voice and say, "It's like this. R.J. always had two kinds of womens. Plain girls to stay with and hot tamales to fool around with. This time, he picked the wrong honey for sure, because it turns out she go with the very motherfucker that own the juke at Three Forks."

"We don't need that kind of talk," Mister Hemplewhite said. "Let's have some respect for the dead." But Honeyboy didn't pay no mind, just catch his breath and go right on.

"They give R.J. a bottle of whiskey that had strychnine in it," he said. "Sonny Boy Williamson was playing mouth harp with him, and when the first bottle come, he knocked it out of R.J.'s hand and said, 'Don't ever drank from a bottle that's already open.' R.J. said, 'And don't you ever knock a bottle out my hand again.' Pretty soon they come back with another bottle and R.J. drank it down. He seem like he all right for a while, but about two thirty in the morning he have to put his guitar down and go outside to vomit. He got worse and worse so we brung him back here. It was strychnine killed him, sure as I'm standing here."

"If you knew it was strychnine, why didn't you call the law?" asked Hemplewhite.

Honeyboy didn't have no answer for that.

"When are you people going to learn? When you got a problem, call the law," Hemplewhite said. "I can't go changing the cause of death. I done wrote it down." Then he signed his name to the report and passed it over for me to do likewise.

Honeyboy stepped up to me with his voice all trembly and said, "What's your name, boy?"

"Vernon Pruitt, Junior," I said. "Associate Director of the Pruitt Funeral Home."

"Look here, Pruitt," he said. "If you sign that, you letting the man from Three Forks off the hook. He killed him. He killed my man R.J."

"He don't have no say in it," Hemplewhite said. "I'm the coroner and I done wrote it down."

We carried the body down to the hearse and since this was an indigent case for the county, we took charge of the personal possessions for the time being—a guitar, a valise, and an old coach trunk full of something so heavy it took me and Maurice both to lug it down the steps.

By the time we got ready to go it was a number of people crowding around in the yard, most of them women crying and carrying on. The girl come down from the house and hung onto the hearse to where we couldn't leave til her mama pull her off.

As we was leaving, Maurice looked back in the rearview mirror with that nasty smile of his and said, "Reckon if I played and sang the womens would cry for me too?"

"I doubt it," I said.

Back at the funeral home, Maurice asked could he leave early because he have to take his mother to get her feet scraped or otherwise she wouldn't be able to stand up in the choir on Sunday.

It's just like Maurice to claim some kind of mercy doings he knows I can't dispute.

The county won't pay for embalming on an indigent case, just a pine box and a hole in the ground. Still, I try to carry out these preparations with as much dignity as I can and so I looked through the boy's things til I found him a clean shirt and tie. Unfortunately the jacket to the pinstripe suit was wadded up with stains all over it, so I took it in the back to sponge it clean and go over it the best I could with the steam iron.

When I come back in with the clothes, Elnora was standing over the boy's body with her head bowed, moving her lips so soft I couldn't make out what she was praying. When she finish and turn around I could see her eyes was all puffy.

"You going to have to do this one by yourself," she said. "It hurt too bad to see him this way."

"Where you know him from?" I asked.

"Three Forks," she said. "Me and some friends of mine went down there to hear him sing."

"Is that where you go with Lonnie Earl?"

"Why can't you leave me alone?"

"He's never going to treat you right. A man like Lonnie Earl don't give a damn about nobody but hisself."

"That's for me to worry about," she said. "Listen, Vernon. I can't work here no more with you disapproving me all the time."

"You don't have to go," I said. "I'll stop."

"No, you won't," she said. "You can't help yourself. Please tell your daddy I'm sorry but I have to go."

Elnora gathered up her things and then she was gone, leaving me to casket the boy by myself. The coach trunk caught my eye. I opened it out of curiosity and it was full of records. I picked one out and took it to the chapel where we have an electric phonograph.

Sitting in a pew by myself, I listened to his music. How could one man squeeze so much sound out of nothing but a plain guitar? Raw and driving on the bottom, sweet and tinkly on the top. When he sang, his voice was rough as a field hand and soft as a seraphim—

When the train rolled up to the station
I looked her in the eye
When the train rolled up to the station
and I looked her in the eye
Well, I was lonesome, I felt so lonesome
and I could not help but cry
All my love in vain

When the song was over, I sat a long time, listening to the needle scratch and pop. Then I got up, turned off the phonograph, and went back in to finish the preparations.

It took some doing to get the suit on him, being that his back was so stiff and arched up from struggling to breathe. Maybe Honeyboy was right. If he did get a dose of strychnine it could of wore him down til he caught the pneumonia later. People think the poison kills a man's brain but what it really does is rob him of his breath.

I knotted his tie, smoothed out his lapels and fluffed up the handkerchief in his breast pocket.

"Why you? Why do all the women love a man like you? What is it they see in bad men, dangerous men like you and Lonnie Earl? Why you? Why you and not me?"

I flexed and worked his hands, stretching out those long elegant fingers, smooth as a girl's except for the calluses on his fingertips from where he fretted the guitar. I folded those hands, then leaned down close and whispered—"A lot of good it done you, pretty boy. Look at you now."

As soon as it passed my lips, a wave of sorrow come over me. I closed the pine lid and nailed it shut, driving each nail straight so as not to split the wood, the bang of the hammer pounding in my head. When I finally stopped and let go, I wasn't sure if I was crying for the dead boy, or for my own sorry self.

3 Nine Below Zero
Ace Atkins

THE DEPUTIES HAD COME AND GONE, trying to track a couple of meth-heads boosting anhydrous ammonia from a holding tank down the road. The sheriff had his boys in four-wheelers out in the snow zipping up and down the Sunflower River and along Highway 49, but we paid the whole thing little mind, turning back to cold Budweiser, warm Jack, and endless cigarettes. This was as cold as the Delta had been in fifty years, and it seemed even colder inside the cavernous space of the old Hopson Commissary.

The only illumination shone from a strand of Christmas lights snaked through dusty booze bottles and the heavy fire glow pulsing from a pot-bellied stove trying its best to heat a room as large as an airplane hanger. A stereo played some vintage Muddy Waters.

"So," said the man at my elbow. "You just took up and left New Orleans? Just like that? Nothing but your truck and that old trailer?'

"I didn't have the trailer then," I said. "I found that Airstream over in Pocahontas."

"What about all your things? Personal items and such."

"I took what survived the storm, a couple books and a Stones album. Most of my clothes had been looted."

"What was it?"

"What was what?"

"The album?"

"*Exile.*"

"Si. Si."

I nodded. Ice had formed hard and stiff in the corner of a small window glowing red with a Budweiser sign. My thick jacket felt as if it were made of paper.

"You sound a little angry."

"It is what it is."

"That whole thing was a mess, my friend. You think it will ever be the same?"

"Nope," I said, and toasted the fella with half a Budweiser, feeling confident in a nice steady buzz.

The commissary had been part of the plantation back in the day and had since been turned into a local juke joint and gathering place for town misfits and out-of-town travelers. The owner, a fella by the name of James Butler, had kept the place about as original as he could, leaving the old post office toward the front of the building and even keeping the odd hay bale near the main stage where bluesmen like Pinetop Perkins and Big Jack Johnson sometimes played. Old farm equipment and rusted Delta relics hung from the wall. Muddy kept on singing.

"And you've been right here?"

"I went to France for a while."

"What was in France?"

"A girl."

"I knew a girl from France once," he said, staring into nothing. "Big blue eyes and fantastic ta-tas."

"How big?"

"Big enough."

The back door opened, and in walked a shirtless man, slathered in mud, with red eyes and blue lips. His thin chest looked as light as a bird's and just as bony, and he stood and shivered, seeking the heat of the old stove. He stood there for several moments, trying but failing to hold onto a cigarette, and I watched him as he planted his feet, dead-eyed, and tried to revive his blue skin.

I looked back to my drink and signaled to James for another round for me and my drinking partner. It was about a quarter til midnight. Muddy kept on. One More Mile. One More Mile.

"Mr. Thoreau once said, "A man is rich in proportion to the number of things he can afford to let alone.""

"I don't feel too wealthy, brother," I said.

Out of the corner of my eye, I watched the shirtless man stare at the clock over the bar. Toward the front of the commissary, the big door blew open and another man, just as scrawny as the other, but this one wearing a long black trenchcoat, wandered in and nervously looked all around, everywhere but at the man by the stove. Same mud all over him, same bad teeth and hollow face with stubble.

"I admire you. No possessions. Nothing to hold you down."

"God bless you," I said.

"May I buy you this round?"

"I won't fight it."

"What did you do before you ended up here?"

"I was a teacher."

"No more?"

"Some things happened down there."

"Like the man said, 'However mean life is, meet it and live it.'"

I NODDED, but the nod turned to a shrug. I rubbed my face and drank more. I watched the clock's second hand. In the bar's mirror, the two men finally met at the stove, drawn by the heat and muttering to each other like little insects working in their own secret language. One of the men nodded towards the bar and I saw that in his dirty little hand he held a shitty little revolver.

"Something happened to you? Right? Please, I don't mean to pry."

"You're not prying."

"But you just stay in that trailer. I didn't even know you lived here til tonight."

"It's pretty goddamn cold tonight."

"Did you want to get out?"

"It's goddamn cold."

"From the trailer."

"I wanted a drink."

"Si."

The man in the trench had ice in his hair and he ambled over to the bar, his teeth chattered hard, whirling some tale to James about his car breaking down. Broke down near the crossroads. As he spoke, the ice melted from his greasy hair and fell to the floor.

Deer antlers held a twelve-gauge shotgun beautifully above the beer cooler. I glanced at it and then back at my new friend.

"Are your people here?" he asked.

"I know some."

"Where are your people?"

"Mostly dead."

"Si. Si. Well, that's something that happens. But you have to live your life."

"I'm not hiding."

"I didn't mean that, friend."

"There was a—aw, hell."

The man in the trench nodded to his friend and turned back to the bar. You could see all this in the mirror, the whole pirouette and shape of it.

The minute hand on the clock turned.

I looked at the whiskey, still feeling the cold.

I looked at the gun.

Another drink was laid down, James leaned in and whispered, "Phones are dead. I can't get a signal on my cell."

I met his eyes and then turned back to my drinking companion whose mouth formed an O, seeing it all come to shape.

The man in the trench had started to pace, the gun loose in hand, more ice melting from his hair as he smoked a cigarette. He quashed it underfoot and then started another.

The clock headed toward midnight.

Muddy kept on. *One more mile. One more mile.*

"It's as hard to see one's self as to look backwards without turning around," said my drinking companion.

"What's that?" I asked.

The mirror was unreal. The second hand moved and the music filled the cold, timeless and still.

The wiry fella drew the gun and yelled in a shaky voice for all of us to come to him and get down on our knees. "Who called the police? Who's the goddamn bright boy that called 'em?"

I slid from the bar stool, hands up, and turned to him.

"On your knees."

My friends looked to me. I remained standing.

"They're coming for you," I said.

"Who called 'em?" His gums purple, teeth blackened. "You?"

"Does it matter?"

"On your knees," he screamed.

I shook my head. No one moved.

He thumbed back the hammer. The gun looked like it might break apart in his trembling, cold fingers. You could hear the wind outside, sliding across the curved metal roof; hollow whistling sounds came from the holes in the commissary attic.

The man snarled and spit and came for me, gun outstretched, calling me a "dead brightboy sonofabitch" until my drinking companion moved between us and said, "Sit. Let's drink. No one wants to go back out there."

I stepped back toward the bar, feeling my weight against the length of it. The album had played out, the silent hiss of the stereo blending with that cold, lonely wind and the broken voices, nonsensical words coming from the men's rotted mouths.

I met James' eyes and glanced up at the shotgun. He nodded and moved backward, slight and slow toward the antlers.

"I said, 'On your knees,'" the shirtless man said and shuffled toward us, his breath rancid as rotting fish. He swiped the Jack from the bar, taking a hit of booze, and tossing the rest to his buddy, who drained the bottle. "Hands behind your head."

For a moment, the whole building felt as if it might blow away, leaving nothing but the frame—the haze of whisky and fear blending into a shaky, unreal film strip that comes at you with broken patterns of light, some unrecognizable, until it all clicks into place and the reel starts rolling again, with new images, some of them broken and jumpy but moving forward just the same.

I waited. James stood under the gun.

The second hand of the clock seemed to echo the pumping of my heart.

I took a deep breath and nodded ever so slightly.

One More Mile.

4 Cuttin' Heads

Alice Jackson

FAYE MAE WATCHED Daddy Ray's callused fingers slide down the list of names and figures her granny kept behind the bar. His mouth chomped at the unlit stogy clamped between his gold teeth, warning her she was striding into deeper water.

Considering her next move, Faye Mae turned to fiddle with the dials of the old tube radio Granny had set on the bar. A peckerwood voice blared from KFFA, across the river in Helena, Arkansas. She turned the sound louder, ensuring Granny wouldn't hear her conversation with Daddy Ray. Granny loved listening to the blues on King Biscuit Time, mainly cause most of the ole blues singers and musicians had played right here at the Dew Drop at least once way back before some of the white places up in the big northern cities had begun hiring them.

"That was J.D. Short and Son House, pounding out their latest single, "You Been Cheating Me." Those men have a gift, a mighty gift, shore nuff, and remember, you hear the blues more right here on KFFA, 1360 on your dial," the nasal deejay rambled.

Faye Mae's older brother Levon had confided to her that Granny had known Robert Johnson before he up and found himself down at the Crossroad, trading songs with the Boogey Man. Levon had told her the story last Halloween, and while she wasn't certain of its truthfulness, she suspected it had some basis in fact. When she was five, Levon had told her all about her mama, how she used to sing the blues at the Dew Drop and how she'd been attracted to the men who arrived with battered guitars, hoping for a few dollars, food, whiskey and, most of all, attention.

The summer of 1963 was blue blazing hot, and the afternoon Delta heat poured through the doorway Granny had opened in order to air out the Dew Drop. She did it every Friday, regular as clockwork, getting ready for the payday customers like they were relatives from far away. It was one of the many things Faye May loved about the Dew Drop. The sunlight brightened the pine floors scarred by years of dancing, loving, fighting and killing. Faye Mae had not seen it happen, but she knew the dark spot near where Daddy Ray's old blue tick hound Rex now laid was the place of last repose of a no-good two-timer who had stolen money from Granny.

The bar had been Faye Mae's home since her mama had dropped her off as a baby. Just up and left her with Granny, who'd kept her wrapped and warm in a wooden beer delivery box behind the bar while Granny waited on the payday customers. Faye May didn't remember any of that, but she loved the stories Granny told, especially how the customers dropped extra coins into the tip jar to pay for her baby food. By the time she was in first grade, Faye Mae was permitted to open the co-colas, but only during the early hours of the evening. She'd even managed to intercept a few of the coins before they fell into Granny's jar. Nowadays, Granny rarely let her come into the bar when customers were there. Granny was always mumbling stuff about how bad things happened to growing girls who found themselves in the wrong place. Granny was especially watchful to keep her away from the occasional musicians who still came to the Dew Drop to play the blues.

"I learned my lesson with your mama about those men," Granny said. "Those musicians ruined her sure as I'm telling this, and you ain't gonna go like that."

Most of what Faye Mae knew about her mother, she heard from Levon. The rest she learned by keeping her ears open and pressed against closed doors when Granny and Daddy Ray thought they were all alone in the Dew Drop. That's how she came to discover her mama was really Daddy Ray's and Granny's daughter, even though Daddy Ray was a white man with a white wife, white children and white grandchildren.

He and his white family lived in a big house whiter than they were, set back among towering oak trees on one of the finest streets in Greenwood, Mississippi, practically the heart of the entire Delta. Just a few weeks ago, she'd seen Daddy Ray and his white granddaughter, Claire, walking down Main Street. Faye Mae recognized Claire—she'd once seen her modeling a pink Easter outfit in Bonner's Department Store. Claire's blond hair was almost as white as her skin. Faye Mae had wanted to talk to Claire, but when she got close enough to speak, Claire turned up her little white nose and spun around so fast her crinoline petticoat twirled in a circle before she stomped away in her white patent leather shoes.

That day in Bonner's Department Store had taught Faye Mae the real difference between white folk and people like her and Granny. Claire's insult had hurt, but Faye Mae wasn't going to always be ignored. A month earlier, civil rights activist Medgar Evers had been gunned down in front of his wife and children at their home in Jackson. That horror was causing white people from up north to slip into the Delta, encouraging black folks to register to vote. And Dr. Martin Luther King over in Alabama was shaking up all kinds of things. Even President Kennedy was helping him. When Dr. King had been jailed, President Kennedy had called, asking him if he needed anything. That's when Granny got photos of both men and hung them in her living room at the back of the Dew Drop. "These men are gonna make your life different than mine was," Granny had promised when she nailed the photos to the bare pine walls.

That was exactly why Faye Mae wanted to talk to Daddy Ray. She was planning to change some things herself. In the long run, all she wanted was for him to give her a special birthday present.

"Daddy Ray, I promise. It'll take just a little while. No more than ten minutes. Please, Daddy Ray," Faye Mae whined.

Daddy Ray's cigar froze. He yanked it from his mouth, then tossed it into one of the old soup cans Granny set along the bar for ash trays. The deep blue of his eyes sparked as he grabbed one of Faye Mae's tiny brown arms, squeezing it hard enough to bruise.

"Young'un, I swear you got only about half the brains your mama did!"

Daddy Ray shook her like he did Rex when the old hound failed to do exactly as Daddy Ray wanted. "Didn't your granny tell you why I can't go shashaying up the main street of downtown Greenville with you?"

Rex raised his head and groaned. Faye Mae squeezed her eyes shut, willing Rex to jump up and bite Daddy Ray. Not too hard, of course. She didn't want Daddy Ray to be hurt so badly he couldn't give her what she wanted for her birthday.

"Daddy Ray, you're hurting me!" Faye Mae screamed.

"You hush now," Daddy Ray hissed into her ear. "You're going to rile up your granny."

Faye Mae screamed again, louder this time. Because of Granny, she never truly feared Daddy Ray. Levon had told her Granny kept a pistol somewhere in the Dew Drop, and although she'd never been able to find it, she believed him.

Bent over from the waist, trying to wench away from Daddy Ray's grasp, Faye Mae relaxed when she saw a slender shadow darken the Dew Drop's doorway.

"You let that girl go right this instant!"

Daddy Ray released her and pushed her away. "Go on to your granny, you little whiner. You little baby."

Faye Mae ran and flung her arms around her grandmother's waist, burying her head into the calico apron that covered her dress. Granny's silence was deafening, scaring Faye Mae.

"Ed Ray, don't you ever again put your hand on this child!" Granny's voice was so cold it sounded like someone Faye Mae didn't know.

Daddy Ray took a deep breath, exasperated. "You don't know what that young'un just asked me to do."

"I don't give a fartin' damn what she asked you to do," Granny replied. "I run this joint. I make the money you're countin' there. I take care of you. I take care of your high-falutin' friends and their whores. You will never, ever touch this child like that again. Do you understand?"

Granny grabbed Faye Mae and spun her towards the doorway. "Girl, you go on outside and git those chores done before dark falls."

Faye Mae skedaddled, the Dew Drop's front door almost catching her as Granny slammed it shut.

FAYE MAE STRAINED to lift Granny's bottle opener off the nail behind the bar. She carefully opened four bottles of Dixie beer, then returned the opener to the nail. Faye Mae wanted everything to be just perfect since Granny had left her in charge. She placed each of the cold bottles on the oval tray, added a bowl of Granny's salted peanuts and a handful of napkins. Watching every step, she headed to the table where Daddy Ray sat with Big Jim and his guests, who were from New Orleans. Faye Mae thought she had heard Big Jim call the older man Mr. Banner and the younger man Lee. No mister for him. Big Jim always brought men to the Dew Drop to talk politics. Daddy Ray said a U.S. Senator as important as Big Jim needed a private place to meet with people, and Daddy Ray was happy to provide the Dew Drop. Like most of Big Jim's guests, Mr. Banner didn't seem to step and fetch for Big Jim, but Lee was different. He was as jumpy as a country whore in church.

"Ray, you know well as I do things are changing. That's why it's got to be done this way. Carlos is in total agreement, and his boys will help us." Big Jim's fat hands sliced the air as he talked. "Guy here will make all the arrangements. Let him be seen. Let a few people get to know him a little. At least enough to remember him when the time comes for it."

It wasn't often Big Jim had to work hard to convince Daddy Ray of anything, and Faye Mae was determined to learn what they were up to. As she neared the table, Daddy Ray hushed the senator with a tilt of his head in Faye Mae's direction.

"Gal, I declare you are the spitting image of your Granny," the senator said, turning to give Faye Mae room to slide her tray onto the table. He leaned down to her and whispered loud enough for Daddy Ray and the other man to hear, "Now, you pay attention to how your Granny kept her legs together. Don't you go spreadin' 'em like your mama did!"

Daddy Ray burst out laughing along with Big Jim and Mr. Banner, laughing at Granny, Faye Mae and her mama just like he always did when white visitors came to the Dew Drop. Only Lee looked embarrassed. Faye Mae knew if Granny had been serving them, Big Jim wouldn't have said such a thing, but Granny refused to serve Big Jim anymore. Now days, Granny left the Dew Drop long before Big Jim and his friends arrived to talk business with Daddy Ray. Faye Mae didn't really mind. Occasionally, Daddy Ray's friends left her tips.

"Do you ride the streetcars in New Orleans, Mr. Banner?" Faye Mae blurted out to the older, gray-haired man. "I want to see New Orleans. My teacher last year, Miss Johnston, says it is one of the best places in the whole United States."

Clearly, Faye Mae's comments upset the man, who sighed and looked to Big Jim in exasperation.

"Shut up, young'un!" Daddy Ray yelled, slamming his fist on the table hard enough to rattle the Dixie bottles. "His name is not Banner. Do you hear me?"

Daddy Ray had been bringing Big Jim and his friends to the Dew Drop as long as Faye Mae could remember. Most of them were from places that Faye Mae had only heard about. Places that she hoped to visit one day. This was the first time her questions had made Daddy Ray angry. Something was up!

"I thought I heard you call him Mr. Banner … "

"What in the hell did I just say to you, girl? His damned name is not Banner," roared Daddy Ray.

Before Faye Mae knew it, Daddy Ray had her arm in his grasp, shaking her so hard the blue barrettes on her pigtails jumped, his face as red as one of Granny's June tomatoes.

"I was jus wantin'—"

"You don't want nothing. Do you hear me? You don't know this man. You have not seen this man. Do you understand?" His fingers bore into the skinniness of her forearm.

Faye Mae nodded her head and tried to back up.

"Ray, let the child go now." Big Jim's voice was smooth. "Let's not make trouble that'll be remembered further than today."

Daddy Ray nodded, keeping his eyes fixed on hers as he eased his grip.

"Course, you're right, Senator," Daddy Ray said, easing back into his chair. "I just got carried away. You're right, of course."

Big Jim reached into his pocket and brought out a shiny half-dollar that he held out to Faye Mae.

"Look here, gal. I got this over to the U.S. Mint last week. Not many people can do that, but ole Big Jim's got his ways." He nodded reassuringly to Faye Mae when she hesitated.

"Why don't you go on outside and visit with your brother while we men talk about all this stuff you're not interested in?" he continued. "Levon'll tell you some stories about Washington, D.C. Now, gal, that's a real city! Don't you want to hear about Washington?"

Faye Mae snatched the coin from his fingers and headed out the Dew Drop's front door as Big Jim proceeded to mouth whip Daddy Ray.

LEVON WAITED in the Dew Drop's parking lot, polishing Big Jim's black Caddie. It was the first time she'd seen him in weeks. He whistled "Big Legged Mama" in time to the white rag he pushed around the chrome.

"If you got another rag, I'll help you," offered Faye Mae.

Levon looked up with a grin. "Now, that's the kind of welcome home I like. Come give your brother a hug." He smelled of Turtle Wax and Big Jim's cologne. Faye Mae wrinkled her nose as he stooped and wrapped his long arms around her.

Levon had a different daddy than Faye Mae. His skin was so light he passed as white in some of the places where he drove Big Jim. When he couldn't pass, he helped Big Jim with people like her and Granny. Faye Mae was smart enough to know, even if Levon wasn't, that was one of the reasons Big Jim had hired him. That and his connections with Daddy Ray. And, like Daddy Ray, Big Jim never did anything for other people unless he got more out of it than they did. Still, Faye Mae knew enough to not burst Levon's bubble with all these facts. What she really wanted was to find out why Big Jim and Daddy Ray were acting all weird about Mr. Banner and Lee from New Orleans.

Levon stepped back and looked Faye Mae up and down. "My,

you're getting big, Little Bit. The boys'll be fightin' over you before long."

Faye Mae tried to act disinterested. Seemed every man she
met these days felt compelled to say the same things. Thank heavens no one said those things in front of Granny, or she would
never see life beyond the Dew Drop again.

"Say, are the gentlemen from New Orleans relatives of Big
Jim's?" Faye Mae picked at lint on her cotton shorts, pretending
like she could care less who the pair was.

Levon's response was to spin his head around, searching the
Dew Drop's yard like a scorched dog looking for water. Satisfied
they were alone, Levon turned back to Faye Mae with an angry
face the likes she'd never seen on her brother. "You don't need to
be asking nothing about them men from New Orleans. You forget who they are and where they're from. You understand me?"

Faye Mae solemnly nodded her agreement and smiled for
Levon's benefit. As always, the best way to deal with Levon was
to turn the conversation back to him.

"Say, would you like one of those cold beers Granny put out for
Big Jim and them? There's more in the Frigidaire than they'll drink."

Leon pulled off his black chauffeur's hat and touched the polishing rag to his brow.

"You are a genius of a hostess, Faye Mae. Yes, I'd like one. The
sun's hot enough to burn the cotton in the fields. A cold bottle of
beer would do me nicely."

Levon had been around Big Jim for so long he was beginning
to sound and act like him. In the old days, Levon shared all his
secrets with Faye Mae, but he'd worked for the senator since he
reached legal driving age. He was still Levon, but he was different too. He was too young to be drinking, especially in a dry
county where liquor and beer were illegal, but Faye Mae wasn't
going to remind him. Breaking little laws was just another perk
of being Big Jim's driver.

"If you'll play for me, I'll sneak around to the kitchen and go in that way so I don't disturb Big Jim, Daddy Ray and, uh, their guests," Faye Mae said.

"Shore I'll play whatever you like." Levon popped open the Caddie's trunk to reveal the guitar Granny had given him years ago. He pulled the instrument out into the sunlight and lowered his voice for only Faye Mae's ears. "Don't be asking no more questions, you hear?"

Big Jim brought guests to the Dew Drop all the time, but nobody had ever been so skittish about them before. "Sit down. Rest and cool off til I get back," Faye Mae said. "You owe me two songs."

A few minutes later, Faye Mae was sneaking away from the Dew Drop's bar, Levon's two bottles of beer resting in the crook of one arm, when she realized Mr. Banner was speaking. Pausing, she strained to make out his words above the whir of the barroom's old ceiling fan.

"Nobody will ever figure this thing out. I can promise you that. That's why it's so important for us to muddy the waters. In a few weeks, it'll all die down. Levon simply has to drive Lee around the Delta so he can get out of New Orleans for a while and apply for some jobs. It's that simple. Nothing will happen to Levon as long as he drives and doesn't ask questions."

Daddy Ray grunted, then mumbled something Faye Mae couldn't decipher. Big Jim jumped in.

"Ray, you just keep your head down. I'll take care of Levon. He's a good boy. Look, the people in New Orleans want what we want, just like Guy here says. We've got to do it for the good of the country. Folks don't know it, but they need men like us to do the right thing here."

The blood pounded in Faye Mae's ears as she strained to hear more, but the scraping of chair legs against the Dew Drop's floor told her someone was getting up from the table. A trip to the men's bathroom would mean someone was likely to see her. Careful not to creak the old floorboards, Faye Mae hurried out of the Dew Drop.

Levon sat beneath Granny's favorite pecan tree, using his polishing rag to wipe dust from his fancy black patent chauffeur shoes. To his right, the guitar sat in the open case. To his left sat Lee, who looked strained and edgy.

Faye Mae handed each of the men a Dixie bottle. Levon took a long swig, closed his eyes and leaned back against the pecan tree. Lee sniffed the lip of his bottle and wiped it with his shirt before putting it to his lips.

"That sure is refreshing in this heat. I do thank you for coming up with this idea." Levon again used his best Big Jim imitation, showing off for Lee. Faye Mae wondered if Levon ever slipped into it in front of Big Jim.

"Say, Little Bit, don't you have a birthday coming up soon? What do you want your big brother to buy you with some of this mess of money he's making from the senator?"

Faye Mae had momentarily forgotten her obsession with her birthday wish in her desire to learn more about Mr. Banner. She shifted gears. "I want the same thing I wanted last year and the year before that, and the year before that … "

"Little Bit, grow up! You know Daddy Ray isn't gonna do that. Quit making him mad every year. Ask him for something appropriate for a young lady. Ask him for jewelry. That's what you need to do."

Faye Mae stuck out her tongue at Levon, who reached as though to snatch it out of her mouth. Levon wasn't going to be any more help with her birthday this year than last. She could see that, and she was tired of his actin'. It was time to change the subject. "Who is that Mr. Banner from New Orleans?"

Levon sat up so suddenly a little of his beer sloshed out of the bottle. "Whoa! I warned you to mind your own business, little sister!"

Faye Mae turned to Lee, who ignored her gaze. "What are you men up to? A few minutes ago, Daddy Ray almost whipped me when I asked about him being from New Orleans. Why does he make all of you so nervous?"

Levon resettled his beer bottles, winked at Lee and chuckled. "Now. Now. There's nothing wrong with, er, … Mr. Banner. I guess he and Big Jim are just doing political business for the first time. That sort of thing makes everybody a little jumpy. If you were around it like I am, you'd understand it more. Why, when Big Jim gets up in Washington—"

Faye Mae didn't care about Washington. "I understand Daddy Ray's got no need to go all crazy when I asked Mr. Banner about New Orleans."

Lee's dark eyes snapped at her as he poured out his beer, then stood to sling the bottle across the yard into Granny's rose bushes.

"You need to keep your little sister quiet, or other people will do it for you," Lee warned before heading back for the Dew Drop.

"I knew y'all were up to no good. Granny isn't going to like—"

"You shut up, Little Bit!"

Levon had never spoken to her in that tone. Tears filled Faye Mae's eyes.

Across the yard, Lee started for the Dew Drop, then changed his path to the old barn down the road. Levon eyed him nervously before turning back to Faye Mae.

"Look, Little Bit, these big political guys have all kinds of secrets. I hear a lot of them, and I have to keep quiet. Why do you think there's a glass partition between the front seat of the Caddie and the back? It's so Big Jim can keep me from hearing him talk when he wants to."

Faye Mae shook her head. What needed so much secrecy? "Granny isn't going to like it. We need to tell her." Faye Mae's tone was pleading.

"Whatever Daddy Ray and them is talking about, you don't need to worry about it. Let them handle it. Why, some of the stuff I hear, I just put it out of my mind because it's too big and too scary to think about." Leon took another long pull off the Dixie's neck, tilting it so far back the bottle's sweat fell onto his cheeks like tears.

"What kind of stuff?" whispered Faye Mae. "Is it the Russians? Miss Johnston told us all about them last year in fourth grade. How they spy on us all the time and want to bomb us and how jealous they are because we make better rocket ships than they do."

Levon leaned around Faye Mae to peer back towards the Dew Drop, making sure one more time that they were alone. When he spoke, his voice was a conspiratorial whisper.

"It's kinda the Russians, but again, it's not exactly them. You wouldn't believe the things Big Jim is mixed up in. The things he has to do in order to keep all of us safe. Why, one day last month I even drove him to the White House to talk to President Kennedy."

Faye Mae's eyes were as round as Big Jim's silver dollar tucked inside a pocket of her shorts. "Did you meet President Kennedy? What did y'all talk about?"

Levon looked around the tree again. "Miss Johnston ever talk to you kids about Cuba?"

"Of course she does. But, what does that have to do with Big Jim?"

Levon sat his lips in a straight line, looking for all the world like the older brother who thought his baby sister was too young to know adult secrets. Instinct told Faye Mae to relax. Levon had never been good at keeping secrets. She held her breath until he began talking again.

"Now, Faye Mae, you can't ever tell anybody what I'm going to tell you. Not even Granny," warned Levon. "You gotta remember. Big Jim would fire me and kill me if he knew I told you these things."

"I promise on Robert Johnson's grave and the night he made his deal with Mr. Devil," said Faye Mae, quoting one of Granny's favorite sayings.

"One night I drove Big Jim down to Biloxi, and he met with some men who'd come in on a boat. They were from Miami. They spoke Spanish," Levon whispered. "I think they were Cubans. I didn't hear everything, but I guarantee you from what I heard, Big Jim is gonna fix this mess with Castro."

"Is Mr. Banner part of that? Is that why Daddy Ray got so mad that I knew his name?"

Anger clouded Levon's eyes. "His name is not Mr. Banner, Faye Mae, and if you know what's good for your dark hide, you'll forget about him and what I just told you. You especially won't be mentioning this to Granny."

She stuck out her lower lip and started to invoke Granny's name again, but suddenly Levon's face softened. When he spoke, it was in his best Big Jim voice.

"Say, I seem to recall that birthday present you've wanted for years, but nobody would let you have it. Do you still want it?"

"You know I do! You're gonna do that for me? No lyin' now!"

Levon leaned back against the tree's trunk. "If you can keep this secret from everybody you know, you'll get that birthday present. I'll see to it personally."

Faye Mae was skeptical. This was obviously a huge secret she was being asked to keep. "You better not bum out on me. If you do, I'll … "

Levon lifted his Dixie bottle in salute. "I swear on my own grave I'll give you your special birthday wish, but only if you keep our secret."

Faye Mae's head bobbed up and down.

FALL FROSTED THE DELTA, and Faye Mae had forgotten about Mr. Banner. Her birthday was fast approaching, and she reminded Levon of his promise every time he dropped by the Dew Drop. Lee was living in Granny's backyard, and Levon was driving him all over the Delta to apply for jobs. Faye Mae was curious about the man, especially since she'd overhead Daddy Ray warning Levon against being seen with Lee. Daddy Ray had advised Levon to drop Lee off, let him apply for work and pick him up later at another location. It was all so strange.

Faye Mae hurried into the weathered barn next door to the Dew Drop, taking care no one was watching. Granny had banished Lee to the barn's dusty old tack room shortly after his arrival, then warned Faye Mae to keep her distance. A couple of hours earlier, Granny had headed out to buy groceries, and Lee had left with Levon. No doubt to apply for more jobs that never panned out.

The time was right to do a little searching of Lee's things, but if Granny caught her, she would kill her on the spot. Holding back information from Granny would be bad enough. Snooping through someone else's things was a killing offense. Granny was Baptist, hard-shelled, and there wasn't leniency for certain crimes.

Sunlight sneaked through the old planks enough for Faye Mae to see. The cot Daddy Ray had brought for Lee was made up so tight she could have bounced one of Big Jim's silver dollars off it. An upended wooden crate was a makeshift nightstand, and a kerosene lamp with a smoked chimney sat atop it. Not much to discover, unless there was something in the long, black box stored beneath the cot. Faye Mae thought it was a guitar case, but as she pulled it out into the light, she saw it was too slim. If it was a suitcase, it was the skinniest one Faye Mae had ever seen. She popped its latches and slowly lifted the top.

Nestled into a cloth cutout was the biggest and shiniest rifle Faye Mae had ever seen. A lot of the men she knew hunted for food, especially during the winter, but none of them, including the white men who pretended to hunt when they were spending time with their girlfriends at the Dew Drop, had ever carried a rifle like this. It even had a little eyeglass for the shooter to look through just like Audi Murphy used in the old movies Granny liked to watch.

Tires crunching on gravel terrified Faye Mae into action. It had to be Levon bringing Lee home. She slammed down the case's lid and shoved it back under the cot without realizing she had failed to close the latches.

"You found a job yet?" Faye Mae asked as she stepped out into the sunlight. She pushed a rickety old bicycle that had belonged to Levon years ago. Her heart beat like an injured sparrow's.

Lee's eyes narrowed, and for a second Faye Mae thought he was mad, but the moment passed, and he only shook his head.

"My friend Ratchet said his daddy found a job over at the little sawmill in Shelby, and Ratchet's daddy is a no-good drunk. You might have a chance there 'cause you don't seem like a drunk to me." Faye Mae pushed the bike toward him.

The corners of Lee's mouth turned up enough to suggest maybe he could smile, if he set his mind to it. "No, I'm not a drunk. I don't do sawmill work either."

"What kind of job you looking for? Maybe we can help. Granny knows bunches of people." Lee looked like he needed a job real soon since he was so skinny, and he wore the same pants, shirt and light-weight jacket every time she saw seen him.

"I'm not really looking for a job," he said. "I'm here because I already have a job, but I can't tell anyone what it is. What you been doing in the barn?"

Faye Mae's hands sweated on the rust of the bicycle's old handlebars. She was going to be killed right here within sight of the Dew Drop, and nobody would ever know what happened.

Lee took a step forward. "Why are you so curious about me?"

The sound of Granny's approaching footsteps stopped the conversation, and Faye Mae silently promised God she would be good for the rest of her life. In fact, maybe God had let Granny show up as a sign Faye Mae should confess everything to her.

"What are you doing out here?" Granny demanded of Faye Mae. She turned to Lee. "Weren't you told to stay away from my granddaughter?"

Lee gave Granny the same little shit-eating smile he'd given to Faye Mae earlier.

The last thing Faye Mae wanted was for Granny to get into a fight with him now. She wasn't certain if her guess about Lee was correct, but the hairs were rising on the back of her neck, and that grin of his wasn't calming her any.

"Granny, a tire went flat on my bike, and I remembered this ole one of Levon's. I thought I maybe could use one of the tires," she stammered.

Granny glared at Lee as though she were going to throw him off her property but thought better of it. She turned her attention back to Faye Mae.

"Levon said he'll be back up here next week." Granny nodded at Lee. "He had a message for you, Faye Mae. He said to tell you he remembers about your birthday."

"That's right, Faye Mae. Levon told me he has a special gift for you," Lee said, his tone a warning only Faye Mae understood. "But, he said you get it only if you're a really good girl. Did he tell you that?"

Faye Mae could almost feel the blood pulsing through the veins in Granny's neck.

"Nothing for you to worry about," Granny shot back at him. "Maybe you'll be long gone before we celebrate her birthday. Faye Mae, move that bike. I need you to help me get ready for tonight's customers."

Faye Mae barely got out a "yes ma'am" before Granny was gone. It was the first time Granny had ever walked away from throwing someone she disliked off her property. That was all Faye Mae needed to confirm her suspicions about Lee. He was here on nasty business, Daddy Ray was part of it, and they were using Levon. If Granny knew Levon was involved in anything with a gun, she'd put Lee on the road. Faye Mae wanted to tell Granny everything, but she also wanted that birthday present. She would just have to trust Levon to do the right thing.

THE NOONDAY SUN warmed the Delta dirt tilled in preparation for winter crops, sending its scent drifting into the Cadillac's open window. Faye Mae, wearing the new red plaid shift dress and white blouse Granny had given her, sat in the front seat between Levon and Lee. It was her tenth birthday, and she was heading to an afternoon party at the house of Norma Jeanette, her best friend. Levon was driving Lee to see someone, but she didn't know who. She only knew that Levon had reassured her that Lee was nothing more than a political organizer for Big Jim, and if he had a gun it was likely for his own protection. For the first time in a week, her mind was at peace.

The radio played blues from KFFA something fierce.

"Whew, that's real music, Lee. The stuff down in New Orleans is good, but it can't hold a candle to the Delta blues," bragged Levon.

"I'm not a big music fan." Lee focused straight ahead.

"You need to drop by the Dew Drop when some of these ole guys are cuttin' heads, and they'll make a believer out of you."

"Cuttin' heads? You mentioned that the other day. What is that?"

Levon chuckled. "Where you from? Y'all don't cut heads down in New Orleans? That's when two blues players want the same crowd, so they outplay each other, forcing the audience to pick one of them as the better player. Round these parts, it also means anyone who's trying to outdo someone else. Or when two people are working together, but they got different intentions."

Levon stretched to turn down the blues song that blared from the Caddie's radio. "When I pick you up after the party, you finally get that birthday present I've been promising you," he said to Faye Mae.

Faye Mae could hardly wait. She'd gotten nice clothes from Granny, a doll from Daddy Ray, and she was looking forward to the party, but Levon's present was the one everyone had told her she'd never receive. Faye Mae crossed her arms and stared dead ahead at U.S. 61, watching the Caddie gobble it up.

FAYE MAE SHIFTED HER BIRTHDAY GIFTS in her arms as the Caddie rolled to a stop in front of Norma Jeanette's house. The sun was sinking low, and Levon was late picking her up. To her astonishment, Lee was behind the wheel instead of Levon, who was nowhere to be seen. Faye Mae had never seen anyone but Levon drive Big Jim's Caddie.

"Your brother didn't finish with his business. He told me to pick you up and take you home. Did you enjoy your party?"

"Yes, it was nice. We played spin-the-bottle, and I outran every boy there," Faye Mae said. "Levon promised he would give me my birthday present now!"

Lee opened the Caddie's trunk and motioned for her to put her presents inside. Faye Mae almost dropped them when she spied Levon's guitar case. Levon never went anywhere without it. She tightened her hold on the presents.

"I don't think I should go anywhere without Levon." She backed away from the Caddie. "I can wait here til you bring him."

"Levon not being here is part of your present. He needed Big Jim to set it up, and he's doing that now." Lee took the gifts from Faye Mae's arms and placed them inside the trunk. What Lee had said was true. Levon was always so correct, and seeking Big Jim's help made sense to her.

When the Caddie reached Greenwood's largest intersection, Lee turned it away from the highway that headed home. Parking right in front of Barclay's Drugstore, Lee came all the way around the Caddie to open and close the door for Faye Mae. Together, the white man and the young black girl headed up the sidewalk of downtown Greenwood. Faye Mae could feel the stares of every person who passed them.

Faye Mae had walked by the drugstore many times, always looking inside to see who was eating ice cream at the soda fountain. Sometimes she'd seen Daddy Ray and Claire sharing a hot fudge sundae. Suddenly, Faye Mae took a step backward and shook her head at Lee.

"I can't go in there. I'm not allowed. We could get in big trouble." Faye Mae's voice shook. Granny would kill her if she started this kind of mess in Greenwood.

Lee opened the shiny bronze door and laid a firm hand on her shoulder. "It's fine for you to come in today. Big Jim and Levon worked it all out for you."

Big Jim had never done anything for Faye Mae, but apparently he would if Levon asked him. Maybe Big Jim wasn't as bad as Granny had warned her.

"You promise? I don't want Granny getting all mad at me."

"I promise," Lee said. "The manager knows we're coming. Big Jim called him. He knows how to handle these things. Nobody crosses Big Jim around these parts. Now, how can your Granny get mad at that?"

Faye Mae let him guide her into Barclay's past the perfume counter with its boxes of Evening in Paris already stacked up for Christmas, past the gift counters with boxes of flowery stationery and cards, then finally into the soda fountain area with its black and white tile floor and small tables, each surrounded by four wooden chairs and set with glass holders of straws and napkins. Faye Mae moved like she was in a dream. Self-conscious over how she must look after the raucous party, she smoothed down her pigtails and stood a little taller. She wished Norma Jeanette were here to see this. She would just die with envy.

"We don't need a menu, ma'am," Lee told the teenaged blond who came over to take their order. "I believe the Senator called in our order."

Faye Mae watched how the girl kept her eyes only on Lee, never looking in her direction.

"Yes, sir. He called. And, he said you and … uh … the young girl would want a hot fudge sundae each. I'll get 'em for you right away." She scurried off, still avoiding Faye Mae until she got to the kitchen. Then, she turned and stared through its square of glass like Faye Mae was some wild animal on the prowl.

"That girl is upset," announced Faye Mae.

"We don't really care," replied Lee. "We're Big Jim's guests, and they know that. Enjoy your birthday present."

"I wonder why nobody else is in here. I've never seen Barclay's empty before."

"Don't worry about that either," Lee said. "Worry about how you're going to eat all this sundae."

The blond girl sat a huge paper cup, filled above the rim with ice cream and chocolate syrup, in front of Faye Mae. In front of Lee, she sat a pretty glass dish that sparkled with vanilla ice cream, chocolate syrup and cherries atop it. Faye Mae's sundae lacked cherries.

"Young lady, I believe you mixed up our orders." Lee's voice was quiet and firm. "I believe Big Jim was explicit in the directions he gave your manager."

Rolling her eyes, the blond quickly swapped the two sundaes. "Don't tell anyone I did that," she said before heading back to the kitchen to resume her position behind the door.

Digging into the rich whipped cream and cherries, Faye Mae knew this was the best birthday she was ever going to have in her entire life, even if Big Jim did make it happen and even if Daddy Ray and Claire weren't there to see it.

GRANNY'S SCREAMS woke Faye Mae before midnight. Before she could get her feet on the cold wooden floor, Daddy Ray was barging into her bedroom, and she smelled the Southern Comfort before he pulled on the overhead light.

"Get up. Granny needs you," he slurred, almost falling on top of her.

Faye Mae knew Daddy Ray drank, but this was the first time she'd ever seen him drunk, and it scared her to death. No doubt he'd discovered she'd been sitting up in Barclay's Drugstore having a hot fudge sundae. Maybe he was drunk because it would make it easier for him to kill her. He certainly was mad enough.

Faye Mae ran to Granny, who sat in her rocking chair with a photo frame clutched to her breast. Her salt and pepper hair, normally brushed smooth and knotted into a bun, stood out around her head in clumps where she had run her hands through it. The chair's rockers beat a steady whamp whamp on the hard floor in time with her crying and wailing.

"Lord, young'un, what're we going to do? It's the end. The end." Granny reached out a hand to pull Faye Mae closer, but she was reluctant to let either adult lay hands on her until she knew what they'd heard about the Barclay's Drugstore incident.

"I'm sorry, Granny. I know I shouldn't have done it. I didn't mean for anything bad to happen."

Granny's feet halted the rocker's rhythm. She lunged from the chair, but Faye Mae was quicker. Granny threw her hands heavenward as though praying an incantation. "Please, Lord, reveal to me what this child had to do with the killing of my beloved baby,

Levon. Reveal it to me here and now, Lord, and if she deserves it, strike her dead for what's she's done!"

Levon was dead? Faye Mae ran to her grandmother, burying her head into the soft bosom.

"I didn't do anything to Levon. I thought you were talking about something else. Please, please don't let Levon be dead."

Granny tilted Faye Mae's chin upward until their eyes met.

"Child, your brother is as dead as my womb. They found his body tonight out near the river, strung up like they always do us." Her hold tightened on Faye Mae. "Now tell me the truth if you knew one single thing to do with that!"

"I didn't Granny. I swear I didn't." Tears poured from Faye Mae's eyes. "I loved Levon. You know that Granny."

"Well, then why were you so afraid and all ready to confess?"

Faye Mae closed her eyes and took a deep breath, preparing herself to meet Levon in the hereafter.

"Because I went into Barclay's Drugstore in Greenville this afternoon and had a hot fudge sundae. Lee took me. He made me go, but I knew you wouldn't like it. I'm sorry, Granny. I'm so sorry."

"Lee? You say he took you?"

"Yessum. He said Levon had Big Jim set it all up for my birthday so it would be okay and they wouldn't throw me outta there. It must have been true because the white people were as nice as pie to me. Lee said Levon couldn't come because he had to get Big Jim to set it up."

Granny let go of Faye Mae, then suddenly reached her arms around her, drawing her into a tight hug.

"Oh, child, child, child," Granny murmured, stroking the little girl's hair. "I want you to tell Daddy Ray this. It's his evil that's done this. His and Big Jim's. Not you."

LEVON WAS BURIED in the graveyard where most of Granny's relatives had been taken since they were freed. At the end of the service, Daddy Ray left Granny's side to speak to Big Jim, who'd arrived with his new chauffeur, a light-skinned young man from Greenville. The two old men shook hands and hugged, burying the truth behind Levon's murder deeper than his coffin in the Delta dirt.

Granny grabbed Faye Mae's hand, yanking her along past the two men as they headed to the Caddie.

"Laura Mae, I'll be along to the Dew Drop in just a minute," Daddy Ray said to Granny.

Granny didn't veer from her course, and her eyes never rested on Daddy Ray again after that moment. "Don't trouble yourself, Ray, you stay here with your kind. You'll never be needed at the Dew Drop again, ya hear?"

LEVON HAD BEEN IN THE GROUND five weeks when Miss Harding announced to Faye Mae's class that President Kennedy had been shot, and students were being released early. The cloudy November day matched Faye Mae's spirits as she walked into the Dew Drop. Since Levon's death, Granny had taken to the living room sofa rather than sit in her rocking chair, and she was there now, watching news reports from Dallas about President Kennedy.

As darkness fell, Faye Mae heated a can of soup for Granny. Several hours later, the bowl of soup remained untouched. Granny hadn't said a full sentence since Faye Mae got home from school.

"Granny, you need to eat something. I'll heat this soup back up."

Before Faye Mae got to the kitchen door, a familiar voice sounded across the room.

"I did not shoot the President. I'm asking an attorney to come forward to represent me. I'm a patsy." Lee's voice was soft but clear. Faye Mae hurried to look at the television.

Handcuffed and standing in the Dallas Police Department, Lee was surrounded by angry-looking policemen and unruly reporters who kept flashing cameras at him. His eye was blackened.

"Oh, Lord, my Lord." Granny gripped her old rag quilt tightly around her. "I knew that man brought nothing but the Devil's trouble. I knew it. I knew it."

"I WANT TO GO UP TO THE FRONT DOOR, ya hear?" Granny insisted.

Granny's feet barely held on the icy lawn of Daddy Ray's white house. Ever since Levon and President Kennedy had died, Granny had been sinking out of life. Faye Mae held tightly to her arm, guiding her. Faye Mae had barely knocked against the leaded glass door before it was opened. Claire, wearing a black velvet dress with black velvet bows in her blond hair, stood solidly in the opening, staring at her and Granny like they were beggars.

"Claire, darlin', now you get on back to your room while I take care of these folks," said the large black woman dressed in a white uniform, who descended a huge staircase just beyond the door. Claire stood rooted like one of Granny's pecan trees. "Shoo now, missy!"

Turning up her pert nose without speaking, Claire retreated. The door swung wide for them. The black woman smiled and gently waved them towards the stairs. "Doc Brumfield says you got just a little time 'fore he passes."

Daddy Ray laid in the biggest bed Faye Mae had ever seen, surrounded by mounds of white pillows. Rex was sprawled across the foot of it, and he raised his head to greet Faye Mae. The room's heavy blue curtains were drawn against the winter day. A fire burned low in the fireplace, and the maid moved to stoke it back to a blaze. A bandage as white as her uniform covered Daddy Ray's bare chest.

The maid had found Daddy Ray seconds after she heard the gunshot from his study. Even so, he couldn't survive the self-inflicted wound.

Granny stopped a good two feet from the edge of the bed. "We're here, Ed Ray, what do you want with us?" she demanded.

Daddy Ray's eyes flickered, then tried to focus on them. "Need to know truth," he barely got out.

"Well, you'd be the last one to see about that," Granny snorted, leaning more onto her walking stick.

"Levon. He knew too much," Daddy Ray wheezed before a coughing fit brought the nurse to his side. She turned him slightly, then backed away again. Daddy Ray looked to Faye Mae. "When did you find the gun?"

Granny beat her walking stick against the floor. "Ed Ray, shut up your nonsense. This girl don't know nothin' about a gun. You're out of your head!"

Daddy Ray's eyes pleaded to Faye Mae until she hung her head in shame.

"I went looking in the barn. It was under his cot. I wanted to know what y'all were up to," Faye Mae admitted.

"So she found a gun. What does that mean?" Granny shouted.

Daddy Ray took in a breath that rattled on the way out of his chest. "Lee told Big Jim. That's why Levon died. He knew too much…" The coughing began again, and Faye Mae smelled death, like when Levon used to bring home dead squirrels in a gunny sack.

"Faye Mae was supposed to have died too. Instead, he took her to Barclay's."

Faye Mae sputtered. "But he said Big Jim set it all up. There was nobody else there. They served me. Only Big Jim…"

"Hush, young'un!" Granny spat. "For once in your life! Be quiet!"

Daddy Ray lifted a hand, motioning her to the bed. "Things … never … what … they … seem." Daddy Ray's chest rose and fell beneath the bandage. Quiet blanketed the room.

Granny stepped forward and touched Daddy Ray's arm while Faye Mae squeezed his hand, willing him to hang on.

Daddy Ray's voice was thready and weak. "I'm…sorry… Laura Mae. He was…my boy, too."

Daddy Ray's eyes fluttered, then rolled halfway down. Faye Mae watched his eyeballs glaze into nothingness.

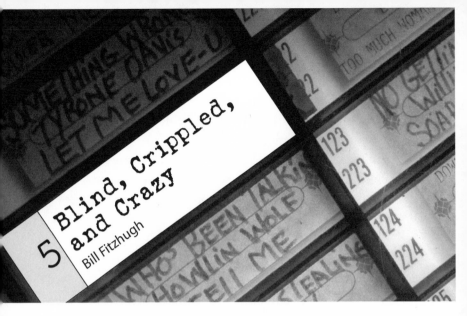

5

Blind, Crippled, and Crazy

Bill Fitzhugh

1959

WADE EASLEY was in the Whites Only car when the Delta
Eagle left Memphis with fifty-eight passengers on board. A
wormy man with one lazy eye, he wore a grey suit and took a seat
by the window, his briefcase clutched in his lap like a paperweight
to keep him from blowing away.

The train crossed the Mississippi on the Harahan Bridge then
tacked south through Arkansas with stops in Helena, McGehee,
and Lake Village, just across the river from Greenville, Mississippi where Wade Easley had some business.

He was one of twelve passengers to get off in Lake Village. It
was hotter than he had expected, more humid too, with the sun
coming down at the same angle from which one is bludgeoned to
death. As he waited on the platform for the porter to hand down
his suitcase, Mr. Easley dabbed his forehead with a handkerchief
and wondered why anyone would live here voluntarily. He
thought about how good a cold beer would taste and hoped he
wasn't in one of those counties that didn't sell alcohol.

What happened next happened suddenly. A man wearing sunglasses and a thick mustache bumped into him roughly from one side, throwing him off balance. The man grabbed for Mr. Easley as if to make sure he didn't fall. He quickly apologized and smoothed Mr. Easley's jacket, asking if he was okay.

Before Easley could tell the man to watch where he was going, he noticed another man approaching hurriedly, pointing a finger and shouting, "You there! Stop!"

The man with the mustache tried to run but this second man grabbed him, spun him around. There was a struggle. Wade stepped back, his grip tightening on his briefcase as he watched the fight with his good eye. The man with the mustache threw a punch, knocking the other man to the ground. Then he turned and scrambled into the station.

The whole thing was over in seconds.

The porter jumped to the platform to help the second man to his feet, saying, "You want me to call the po-lice, Mister?"

"No," the man said, brushing himself off. "No need for that."

Wade, unsettled by the sudden and unexpected violence, gathered himself and approached the man to ask what the ruckus was all about.

The man smiled and held up a wallet. "I believe this is yours, sir."

Mr. Easley quickly frisked himself. "What the—"

"Pickpocket," the other man said. "I saw the whole thing as I got off the train." He handed the wallet back to Mr. Easley.

"I'll be damned," Easley said. "Thank you, sir. I, I don't know what to say."

"No need to say anything. You'd have done the same, I'm sure." Stuffing his handkerchief into his pocket, he offered his hand. "I'm Wade Easley."

"Charlie Clanton," the other man said. "Nice to meet you, except for the circumstances." He rubbed his jaw where the pickpocket had landed the punch.

They stood there awkwardly for a moment before Mr. Easley opened his wallet and fingered some bills. "Here, I owe you a reward."

Charlie Clanton held up his hands, said he wouldn't think of it. Completely unnecessary, just doing the right thing. But Mr. Easley insisted, said he wouldn't feel right otherwise. Charlie said he understood but simply wasn't going to accept money just for doing the right thing. Said it's the way he was raised.

"Well, okay, all right," Wade said, putting his wallet away. "But I insist you let me buy you dinner tonight, at the least. I'm staying at the Hotel Greenville. What do you say?"

Charlie Clanton smiled and said, "That's fine and generous, Mr. Easley. I accept. What time is good for you?"

THAT EVENING, when Charlie met Wade in the lobby of the hotel, the first thing Wade said was, "I'm sorry to say I just discovered this is one of your dry counties, Mr. Clanton. I had hoped to enjoy a few drinks with you before dinner. That is, if you're a drinking man."

Charlie winked and said, "Not to worry, Mr. Easley, things are not as dry as they appear." He gestured toward the door. "Let's take a walk, see if we can't find a little somethin'." They went up to Nelson Street where there seemed to be a lot of action for a place where prohibition was still the law. They stopped at a storefront with blacked-out windows. Charlie knocked on the door. A panel slid open. Charlie winked at Wade then leaned toward the open slot and said, "We're here to see the blind pig."

The man behind the door said, "Cost a dolla' each."

They paid their fee and stepped inside. The room was cool with black and white tiles and a long bar on which sat a child's stuffed pig with the eye buttons removed. They ordered gin and sat at a table in the corner where Charlie explained how the county sheriff made out like a bandit allowing the sale of liquor as long as he got his cut, same as with the cocaine and the gambling and everything else in Washington County, the way it had always been.

They made a toast to local law enforcement and ordered another round.

The gin loosened things up pretty quick. Charlie eased into asking this and that. Found out Wade was in Greenville to meet with a man by the name of Tucker Woolfolk, see about buying his farm. It wasn't long before the gin got Wade to let Charlie in on a little secret. "See, I got an old friend at the chancery clerk's office, tips me off when one of these dumb crackers's about to default on his loan. I get here before the bank does a foreclosure auction, get it on the cheap, then I turn around and sell it to corporate farming interests."

"Hey, that's pretty damn slick," Charlie said in admiring tones.

"Can you imagine?" Wade shook his head in contempt. "Like this Woolfolk I'm here to see, living on the richest farmland on earth and he can't make a go of it as a farmer?"

"Hard to believe, alright," Charlie said.

"I mean, I hate to say it, but, hell, you can't grow a crop here, you probably oughtta be doing something else."

"Really, you're just helping 'em out, then, right?"

"That's the way I like to see it."

Charlie seemed mighty impressed. He pointed at Wade. "Say you're the first guy to the door when opportunity knocks, huh?"

Wade shrugged as modestly as he could, but he had to admit he was pretty sharp.

Charlie seemed intrigued by the whole thing, said it sounded like some real sophisticated business, encouraging Wade to carry on about how he'd developed some clever sales techniques. Said one of his tricks was carrying lots of cash to his meetings because, he said, people are willing to sell for less when they see they'll get the money right on the spot. "That's what I call my bird-in-the-hand technique."

Charlie said, "Well it's a good thing we stopped that pickpocket."

Wade laughed at that. "Charlie, my wallet ain't big enough to carry the kind of money I'm talkin' 'bout." He shook his head like Charlie had no idea. "I got a briefcase back in the hotel safe for that."

Charlie was more and more impressed with every word out of Wade's mouth. Said he figured Wade for a regular real estate genius.

Wade soaked it all up with the gin and they got another round before Wade got around to asking Charlie what he did.

Charlie allowed as how he used to work for the Library of Congress, making field recordings of American folk musicians. "I'm considered something of an expert in the field."

Wade said, "Folk? Like that Woody Guthrie? People like that?"

"Well, some like that, but mostly blues players. You heard of Honeyboy Edwards or Dusty Brown or Muddy Waters?"

"I think I've heard of that last one, that Muddy Waters," Wade said. "But I can't say I'm too familiar with that music. I'm more of an Elvis fan."

"Well, you know a lot of what Elvis does comes straight outta the blues."

"No."

"Oh yeah. I mean, for example, 'That's All Right Mama.' That was written by Arthur Big Boy Crudup, one of Elvis' favorite blues players." Charlie talked about the blues for a while before he said, "You know it's funny, the blues originated right here in the U.S., but the only place you can sell the records, in big numbers anyway, is overseas."

"Is that right?"

"Oh yeah, Europeans and Japanese can't get enough of it.

That's why I became a record producer. See, with my background, I was able to get standing contracts from half a dozen foreign record companies if I manage to locate and record specific artists."

"No kidding? For good money?"

"Well, probably not the kind of money you're dealing with your real estate, but good enough," Charlie said. "Of course, depends who the artist is. Some contracts are just a few thousand, but I've got one for a ten thousand advance and royalties that can add up to four or five times that."

Wade let loose with a long, low whistle. "That's some good money."

"Hey!" Charlie rapped his knuckles on the table like he'd had an idea all the sudden and said, "I tell you what, I'm going to a place outside of Leland tomorrow night, meet a local contact who's helping me track down some old recordings. Why don't you come along? Bound to be somebody playin', we could have us some fun. Have a drink, maybe throw some dice? Give you a story to tell about the night you spent in a real Delta juke joint."

The next night they drove up Highway 61, a few miles north of Leland, eventually pulling into the parking lot for the Starlighter's Lounge, a squat cinder block affair surrounded by cotton as far as you could see.

The joint was jumping. Skin game going at one table, Florida Flip at another, and dice in the corner. Some couples laughing and dancing to the jukebox. Charlie and Wade were the only white faces in the place. Charlie got a bottle and they sat in a booth, started talking. Wade allowed as how it sure seemed authentic even though he didn't have anything to compare it to.

"Oh yeah," Charlie said. "This is the real deal. Bartender tells me Automatic Slim's supposed to play later tonight. Got a real distinct style."

"He somebody you're looking to sign?"

"Naw, I'm here to meet a fella sent me a telegram last week, said he got a hot lead on some recordings we been looking for." He leaned forward conspiratorially. "And if he does, me and him're gonna be shittin' in some tall cotton," Charlie said with a wink.

Wade laughed and asked what the lead was. Charlie played coy, said he couldn't talk about it. But Wade kept pestering until Charlie relented. He poured Wade another drink, glanced around, then leaned onto the table, lowering his voice. "All right, you ever heard of the Blind, Crippled, and Crazy sessions?"

Wade shook his head and leaned in close to hear the story.

After a furtive look around the room, Charlie said, "Well, there're some tape recordings out there that have what you might call a mysterious provenance. There're actually two different stories about these tapes. The first one, and the one most people believe, is one that goes back to the night when a man named Lamar Suggs was murdered."

"This Suggs was one of these musicians?"

"No, he was a bootlegger and occasional pornographer," Charlie said. "Anyway, the story goes that these three guitar players—Blind Buddy Cotton, Crippled Willie Jefferson, and Crazy Earl Tate—got together that night under mysterious circumstances and recorded as a group, which was highly unusual, since they're all famous for being solo players."

Giddy on the gin, Wade was hanging on every word out of Charlie's mouth. He said, "What kinda mysterious circumstances?"

"Well, the story goes that a fella name of Pigfoot Morgan was driving Cotton, Jefferson, and Tate up to Memphis so they could catch a train to Grafton, Wisconsin, where they were gonna record for the Paramount label. Well, on the way, they came across the body of Lamar Suggs out on Highway 61. The four men got out to investigate. A minute later they saw the sheriff's car approaching. Well, when Pigfoot Morgan saw the sheriff's car coming, he drove off, leaving the other three men behind."

"Boy that's a bad case of wrong place at the wrong time."

"You ain't kiddin'," Charlie said. "A Mississippi sheriff finds three jigs standing over the body of a dead white man, everybody knows the deal. Anyway, once he figured out who these three were, the sheriff got an idea. Instead of takin' the three of them to jail, he took them to the local radio station, which was owned by his uncle. He figured as long as he had these fellas between a rock and a hard place, he'd blackmail them into cutting a few sides and make a few dollars."

"Blackmail 'em how?"

"He threatened to arrest 'em for Lamar Suggs' murder if they didn't do two things: first, they had to make a few recordings, and second, they had to sign statements that Morgan was the killer, even though the sheriff knew it wasn't true."

"How'd he know this Pigfoot Morgan hadn't done it?"

"Because the sheriff had killed Suggs himself about five minutes before they showed up. Seems that he found out Suggs was seein' his wife," Charlie said. "The back door man, as they say."

"That's a helluva story."

"Yeah, and if the tapes are as good as people say, they're pretty valuable. But see, here's the best part. For years, there's been this rumor that these tapes were actually recorded back in 1932 out at Dockery Plantation and that it's a recording of Charlie Patton, Tommy Johnson, and Son House playing together. Three of the most important names in the blues. And if that's the case, the tapes are virtually priceless."

"How priceless?"

"Who knows? A quarter million, a half million. It's impossible to say."

Wade's jaw dropped. "You gotta be kiddin' me."

Charlie shook his head. "People say the tapes leave you speechless. Collectors have been trying to find them ever since.

Matter of fact … " Charlie reached inside his jacket and pulled out a document. "Record company out of London sent me this contract, said they'll pay a ten thousand dollar advance against the standard—" Charlie stopped when he noticed a man had stopped at their table.

The man snatched the contract from Charlie's hand and said, "Charlie, what the hell're you doin'?"

Charlie looked up casually. "Oh, hey, Travis. I was wonderin' where you were." He snatched the contract back and returned it to his inside pocket.

For a moment Wade thought he'd seen this man before but he couldn't figure where and he let it go.

Travis sucked so hard on his cigarette his cheeks sunk in. He pointed at Wade and said, "Who's this guy?"

"Relax." Charlie gestured at a chair. "Sit down. This is Wade Easley. We both came in on the Delta Eagle, that's all. Wade's in real estate. He ain't after the tapes."

This seemed to satisfy Travis and he joined them at the table. "If you say so." He shook Wade's hand and said, "Nothin' personal."

Wade shrugged it off. "Have a drink."

"So," Charlie said. "Whatcha got?"

"Good news and bad," Travis said. "Good news is … I found the tapes."

Charlie nearly jumped out of the joint. "Jesus! Where? Who has 'em?"

"Crazy Earl Tate's had 'em all along," Travis said. "And he's willin' to sell."

"Did you hear them?"

"Of course I heard them," Travis said. "And every word is true. I got goose bumps. Hair on the back of my neck was standing on end."

"You think it's Blind, Crippled, and Crazy or Patton, Johnson, and Son House?"

"Tate said it wasn't him and Willie and Buddy, so draw your own conclusion."

Wade's head bounced back and forth as the conversation unfolded.

"So what's the bad news?"

Travis sucked hard on his cigarette again, said, "Fontaine's in town and he knows Earl's got the tapes."

"Shit. Fontaine?" Charlie buried his face in his hands for a moment before he looked up. "Are you kiddin' me?"

Travis shook his head. "I made the offer, like we talked about, but Earl said Fontaine's willing to pay more."

"God—" Charlie slammed a fist on the table then looked at Travis. "He say how much more?"

"Five more."

"I don't suppose you mean hundred."

Travis shook his head again. "Thousand."

"Jesus, Mary, and—"

A sly smile crossed Wade's face.

Travis stubbed his cigarette out. "Earl said he'd give us til tomorrow night to match the offer since we got there first."

"Oh that's just peachy. Where the hell're we gonna get that kinda money in the next twenty-four hours?"

That's when Wade nudged Charlie and cupped a hand to one ear. He said, "You hear that?"

Charlie looked distressed and distracted. "Hear what?"

"If I'm not mistaken, it's the sound of opportunity knocking."

"What're you talking about?"

"I'm talking about the solution to your problem."

"I don't follow."

"You said it yourself, Charlie. Who's the first guy to the door when opportunity knocks? Me, right? Well, you got a venture and you need some funding. And I've got funding for a venture."

Travis lit another cigarette and said, "I don't like where this is goin'."

"You got your real estate to deal with," Charlie said. "We'll figure this out."

"Hell, it's my money," Wade said. "I ain't gotta invest everything in real estate. This looks like a good deal to me. You got that contract. You found the tapes. All you need is the rest of the financing."

Charlie looked at Travis like he might be considering the idea.

"Are you outta your rabbit-assed mind?" Travis shook his head. "No way! We ain't cuttin' this sumbitch in on this. Don't even start." He slugged down his drink, reached for the bottle.

Charlie shrugged, said, "Fine with me, Travis, but we gotta get the money somewhere or kiss the tapes goodbye. You got an extra five grand?"

Travis stared hard at Charlie for a second before he cursed and said, "I knew something like this was gonna happen."

"You knew what was gonna happen?"

"I don't know. Just…something. We let this sumbitch in and we gotta make the split three ways."

"Well Travis, would you rather split *something* three ways or keep *nothing* all to yourself?"

Wade smiled and slapped the table top. "Now you're talking." He rubbed his chin for a second before he pointed at Charlie. "Lemme ask, you know how this Fontaine character plans to pay?"

"Same as us, I 'spect." Charlie shrugged and poured another round. "Standard contract, small cash advance with the rest due based on royalties over time."

"So that extra five grand he's offering is in the royalties?"

"Yeah, it's all on the back end." Travis nodded. "That's what Earl told me."

Wade smiled and said, "Bird in the hand, Charlie." Wade rubbed his finger and thumb together. "Instead of that small advance, we show this Earl Tate he's gonna get that money up front instead of that pie-in-the-sky pitch. I guarantee we get those tapes."

Charlie scratched his head. "I don't know…"

"Trust me," Wade said.

THEY WENT BACK to the Hotel Greenville so Wade could get his briefcase out of the safe. Then they drove out to Crazy Earl's shack near Milestone Bayou. They parked on the side of the road and started down a narrow path leading to a field beyond a stand of cypress.

Wade had never been so far back in the woods. Charlie and Travis were a few feet away but in the darkness he could barely see them. The drone of frogs and cicadas was so loud and constant that he couldn't hear himself think. Somewhere out in the moonless bayou, a big cat let loose with a murderous screech. It chilled Wade to the bone and made him think this was the sort of darkness into which people fall and are never seen again.

They picked their way slowly through the dark and weedy field that led to Earl's shack. Ahead they could see the golden glow of candles flickering in the window.

Charlie said, "Wade, just so you know, Crazy Earl didn't just draw his name out of a hat."

"'Zat right?" Wade was holding his briefcase against his chest like a shield.

Travis tapped a finger to the side of his head. "Says he's a conjur doctor, you know? Makes charms and hands."

Wade peered over the top of his briefcase. "Hands?"

"Yeah, talismans, amulets, things like that. There's people swear he's cured 'em of stuff. And, hell, who knows. World's full of strange things."

They stopped at the steps leading to the porch. Charlie called out, "Hey, Earl? It's Charlie Clanton. Came out to talk about them tapes."

There was no response. But after a moment the door creaked open and Earl stepped out, all red-rimmed eyes and bitter scowl. His face was an angry mug shot. He wore a long Prince Albert coat and a stove-pipe hat, cocked all acey-deucy. He looked into the darkness beyond the men, like there might be something dangerous behind them and he said, "You come in but you gone have to wait til I'm done making this hand."

They followed Earl into his murky shack and sat down on a couple of mismatched chairs and a milk crate. Fear was creeping in on Wade as he looked around. The shack was overflowing with clay jars and tin cans and odd little boxes filled with bird wings and the jaws of small mammals. There were ashes and powders of things burned on red-hot metal, dirt from the graves of the old and wicked, congealed blood from pig-eating sows, patches of red flannel, and all the other ingredients necessary to bring about everything from love to sorrow to death.

Earl sat at his table and dropped some snakeroot into an old Silver Crest lard tin, then he set it over a candle and added a pinch of sand-burr. After that he dropped in a broken black cat bone and two rusty coffin nails. As the smoke rose from the tin, Earl closed his eyes and said, "Eh! Eh! Bomba, hen, hen! Canga bafio te! Canga li!"

He breathed the smoke and began to tremble and jerk. Then he turned and looked directly at Wade, a crazy look in his eyes. "I been marked," he said as his jaw began to wobble. "I'm a blue-gummed nigger could kill you with one bite!"

In the flickering candle's glow Wade nodded like a frightened child. He had no doubt it was true. He was halfway hiding behind his briefcase now, just hoping the voodoo was almost over so they could get down to business and get the hell out of this dark little shack and the crazy man with the Judas eye.

After a moment, Earl seemed to return to his own mind and body. He stood and went to one of the shelves behind him where he took down a handmade box lined with flannel. Charlie and Wade looked at Travis, who nodded his affirmation that it was the box containing the tapes.

Earl said, "That Mr. Fontaine is coming with his contract tomorrow night. I s'pose you gone try to talk me outta takin' his deal?"

"You got us all wrong," Charlie said, pulling a pen and a document from inside his coat. "We got a new offer." He laid it on the table in front of Earl, the pen off to the side. "We knew we had to sweeten the deal, show you we're serious."

"Whatchoo mean, sweeten it?"

Charlie reached for the briefcase and Wade just about threw it to him. Charlie popped the latches and set the open case on the table facing Earl.

AN HOUR LATER, they were back at the Starlighter's Lounge, drinking gin and having a laugh about the whole thing. The handmade box with the tapes sat in the middle of the table.

Wade rapped his knuckles on the box and said, "What'd I tell you?"

"Bird in the hand," Charlie said, tilting his glass at Wade. "You sure know your stuff."

"That's right," Wade replied. "You see how quick he signed that contract?"

Travis sucked on his cigarette and said, "He did move pretty fast once he saw that cash."

Wade opened the box and looked at the dusty reels of tape. "How long before they get these out as a record?"

Charlie started to explain the process of mastering and printing albums and how the distribution would work. After a minute, Travis got up to go chase after some woman he'd had his eye on. He said, "Charlie, I'll catch up with you later." He pointed at the box. "Make a copy of those before you ship 'em off." He shook hands with Wade, then followed the woman out the door.

Charlie poured two more glasses and set the bottle on top of the box. "Wade, you wanna go listen to our investment? I got a friend with a tape machine, probably let us use it, we bring him some of this gin."

"Good idea," Wade said.

"All right then." Charlie stood up. "I'm going to the men's, then we'll go hear what all the hoopla's been about all these years." He pointed at Wade, then the box. "Don't run off."

Wade draped an arm over the box. "I'll be waitin' right here."

He sat there for good while, drinking and considering all the ways he was going to spend his money. He was drunk enough that he didn't care how long Charlie had been gone. Didn't even think about it, just leaned on that box and waved his empty glass to get a refill.

By the time he started to wonder what had happened, Charlie and Travis were miles away, pulling down a dirt drive onto somebody's farm, right past a mailbox with "Woolfolk" painted on the side. There was a car parked out front. Earl Tate got out with the briefcase and greeted Charlie. As he handed it over, Earl chuckled and said, "Bird in the hand." Charlie laughed too.

WADE FINISHED HIS DRINK and looked around the bar. He started to get a funny feeling, so he picked up that box and went to the men's room.

Charlie walked up the steps to the farmhouse, knocked on the door. "Uncle Tucker?"

The men's room was as empty as the sudden feeling in the pit of Wade's stomach. He ran out to the parking lot but Charlie's car was gone. He looked all around and there was nothing but cotton as far as the eye could see.

6 Big Midnight Special

James Lee Burke

YOU KNOW HOW SUMMERTIME IS down South. It comes to you in the smell of watermelons and distant rain and the smell of cotton poison and schools of catfish that have gotten dammed up in a pond that's about to be drained. It comes to you in a lick of wet light on razor wire at sunup. You try to hold on to the coolness of the night, but by noon you'll be standing inside your own shadow, hoeing out long rows of soybeans, a gunbull on horseback gazing at you from behind his shades in the turn-around, his silhouette a black cutout against the sun.

At night, way down inside my sleep, I dream of a white horse running in a field under a sky full of thunderheads. The tattoos wrapped around my forearms like blue flags aren't there for orna-mentation. That big white horse pounding across the field makes a sound just like a heart pumping, one that's about to burst.

In the camp, the cleanup details work til noon, then the rest of the weekend is free. The electric chair is in that flat-topped off-white building down by the river. It's called the Red Hat House because during the 1930s trouble-makers who were put on the levee gang and forced to wear stripes and straw hats that were painted red got thrown in there at night, most of them still stinking from a ten-hour day pushing wheel-barrows loaded with dirt and broken bricks double-time under a boiling sun. The boys who stacked their time on the Red Hat gang went out Christians—that is, if they went out at all, because a bunch of them are still under the levee.

The two iron sweat boxes that were set in concrete on Camp A were bulldozed out about ten years ago, around 1953. I knew a guy who spent twenty-two days inside one of them, standing up, in the middle of summer, his knees and tailbone jammed up against the sides whenever he collapsed. They say his body was molded to the box when the prison doctor made the hacks take him out.

Leadbelly was in Camp A. That's where prison legend says he busted that big Stella twelve-string over a guy's head. But I never believed that story. Not many people here understood Leadbelly, and some of them made up stories about him that would make him understandable, like them—predictable and uncomfortable with their secret knowledge about themselves when they looked in the mirror.

Wiley Boone walks out of the haze on the yard, his skin running with sweat, his shirt wadded up and hanging out of his back pocket, the weight sets and high fence and silvery rolls of razor wire at his back. He has a perfect body, hard all over, his chest flat-plated, his green pin-striped britches hanging so low they expose his pubic hair.

"You still trying to pick 'The Wild Side of Life'?" he asks.

"Working on it," I say.

"It's only taken you, what, ten goddamn years?"

"More like twelve," I say, smiling up at him from the steps to my "dorm," resting my big-belly J-50 Gibson across my thigh.

"Jody wants to match the two of us in the three-rounders up in the Block."

I lean sideways so I can see past Wiley at the group out by the weight sets. There's only one chair on the yard, and Jody Prejean is sitting in it, cleaning his nails with a toothpick, blowing the detritus off the tips of his fingers. Jody has the natural good looks of an attractive woman but should not be confused with one. I mean he's no queer himself. Actually he has the lean face and deep-set dark eyes of a poet or a visionary or a man who can read your thoughts. Jody is a man of all seasons.

"Tell Jody I'm too old. Tell him I'm on my third jolt. Tell him I didn't come back here to take dives or beat up on tomato cans." I say all this with a smile on my face, squinting up at Wiley against the glare.

"You calling me a tomato can?"

"A bleeder is a bleeder. Don't take it personal. I had over fifty stitches put in my eyebrows. That's how come my eyes look like a Chinaman's."

"I'll do you a favor, Arlen. I'll tell Jody you'll be over to talk with him. I'll tell him you weren't a smart-ass. I'll tell him you appreciate somebody looking out for your interests."

I form an E chord at the top of the Gibson's neck and start back in on "The Wild Side of Life," running the opening notes up the treble strings.

When I look back up, Wiley is still standing there. There are a series of dates tattooed along each of his lats. No one knows what they represent. Wiley is doing back-to-back nickels for assault-and-battery and breaking-and-entering.

"Jimmy Heap cut the original song. Nobody knows that. Most people only know the Hank Thompson version," I say.

Wiley stares down at me, his hands opening and closing by his sides, unsure if he's being insulted again. "Version of what?"

"The Wild Side of Life," you moron, I think, but I keep my silence. Saying my thoughts out loud is a disease I've got and no amount of grief or 12-step meetings seems to cure it.

"Wiley?"

"What?" he says.

"Chugging pud for Jody will either put you on the stroll or in a grave at Point Lookout. Jody goes through his own crew like potato chips. Ask for lockup if you got to. Just get away from him."

"One of the colored boys ladling peas owes me a big favor. Don't be surprised if you get something extra in your food tonight," he says. He walks back to the weight sets, pulling his shirt loose from his back pocket, popping the dust and sweat off his back with it. There's already a swish to his hips, double nickels or not.

THE BOYS WITH SERIOUS PROBLEMS are called big stripes. They stay up in the Block, in twenty-three-hour lockdown, along with the snitches who are in there for their own protection. Jody Prejean doesn't qualify as a big stripe. He's intelligent and has the manners of a dapper businessman, the kind of guy who runs a beer distributorship or a vending machine company. His clothes are pressed by his favorite punk; another punk shampoos and clips his hair once a week. His cowboy boots get picked up at his bunk every night. Before sunup they're back under his bunk, their tips spit-shined into mirrors.

His two-deck bunk is in a board-plank alcove, down by the cage-wire that separates us from the night screw who reads paperback westerns at a table under a naked light bulb until sunup. On the wall above Jody's bunk is a hand-brocaded tapestry that reads: "Every knee to me shall bend." I lean against Jody's doorjamb and look at nothing in particular. Jody is sitting on the edge of his bunk, playing chess with a stack of bread dough from Shreveport named Butterbean Simmons. Butterbean talks with a lisp and is always powdered with sunburn. He has spent most of his life in children's shelters and reformatories. When he was nineteen, his grandmother tried to whip him with a switch.

Butterbean threw a refrigerator on top of her, then tossed her and the refrigerator down a staircase.

It takes Jody a long time to look up from his game. His dark hair is sun-bleached on the tips and wet-combed on his neck. His cheeks are slightly sunken, his skin as pale as a consumptive's. "Want something, Arlen?" he says.

How do you survive in jail? You don't show fear, but you don't ever pretend you're something you're not. "I do my own time, Jody. I don't spit in anybody's soup."

"Know what Arlen is talking about?" Jody asks Butterbean.

Butterbean grins good-naturedly, his eyes disappearing into slits. "I think so," he replies.

"So tell me," Jody says.

"I ain't sure," Butterbean says.

Jody laughs under his breath, his eyes on me, like only he and I are on the same intellectual plane. "Sit down. Here, next to me. Come on, I won't hurt you," he says. "You were a club fighter, Arlen. You'll add a lot of class to the card."

"No thanks."

"I can sweeten the pot. A touch of China white, maybe. I can make it happen."

"I'm staying clean this time."

"We're all pulling for you on that. Where's your guitar?"

"In the cage."

"A Gibson, that's one of them good ones, isn't it?"

"Don't mess with me, Jody."

"Wouldn't dream of it. Your move, Butterbean," he says.

I BUTCHER CHICKENS AND LIVESTOCK with a colored half-trusty by the name of Hogman. He has bristles on his head instead of hair, and eyes like lumps of coal. They contain neither heat nor joy, and have the lifeless quality of fuel that's been used up in a fire. His forearms are scrolled with scars like flattened gray worms from old knife beefs. He owns a mariachi twelve-string guitar, and wraps banjo strings on the treble pegs because he says they give his music "shine." Some days he works in the kitchen and delivers rice and red beans and water cans to the crews in the fields. While we're chopping up meat on a big wood block that provides the only color inside the gloom where we work, he sings a song he wrote on the backs of his eyelids when he was still a young stiff and did three days in the sweat box for sassing a hack:

My Bayou Caney woman run off wit' a downtown man,
She left my heart is in a paper bag at the bottom of our garbage can.
But I ain't grieving 'cause she headed down the road,
I just don't understand why she had to take my V-8 Ford.

"You're a jewel, Hogman," I say.

"Lot of womens tell me that," he replies. "Was you really at Guadalcanal?"

"Yeah, I was sixteen. I was at Iwo in '45."

"You got wounded in the war?"

"Not a scratch."

"Then how come you put junk in your arm?"

"It's medicine, no different than people going to a drug store." I try to hold my eyes on his, but I can't do it. Like many lifers, Hogman enjoys a strange kind of freedom; he's already lost everything he ever had, so no one has power over him. That means he doesn't have to be polite when somebody tries to jerk his crank and sell the kind of doodah in here that passes for philosophy.

"You was struck by lightning, though? That's how you got that white streak in your hair and the quiver in your voice."

"That's what my folks said. I don't remember much of it. I was playing baseball, with spikes on, and the grass was wet from the rain. Everything lit up, then I was on the ground and my spikes were blown off my feet, and my socks were smoking."

"Know what you are, Arlen? A purist. That's another word for hardhead. You t'ink you can go your own way, wrap yourself in your own space, listen to your own riffs. Jody Prejean has got your name on the corkboard for the t'ree-rounders."

"Run that by me again?"

"Jody put your name up there on the fight card. You going against Wiley Boone. You cain't tell a man like Jody to kiss your ass and just walk away."

"Jody is a gas bag," I say, feeling the words clot in my wind-pipe.

"He'll break your thumbs. He'll get somebody to pour Drano down your t'roat. You can ax for segregation up in the Block, but he's got two guys over there can race by your cell and light you up. Jody can walk t'rew walls."

"So screw him," I say.

"See, that make you be a purist. Playing the same songs over and over again. You got your own church and you the only cat in it. The world ain't got no place for people like you, Arlen. Not even in here. Your kind is out yonder, under the levee, their mout's stopped with dirt."

Hogman slams his cleaver down on a slab of pig meat, cracking through bone and sinew, covering us both with a viscous pink mist.

FOR SUPPER THIS EVENING we had rice and greens and fried fish. The warden's wife is a Christian woman and teaches Bible lessons up in the Block and oversees the kitchens throughout the prison farm. Sometimes through my window I see her walking on the levee with other women. Their dresses are like gossamer, and the shapes of their bodies are backlit against a red sun. The grass on the levee is deep green and ankle-high, and the wind blowing off the Mississippi channels through it at sunset. The sky is piled with yellow and purple clouds, like great curds of smoke rising from a chemical fire. Far across the water are flooded gum and willow trees, bending in the wind, small waves capping against their trunks, marking the place where the world of free people begins. The ladies sometimes clasp hands and study the sunset. I suspect they're praying or performing a benediction of some kind. I wonder if in their innocence they ever think of the rib cages and skulls buried beneath their feet.

My J-50 Gibson has a mahogany back and sides and a spruce soundboard.

The bass notes rumble through the soundboard like apples tumbling down a chute, and at the same time you can hear every touch of the plectrum on the treble strings. The older the J-50 gets, the deeper its resonance. Floyd Tillman signed my soundboard in a Beaumont beer joint. Brownie McGhee and Furry Lewis and Ike Turner signed it in Memphis. Texas Ruby and Curley Fox signed it at Cook's Hoedown in Houston. Leon McAuliffe signed it under the stars at an outdoor dance on the Indian reservation in the Winding Stairs Mountains of East Oklahoma.

My only problem is it takes me ten years minimum to get a piece down right. I started working on Hank Snow's "Movin' On" in 1950. Eleven years later I saw him play. Know how he created that special sound and rhythm that nobody can imitate? His rhythm guitarist used conventional tuning and stayed in C sharp. But Hank tuned his strings way down, then put a capo on the first fret and did all his runs in D sharp. Is that weird or what? What the rest of the band was playing in was beyond me. The point is Hank broke all the rules and, like the guy who wrote "The Wild Side of Life," created one of the greatest country songs ever written.

My bunk is military tuck, my snacks or "scarf" and my cigarette papers and my can of Bugler tobacco and my cigarette-rolling machine and my magazines all squared away on my shelf. The big window fan at the end of the building keeps our dorm cool until morning. After a shower and supper and a change into clean state blues, I like to sit on my bunk and play my Gibson. Nobody bothers me, except maybe to ask for a particular song. If you're a "solid" con, nobody usually bothers your stuff. But a musical instrument in here can be a temptation. Just before lights go out at nine o'clock, I always give my Gibson to the night screw, who locks it in the cage with him, along with the soda pop and candy bars and potato chips and Fritos for the canteen.

Tonight is different.

"Cain't do it no more, Arlen," he says. He has a narrow face and sun-browned arms that are pocked with cancerous skin tissue. One of his eyes is slightly lower than the other, which makes you think you're looking at separate people.

"That kind of jams me up, boss," I say.

"It ain't coincidence you're down on the 'bitch, boy. If you followed a few rules, maybe that wouldn't be the case."

"Don't do this to me, Cap."

"Don't degrade yourself. You're con-wise and a smart man, Arlen. Adjust, that's the key. You hearing me on this?"

"Yes sir."

Jody got to you, you lying bastard, a voice inside me says.

"What'd you say?"

"Not a thing, boss," I reply, lowering my eyes, folding my arms across my chest.

"By the way, you're not working in the slaughter house no more. At bell count tomorrow morning, you're on the truck."

AT SUNRISE I wrap my Gibson in a blanket, fold down the ends along the back and the soundboard, and tie twine around the nut, the base of the neck, and across the sound hole. I put my Gibson under my bunk and look at it for a long time, then go in for breakfast. We have grits, sausage, white bread, and black coffee, but it's hard for me to eat. Just before bell count on the yard, I look at my Gibson one more time. The morning is already hot, the wind down, clouds of gnats and mosquitoes rising from the willow trees along the river. Three U.S. Army surplus trucks clang across a cattle guard and turn into the yard. In the distance I can see the mounted gunbulls in the corn and soybean and sweet potato fields waiting on our arrival, the water cans set in the shadows of the gum trees, the sun coming up hard, like a molten ball lifted with tongs from a furnace. Some of the gunbulls are actually trusty inmates. They have to serve the time of any guy who escapes while under their charge.

At noon I see Butterbean Simmons hoeing in the row next to me, eyeballing me sideways, his long-sleeve shirt buttoned at the wrists and throat, his armpits looped with sweat. "The money is on Wiley in the three-rounder," he says. "I'm betting on you, though. You'll rip him up."

The soil is loamy, cinnamon-colored, and smells of pesticide and night damp. "Tell Jody he touches my box, we take everything to a higher level," I reply, my hoe rising and falling in front of me, notching weeds out of the row.

"Man, I'm trying to be your friend."

My oldest enemy is my anger. It seems to have no origins and blooms in my chest and sends a rush of bile into my throat. "Lose the guise, 'Bean, and while you're at it, get the fuck away from me."

The night screw had said I went down on the 'bitch, as in "habitual," as in three jolts in the same state. When you carry the 'bitch with you into a parole hearing, there's a good chance you're not even going out max time; there's a good chance you're going to stack eternity in the inmate cemetery at Point Lookout. Why am I working on my third jolt? I'd like to say it's skag. But my dreams aren't just about white horses pounding across a field under a blue-black sky forked with lightning. My dreams tell me about the other people who live inside my skin, people who have done things that don't seem connected to the man I think I am.

By quitting time, I'm wired to the eyes. After we offload from the trucks, everyone bursts into the dorm, kicking off work shoes, stripping off their clothes, heading for the shower with towels and bars of soap. I head for my bunk.

My Gibson is still there, but not under it, *on* it, like a wrapped mummy stretched out on the sheet. I put it back under my bunk, undress, and go into the shower. Wiley Boone stands under one of the pipes, a stream of cold water dividing on his scalp, his body running with soap, braiding in a stream off his phallus.

"Who moved my box, Wiley?" I ask.

"Guys cleaning up? The count screw?" he replies. "Maybe it was an earthquake. Yeah, that's probably it."

"You're planning to lay down in the three-rounder, aren't you?"

"I'm gonna hand you your ass is what I'm gonna do," he says.

"Wrong. I'm going to hold you up. And while I'm holding you up, I'm going to cut you to pieces. Then I'm going to foul you. In the balls, so hard your eyes are going to pop out. So you're going to lose every way possible, Wiley. When you figure all that out, go tell it to Jody."

"You got swastika tats on your arms, Arlen. Hope nobody wants their ink back. You ever have to give your ink back? Thinking about it makes my pecker shrivel up."

The night screw said I was con-wise and smart. After trying to bluff Jody by going at him through Wiley, I had to conclude that the IQ standards in here are pretty low.

BUT I'D SCREWED UP. When you're inside, you never let other people know what you're thinking. You don't argue, you don't contend, you don't let your body language show you're on to another guy's schemes. You wrap yourself in a tight ball and do your time. I'd been a club fighter. Our owner took us from town to town and told us when to stand up and when to lie down. That's how it works, no different than professional wrestling. I'd shot off my mouth to Wiley and tipped him to what I'll do if Jody tries to make me fight by stealing my guitar. That was dumb.

Just before lights-out, I go into Jody's alcove. He's wearing pajamas instead of skivvies, eating a bowl of blackberry pie and cream with a spoon. "You won't have any trouble with me. I'll be on the card and I'll make it come out any way you want," I say. My eyes seem to go in and out of focus when I hear my words outside of myself.

"I'll give it some thought," Jody says. "A man disrespects me, he puts me in an embarrassing position, even guys I admire, guys such as yourself."

"Yeah?" I say.

"Wish you hadn't created this problem for us. You told Wiley I was gonna put him on the stroll? Why'd you do that, Arlen?"

"What do you want from me?"

He glances up at the tapestry on the wall, the one that says "Every knee to me shall bend."

TUESDAY THE SUN IS A YELLOW FLAME inside the bright sheen of humidity that glistens on the fields and trees. The gunbulls try to find shade for themselves and their horses under the water oaks, but there is precious little of it when the sun climbs straight up in the sky. The air is breathless, and blowflies and gnats torment their horses' eyes and legs. A white guy nicknamed Toad because of the moles on his face collapses at the end of my row and lies in a heap between the soybean plants. It's the second time he has fallen out. A gunbull tells three colored guys to pick Toad up and lay him on a red-ant hill out in the gum trees. Toad is either a good actor or he's had sunstroke, because he lies there five minutes before the captain tells the colored guys to put him in the back of the truck.

I hear Butterbean thudding his hoe in the row next to me, his breath wheezing in his chest, sweat dripping off the end of his nose. He wears a straw hat with the brim slanted downward to create shade on his face and neck. "I didn't have nothing to do with it, Arlen," he says.

"With what?" I say.

"*It.*"

Then I know the price I'm about to pay for going against Jody. In my mind's eye I see a trusty from the kitchen walking through the unlocked door of the night screw's cage, the dorm empty, his flat-soled, copper-eyelet prison work shoes echoing down the two rows of bunk beds. I feel the sun boring through the top of my head, my ears filling with the sound of wind inside a conch shell, my lips forming an unspoken word, like a wet bubble on my lips.

I feel the hoe handle slip from my palms, as though the force of gravity has suddenly become stronger than my hands. I hear the creak of leather behind me, a mounted hack straightening himself in the saddle, pushing himself up in the stirrups. "You gonna fall out on me, Arlen?" he says.

"No sir, boss."

"Then what the hell is wrong with you?"

"Got to go to the dorm."

"You sick?"

"Got to protect my box, boss."

"Pick up your tool, boy. Don't hurt yourself worsen you already have."

When I drop off the back of the truck that evening, I watch everyone else rush inside for showers and supper. I walk up the wood steps into the building and cross through the night screw's cage, wiping the sweat and dirt off my chest with my balled-up shirt. The dorm is almost totally quiet, everybody's eyes sliding off my face as I walk toward my bunk. One guy coughs; a couple of other guys head for the showers, walking naked past me, their eyes averted, flip-flops slapping the floor.

I get down on one knee and pull my guitar from under my bunk. It's still wrapped in the blanket I tied around its neck and belly, but the twine sags and the lines and shape of the blanket are no longer taut. Inside, I can hear the rattle of wood. The contours of my Gibson now feel like the broken body of a child. I untie the twine from the nut and the bottom of the neck and the belly and peel back the folds of the blanket. The mahogany back and sides and the spruce soundboard have been splintered into kindling; the bridge has torn loose from the soundboard, and the strings are coiled up on themselves and look like a rat's nest. The neck is broken; the exposed wood, framed by the dark exterior finish, makes me think of bone that has turned yellow inside the earth.

I sit on the side of my bunk and take my Bugler tobacco can and my cigarette papers and my rolling machine off my shelf and start building a cigarette. No one in the dorm speaks. Gradually they file into the shower, some of them looking back at me, the night screw watching them, then shifting his eyes in my direction. "Better eat up, boy," he says.

"Give mine to the cat, boss," I reply.

"Say that again."

"Don't pay me no mind, Cap. I ain't no trouble," I say.

A FEW DECKS of Camels or Red Dots (Lucky Strikes) will buy you any kind of shank you want: a pie-wedge of tin or a long shard of window glass wired and taped tightly inside a chunk of broom handle; a toothbrush heated by a cigarette lighter and re-shaped around a razor blade; a sharpened nail or the guts of a ballpoint pen mounted on a shoe-polish applicator. Cell house shakedowns probably don't discover a third of the inventory.

Molotov cocktails are a different matter. The ingredients are harder to get, and gasoline smells like gasoline, no matter where you hide it. But a guy up in the Block who works in the heavy equipment shed knows how to stash his product where his customer can find it and the hacks can't. It's a package deal and his product never fails: a Mason jar of gas, Tide detergent, and paraffin shaved into crumbs on a carrot grater. He even tapes a cotton

ignition pad on the cap so all you have to do is wet it down, touch
a flame to it, and heave it at your target. There's no way to get the
detergent and the hot paraffin off the skin. I don't like to think
about it. Ever hear the sound of somebody who's been caught inside a flamethrower? It's just like a mewing kitten's. They don't
scream; they just mew inside the heat. You hear it for a long time
in your sleep. You hear it sometimes when you're awake, too.

Jody comes to my bunk after supper. Some of his crew trail in
after him, lighting smokes, staring around the dorm like they're
not part of the conversation but lapping it up like dogs licking a
blood spore. "You're starting to get a little rank, Arlen. You're not
gonna take a shower?" Jody says.

"I'll get to it directly. Maybe in the next few days," I reply.

"Some of the guys think you ought to do it now."

"I think you're probably right. Thanks for bringing it to my
attention."

I stub out my cigarette in my butt can and blow the smoke
straight out in front of me, not looking at him, the pieces of my
destroyed Gibson folded next to me inside my blanket. I pull the
corners of the blanket together and tie them in a knot, creating
a large sack. I can hear the strings and the broken wood clatter together when I lift the sack and slide it under my bunk.

"My box is still with me, Jody," I say. "So is the music of all
the people who signed their names on it. Busting it up doesn't
change anything."

"You're as piss-poor at lying as you are playing the guitar,
Arlen."

"I was at Iwo," I say, grinning up at him.

"So what?" he says.

Truth is, I don't rightly know myself. I strip naked in front of
Jody and his crew and watch them step back from my stink. Then
I walk into the shower, turn on the cold water full blast, and lean
my forehead against the cinder blocks, my eyes tightly shut.

WEASEL COMBS is a runner and jigger, or lookout man, for a guy up in the Block who takes grapevine orders and provides free home delivery. Our crew is working a soybean field up by the front of the farm, not far from the main gate and the adjacent compound where the free people live. At noon the flatbed truck from the kitchen arrives, and Hogman and Weasel drop off the bed onto the ground and uncap the stainless steel caldron that contains our red beans and rice. A dented water can full of Kool-Aid sits next to it. Weasel is an alcoholic check writer who always has a startled look on his face, like somebody just slammed a door on his head.

"How about an extra piece of cornbread, Arlen?" he says.

"I wouldn't mind," I say.

"I got that magazine you wanted. It's in the cab. I'll bring it to you when I get finished here." His eyes stare brightly into mine. His denim shirt is unbuttoned all the way down his chest. His ribs are stenciled against his skin, his waist so narrow his pants are falling off. A big square of salve-stained gauze is taped over an infected burn on his stomach.

"I could use some reading material. Thanks for bringing that, Weasel," I reply.

We eat in a grove of gum and persimmon trees, the sky growing black overhead. Down below the road that traverses the prison farm I can see the clapboard, tin-roofed houses of the free people inside the fence, clothes popping on the wash lines, a colored inmate breaking corn in a washtub for the wife of the head gunbull, kids playing on a swing set, no different than a back-of-town poor-white neighborhood anywhere in the South. The irony is the free people do almost the same kind of time we do, marked by the farm in ways they don't recognize in themselves.

The hack at the gate sits in a wicker-bottom chair inside a square of hot shade provided by the small shack where he has a desk and a telephone. He's over seventy and has been riding herd on convicts since he was a teenager. Legend has it that during the 1930s he and his brother would get drunk on corn liquor in the middle of the afternoon, take a nap, then pick out a colored inmate and tell him to start running. People would hear a couple of shots inside the wind, and another sack of fertilizer would go into the levee. His teeth are gone and his skin dotted with liver spots. There's not a town in Mississippi or Louisiana he can retire to, lest one of his old charges finds him and does things to him no one does to an elderly man.

I can hear thunder in the south. The wind comes up and trowels great clouds of dust out of the fields, and I feel a solitary raindrop sting my face. Weasel squats down in front of me, his mouth twisted like a knife wound. A copy of *Sports Illustrated* is rolled in his palm. "There's a real interesting article here you ought to read," he says, peeling back the pages with his thumb. "'Bout boxing and all and some of the shitheads who have spoiled the game." He slips a beautifully fashioned wood-handled shank out of his bandage and folds the magazine pages around it. He lowers his voice. "It's hooked on the tip. You want to hear that punk squeal, put it into his guts three times, then bust it off inside. He'll drown in his own blood."

When the truck drives off, Hogman is looking at me from the back of the flatbed, his legs hanging in the dust, his eyes filled with a sad knowledge about the world that is of no value to him and that no one else cares to hear about.

THE WIND KEEPS GUSTING HARD all afternoon, and lightning ripples silently through the thunderheads, sometimes making a creaking sound, like the sky cannot support its own weight. The air is cool and smells of fish roe and wet leaves and freshly plowed earth and swamp water that is netted with algae and is seldom exposed to full light. The air smells of a tropical jungle on a Pacific island and a foxhole you chop from volcanic soil with an entrenching tool. It smells of the fecund darkness that lies under the grass and mushrooms that can bloom overnight on a freshly dug grave. Again, I feel the gravitational pull of the earth under me, and I have no doubt the voices that whisper in the grass are whispering to me.

I sit on the front steps of our dorm and stare through the wire at the wide rent-dented expanse of the Mississippi River. Inside the flooded gum trees on the far side, a bolt of lightning strikes the earth and quivers like a hot wire against the sky. I think about the day I was struck by lightning and how I awoke later and discovered there was a quiver in my voice, one that made me sound like a boy who was perpetually afraid. But my voice and my deeds did not go with one another. The Japanese learned that, and so did my adversaries in New Orleans, Birmingham, Miami, Houston, and Memphis, or wherever I carried the sickness that lived inside me.

"A hurricane is blowing up on the Texas coast. It may be headed right up the pike," the night screw says.

"Why didn't you protect my box, boss? It's not right what y'all did," I say, my arms propped on my knees, my face lowered.

"Your problem is with Jody Prejean, boy. You best not be trying to leave it on other people's doorstep," he replies.

I raise my head and grin at him. "I'll never learn how to pick 'The Wild Side of Life.' It's not right, boss. It's got to be in the Constitution somewhere. A man has got a right to pick his guitar and play 'The Wild Side of Life.'"

His face clouds with his inability to understand what I'm saying, or whether I'm mocking him or myself. "Your problem is with Jody. You hearing me? Now, you watch your goddamn mouth, boy," he says.

For sassing him I should be on my way to segregation. But I'm not. Then I realize how blind and foolish I have been.

THAT NIGHT, as the rain drums on the roof, I catch Jody in the latrine. He's wearing flip-flops and skivvies, his skin as pale as alabaster, his dark hair freshly clipped. "The hacks are setting you up," I say.

"Really?" he says, urinating into a toilet bowl without raising the seat, cupping his phallus with his entire palm.

"Wake up, Jody. They've made me the hitter."

"This is all gonna play out only one way, Arlen. You're gonna be my head bitch. You're gonna collect the stroll money and keep the books and be available if and when I need you. You're gonna by my all-purpose boy. I'll rent you out if I have a mind, or I'll keep you for my own. It will all depend on my mood."

As I watch him I think of the shank I got from Weasel, the piece of glazed ceramic honed on an emery wheel, dancing with light, the tip incised with a barb that will tear out flesh and veins when the blade is pulled from the wound. I want to plunge it into Jody's throat.

"Why you looking at me like that?" he says.

"Because you're stupid. Because you're a tool. Because you're too dumb to know you're a punch for the system."

He shakes off his penis and pushes at the handle on the toilet with his thumb. He wipes his thumb on his skivvies. "It's just a matter of time. Everybody gets down on his knees eventually. You didn't go to Sunday school?"

THE RAIN QUITS AT SUNRISE, at least long enough for us to get into the fields. Perhaps fifty of us are strung out in the soybeans, then the wind drops and the sky becomes sealed with a black lid from one horizon to the next. Seagulls are tormenting the air as though they have no place to land. In the distance, a tornado falls from a cloud like a giant spring and twists its way across the land. A bunch of trucks arrive, and the gunbulls herd us to the levee and we start offloading bags of sand and dropping them along the river's edge.

The river is swollen and yellow, and the willow trees along the banks make me think of a mermaid's green hair undulating inside a wave.

More guys are brought up from the Block, snitches and even big stripes from lockdown and malingerers from the infirmary, even Jody Prejean and his head punk, Wiley Boone, and Hogman and Weasel—anybody who can heft sixty-pound sacks and carry them up a forty-degree incline and stack them in a wall to stop the river from breeching the levee.

I think about all the dead guys buried in the levee, and I think about the hacks who set me up to kill Jody Prejean. I think about the Japs I potted with my M-1 when I was sixteen, some of it just for kicks. I think about what I did to a dealer in the French Quarter who tried to sell me powdered milk when I was jonesing and couldn't stop shaking long enough to heat a spoon over a candle flame. I think about what happened to a Mexican in San Antonio who tried to jackroll me for my Gibson. I remember the look in the eyes of every person I have hurt or killed and I want to scrub my soul clean of my misspent life and to rinse the blood of my victims from my dreams.

I want to pick "The Wild Side of Life" the way Jimmy Heap used to do it. I drop the sandbag I'm carrying onto the levee.

"Where you going, Arlen?" Butterbean says.

"Stay off those porkchops, 'Bean," I reply.

I walk down the levee into the shallows, my hands open to the sky. The wind is whipping through the willow trees, stripping leaves off the branches, scudding the river's surface into froth along the shoals. I feel small waves slide over my pants cuffs and the tops of my work boots.

"You lost your mind, boy?" a gunbull hollers.

I wade deeper into the river, its warmth rising through my clothes, raindrops striking my scalp and shoulders as hard as marbles. The surface of the river is dancing with yellow light, strings of Japanese hyacinths clinging to my hips, clouds of dark sediment swelling up around me. Far beyond the opposite shore, the thunderheads look like an ancient mountain piled against the sky.

I hear the pop of a shotgun in the wind, and a cluster of double-aught bucks flies past me and patterns on the water. The river is high on my chest now and my arms are straight out as I work my way deeper into the current, like a man balancing himself on a tightrope. A floating island of uprooted trees bounces off me, cracking something in my shoulder, turning me in a circle, so for just a moment I have to look back at the prison farm. All of the inmates are on their knees or crouched down in fear of what is happening around them. I see the night screw pull a shotgun from the hands of a gunbull on horseback and come hard down the levee, digging his boots into the sod.

Just as he fires, I smile at him and at the wide panorama of his fellow guards and their saddled horses and the convicts who seem to dot the levee like spectators at a ball game. In my mind's eye the twelve-gauge pumpkin ball flies from the muzzle of his gun as quickly as a bird and touches my forehead and freeze-frames the levee and the people on it and the flooded willows and the river chained with rain rings and the trees of lightning bursting across the sky.

One of my sleeves catches on the island of storm trash, and as I float southward with it, my eyelids stitched to my forehead, I think I see a mountain looming massive and scorched beyond the opposite shore, one I saw many years ago through a pair of binoculars when six of my fellow countrymen labored to plant an American flag on top of it.

My Own Little Room in Hell

Dean James

EVERYTHING FELT HEAVIER TODAY. Her right shoulder twinged hard as she lifted the iron from the wood-burning stove to carry it to the ironing board near the window.

Wincing, she set the iron on a trivet at the broad end of the board. She unwrapped the cloth from around the handle of the iron and wiped the sweat from her forehead. The upper half of her thin cotton shift stuck to her body.

The mid-August day was hot and still. There was little relief from the open window. She could see the shimmer of the heat over the cotton fields that stretched endlessly into the distance.

Sometimes she imagined the whole world was nothing but one big cotton field. Didn't matter which room of the house she was in, when she looked out a window, all she could see was neat rows of cotton.

With a sigh she turned away from the kitchen window to pick up the iron. Pain danced across her back as she bore down on his shirt, smoothing away wrinkles. She tried to ignore the aches. If the shirt didn't turn out just the way he liked it, she'd have worse pain to worry about.

She wished she could do this chore in the parlor. That's where his radio was. The time sure would pass quicker. There was a station in Memphis that played some blues music. One over in Arkansas too.

But he didn't like her touching the radio. He'd saved up for it, watched over it like a jealous lover. Radios had been hard to come by, til the war ended two years ago. Too bad he hadn't been in the war. A Jap or German bullet through his head would have saved her plenty of pain.

She'd learned to be real careful with the radio. Most days he was gone from sunup to sundown, but sometimes he surprised her. He'd caught her twice listening to her blues.

He made fun of her for wanting to listen to nigger music. That's what he called it. Accused her of being a nigger lover, wanting to spread her legs for the first black buck that looked at her sideways.

No use in letting those memories shame her. She sang a song she'd heard Johnny Blue perform one time:

"Got my own little room in Hell,
Drinkin' the devil's wine.
Got my own little room in Hell,
Just trying to pass the time."

DIDN'T MATTER that her singing was all off-key. It served its purpose. Being in that room with Johnny Blue made it easier somehow.

She bore down with the iron again.

Every time she ironed, she thought about her mama.

Her mama had taught her to iron when she was nine, hardly big enough to lift that big old thing. She'd learned to do the job real good, though. She'd had to, with her mama laid up in bed with one baby after another in the six years since. There were ten of them now, three older than her, and six younger. She guessed her mama would stop having babies soon. Last she'd heard Mama was starting to go through the change.

These thoughts hurt. She hadn't seen her mama since she'd gotten married over a year ago. She hadn't seen her daddy either, but him she tried not to think about. She'd never be able to understand what he'd done to her.

Mama had tried to stop her daddy, but her mama was weak with Daddy. He could always get around Mama. Course, he didn't tell Mama the real reason she was marrying Mr. Charles McAlister. That would have been too shameful.

She'd promised her daddy she wouldn't tell Mama either. She regretted that now. Mama thought she wanted to marry Mr. Charles McAlister awful bad, even though he had to be twice her age, at least thirty. He was real handsome, and probably most girls would've been happy to marry such a good-looking man. He had a good job, too, overseer on one of the big Delta plantations.

If only her daddy didn't like to drink and gamble so much. He lost a lot of money—money he should have been spending on Mama and the babies—to Mr. McAlister, and he had no way of paying the man back.

Except with her.

Mr. McAlister said she was beautiful, with her long brown hair and big green eyes. Her bosom had already developed, like her two older sisters. Mr. McAlister couldn't take his eyes off it.

She burned with shame at the thought of her so-called wedding night. The things Mr. McAlister had forced her to do. She'd never heard tell of such, even with her two big sisters already married. They'd never said a thing to her about such disgusting practices.

Daddy hadn't been able to look her in the face when she'd married Mr. McAlister at the justice of the peace's office. He kissed her on the cheek once the ceremony was done, and he hurried out of there like a demon from hell was on his tail.

Sometimes she wished a demon from hell would find her daddy. Sometimes she thought she was married to Satan himself.

After the first shock of finding out she was going to marry Mr. McAlister wore off, she thought it might be nice to be a married woman in her own house. She could have her own babies to look after.

The wedding night destroyed any dreams she had of a happy marriage.

If that hadn't been enough, the first beating three days later did it for her.

She couldn't remember why any more. There'd been too many other beatings since. He never left a mark on her face or her arms, only on places nobody could see.

She smiled bitterly at that. She hardly ever saw anybody besides him, unless he took her in to town to do the shopping. Most of the time he brought the groceries home.

She preferred it that way. If she dared to look at anyone in town, especially a man, he got real mad. No matter how she protested, he wouldn't listen. He said she was just looking around for another man to spread her legs for.

The thought of that made her sick.

She set the iron back on the trivet and examined the shirt. Satisfied, she put it on a hanger and carried it from the kitchen, across the hall of the shotgun house and into the bedroom.

She hung it in the closet and walked back to the kitchen. Two shirts to go and she'd be done with the ironing.

The iron needed heating up again. She moved it back to the stove. Wanting air, she walked from the kitchen into the hallway. Both the front and back doors were propped open, and a tiny breeze wafted down the hall.

Better than nothing, she thought. She moved to the back door and gazed out. The backyard ended six feet from the steps, and the cotton fields began.

She squinted up at the sun. She reckoned it must be about three o'clock.

Soon as she finished ironing she'd have to start on his dinner. Had to be ready the minute he got home. Today was Tuesday, so he wouldn't stay out late tonight. He'd be home around five thirty, hot, tired, and hungry. After he ate, he'd go back to the fields, make sure the men were still hard at it.

At sundown he'd be back. She always hoped he'd be in a good mood, but the men usually managed to piss him off someways. She wondered if he beat them, too.

Half an hour later, finished with the ironing, she put board and iron away. She grabbed a bucket and went out to the back-yard to the pump. She used one hand and put the other under the faucet. The cold spring water felt so good.

She filled the bucket, cupped some water for her face. Let it drip down. Splashed more on her chest, soaking her shift even further.

Sometimes she thought about filling that big old bucket with water and sticking in her head until she drowned.

Or maybe filling the old tin tub they used for bathing and slipping down under the water.

But if she did that, what would he do? He'd threatened more than once to kill her mama and daddy if she didn't do what she was told.

She didn't think he'd really do that, kill somebody, though he'd come purt' near to killing her one time. She'd been laid up in bed for three weeks. From time to time her insides still ached.

Back in the kitchen she dipped water into a boiler. On Tues-day nights it was always fried chicken, biscuits, rice and gravy. Mama had taught her how. He always said she cooked real good, so that was a mercy.

She pulled the rice canister off the shelf and opened it. Star-ing inside, she started trembling. Almost empty. No. Lord no.

Frantically, she searched the shelves, looking for more rice. How could she have forgotten?

She stumbled over to a kitchen chair and sat. The floor seemed to come up to meet her. She put her head down between her knees for some time.

Gradually her head cleared, and she sat upright. Town was too far. Even if she ran as hard as she could, she'd never get there and back in time.

Only one thing to do.

Three minutes later, hastily dressed, still barefoot, she headed out the front door.

She ran the three-quarters of a mile to where an old black woman, Miz Hattie May Carson, lived. Miz Hattie had helped her out before. She was a kind, wise old lady who made home remedies. Even Mr. McAlister would sometimes ask for Miz Hattie's help.

Miz Hattie helped nurse her through that bad spell, when she was laid up for three weeks.

Panting, she slowed to a walk fifty feet from Miz Hattie's old house. Stopping in the shade of an old oak, she rested and caught her breath. She liked Miz Hattie's trees, wished they had some around their house.

She heard talking coming from inside the house. Sweating, her legs caked with dust, she slowly mounted the steps to the front porch.

A woman's voice floated out as she stood, hand raised to knock.

"They's gonna be hell to pay, Miz Hattie. Them boys is so riled up, they's gonna be something terrible happen fo' long. You jes' wait and see."

"And don' nobody know who did it?" Miz Hattie asked, her deep voice full of concern.

"No, ma'am, they sho' nuff don't," the other woman said. "But they gots their suspicions."

She knocked at the door, wondering what the women were talking about. She hated to interrupt, but time was passing quickly.

"Come on in." Miz Hattie's voice rang out.

"Thank you, Miz Hattie. It's just me." She stepped through the screen door, let it shut gently behind her.

"Chile, back in the kitchen," Miz Hattie said. "Come on back."

She walked down the hall and into the kitchen. Miz Hattie, her grizzled head bent over a bowl on the table, was saying, "You'd best be gettin' on, Raylene."

The other woman, maybe forty years younger than Miz Hattie, said, "Yes'm." She acknowledged the newcomer's presence with a quick nod before disappearing into the hallway. Moments later the screen door snapped shut.

"It's nice to see you, chile," Miz Hattie said, putting aside the bowl of green beans she'd been snapping. "How you doin'?"

"I'm okay, Miz Hattie," she said, moving slowly forward. "I hate to bother you, but I need some rice real desperate-like." She reached into the pocket of her worn dress and pulled out some change. "I can pay."

"Don't you be frettin' so." The wise old eyes examined her with kindness, and she blushed. "I got some rice, and you's welcome to it. I reckon you run out unexpected like, and he wants him his rice for supper."

"Yes'm," she said. Miz Hattie understood all too clearly.

"Jes' reach up on that shelf over there," Miz Hattie instructed her in a light, friendly tone. "Yes, lamb, that one there. Did you bring something to put the rice in?"

Stricken, she turned to her benefactor as she set the jar of rice on the table. "Oh, Miz Hattie, I was in such a terrible hurry I didn't even think." She glanced down at her dress. "I reckon I could carry it in my pockets."

Miz Hattie chuckled. "Lord, chile, Heaven knows I gots all kinda jars jes' sittin' around this house. You find one over there and get the rice you need, baby."

Hands trembling, she did as she was told, measuring out what she needed for tonight's meal, pouring it into a small jar.

She tried to pay Miz Hattie, but the old lady wouldn't accept it.

She needed to get back home, but curiosity got the better of her. He never told her anything much, so she was always starved for news. Any kind of news.

"Miz Hattie," she began, her hands rubbing the jar of rice like a talisman, "I couldn't help hear, when I came up to your door, that something terrible's happened."

Miz Hattie's gaze grew dark, and she glanced away for a moment. "You's better off not knowing about such things, baby. Stay in yo' house, and don't even stick yo' head out of it for a while."

"Please, Miz Hattie." She'd never seen her only neighbor in a mood like this. "What's goin' on?"

Miz Hattie shook her head. "Oh, chile, they was a killin' two nights ago at one of them juke joints."

"Who got killed?"

"Johnny Blue."

Stunned, she reached for the table to steady herself, almost dropping her jar of rice. She set the jar down and then lowered herself into a chair.

Johnny Blue. He'd been in her thoughts earlier. He was a boy from around Clarksdale with a whisky-roughened voice. She'd heard him perform once, before she was married. She'd sneaked out of the house one night along with her friend Bobbie Sue, and they'd walked the two miles to a joint where they'd heard he'd be singing.

She and Bobbie Sue sat outside, too young even to sneak in, and strained their ears to hear what they could. The raw emotion in Johnny Blue's voice made her heart ache.

Many a night since, she'd lain awake, listening to that voice in her head. She'd heard him on the radio a few times. He sang to her, even if he didn't know it. He knew her pain, her fear, the longing she had.

And now he was dead.

She burst out crying.

"Lord, chile," Miz Hattie said, alarm in her eyes. "What you carryin' on so for? How come you cryin' for some black man you don't even know?"

The old woman reached out a hand, and she grasped it. Trying to contain her sobs, she managed a few words. Miz Hattie seemed to understand. She handed across her handkerchief.

"Wipe yo' eyes, lamb."

She handed back the sodden handkerchief, and Miz Hattie laid it aside.

"Why would somebody kill him?"

Miz Hattie stared at her, and she read the pity in the old woman's eyes. "Oh, Lord, girl, when do a white man need a reason to kill a black man? Nobody don' know for sure who done it. But they reckon it was a coupla white men done jumped him late that night when he be on his way home."

She shook her head, still trying hard to understand it all. "Why?"

"Don' know why, girl, don' keep askin' me." Miz Hattie got stern with her. "But you keep yo'self in that house, and don' be goin' nowhere or talkin' to nobody. They's something bad gone happen. Peoples is mighty angry. Johnny Blue had a lot of friends."

"Yes'm." She nodded, reaching for her jar of rice. Miz Hattie had said all she was going to say, she could see that.

"You best be gettin' on home, baby," Miz Hattie said. "It be almost fo' thirty."

Alarmed, she jumped up. She couldn't be late serving him his dinner. "Thank you, Miz Hattie," she said, her breathing already coming hard.

She darted out of the kitchen, jar clutched in her hand, slowing down only to open the screen door. She didn't mean it to slam behind her, but she didn't have time to waste.

She raced home, in a tizzy to get his dinner ready. Stopping only long enough to wash away the dust from her bare legs and feet, she set to work.

It was close to six o'clock when Mr. McAlister made it home. She thanked the Lord for small mercies as she set his plate in front of him.

He started in without even a word to her. She went back to the stove to fill her own plate. She sat down across from him and started eating. She never dared take a bite first. He didn't like it.

His plate empty, he shoved it toward her. She got up and refilled it, set it down in front of him again.

She couldn't watch him while he ate. He always shoved food in like he wasn't ever going to eat again. If she looked at him, she wouldn't be able to eat her own plate.

Finally, he was done. He drained his water glass and sat back. She put aside her fork. Once he was done, she was done.

"That was good," he said. "You cain't do much else, but you can cook."

"Thank you." She glanced at his eyes. This was going to be one of the bad nights.

"How was your day?" Sometimes he liked it if she asked him about his work. It could put him in a mellower mood.

Not tonight, she could tell at once. His face darkened.

"Them damn niggers were 'bout as useful as tits on a boar hog today. They ain't much good the best of times, but today and yesterday, I swear they wasn't even worth killin'." He shook his head. "But ain't much I can do about it. Mistuh Bell won't let me use a whip on 'em."

Mr. Bell was the general manager of the whole plantation and Mr. McAlister's boss.

"They upset about something?" She tried to sound like she didn't know nothing, but she couldn't tell if she fooled him.

"Oh, yeah," Mr. McAlister said. He grinned real big. "Somebody beat the shit out of some singin' coon and killed him. They're all riled up about it, mutterin' and carryin' on. Ain't a damn thing they can do about it though." He laughed.

"That's terrible," she said, realizing her mistake the second the words were out of her mouth.

THE NEXT MORNING she could barely get out of bed to cook his breakfast. He didn't speak, wouldn't even look at her. He was always this way the next morning.

After he left for the fields, she cleared away the remains of the food. She couldn't eat anything. It was all she could do not to vomit all over the stove while she cooked.

She cleaned herself as best she could, wishing she dared heat water for a bath. But he'd know she'd used the wood, and that wouldn't do.

During the night she hurt too much to be able to sleep, so she'd had time to think.

Once he was safely gone, she dressed, this time putting on her shoes and sticking what she needed in an old carpetbag. She didn't run this morning. She couldn't.

The heat made breathing even harder. By the time she reached Miz Hattie's house her dress was soaked through, and she thought she might faint before she could make it up to the front door.

But she got there. Leaning against the frame, she knocked, unable to call out.

"Come on in," Miz Hattie called.

She knocked again. She didn't have the strength to move.

Miz Hattie came bustling up to the door moments later. One look, and she knew what had happened.

Gently the old lady led her inside and into the kitchen. She sat, numb and exhausted, while Miz Hattie gathered what she needed.

By the time Miz Hattie finished her ministrations, she felt better. Her head had cleared, thanks to a drink the old lady had given her. She still hurt, but she felt stronger.

"Thank you." Her voice came out as a whisper. Miz Hattie served her more tea, and she drank.

"Po' little chile," Miz Hattie said. "That man, he be the devil himself. Ain't no call for him to be beatin' on you like this. May the good Lord strike him dead."

She smiled faintly. She had little faith that the Lord would stir Himself on her behalf. It was up to her to find a way out of her little room in hell.

She reached for her bag and pulled out one of Mr. McAlister's white shirts. She thrust it at Miz Hattie.

Puzzled, Miz Hattie took the shirt and unfolded it. Together they stared down at the bloodstains all over the front of it.

"I found it this morning," she said. "I got to countin' up, and I knew there was one missing. I finally found it stuffed behind the bureau."

Miz Hattie pulled the shirt closer, one gnarled black finger tracing the outline of blood spatters. She shook her head and looked up.

She could hardly breathe while the old woman thought about it. Miz Hattie nodded. "Yes, chile, I see. I do see." She folded the shirt with care and laid it aside.

"Thank you," she whispered.

Miz Hattie nodded again. "Now you go on home, girl. You take it easy." She got up from the table and fetched a jar. "You put this on you when you start hurtin', and you'll be feeling better soon."

"Thank you." This time her voice was stronger, and when she stood, she didn't hurt near as much.

Out on the road, she glanced back once to see Miz Hattie standing in the doorway of her house, watching her. She didn't wave, just turned and headed down the road to home.

That night he didn't make it in til sundown. She had his pork chops, sweet potatoes, collard greens, and cornbread ready. He ate without talking, still not looking at her.

While she cleaned up in the kitchen, he went into the parlor and turned on the radio. He'd listen to a baseball game, she knew. Probably the St. Louis Cardinals. They were his favorite team.

The sun faded away outside, and she stood at the kitchen window with the light off. She fancied she could see the rows of cotton, marching ever forward. The moon was dim, but she could make out the first few feet of cotton. She stood there for a long time, not moving, simply waiting.

Must have been well after nine when she heard a loud thud from the front of the house. The radio switched off, and Mr. McAlister started yelling. She paid no attention to the words.

Moments later she heard him open the front door. He was too arrogant to be afraid. She could just see him, out on the front porch, defiant, unwilling to back down.

Her legs suddenly weak, she eased herself to the floor beneath the window. She heard the commotion, angry voices, Mr. McAlister's among them.

Then the shotgun blasts. She didn't try to count them.

The night grew quiet around her. She sat under the window for a long time.

SHE HANDED THE DRIVER HER TICKET and climbed into the bus. With the money she got from selling his radio, plus the money Mr. Bell gave her—saying it was back wages, though she knew better—she was able to buy a ticket to Oklahoma City. She even had enough to tide her over until she found a job.

It was too bad about the radio. She could listen to whatever she wanted to now. But she needed the money more. She could always buy a radio for herself sometime. She smiled.

She'd been thinking a lot about Johnny Blue. Especially his song about his own little room in hell. She'd been there, but now she was free.

She stared down at her left hand. The cuts in her fingertips had had a week now to heal. He'd beat her pretty bad that night, but not enough to draw much blood.

She'd had to cut herself. She hardly noticed the pain at the time, even though the sight of the blood made her faint-headed.

Some day she might have regrets. But she didn't think she would.

Mr. McAlister had found his own little room in hell, and welcome to it.

Baby did you see that fire burnin'
Straight up in that black Oklahoma sky
O now did you see that fire burnin'
Straight up in that black Oklahoma sky
Lord I seen them buildings all come-a crashin' down
And I reckon somebody gots to die …

AIN'T BUT TWO THINGS my father left for me in this world: a beat up old no-name six string, and a .38 Smith & Wesson. Just like the old man I keeps the pistol stowed away inna same guitar case I now tote cross my back. Everywhere I go. Heavy load, sure nuff, but it done served me well.

Most folk know me as Plow Boy Lewis. Been also called the Oklahoma Ox from time to time. But to other guitar pickers, this here Big Junior Slides at your service. Yes indeed. I can sings and plays any old tune you might like to hear, and swearing on a stack of Bibles, it won't be like nothing you ever done heard before. You see, when I gets to playing this here guitar I keeps a three-inch length of brass pipe on my ring finger, and a sawed-off bottle neck right there onna middle. I'm the onliest one who play that way, so far I ever seen. Give me a real special sound when I switches back and forth tween the two, howling like a cold wind or grinding like a buzzsaw blade.

Ain't no gimmick or stage trick, you understand. A heavy boot heel on my right hand nigh on to fourteen year ago, that there were the mother of my invention. Since then them two fingers been stiff as copper rods, and I can't fret no chord or ball up a fist to save my soul. All on count of a man who come to call one hot black night in Tulsa.

I ain't killed no man, Lord
But I come doggone close
Said I ain't yet killed a man, no
But I come doggone close
And if that man git to me first Lord
He gonna hafta reckon with my ghost ...

Reckon I believes in God almighty, hear. Reckon I do. But he ain't nothing I can rightly speak on. Never seen his face. But I sure nuff seen Devils. Seen them all my day. Devils all over. One here, one there, walking just like man. Some come in white hoods, you understand. Some with a badge and uniform. Some Devils, they be seen in real fine suits. Yes sir. Some don't come in no costume at all, all right, but you will sure nuff know them by the Hell they unleash.

O preach'm now ...

It were the end of May, nineteen-hunnet-twenny-one. Back then they call the Greenwood side of Tulsa the "Negro Wall Street," and me and mine, we was right there in that good life. Bertie, she ten year old at that time, and Ethel just turning thirteen that day of the thirty-first. Our father, he run his very own shoe store, and us four we all done our share round the shop. Had usselves a real nice place right upstairs, yes we did.

My two sisters and me, we was setting places for Ethel birthday supper (on that same kitchen table Mama died on giving birth to yours truly seven years before) when the first shots rung out.

"Daddy," Ethel say with a start, "what that noise out yonder?!"

"Ethel, you take your brother and sister to the back bedroom and you hide under that bed now. And don't you make no sound, hear!"

"But Daddy!"

"Now, girl! Don't you make a peep and don't come out til I says! GO NOW!"

We run off quick as jackrabbits as old man snatch up his pump-action shotgun and head on downstairs and on outside. My sisters both crying, shaking and quaking, and I had a mind to do likewise. But them tears just ain't come. Froze solid and still, sure nuff. Old man said don't make a peep, and I weren't bout to. Huddled inna dark under that bed petrified like three little old hound dogs in a thunderstorm, we could hear it all coming down outside: screaming, gunfire, busting up like war. And the louder it grow the hotter it done got. Damn blasted hot. I knew they done splitted Hell wide open outside.

"O Daddy …Daddy …" Bertie got to sobbing. "What if he don't never come back?"

"Hush up that mess, Bertie," Ethel say.

As for me, I ain't had no words of comfort nor words of fear. I ain't have no words at all.

"Imma catch me a look," Ethel say, and she done slid out from under the bed.

Just then the door slam open, and pale as death, two white mens lumber in. Staring hard with Lucifer eyes. I couldn't barely make them out laying down there where I be, but I seen the one were fat as a brood sow set to pop with piglets, wearing blue coveralls and swinging a kerosene lamp. T'other, he were built right from bricks carved thick and sharp, his pitch black hair cut straight cross the top his head just like a push broom.

"Now…what we got here?" the bristle-headed one say, grinning dark and broke-tooth, giving Ethel the old wild-eye and pointing his revolver at her bosom. She lock up tighter than a snare drum and press against the north wall. So he stomp on over her way, real slow and heavy, and don't you know one them mud-caked clompers was gonna crunch down on my right hand, snapping them two fingers like brittle old twigs in a dry autumn. Bertie, she slap her hand cross my mouth for to keep me silent … but I weren't fixing to make no sound any old way, even though that pain were hacking paths all through my skinny little frame. That man he ain't notice, though, on count of his eyes being dead set on my sister's trembling young body.

"Come on, Whitney," the fat one got to grunting. "We ain't got no time for no fornication."

"Just…just do your business quick and git gone, hear?" Ethel say, putting on a right brave face.

"Let's just see how it goes, little girl," that man hiss, reaching his hand toward Ethel top button.

Right then Senior Lewis come on busting through the door swinging his shotgun like a club and he catch the hog man in his blubbery gut with one swoop. Swinging the lamp so hard the wick blow out, that fat hunky retch out a dribble of blood, drop his lamp, and stumble off down the hall wheezing and groaning like a beat down pack mule. Father were just set to cocking his rifle as that other white man turn the revolver on him, and open up his chest wide with one shot. Old man slam against the south wall, dead as a rock inna sea, smearing a thick trail of red right cross the paint. Room smelling from sulfur, flint, and kerosene.

Bertie, she got to screaming loud, "Daddy! Daddy!" and Ethel slide down the north wall just sobbing. The white man look back at Ethel, strike a match with his thumb that he done pull from his pocket, drop it inna kerosene and say, "Y'all cook real good now." And make his exit.

I don't member much else but the flash of fire and watching my father go up in flames. We fly from the room, down them stairs into the shop, and out the door.

Outside Greenwood Avenue weren't nothing but a mass of fire so far as your eye could see. Whites there rounding up Negroes all long the way, just like livestock, and carting them off to parts unknown. Folk who resist was shot on site. And there it were, whole colored side of the Frisco tracks burning, crumbling, falling away to nothing, the night sky above filling with smoke and black dust.

"We making our stand at Stovepipe Hill!" someone were heard to shout. But what that mean to three small childrens who just seen they only parent knock down dead as a old stone and they home disappear in one blazing flash? It ain't mean nothing at all, I tell you that. So we just to stood there, eyes wide like six burning suns, as the whole goddamn world die all round us.

All sudden a wild spirit up and grab me and I done found myself to running right on back inside that burning shop.

"Junior! No!" Ethel holler. But I ain't pay her no mind.

I gone straight on behind that front counter, grab up my father guitar case and kept right on to running back outside. That there case, I couldn't hardly lift it, and my two broke fingers got to throbbing and pounding something evil. But I's needing what was in it. I done knowed that I did.

No sooner I be outside again a black automobile screech to a stop right by us, and a young, well-dressed Negro man we ain't never seen fore in our lives jump right out.

"Y'all okay?" he axe. "Get inna car. Imma git you out of here now."

We ain't move a hair.

"Y'all stay here and you gonna burn right up," he say. "Either that or them white men gonna haul you off to a camp. You want that?"

Not so much as a twitch, you hear. Just three little old scarecrows swaying inna hot breeze of a flaming city.

"Ethel?" he say. "Bertie? Junior? Last chance now."

After a short breath of hesitating, we crawls on into that vehicle. Yes we did. Nothing to lose, you understand. The young man he shut the door for us, jump on in his own self, and we speed off into the night.

"Where you need to go?" he axe further. "You got family anywhere close by?"

Only family I ever did know was Ethel, Bertie, and our old man. But Ethel she manage to squeak out, "We g-gots kin in … in Doddsville."

"Doddsville? Mississippi?"

"Y-yes sir."

"Goddamn…that's a long haul. But…I'll take you there."

"Th-thank you sir."

"This is bad…" he mutter under his breath, pressing the pedal and sending us off with a screech. "Worse than '92. Worse than '65. Haven't seen it like this since 1896."

I ain't had no earthly notion of what he saying. But I ain't truly care none. Shock had me closed up good.

And so we done drived all through the night, not speaking nother solitary word, leaving a burning Tulsa and every last bit of life as we done knowed it far behind. And there I set clutching all I had left of old man in my one good hand, t'other hand aching and stinging for what his killer done left me with.

COME SUN UP the man he drop us off at Aunt Bessie house. She come crying and wailing offa that front porch just grabbing us up so tight we bout like to smother, and screaming Why Lord why O sweet Jesus?

Aunt Bessie led the girls on inna house, and I be fixing to follow, when that man he lay his hand on my shoulder. I turn round to face him.

"You gonna carry that with you, Junior?" he axe, pointing at my father guitar case I gots clutched tight cross my chest. I nod my head yes. "Figure you gonna use that machine in there?" he tap the case. "Use it like your father did?" I nod again. He smile wide. "Well in that circumstance, I reckon we'll be meeting each other again. We'll likely have to strike up a deal when you get grown. I can help you, Junior. I can help you when you need it. *And you gonna need it.*"

That young man he say fare thee well, and set off inna dust of the morning. Never even done give his name.

Clarksdale callin', baby
Don't you know I be on my way...

I AIN'T THAT BONEY LITTLE BOY NO MORE. No sir. I's well a full-grown man these here days, and believe that I sure enough got my growth. I ain't called The Ox for no damn reason, hear?

Us three, we shuffle round tween aunts, uncles, and cousins til we old enough to make our own ways. Both my sisters they done settle down in Selma, Alabama with husbands and childrens in tow. I use to see them round holidays and such. But I don't see them no more. Folk grow apart. It be that way sometime. Me, I drived a mule-plow inna fields all through the South while I's raising up, spending my weekends picking my father guitar in jooks when I gots the age to do it. Time come I made my way riding onna music alone. Weren't long fore my crazy two-slide playing ways had folk packing joints everywhere this side of the Mississippi. Everywheres cepting Oklahoma. Swore on my father unmarked grave I weren't never setting foot in that town again.

I do admit I done had occasion to fall into them old traps of
The Blues Man: fighting, drinking, gambling, kicking the gong
round, having to stomp a body or get my own self stomped for
making time with Mr. So-and-so wife. You understand. Ain't nothing I's proud of, that just be the life of a rambling man. Yes sir.

But things they do haunt me. Things that got this boy shaking and sick at night, trying to cry even as a full grown man, but
ain't got what it take to do it. It be locked up in my throat and I
can't push it on out. That night in Tulsa burn through my very
dreams, and I can't never shake it. That look inna eyes of my father when that bullet done rip through his chest, his life leaking
out his back all down the wall. Way that ofay who kill old man
look hard on my sister with some manner of lust and hate the
likes of which not a body alive should have put down on them.
That old Whitney, with his intentions. It weigh down hard on
me, like that load I tote cross my back. It gets to aching all
through me, like them two wrecked up fingers on my right hand.
Ain't no liquor brewed up by man gonna give me the cure I be
needing. No sir. Ain't not a one. Though I tries to find it all same.

Something else haunt me s'well, if haunt the proper word for
it. Some nights when I be playing my songs for the people to
dance to, I sometime look out and see that man who done drived us to Mississippi. Never don't talk or nothing, he just out
inna crowd. Somewheres inna back. Sometime he tip his hat and
smile. But I gits to looking down at my picking hand for one little old second, look up...and he gone.

It weren't just at jooks I seen him at. No sir. Even as just a boy
I be out plowing or picking inna fields and I would have to swear
to holy Jesus that I would see that man out yonder far off. He be
right there. But I blink my eyes, turn my head just so, and he
ain't there no more when I look on back. Figure that he would
stroll on out where I be and chew the rag a spell. I thank him for
his kindness. But always he done gone like a wisp onna wind. I

ain't seen him again for many a year, til I start to playing jooks. And then it be just a moment here and a moment there.

He done said that we meet again, but we don't never meet. I be seeing him, but then he gone.

Thing that trouble my mind, though, is that he … he don't never seem to get no older. From seven year old to twenny-one I done seen this man off and on, and he don't ever age a solitary day. My death right now if I tells a lie.

> *Just like a dog inna thunder Lord*
> *Can you hear me weep and moan*
> *Just like a dog inna thunder*
> *Lord Lord Lord*
> *Can't you hear me weep and moan*
> *There be a roar of hellfire all round me, Lord*
> *And I's out here on my own...*

And so it come to pass that I finds myself right there in Clarksdale, Mississippi. Some colored folk working fields right onna outskirts of Coahoma County was fixing to pitch a ball out at a old farmhouse, and some ruckus was sure enough a cinch to go down. For such affairs as these a loud, hard-driving guitar player be needed, and there plenty to pick from round Clarksdale. But come on now. Ain't nobody to call on in that situation but the Plow Boy hisself. And let me tell you, them folks ain't disappoint, and I ain't disappoint them. The Spirit were sure nuff moving all over that joint, but weren't nothing holy bout it, no sir. Got paid in a fine hot meal and a good bit of jingle for my pocket. And the lady of the house she tip me a bit more on top. You understand.

Next day I gits up and heads off inna town for to buy me a new hat and walking shoes. Just cause the notion please me. So light in my step I was right then I ain't even barely notice all them ofays milling bout they business. Turning right up East Second Street…that there where I done seen him.

Climbing up inna driver side of a flatbed truck I seen that square flat top first off. Same push broom haircut I seen fourteen year ago, now with a good helping of salt mix in that block of black pepper. Softer rounda middle too, but still hard cut like a rock. And just so as I can be sure of what I be seeing, I hears, "Come on, Whitney, move on over and let me drive," a younger white man say huffing up to the vehicle.

"Shut the hell up and git in," old Whitney he bark back at him, and the kid do just that. My slide fingers got to throbbing just to see the man, and he musta felted my stare on him right then cause he turn them Devil eyes right on me and he say, "You need something, boy?"

I just kept on to looking and not moving one muscle. 'Fore too long he just drive away.

Next eight hours or more I set right onna side of that street there just playing my guitar. And thinking evil. Ain't git up to eat or make water or nothing. Just set and play til the sun start to setting. Couple folk drop a coin or two, but most just walk on by. Don't make me no nevermind one way or t'other. I just had to set and play and that alla what I could do. Thinking on Tulsa, thinking on Senior Lewis, thinking on the life we all done had. Thinking on what be all gone now. Thinking evil.

I ain't know if he were coming back. Old White Whitney. But I had a notion that he just might. And come sundown I seen that flatbed truck once again. Both them mens git out from they vehicle sweating and dusty, and head on into a white folk tavern.

"HELLS BELLS you a big'n, ain't you?" Barkeep say to me, sizing me up and stepping on back a piece. "Can I help you?"

Old Whitney there with his young friend, and there I be, standing right behind that pale old rat as he set stuffing his mouth with corn bread. So close I coulda snap his goddamn neck right then. Barkeep eye me real nervous-like and I stands there holding my guitar with my left hand, clicking my slides together with my right. Clickclack. Clickclack. Don't think I could stop the clicking even if I's wanting to.

"Well, sir," I says smiling real wide, "name of Plow Boy Lewis at your service. I be just to passing right through your fine town here and I gots a bit of rumbling in my belly. Now, I ain't got too much inna way of money to pay, but I were hoping that maybe I could set yonder and play a coupla tunes for your patrons here in exchange for a meal or the like. I surely don't mind setting out back to eat. No sir. Don't mind at all."

Horse shit, you understand. I weren't hungry. I couldn't eat nothing just then nohow. But I had to see up close with my own eyes that man. That man who done set the fire and pull the trigger that done took my whole life away.

"We don't have that kind of music here, and we don't serve your … kind of food here neither. You just go on git now."

I stood right still, holding a molded grin on my face.

"Is he gonna hafta tell you again, boy?" Whitney grunt, turning toward me. "You simple? You deef? The door's thataway. Consider yourself warned for the last time."

So I smile, nod my head real nice, and make my way on outside.

And inna dark, I waits.

People be coming and going mosta night. Time come and folk got to be leaving and no one new replace them. I seen that younger white man come stumbling out and walk on his way alone. And then finally … there he. My man. The one I be waiting on. Out onna streets by hisself. And with not a care in his heart, I reckon. And nothing else neither.

At his truck I were there waiting fore even he git there his own self.

"Don't turn round," I say.

"What the goddamn—"

"And don't make one more noise. Just git to walking."

And that's just what he done with nary another word from me—.38 pressing right on inna curve in his back saying all what need to be said.

SO WE GOT TO WALKING. Offa street. Outta town. Inna dust. Into the thick of trees. Frogs and insects screaming out inna night. He in front, me behind toting that guitar on my back, alla while the muzzle of my father pistol pointing straight at his goddamn head.

And we don't say nothing for long time.

"You pull that trigger you gonna swing, boy," he say after we got to walking a fur piece. "You know that, right."

Imma swing if I pull the trigger or not, I says inside my own mind. But I don't mutter not a word out loud. We just walk. Deep into the black of the night. I hears his breathing git heavy. He start to jabbing his heels inna soft ground further we go. Just a little old protest, I reckon. But we keeps on moving.

"I can git you money, if that's what you want, boy," his voice git to cracking.

I laughs a bit onna inside. But I don't say nothing and we just to keep on. *Keep on. Keep on ...*

"TURN ROUND," I says finally.

And he do. I holds that .38 on him with my left hand just as still as you please.

"Reckon both us done rambled to Clarksdale," I says some more. "Now who would figure such a thing? Reckon it's fate?"

"I just f-follow the work," he stutter.

"Well, Mister, that make two of us. You knowing me, Mr. Whitney?"

"Can't say that I do," he say real quiet like. "Should I?"

"Some might to say that yes you should. Sure nuff. Yes indeed. Uh huh. So ... question for you."

"All ... all right."

"You gots dogs at home, Mr. Whitney?"

"How's that?"

"Answer my question now."

He scratch the back his head and spit onna ground.

"I'm afraid I don't r-rightly understand yer question."

"Now, Mr. Whitney. It surely ain't no hard thing to answer. Mean to say, you either gots dogs or you ain't. So, do you gots dogs at your home? Yes or no?"

"I keep ... two mutts for hunting, yes I do."

"Do they git to crying and whimpering come a thunder storm?"

He blink hard twice, eyeing my .38.

"What now?"

"DO THEY CRY AND WHIMPER IN A THUNDER STORM!"

That rage just got to flooding all through my body, you understand. My right hand got to shaking, and that glass slide got on to clackety clack clacking against the brass. *Clack clack clack clack. Clack clack clack clack.* For a moment, but for the crickets and tree frogs, it were the only sound.

"I ... I suspect they do."

Clack clack clack clack clack.

"Even the biggest, meanest dog inna world will git to whimpering and wailing in a storm, won't he, Mr. Whitney?"

"Um ... I reckon. I reckon he will at that, yes."

"Now, Mr. Whitney, why do you suspect that be?"

Clack clack clack clack clack clack.

"Don't ... don't rightly know."

Clack clack clack clack.

He git to fidgeting with his fingers as he can't seem to take his eyes offa my right hand shaking harder now. *Clack clack clack clack clack clack clack.*

"Well, Mr. Whitney … I gots a notion I git to studying on from time to time. Don't call me a expert now, it just a notion. But it seem to me that a house dog will cry all through a storm … just cry cry cry … cause thunder make him come to realize … that he alone. You understand?"

"Um."

"Dogs is just like us, hear? They lie to they own selfs, just like we do. Most time your dog he think the life he gots in your house, it's just fine and dandy. And he think on you and your kin and the other dogs inna house as his pack, all right. But you ain't. We ain't. We ain't no kin for a dog. Out inna wild, dogs and wolfs they run in packs of they own. And in a storm they locks in close together for to keep warm and safe.

"But house dog ain't got no pack … and the sound of thunder draw out that fear and pain like dredging a dark, cold lake. You alone inna world, thunder say to a dog. All. Alone. All alone. So … he cry."

With that I squeeze the trigger just as I pulls my arm to the left, sending that bullet blasting just over his right shoulder. He jump with a start, bugeye, and git to trembling.

"You hearing that dog thunder, Whitney? You hears it? I do. Yes sir. I hears it. I hears it ALLA TIIIIIIIIIIIIIIIME!"

Right then that man he git to shaking hard, worser than my right hand. Mouth quivering like jelly on a spoon.

"Look here," he say, "I … I don't know what it is you want from me, but you just name it. All right? Just name it now."

So many things I could name right then. So many. But instead I just squeeze the trigger again.

And I pull that shot just like the first. Stack of Bibles I did. Sure as I live and breathe I done sent it over his shoulder again.

But that ain't where it done gone. Goddamn if that bullet ain't break right on through his left cheek.

He stumble back with the wild-eye in dead shock. Then fall flat to the ground.

And you know I done stood over him firing off them last four shots right on into his skull til his head weren't nothing but tomato pulp and little cut honeydew rinds.

I DROP THE PISTOL, stumble on over to a thick patch of grass, and fall to my knees crying deep and heavy. Retching up what left of last night supper I stays on to crying and I cannot stop. I retches some more, all right. And more. But ain't nothing but spit and noise after a spell. All hollow inside.

Got my payback, sure nuff did. Got that payback ... but it ain't mean nothing. He dead ... and I might just well be dead same as him.

But there ain't no bullets left.

"ALL RIGHT NOW, JUNIOR?"

I looks up, still on my knees inna grass. And who do I sees walking up to me, but that young Negro who drived us from Tulsa. Same as I ever done seen him and not a day older.

"Toppa the world, Mister," I says wiping my hand cross my lips. "Ain't that plain to see."

He smile and nod.

"Looks like you made a bit of a mess there, son," he say tipping his head at old Whitney body laying there. "Everything better now?"

"Ain't nothing better now," I says clenching my teeth hard. "Nothing. Likely worser, in fact. You looking at two dead mens here inna grass, friend-boy. Ain't just one. Ain't just him."

"That's probably true."

"Got a name do ya?"

"Chances are good. But you can just call me Jerome."

I git to standing up straight and look him dead inna eyes.

"You ain't age a minute since Tulsa, Jerome. How you count for yourself?"

"Just lucky I guess. So tell me, Plow Boy. What's your plan here? How far do you think you can go before they trace this jackass corpse right to you?"

"Reckon I might just well turn myself on over. All right?" I raise up my hands, surrendering to the Lord. "Let this just end now … Less then you gots a different notion. I be all ears, all right, yes indeed."

"That's what I like to hear," he say grinning wide. "You follow me. I know a path that'll take you FAR from here. None of these mothergrabbing fools will ever find you. Of course … it's gonna cost a bit. This ain't free, like Tulsa. You ain't a boy no more, and this is a different kinda walk. You understand."

"I ain't got no ways to pay you."

"You'll find a way."

"So I follows you … and the Devils be offa my trail for good?"

"Well … you'll kinda be trading one set of devils for another. But you follow my lead, and don't make a big show of yourself, and you'll be just fine. Eventually."

"You … huh … you Satan, ain't you?"

"Ha-ha-ha!" He git to laughing, doubling over on hisself. "O shit! Ha-ha-ha! You are the first to ever just come right out and ask! Well … that's a damn good guess anyway!"

Inna distance I see them lamp lights just to floating inna trees. Getting closer and closer. And them devil voices get louder,

"Right out yonder is where I heard them shots!" a voice say. "Follow me! Keep them rifles at the ready."

"Goddamn," I says.

"Goddamn indeed," Jerome reply.

"This it, I reckon."

"You could try to run, yes you could. But come on now. How far do you think you'd git on your own? You stay here and they are gonna burn you up. Or string you up. Or both. Choice is yours, Junior. Last chance, now."

"But ... where we gonna go?"

"What's your pleasure? Big city? Ain't so much the *where*, it's the *when*."

"I heard something!" another voice holler. "Thisaway!"

"Where your automobile at?"

"O, we ain't driving, Plow Boy. It's a long dark path we're walking."

I bends over to fetch my .38 and sling that guitar cross my back one time again.

The voices float closer. "This way! I see something moving! Come on! Hey! Y'all out there freeze!"

"We best git a move on, Junior. It is now or never."

SO WE DONE JUST THAT. Ducking on out into the brush, dodging the devils, quick and silent til we inna clear. Then walking. Walking all through the night. Not speaking nother solitary word. Leaving old corpse ... and old Clarksdale ... and every last bit of my life as I ever done knowed it far behind.

9 Songbyrd Dead at 23
Suzann Ellingsworth

THE DEPRESSION, folks what call it that has a roof overhead and jobs to get up for of a morning. Most everybody else says it's the Hard Times and they come on years afore them Yankee banks chained their doors.

I don't recall no Soft Times.

I might've if my brothers kept sending money home, like they'd promised. After Mama died, my big sister, Mary Sarah, said she was goin' to town to find work. I was to stay put and see to the chores, like I was a servant and our cabin in the Boston Mountains ever shined from hers and Mama's scrub and polish.

Along about the third day, I notioned to learn "Once I Had A Fortune" on daddy's old mandolin. It was Mary Sarah's favorite. Sulled up as she was when she left, she'd be tickled to hear it when she stepped through the door.

The peculiar thing about teaching your fingers the song in your head is the tune and the words gets chopped up and stretched out to nonsense. Then all of a ziggety-zam, I was pluckin' and singin', "My sweetheart has a new fella, and me, she has turned aside. Farewell, farewell, my dearest lil' darlin', I'll go where the world is wide ..."

Quick as that, I lit for Winslow, the neck of that mandolin clenched so tight it's a wonder it didn't crack in two.

"Mary Sarah Comstock?" folks said, time and again, like I had a hundred sisters who'd swore to Mama they'd take care of me. "Why, I haven't laid eyes on her in a month of Sundays." The world is wide, sure enough. Never once did I think to ask *what* town she was venturing off to before she slammed out the door.

It was too dark to walk home, as Arkansas was famed for haints and jimplicutes that breathed fire and prowled the woods of a night. I snuggled into the brambles by the railroad tunnel, hugging the mandolin and wishing Mary Sarah was in the ground, same as Mama and Daddy.

That's where Books poked me with a stick to see if I was alive. I'd never met up with a hobo before. Him and two others laid a fire between the tunnel's maw and a boulder. A lard can plundered from a trash heap boiled bits of vittles they'd scrounged.

Mulligan stew it's called, irregardless of what's in it and what jungle it's cooked in. For the past two years, I've swallowed down gallons of it. Nowadays whole entire families are flipping freights to find work, the Promised Land or, God be merciful, both in the same spot.

Cleburne, Texas ain't it, but seemed middling prosperous with sun in my eyes. I found me a corner to panhandle on and slid off my knapsack jerry-rigged from a flour sack. What worldly possessions I had were in it, since anything that can't be toted in a bindle or pockets owns you, instead of the other way 'round.

Folks that thought me a farm boy were startled when I whipped off my flop hat and the hair flew wild, pert-near to my waist. Daddy's old mandolin had more nicks than a blind barber's first shave. I blew off the cinders, plucked it for tune, then lit into "Old Dan Tucker."

Toes tapped along and hands clapped louder than just polite. Hard coin tinking in my cup made its own music. I sang another two before packing up, saying my throat was parched dry.

A fat jake behind the grocery counter watched me fish a Coca-Cola outta his cooler's rank slush. He palmed my nickel, then said, "Best you hitch onto the next train. We don't abide tramps around here."

Towns a-bristle with churches bigger'n a courthouse seldom did. Him bluffing curt didn't portend trouble, but I put a block between me and the store and crossed the street. Wouldn't you know, the apples I'd took from his bin was wormy. Naught wrong with the Baby Ruths nestled in with 'em.

I strummed, sang to a fare-thee-well, and started begrudging that nickel in the grocer's till. What lands in the cup is for show. Pickin' pockets is dicey, lest I draw a crowd. Then I can lay down the mandolin and take a rube for a do-si-do. Dancin' bosoms behind my overalls' bib do take a man's mind off the cash he's carryin' and nimble fingers dousing after it.

So far, the sodbusters I'd seen didn't have squat in their pockets save lint. As if that wasn't irksome enough, a gent in a Model T drove by a second time and parked at the corner. I suspected him for the law, but he just sat, arms folded on the window ledge, working his mouth funny, like his jawbone needed grease.

"'Back Water Blues,'" he called. "Do you know it?"

I shook my head, like I didn't. Somethin' for nothin' I don't give.

Presently, he walked up flipping a half-dollar off his thumb. His necktie hung loose, but he'd shrugged on the suit coat to his pin-striped trousers. He hummed a piece of "Crazy Blues" off-key. "Please, miss, won't you sing it for me?"

"Please" was as rare as fifty cents all at once. Stupid I wasn't. Sure as I got to get myself a gun, shoot myself a cop, he'd pull a tin star. "Can't, mister," I said. "It ain't fit for a mandolin."

"Just sing." To the lollygaggers, he said, "You'll pay to hear it, won't you?"

A couple of biddies flounced off, whilst spare change rattled into my cup. The Good Book says the price of wisdom is above rubies. I sold mine cheap.

He clapped hard enough to break the skin. "Never have I heard such a voice from a woman, much less a child."

"Eighteen's no child, mister." I snatched his coin lickety-split. "Thankee kindly," I told them, looking walleyed from me to him.

"I'll be fifty before you see eighteen, hon." He was fresh-shaved and smelled nice of hair oil and Witch Hazel. Rooster-tracks forked deep when he smiled. "I'd like to buy you dinner and talk a little business."

"Uh-huh." I stowed my possibles and twisted my hair to smash under my hat. "We'll get on down the street and you'll say, 'I done forgot my billfold in the hotel room, so's let's us go fetch it.'"

Once you've been orphaned, decked boxcars the country over, been jailed, left a baby in a bloody bucket, been shot at and stabbed a time or two, there's no tricks to learn, or learn from.

"I won't lay a hand on you, miss." The card he gave over had Tom Vance Hickam in tall letters and Independent Talent Scout in shorter ones. "I came here to audition a lady who sings and tells bawdy jokes. Then I heard you."

My heart kicked up a beat. Real casual, I held out the card. "Then you ought'n not keep her waiting, Mr. Hickam."

That scowled his face. "Aren't you ever tired of being broke and hungry?"

I wasn't and hadn't been, since I hopped that first boxcar back in Winslow. Workin' stiffs fret payin' rent and gas bills and what in creation they'll do, if'n the boss man gives 'em the boot.

Life's for livin', not killing yourself makin' one.

Mr. Hickam yapped at my heels. "I'm trying to tell you, there's money in your voice. Plenty more than that cup holds."

I TOLD THE WAITRESS at the diner I'd have an egg salad sandwich and water to drink. Tom scratched it for two blue plate spe-
cials and two glasses of milk. We'd have coffee with our raisin pie.

I hated milk. He doctored his from a pocket flask. "Here's
your first lesson about the music business, Dwaynetta. Don't
skimp when someone else is paying the tab."

Playing humble makes a generous giver, but what he didn't
know wasn't mine to teach. I tucked into my roast beef supper,
whilst he prattled as how Jimmie Rodgers, Maybelle Carter and
her kin, and others had the jump on hillbilly music. A smart
manager and a gimmick were needed to make a splash.

"Topsy-turvy—that's our gimmick. First off, you sound
blacker than Bessie Smith."

Mama said singing woeful for what's gone or unlikely to be
blisters the heart. What my daddy would've done to him for
sayin' his li'l angel sang like a nigger would take the better part of
a day to die of.

"I ain't Bessie Smith. And it ain't just 'cause she don't play
mandolin."

"That's the beauty of my topsy-turvy idea, hon. Who do you
think buys theater seats to hear her sing? Negroes?"

A black hobo by the name of Big Bill told me nigh the same
thing. We'd met up when he hopped the Illinois Central with a
guitar slung 'round his neck. Rode the line regular, betwixt
workin' in Chicago and visitin' his wife and family in Langsdale,
Arkansas.

Big Bill said once a plantation owner hired him for a three-day
picnic, there wasn't no playing at the jooks. Whites paid extra for
the best and the best was too good for niggers. A blues dive in
Chicago was the first place he'd played for his own kind.

He went on about how you had to be black to sing blue. He
said whites liked the music, but don't feel the words, 'cause they
ain't lived 'em. I'd laughed, seeing as how we were eatin' the same

stew from tin cans on the wrong side of the tracks. "Looks to me like hard times is color-blind," I said.

"Mebbe so." He sucked his teeth. "But people ain't."

I never seen him again on the IC Line. Might be his uppity mouth run a tad faster than he could.

Tom thanked the waitress for sloshing us more coffee boiled from yesterday's grounds. The flask topped off his cup. "Her hair. Did you notice? The day Volstead made liquor illegal, women cut off their hair like boys. Why, I can't imagine."

He lit a cigarette and blew out the smoke all of a gust. "That's why yours stays long. Shorter, but long. Topsy-turvy." He smiled. "A long gown, too. There's curves under those rags and dirt. I'll bet our future on it."

The way he talked, stared through me, worked his mouth funny again, was like seed ticks creeping 'neath my shirt. It wasn't on accident the diner's screen door was a hop-skip away from run like hell.

"Dwaynetta, though …" His hawk-nose crinkled. "Do you have a middle name?"

"Lurleen," I said around a gulp of pie.

"Dwaynetta Lurleen Comstock." He shook his head. "No insult intended, but that doesn't spell 'songbird' no matter how you slice—" He snapped his fingers. "Lena. Lena … Bird. No, B-Y-R-D. It's classier." His hand clawed and bobbed on air. "Tom Vance Hickam presents, Miss Lena Byrd, Blues Songbird Extraordinaire. One Night Only."

I cocked up a heel and swung my knee past the chair corner. "Call me Robin Redbreast, if'n you care to. I ain't singing no nigger blues—"

He clamped my wrist. "Five hundred a week, hon." His breath stank of bootleg whiskey and scorched tobacco. "Believe you me, chances like this don't come along but once. If ever."

"Five hundred *dollars?*" Daddy never earned near that in a year sawyering at the mill.

"Minus expenses, manager's commission ..." Tom turned loose of my arm. "Could be less some weeks. Could be double, triple as much. What do you have to lose?"

Thoughts of spending a stake that fat set my mind a-whirl. Tom said Easy Street was a steep climb, but he'd print handbills with Lena's picture and string them from Texarkana to Mobile and all over the Delta. I'd sing on the radio, whether the station broadcast fifteen miles or five hundred, and invite folks to whichever tent show, music hall, club, taxi-dance, speakeasy or house party I'd be at next.

"We'll have to age you some, though," he said. "Twenty-three seems about right. Young, but old enough to travel with a grown man."

I slipped his billfold from my pocket before he noticed it was missing. Deciding between sure money and a grift was a trial. Especially since I'd be singing my fool head off til I had enough cash to ditch him.

"Sixteen going on twenty-three or not," I said, "what'll Mrs. Hickam think about you jitneyin' Lena Byrd from here to yonder?"

Tom's eyes left mine. "The only Mrs. Hickam was my dear mother, God rest her."

Uh-huh. I nipped the inside of a cheek to stanch a grin. Right off, I'd pegged him for one of them confirmed type of bachelors. I nudged the billfold to the floor, whilst Bessie Smith sang in my head, "I got the world in a jug, the stopper's in my hand."

Not quite yet, it wasn't. But it would be.

TWO DAYS LATER, Tom was parleying with that soda pop bottler when the chink gal seamstress brought the clothes she'd stitched for me.

The radio station dress fit nice, but wasn't flashy, aside from being pokeberry red. After I'd sing live, Tom would leave a special-made record to get around laws against playing them on the air. It'd sound like I was still there, talking up that soda pop, then commence "Lena's Blues."

Tom wrote it. It weren't no prize-winner, but most nigra blues wail about jelly roll and whores and booze. Sing or play one of them on the radio and the bottling company sponsoring the records would have conniptions.

He knocked "Shave and Haircut" on the door, just as I shimmied into the new singing gown I'd wear at clubs and such. The chink gal sewed two alike, copied off a picture-page he'd tore out'n a magazine. They're blue and slit high up a leg and low in the front.

The matching gloves with cuffs at the elbows I'd nixed for a black pair. Slip a single dollar inside them light ones and it'd show clear as day. No sense wearing 'em, if I couldn't dip pockets on the sly for more than was paid to hear me or fell in my tip bowl.

I twirled to show Tom the gown, my side-parted hair puddling on my shoulders, and the paste-diamond eardrops and necklace he'd bought me. Swayin' and singin' "Wasted Life Blues," I pretended to cozy up to this jake and that one.

By Tom's face, you'd swear he'd gone simple. I reckoned a lady's man wouldn't notice me steal his socks out of his shoes.

"The way you look, maybe we should drive straight to Chicago."

He'd already bored me to tears talking about singers lined up to audition for Yankee record companies. Topsy-turvy was gonna get Lena Byrd famous in the Delta. Them bigwigs were gonna arm-wrestle for her on the labels and finagle a headliner spot on the theatre circuit.

Fit to bust as he was about Lena's career, it'd be mean to tell him she'd turn into Dwaynetta again when her new purse with secret pockets had a nice heft. Lena was his dream. Dwaynetta had other plans.

"Chicago?" I said. "But I ain't sung a lick in front of anybody, yet. What if nobody comes to hear me?"

"Oh, they will. I was just thinking out loud."

"Well, quit for five seconds. I've got a surprise for you."

From under the pillow, I took out the box camera I bought with the money he'd left to pay the chink dressmaker. I'd told her Tom forgot, that he'd bring the money to her tomorrow afternoon. We'd be miles across the state line before then.

"Where do you want to take my picture for them handbills? By the window for the light?"

Tom raked his fingers through what hair he had left. "Where the—Lena, honey, snapshots are for scrapbooks. And the film has to be mailed off for developing."

To Rochester, New York, the man at the store said. Bona fide pictures were too flimsy. The exposed cartridge was all the stopper I'd need for Tom Vance Hickam's jug.

He went on, "At dinner last night with Marcus Woollsey—didn't you hear me say he's a professional photographer? A printer he works with can run off the handbills before we leave in the morning."

"I ain't deaf." I plopped down on the bed, hunch-mouthed and sniffly. "But with all the money you're spending on me, I thought I might could save some on my picture."

He hugged my shoulders and gave me his hanky. "I appreciate that, I really do. I'm a far cry from wealthy, but Mother left me several—Listen, why don't you powder your nose and leave the finances to me, okay? Marcus should be here any minute."

On the way to the washroom, I switched on the cathedral radio on the dresser. Tom let Marcus in a tick before an announcer started the farm-to-market report. Neither Tom nor his Nancy-boy heard the washroom door open a crack and the camera clicking away.

Seeing them two steal kisses and pet had me tasting my lunch a second time.

"Big Rock Candy Mountains" was sung frequent at hobo camps. Nigh on as popular was "The Stuff Called Money." Big Bill said he'd wrote it. Whether he did or didn't, it was catchy, and I must've strummed it once too often for Tom. We was drivin' through a cotton field ocean when he ripped Daddy's mandolin out'n my hands and slung it as far as it'd fly.

I told him he ought be glad I'd set my heart on a DeSoto Touring Car a couple months back. If we was still puttering along in his Model T, that mandolin woulda busted on the window post and throwed splinters at his eyes.

It ain't my fault that where we have to be tomorrow is nearly always too far away to stay put of a night. Or that Mrs. Hickam left her funny-turned son barely enough to pay expenses and buy a dandy new automobile.

A songbird needs her rest, don't she? A midget couldn't stretch out in his flivver's front seat. And Tom groused every time the drowsies come over me and he had to wrestle clothes, soda pop-records, and handbill boxes with his bootleg and my medicine hid at the bottom from the back to the front.

The DeSoto's rear floorboard holds our claptrap with room to spare. Under his breath, Tom calls the cloud-soft back seat, Lena's Crib, like I'm Memphis Minnie turnin' tricks between shows.

Hell with him. The top down and wind a-howl is like deckin' a highballin' rattler again. And I will be shortly—to a place that ain't never heard of winter nor Miss Lena Byrd.

My purse is nigh goose plump and Tom's mood went from scared spitless to hateful after he tore apart the Model T searching for my film cartridge. Him and Marcus ain't the only pictures on it. He won't find it in the DeSoto, neither.

Almost plain sight is magical for foolin' the eye. Why, a week or more passed after I sung at Colonel Highfalutin's house party in Vicksburg before Tom saw my paste jewelry was real silver and diamonds. He wouldn't have then, if I hadn't decided to wear Mrs. Highfalutin's bracelet, too.

"Hurry up, Lena."

God, gimme a dollar for every time he's said that and I'll be shed of him in a blink.

"I *am* hurryin'." Like I ever dawdle changing from the radio station dress into a singing gown behind a blanket. Then again, it's a blessing Tom's girly, what with me stripping half-nekkid in front of him three, maybe four times a day.

When I was decent, he folded the blanket and fetched my medicine. A bar-dog in New Orleans put me onto sloe gin to soothe my throat. It surely does, as long as doses is took regular.

"That's plenty," Tom said, as cross as a gut-shot bear.

I swung away from him. "One more swaller." Or two.

He snatched the fruit jar and screwed on the lid. "Later. I can't have you forgetting the lyrics like you did in Meridian. People here in Jackson know them better than you do."

"Oh yeah?" I slashed on lipstick in the DeSoto's side mirror. "Why don't they sing to each other and save me the trouble?"

"Because they've paid three dollars apiece to hear the lovely Lena Byrd, Blues Songbird Extraordinaire." His thumb swiped hard at a lipstick swoop 'neath my lip. "Not counting what she'll steal in her gloves."

I ran the brush through my hair, then threw it on the seat. "You don't like it? Shove off, then. I can hire a driver for a coupla bucks a day and all the pleasurin' he can give."

Tom chuckled low and mean. "And the first place he'd take you is the local sheriff's office."

"It ain't me that writ laws against queers." I patted his cheek. "You'll get your film, by and by. I promised, didn't I?"

"No. I wouldn't believe you if you had." He lit a cigarette and crushed the empty box. "Do I have to beg for a *coupla bucks* before we go in?"

"You should, mean-tempered as you're gettin'." I gave him the five-dollar bill folded in my powder compact. Sweeter'n hackleberry gin, I said, "Is that enough, hon?"

He took my elbow rough to escort me into the dance club. The air was gray-green with smoke and bootleg fumes. People brayed like mules—too loud to think, much less hear the house band. If I didn't know better, I'd swear Tom drove in circles to the same dimlit, rackety, sweat-smelly building every night for months on end.

Then and there, I knew Jackson was Lena Byrd's last performance. Dwaynetta'd had all the singing and smiling and do this and go there she could stomach. She'd stash Lena's stake and live cheap and happy off milking Tom and Marcus Woollsey for a hundred now and then.

'Til Tom said in my ear, "What's the matter with you?" I didn't know I'd stopped dead-bang, a yard short of the stage. "Nothin'. Fetch me a drink, then stand back. Ol' Lena's gonna sing her fool heart out, tonight."

A packed house is apt to set fists and bottles to flying. Tonight folks listened, clapped, whistled like sixty, whilst I belted and crooned every shade of blues and red-hots betwixt. Mr. Talent Scout Hickam says an encore's one song extra. Well, I did "Blue Delta Blues" twice over, and still they hollered for more.

Tom was pulling me outside, when I thought I heard, "Dwaynetta!"

A handbill waved. "Dway-netta, wait!" A woman elbowed through the crowd behind me. Her face was flushed splotchy and mouse-hair a fright.

I caught the alley's steel door before it whanged shut and locked. "Mary Sarah?"

She bowled into me, jabbering like a magpie. "I *knew* that was you." She squinted at Tom. "I asked him, back in Helena, and he said he'd never heard of Dwaynetta Comstock. But the longer I studied on the handbill picture, the surer I was he'd lied."

Tom flinched. "Sorry. Honest mistake."

Uh-huh. We'd took rooms in Helena, after he said he was too drunk to drive on to Arkansas City. Locked eyeballs with somebody was more like it. So did I, and mine was almost as strappin' handsome as the one with Mary Sarah.

Tom planted a shoe on the DeSoto's bumper and fired up a coffin nail. The fresh box was already two-thirds empty. "Every town we're in, a sister tugs my coat, or a cousin, or your long-lost uncle Bob."

Mary Sarah wiped snot on the sleeve of a ratty gray sweater. A brown skirt hung halfway to her bony ankles. She was four years older than me and always was plainer than boiled rice. What this husband of hers, Vic Pelagiano, ever seen in her, I couldn't divine.

From the up-and-down Vic gave me, he didn't rightly recall himself. He doffed a fedora and drawled, "Pleasure to meet you, Miss Byrd, Mr. Hickam." A lazy grin crooked at a corner. "You should've heard the wife yap about her baby sister singing on the radio."

"Ha! You didn't believe me, either, didja."

Her snivelin' sure hadn't changed. Time was, when scarcely a day passed lest she whined the same exact thing to Mama. Daddy'd kiboshed her nonsense, before I was knee-high to a cedar stump.

"I let you drag me to Jackson," Vic said. "*Didn't* I?" It came out gruff, but who could blame him? "Give any thought to how stupid I'd have felt if you'd been *wrong*?"

All of a whoosh, I knew her and Tom lashed together with baling wire wouldn't make a backbone. Vic winked, like he'd read my mind.

"I hate to break up the family reunion," Tom said, "but Lena and I have to scoot on up the road." Damned if he didn't light another cigarette off the butt of the first.

"You do?" Mary Sarah's fingers pecked her sweater. "But we rode the bus all day to see you, and I thought we'd find us an eatin' house, have a good visit, then stay—"

She glanced at Tom, then at the ground. "I bought one-way tickets. Didn't know how long we'd be here, and—"

"Quit your blubbering, for crissake," Vic said. "We'll buy two more at the bus depot."

"Can't, and you know it. The man at the front door wanted six dollars to let us inside. You drank the last two I had."

Vic grabbed her arm. "Will you shut the hell up?" She cringed, like he'd boxed her ear. "I apologize, y'all. I don't know what gets into her sometimes. Y'all go on, now, and—"

"No!" She yanked free of him. "You can't just leave me here, Dwaynetta. You just can't."

I should've laughed. Could've spit between her close-set eyes. "Like you left me? At the cabin?"

She jerked, liked I'd slapped her. "I sent a letter home, soon as I had three pennies for a stamp. You was already gone. Where, nobody knew."

A-carse she'd say that, after I'd made my own way for close onto three years. I'd bet my diamond earbobs, Vic quit warming Mrs. Prissy Do-Right's sheets on their honeymoon. Hot blood ain't satisfied easy, nor for long.

"Would you excuse us, please?" Tom waved me toward the front of the DeSoto. I knew what he'd say before his mouth flapped. "We have to be in Memphis tomorrow. Give the poor woman money for bus fare and let's go."

"*What?* All she come for was a hand-out. Well, she ain't getting it from me."

"She's your sister."

I wrapped the chain handle around my purse. "Yeah, and if I wasn't Lena Byrd, she wouldn't give two hoots about me." My nerves were cracklin' for my medicine. "You feel so all-powered sorry for her, you give her the money."

His face sneered up ugly. "I would, if I had any."

"Ain't my fault you wasted it on smokes and whiskey."

"Nothing is ever your fault, is it, Dwaynetta."

Mary Sarah scurried up, teary eyed and holding her arm. "You're bound for Memphis?"

Eavesdropper. Vic shoulda boxed her ear. Both of 'em.

Tom said, "We have a meeting with a producer and engineer from Columbia Records tomorrow afternoon."

"Well, Helena and Memphis are real close to one another," she whined. "Twenty-some miles off Route 49 would get us—"

"East and clear across the Mississippi." Vic sidled close enough to gander down my dress. He must've liked what he saw, for his voice quivered, when he said, "Not everybody's as dumb as you are, Mary Sarah. Mr. Hickam knows full well, Highway 55 runs due north from Jackson."

Soft as a whisper, his hand caressed my bottom. "But I'd spell you drivin' the long way, if you don't mind to share this fine motorcar."

A sneaky-quick touch of my own had my mouth waterin'.

"Fine with me," Tom said, "if it is with Lena."

I could scarcely nod for thinking how the Desoto's back seat was pitch-dark of a night. I'd make Tom give over his pocket flask, so's Vic and me could have us a drink, relax, and get to knowing each other *real* good.

THE RATHSKELLER in St. Louis was reputed to be the best restaurant in the city. Clay-tiled floors and three-quarter walls dividing the dining rooms kept the noise level as constant as the delectable aromas wafting about.

The creased, *Jackson Daily News* clipping on the tablecloth was a single column wide and under three inches long. A small-point headline read: SONGBYRD DEAD AT 23.

Nearly a month had elapsed since the tragic automobile accident on Route 49. A faulty tire was blamed for the DeSoto veering off the road and crashing into a field-rock corner post. The gasoline tank exploded either on impact or shortly thereafter.

The occupants were burned beyond recognition. The vehicle's license tag and information provided by a Jackson dance club owner aided the county coroner in identifying the deceased as Miss Lena Byrd, 23, an up-and-coming blues singer reportedly from Arkansas, and her business manager, Thomas Vance Hickam, 48, of Elgin, Illinois.

"I'm late, I know, and I'm sorry." Mary Sarah Comstock Pelagiano hastily seated herself. "I wasn't sure you'd be here at all." A faint, musty odor escaped the coat falling over the back of her chair. After tonight, her clothes needn't be bought secondhand.

Her hair was bleached blonde and professionally cut. She still shunned cosmetics, including lipstick, but her eyes no longer resembled an animal's trapped out of season.

She told me that Vic Pelagiano had beaten her like her father did and took every nickel she'd earned from two jobs to his none. She'd understood, though, that beatings don't necessarily bruise or break bone. That tie had bound us when we met in Helena by accident or fate, and talked, commiserated, then conspired.

"I can't stay long." She chafed her hands. "You know, to eat or anything."

"Coffee?"

She hesitated. "Sure. Why not?"

"So, how do you like St. Louis?"

"It's all right." She shrugged. "Colder and bigger than Helena. I got me a job right off, and a little bitty apartment close by on—well, close to here. You?"

"I'm catching a train for Florida in a little while. I can give you an address—"

"No, don't." Pink circles formed at her cheeks. "I mean, there's no need of it, is there?" Her eyes slanted at the clipping. They skittered as she read, then rose to mine. "It still don't seem real."

"Pretend it was a bad dream. You'll sleep better if you do."

The Rathskeller's ashtrays were as deep as soup bowls. A match ignited the clipping. Mary Sarah gasped and reared back in her chair. The reminder of torching the DeSoto was unintentional. She'd assumed the fire was necessary to rid herself of a vicious, whoremonger of a husband.

Technically, cyanide in the pocket flask and in Lena's sloe gin accomplished that. Any second thoughts Mary Sarah might have had evaporated when she saw her husband fucking her sister in the back seat.

"Off in the head" is how she'd described her younger sister. She believed Dwaynetta suffocated their mother while Mary Sarah went for the doctor. House calls were free, if the patient was beyond treatment.

Terrified of her sister, Mary Sarah ran for her life. The letter she'd mailed to Winslow wasn't to Dwaynetta, but to the authorities, accusing her of matricide. Seeing Lena Byrd's picture on the handbill proved God didn't answer vengeful prayers.

God helps those who help themselves. Spawn like Lena and Vic were nothing, if not predictable.

After the accident, discreet inquiries to the coroner and sheriff's office confirmed the car and contents were charred to ashes. The intense heat alone would have destroyed any film, even if protected by a cartridge.

The waiter brought Mary Sarah's coffee and refilled mine.

"What about you, Tom? Do you sleep through the night?"

My cup clattered in the saucer. For a second, I'd have sworn it was Lena mocking me. Fear smoldered in my gut that I'd traded one blackmailer for another.

I opened my suit coat. My train ticket to Los Angeles was in the name of T.V. Hicks, KNX's new, night owl announcer. I pulled out the envelope behind it and slid it across the tablecloth.

The cash in Lena's purse had amounted to slightly over two thousand dollars—minus the hundred Mary Sarah and I split that night.

I'd gambled a pay-off would shut her mouth, until our rendezvous. If her guilty conscience won out, I'd need that two grand to leave the country in a hurry. Damned generous to give her a dime, considering how much Lena extorted from me.

My chair screeched across the clay tiles. "Put that under your pillow. I wouldn't trust a bank, yet."

"You're leavin'? Just like that?"

I flipped a silver half-dollar on the table. "Like I said, hon. I've got a train to catch."

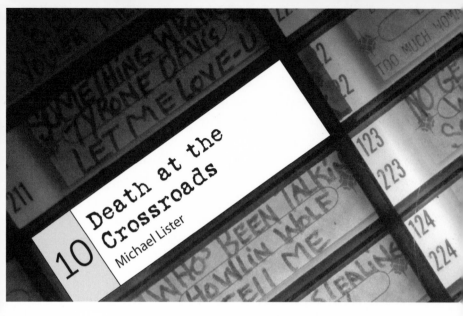

"GET YOU GUYS ANYTHING ELSE?" Maria asked.

Lefty, Sid, and RD shook their heads.

"Lap dance," Jerry said.

Maria jerked her head toward him, her straight blonde hair whipping around to smack the clear complexion of her flawless face.

"What'd I tell you? No ordering off menu. If you think your old heart can stand it, you can get one in about an hour over at Tan Fannies."

Mid-afternoon on a Tuesday at Junior's, the lunch crowd, such as it was, long since returned to work, Maria's boys still in the large U-shaped booth in the corner, table cleared, only their coffee cups remaining.

Little Milton was belting out "They Call it Stormy Monday" from a jukebox in the corner.

Four white-haired men, all in their early seventies, all musicians, all wrinkled and irrelevant, had the distinction of being Maria's boys. Jerry, a guitarist for Son House and Skip James during their resurgence in the 1960s, who had eventually been forced by arthritis to put down his Strat, was the most talkative and the biggest flirt. Tall, thin, soft-spoken, Sid, who built and played cigar box guitars, said the least. He was a recent widower, and she worried about him the most.

"Why *don't* you work at Tan Fannies?" he asked.

"Tits're too small, ass's too white."

As she had expected, her boys were shocked to hear such language coming from their Maria. Gasps, whistles, and grunts accompanied wide eyes that immediately darted to her tits and ass.

Maria Bella had been serving catfish and collards and chicken and trash burgers and mud cake at Junior's for a few years now, was liked by everyone, adored by these old men who met daily for leisurely meals, unrushed conversation, and a bit of flirting, but she was still an outsider—a stranger in a strange land, and always would be—just the way she wanted it.

Junior's had all the trappings of a juke joint—random, catch-as-catch-can furnishings, mostly wobbly tables and hand-me-down vinyl chairs, the booth Maria's boys were in was the only one; a small stage where blues was occasionally played; a couple of pool tables; a bar; cheap booze; strings of Christmas lights strewn around the room; and walls filled with blues memorabilia—but the four old, arthritic men in the booth were the most authentic things in the joint.

The old wooden door in front creaked opened and a young, white tourist walked in wearing catalog clothes and an awestruck expression, and began looking around like he was still at the museum that no doubt brought him to town.

"God, I love it when you talk dirty," Jerry said.

Beneath Maria's big brown eyes, her perfect white teeth peeked out from a repressed smile.

"That's almost as good as a lap dance," Lefty said.

"Better," Jerry said. "I've gotta rush home and change my damn Depends."

Part of what would forever keep Maria an outsider was her mystique, the way she just showed up in Clarksdale one day, took a waitressing job at Junior's, rented a vacant house trailer in the Sunflower Mobile Home Park, and kept to herself, spending her free time at the Carnegie Public Library or the AA meeting in the musty meeting hall of the AME church.

"You've got plenty to work with," RD said. "You look about a billion times better than the best Tan Fannies has ever had."

"Ah, that's so sweet," she said.

She looked over at Sid for a response, but he didn't say anything. He was smiling, though, which was an improvement, and for an instant there seemed to be the hint of a spark in the old blue eyes behind the small glass lenses.

Jerry said, "You could work anywhere. If not Tan Fannies, how 'bout Ground Zero? Anywhere but Junior's. You're the only reason we come in this dump."

She smiled. She would've liked to work at Ground Zero Blues Club, but with Morgan Freeman being a co-owner, it was too risky, too many cameras, too much exposure, too much press, too many filmmakers shooting docs about the blues. It was too bad, too. She could've used someone like Mr. Freeman in her life. There was a stately decency about him, a goodness behind the rounder twinkle in his wise eyes.

"Junior done sucked her in," RD said. "Now she can't get out. Should've started somewheres else when she first come to town."

RD, who actually favored Morgan Freeman a bit, was the only African-American in the group. He had played bass for Maria's all-time favorite blues musician, Howlin' Wolf.

The tourist fed the hungry jukebox and Robert Johnson's "Cross Road Blues" began to play.

"Real original," Jerry said in the direction of the tourist, but not directly to him. "Nice choice. You just come from the big blue guitars or are you on your way? It's not really *the* crossroads you know. Hell, it ain't even *a* crossroads."

"What *did* bring you to Casablanca?" Sid asked Maria.

Her full resplendent smile was as breathtaking as it was un-expected. She rarely smiled, and this was the first full-wattage version the men had ever seen. There was an essential sadness be-neath her beautiful exterior that permeated everything she did—even her restrained smiles. As RD put it, "She the only white woman I ever did know to truly have the blues in her soul."

"My health," she said. "I came for the waters."

The whole town wondered where Maria came from and what had brought her to Clarksdale. Her boys made a game of guess-ing, each continually searching for new and clever ways to ask the young woman who seemed to have read every great book and memorized every good line from every great film.

"Waters? What waters?" Sid asked. "We're in the desert."

"Desert?" Lefty said. "Fuck he say?"

"What he say?" RD asked.

"Sid's lost his goddam mind," Jerry said. "Losing Gwen was too much for him. Sent him over the—"

"Sid," Lefty said loudly. "We're in Mississippi. Big ass rivers full of water everywhere you turn."

"We're repeating lines from one of the best films ever made," Maria said.

"Oh," RD said. "Old Bogart movie. What's the name of—"

Jerry turned to him, exasperation on his face. "He just said it. *Casablanca.*"

"Did he? I missed it."

Over near the entrance beneath the strings of antique Christ-mas lights that hung year-round, two businessmen were growing weary of waiting to be seated. Maria knew it, could sense it in their body language, but didn't rush this, her favorite part of the job.

"I've often speculated on why you don't return to where you came from," Sid said. "Did you abscond with church funds? Did you run off with a senator's daughter? I'd like to think you killed a man. It's the romantic in me."

Even though she knew the line, knew what was coming, a twitch at *killed a man* gave her away.

She could never be a poker player, Sid thought.

A glimpse. Just a glimpse, but a real revelation. Maria was still a mystery. Sid still didn't know much about her, but he knew she was a killer. If Gwen were still here, she'd say he didn't know it, just suspected it, but she'd be wrong. He knew it. What he didn't know was what he was going to do about it.

"SHE KILLED SOMEONE," Sid said.

"Huh?"

He and Lefty were shuffling down State Street past a carwash where a small group of young black men were putting the finishing touches on an enormous purple Cadillac.

"Maria. She's hiding here because she killed a man—or a woman."

"RD's not the only one who's lost his goddam mind. Where we headin'?"

"Hicks. I wanna take some tamales home."

"Good idea. Maybe you haven't completely lost your goddam mind."

Next to Sid, Lefty looked even shorter than he was, his rounded, slightly hunched shoulders subtracting further from his already diminutive stature.

"I never would've used the *Casablanca* line if I thought she'd really killed someone."

"Maria's not a murderer," Lefty said.

"I'm tellin' you, Left, she is. I saw it in her eyes."

"I've known a few in my time. Maria ain't one."

Though no one knew for sure exactly, Lefty, who was never much of a musician, was rumored to have worked for one of the families in Chicago before the blues and old age brought him to Clarksdale to stay. Bagman, enforcer, driver, even errand boy, he'd've seen a hell of a lot more killers than Sid.

"She is. I'm telling you."

"So what if she is?"

"Well," Sid said, pausing a moment, "I don't know."

They padded along in silence for a while, raising their swollen and misshapen hands to wave at passing cars, nodding to approaching pedestrians.

"I want you to find out who she is and where she came from," Sid said.

Lefty shook his head.

"I know you know people."

"If I ever knew people—and I'm saying *if*, they're all dead."

"Come on, Left. What I ever ask of you?"

"I don't know. Why you wanna know?"

"Just curious. Bored. Nothing better to do."

"Whatta you gonna *do* with the information? Don't wanna see Maria get jammed up. I like her."

"Nothing. I swear. I'm just dying to know."

ON A CLEAR SEPTEMBER DAY IN 2001, Maria Bella ended the life of Nancy Most. It was a long time ago now, but in her memory it was always as if it just happened. She hadn't intended to do it, didn't know she was going to the moment before she did it. No one could argue premeditation. And no one ever would. No one in Clarksdale, Mississippi, even knew who Nancy Most was, and as far as Maria knew, no one was looking for her.

But now Sid knew. She'd seen it in his eyes. She knew it. What she didn't know was what she was going to do about it.

Life could be so random. One morning, Nancy Most was working her mall job at Ann Taylor Loft, going about her life, unaware how little of it there was left, and by lunch she was dead.

She was an addict, a user in every sense of the word, a woman who traded on her good looks and wicked hot body to get what she wanted. She'd hurt so many people, done so much damage—but did she deserve to die? Maria thought so. Fate had left the decision up to her, and she'd chosen. Since then, she'd thought about it often—nearly every day—but she didn't regret what she'd done. Given the same circumstances, she'd do it again.

"WE GOIN' ON A LITTLE ROAD TRIP," RD said. "Go with us."

Lunch on a Thursday, and Maria's boys were in their booth. Sid still looked at her funny—though only when she wasn't looking—but the others acted just the same.

Bessie Smith, who died not far from here following a car accident, was on the juke moaning out "Muddy Water."

"Where?"

"Jackson."

"*Jackson?*"

He nodded. "Subway Lounge. We all played there back in the day."

"Everybody did," Jerry said. "It was a real juke—not like this place. Not like all the shit they're tryin' to market to tourists—that ridiculous Crossroads sign, fuckin' casinos, corporate owned blues clubs."

"Buckets of beer," RD added. "Authentic blues, anyone could sit in with the band—House Rockers, King Edwards. Everybody there was there to hear the blues."

"Weren't competin' with a bunch of goddam slot machines while you played," Lefty said.

Jerry cleared his throat and Maria could tell he was about to break professoral and, if true to form, tell her shit she already knew.

"Real jukes started as a place for black sharecroppers to escape their painful existences in a time when Jim Crow kept 'em

out of the white joints," he said. "On the outskirts of town in shacks or somebody's house, they offered cheap entertainment, a chance to socialize and share each other's burdens. Hell, these poor bastards were still essentially slaves and were only off a day and a half from Saturday afternoon til Monday morning."

RD added, "It's why the blues ain't just music, gotta be caught, not taught, and jukes not somethin' some corporation can do."

Maria said, "Didn't they tear the Subway down a few years ago?"

"It and the only place I could stay in back when we's on the road," RD said.

"It was in the bottom of the old Summers Hotel," Lefty said.

"Tell her about the time you got the room in the white hotel," Jerry said, but continued before RD could respond. "He went to this place in—where was it? Some town that only had a hotel for whites. Knocks on the door, middle of the night. Got no rooms, manager tells him. RD goes around the corner to a bar, calls the hotel, changes his voice, pretends to be a white man named LeRoy, tells the manager he needs a room for a guy he's sending over. No problem, manager says. RD goes back a few minutes later, tells him Mr. LeRoy sent him, gets a room."

"What's there now?" Maria asked.

"Huh?"

"Since they tore it down? What're you going to see?"

"Where it was."

"You're driving three hours to where something used to be?"

"Who knows," RD said, "we might bring some instruments and our own buckets of beer and make some music."

"Sounds great, but 'fraid I'll have to pass this time."

"She don't want to hang out with a bunch of saggin' old men," Sid said.

He can't even look at me, Maria thought. Sure as shit doesn't want me along for a road trip.

Bessie's moan gave way to the haunting whine of Skip James' desolate voice accompanied only by the simple sound of an acoustic guitar on "Devil Got My Woman."

When RD finished his burger, only the onions remained on his plate. Jerry slid the plate toward Maria. Looking from the onions to her, he raised his eyebrows and wondered if he'd given her enough to work with.

She thought about it, then smiled. "There was one scene you *did* write."

"About the onions?"

He was obviously pleased with himself. The others turned their attention to them, attempting to figure out what book or movie was being quoted.

"Yes."

"Does Henry mind onions?" Jerry asked.

"I know this," Sid said. "Henry. Henry. Who is—"

"He can't bear them," Maria said. "Do you like them?"

"Is it possible to fall in love over a dish of onions?"

Maria nodded at Jerry. "Well done you."

"You're the one to be commended."

"I know it," Sid said. "Is it a movie or a book?"

"Both," they both said.

Maria added, "It's a scene about a movie in a book that was turned into a movie based on the book—which makes it a scene from a book in a movie, in a movie based on a book."

"The fuck?" Lefty said.

"*The End of the Affair*," Sid said, snapping his arthritic fingers.

"Impressive," Maria said.

He didn't look at her—hadn't since he saw the confession her eyes had made.

"Better than *Casablanca*," Jerry said.

"HOW OLD YOU THINK MARIA IS?" Lefty asked.

Sid shrugged.

Lingering after the others had gone, the two elderly gentlemen with nowhere to be were standing out on the sidewalk in front of Junior's.

"Younger than she looks. There's something in her eyes. I'd say she's had some hard years. Mid-thirties?"

"Eighty-four."

"Goddam. I was wrong, she's aged well."

The two men were silent a moment. When Lefty didn't say anything else, Sid said, "Seriously?"

"I'm serious."

"Left, that beautiful young woman in there's not eighty-four."

"Maybe not, but the woman whose identity she stole is. Or would be if she weren't dead."

"She killed an old woman and took her identity?"

"All I know for sure is Maria Bella lived most of her life along the Outer Banks, taught school, ran one of those little lighthouse gift shops. During the months leading up to her death, she had a live-in companion who helped with cooking and cleaning and offered her some much needed company—a pretty blonde girl who appeared out of nowhere to apply for the job."

"How long ago was that?"

"Just before she showed up here."

"Where was she before she came to live with the real Maria Bella?"

"Should know in another day or so."

Sid nodded, thinking, his gaze drifting up, away. Far away.

"Just curious, right, Sid? Not gonna do anything about it— no matter what we find out?"

"Right. Just wanna know."

"Then stop lookin' like you're figurin' on some kind of goddam plan."

"Why won't you look at me?" Maria asked.

Sid made eye contact with her for the first time in several days. "I look at you. I'm looking at you right now."

They were seated at a round wooden table near the fiction section in a dimly lit back corner of the Carnegie Public Library. On the table in front of Maria, two stacks of reference books blocked Sid's view of the notebook she'd been so feverishly scribbling in when she looked up, saw him, and insisted he join her.

"You know what I mean," she said. "Ever since you saw my reaction to the line you quoted, you look at me differently."

He didn't say anything at first, then, "What're you researching?"

"Just something for a little project I'm working on."

"A project?"

"It's nothing. Really."

He squinted to make out the titles on the spines of the books across the table from him. He made out *Crime Scene Investigation* and *Arson* something or other.

"I'm not who you think I am," she said.

"How do you know what I think?"

"Even if I did some horrible things in the past, isn't it who I am *now* that counts?"

He nodded, but there was no conviction in the gesture.

"Don't people deserve a second chance? Don't we all need one from time to time?"

"We do."

There was an innate gentleness in Sid that shone through his weary, watery blue eyes even behind his glasses, but Maria couldn't find the compassion she was searching for.

"I'm not the person I was, and I'll never be again. Can't that be enough? Can't you just accept me for who I am now?"

"I just want to know your story," he said. "That's all."

"You know it. It began when I got here."

"Then your back story."

"Why? Why does it matter?"

He shrugged.

"I walked out of one life and into another. Can't we just leave it at that?"

He didn't respond.

"I want you to read something," she said, standing up and walking over to a shelf about halfway down the nearest aisle. "Ever heard of the Flitcraft Parable?"

He shook his head.

She returned to the table with a musty, misshapen copy of Dashiell Hammett's *The Maltese Falcon*, opened it to chapter seven, laid it on the table in front of him, and walked away.

He quickly read the passage, holding the book as far away from his eyes as his long arms would allow.

The episode involved a man named Flitcraft who left his real estate office in Tacoma for lunch one day and never came back.

He was supposed to play golf that afternoon, something he had set up half an hour before he left for lunch. His wife and children never saw him again.

He just vanished.

That was in 1922. In 1927, when Sam Spade was with one of the big detective agencies in Seattle, Mrs. Flitcraft came in and told him somebody had seen a man in Spokane who looked a lot like her husband. Spade went over and checked it out. It was Flitcraft all right.

He'd been living in Spokane for a couple of years as Pierce Charles, had a car business, a wife, a baby son, owned a home in the suburbs.

What happened to him? Why'd he vanish?

On his way to lunch, he passed an office building that was being built. A beam fell eight stories down and smacked the sidewalk right beside him. Close, but it didn't touch him. A piece of sidewalk chipped off, flew up and struck his cheek. He still had the scar when Spade saw him. He rubbed it affectionately with his finger as he told Spade the story.

Flitcraft had been a good citizen, husband, and father. The life he knew was clean, orderly, sane, and responsible. But then a falling beam had shown him that life was fundamentally none of those things. He, the upstanding guy, could be wiped out between office and restaurant by a random accident.

He was disturbed by the discovery that in sensibly ordering his affairs he'd gotten out of step with life, and before he'd walked twenty feet from the fallen beam he realized he'd never know peace until he adjusted to this new glimpse of life. By the time he'd eaten his lunch, he'd decided that if life could be ended by a random falling beam, he would change his life at random by simply going away.

He went to Seattle that afternoon, then wandered around for a couple of years before drifting back to the Northwest, settled in Spokane, and got married—and though the second wife didn't look like the first, they were more alike than they were different.

Flitcraft, now Charles, wasn't sorry for what he'd done. It seemed reasonable to him, and Spade suspected he didn't even realize he'd settled into the same groove he'd jumped out of in Tacoma.

"But that's the part of it I always liked," Spade said. "He adjusted himself to beams falling, and then no more of them fell, and he adjusted himself to them not falling."

"WHAT'S IT MEAN?" Lefty asked.

"That she walked away from her life and started a new one," Sid said. "Not because of a beam nearly falling on her. Because she killed someone."

It was midmorning. The two men lingered in front of Junior's on their way to join the others for lunch.

"I don't know, Sid."

"What else you find out?"

"Not much. It's as if she didn't exist before she moved in with old Mrs. Bella."

"See. Like Flitcraft."

"I guess."

"Anything else?"

"She sends anonymous sympathy cards to Alfred and Angie Most up in New York and has flowers put on their daughter Nancy's grave. She also gets checks from the William Morris Agency at a PO box under the name of Nancy Lost."

"She feels bad for killing their daughter, but not bad enough not to use a variation of her name. Checks for what?"

Lefty smiled. "TV scripts. She writes for some true crime show on a chick network."

The fire whistle from the station a few streets over started to blow, and the two men turned to see blackish-gray smoke rising from the Sunflower trailer park.

Jerry and RD rushed out the front door.

"That's Maria's place," RD said.

"She coming?" Lefty asked. "We can walk down there with her."

"She didn't show up for work today," Jerry said. "Come on."

As the four bent and limping men hobbled toward the Sunflower, all Sid could think about were the research books stacked in front of Maria on the library table.

By the time they arrived, the rental trailer was a melted mass of charred, wet debris. What was left of the walls and roof were flat on the floor now.

"Never seen one go that fast," Nate, a volunteer fireman, said.

"Had to have some help," Coy, the oldest of the fireman, said. "Been doing this a long time. Nothing burns that fast without some kind of accelerant—not even a trailer."

"Was Maria inside?" Jerry asked.

"Huh?"

The two firemen were unaware the old men were behind them.

"Was there anyone inside, goddam it?" Jerry yelled.

"*Hey,*" Nate said, holding up his gloved hands. "Simmer down, old man. We don't know anything yet. Y'all need to back away from this area."

"Got something," a fireman yelled from the back of what used to be the trailer.

"What is it?" RD asked.

"We can't see any better than you can," Jerry said. "Just wait a minute."

"Let's move around back for a better look," Lefty said.

They did, making a wide circle around the trucks and coming up in between two other trailers, but when they saw the blackened, molten mass of body, they wished they hadn't.

"Sweet Jesus Christ on a crooked Cross," RD said, turning away.

"The hell happen here?" Jerry said. "Who'd do this to that sweet girl?"

Sid leaned over and whispered in Lefty's ear, "Who'd that sweet girl do this to?"

Lefty turned and looked at him for a long moment, then jerked his head, motioning him away from the others.

"What did you do?" Lefty asked.

"You think I did this?"

Lefty shook his head. "I don't mean the fire. What'd you say to her?"

"Nothing."

"Said you were just curious. Wouldn't do anything."

"I didn't."

"What'd you say to her? You had to push her, couldn't just leave it alone, had to let her know we were on to her, and now she's killed again and disappeared. Whoever that is in there, you're an accessory to her murder."

WHEN SID'S EYES OPENED in the middle of the night, heart pounding, mind racing, he knew he wasn't alone in his dark bedroom.

"Maria?"

"Leave the light off," she said.

Sid wondered if he was about to die, and he realized he really didn't mind all that much. With Gwen gone he went from having a sort of half-life to nearly no life at all. Life is loss, he thought. Ultimately we lose everything. Everything. And I'm nearly there.

"You here to kill me?"

"To ask a favor."

"*Really?*" he asked, the high-pitched surprise clearing the sleepiness out of his voice.

"Don't try to find me," she said. "I'm leaving tonight. Disappearing again. And it'd be nice not to be followed."

"I'm an old man. I won't be following you."

"I mean don't have it done. The police won't know that's not me in the trailer. Don't tell them any different."

"Who is it?" he asked. "Who'd you kill to escape this time?"

"I didn't kill anyone. I swear. I wouldn't expect you to keep quiet about murder. I dug up a recently buried body."

"My Gwen?"

"*No,*" she said. "God, no. I would never. Anyway, this woman was already dead. All I did was dig her up and burn her body. That's awful, I know, but necessary—and nowhere close to murder."

"Won't the police know it's not you?"

"I burned the body before I lit the trailer. It'll be unrecognizable. No one knows me. I haven't left any evidence."

"Guess you're getting pretty good at this by now."

"What's that mean?"

"Maria Bella."

"Yeah?"

"I meant the real one. You killed her."

"I didn't. She was an old lady. Died of natural causes. I took her identity. That's all. I can't believe you know about that."

"Tell me about Nancy Most."

A long silence followed.

"She was a coke head. Strung out most of the time. You can't imagine the things she did."

"Tell me."

"She hurt her parents so much they finally cut her loose. They loved her, were so patient, but…"

She trailed off and they were silent a moment.

"I can't believe you know about her," she added.

"Whatta you write in those cards you send her parents?"

"Lies. That their daughter changed before she died, that they'd be proud—but she didn't. She'd do okay for a little while. Get cleaned up, get a job, get a man, but it wasn't long before she'd be right back on the shit. The last time she got cleaned up, she got a job at the Ann Taylor Loft store in the concourse mall at the World Trade Center. She did fine for a while, but was already headed back down when the planes flew into the towers. Know what she did when the planes hit? Locked up her store and started up Tower I to see her supplier. Imagine. The world's falling down around her, all she can think about is securing her next fix. She would've been in the tower when it came down if a cop hadn't grabbed her in the stairwell and forced her out."

Sid's mind was racing. The woman in the room with him must've had a brother or a dad who was a cop or a fireman or a worker who got killed because of Nancy Most.

"She got out?"

"Before the tower came down? Yeah. Not everyone who died that day was killed by terrorists."

"She was a drug addict, but why'd she have to die? What'd she do?"

"Did you not hear me? She was never gonna change. She got pregnant one time. If that didn't clean her up, nothing would. When she delivered, her little premature, underweight baby had withdrawals. You know what she did? Gave it up for adoption and kept on shoving that shit up her nose."

Sid didn't say anything.

"Will you give me your word as a gentleman you won't tell the cops or try to find me?"

"How can I not report you? Even if I believe you about the victim in the trailer and the real Maria Bella, you murdered Nancy Most."

"I wouldn't call it murder."

"There's got to be more to it than that she was a drug addict. You don't go around killing drug addicts. What did Nancy do to you?"

"*What?*" She sounded genuinely perplexed.

"You didn't just kill her because she was a drug addict."

"I don't understand. I thought you knew. You knew everything else. I didn't literally kill Nancy. I just let people think she was in the building when it came down."

"What happened to her?"

"Flitcraft, remember? Nancy walked out of the building and when she saw it come down, when she realized how many thousands of people who didn't deserve to die were killed and that she was spared, she kept on walking. She walked out of her life and never looked back. I buried Nancy Most on September 11, 2001."

"So you're Nancy—"

"I *was*. Eventually I was Maria Bella. Soon, I'll be someone else. But I'll never look back, never go back to being who I was before, a worthless addict who didn't deserve to live—not when so many who should be alive aren't."

"But that was so long ago. Can't you just—"

She let out a harsh, humorless laugh. "It's today. Right now. Every moment. Don't you get it? Talking heads kill me with their bullshit about a post-nine-eleven world. There's no such thing for people like me. It's always present—explosions, sirens, screams, bodies falling from the sky, fire, smoke, ash, death. So much death. And at least one that was deserved."

"There's no way you were that person, that bad. You're too good, too kind, too—"

"I can only think of her that way."

"Don't worry, Nancy—"

"Don't call me that."

"I won't follow you. I won't tell anyone. I'll miss you. I'm sorry I didn't just leave it all alone."

"Me, too."

"Write me sometime," he said, but there was no reply. She was already out of the room, out of his life. Flitcraft had adjusted to a world of falling beams and when no more fell, had adjusted back. Maria had adjusted to a world with falling bodies and would never adjust back. He liked that about her. In a way, she was the very definition of the blues.

11 | Blues for Veneece
Lynne Barrett

MALLORY SLIDES HER SHOVEL FORWARD, planing one more layer of earth from the interior of the structure the archaeology students have nicknamed "the Kitchen," though whether the Mississippian Indians used it for a cookhouse or to prepare the dead for burial, they don't know. With this motion, the rhythm of excavation, she has worked off her hangover, and the October sun feels good on her back.

Luis watches her: no makeup, serious brows, hair pinned up, tiny silver earrings, big shirt tied around her waist since the morning cool baked away, washed out green tee that says, in pink, *No kidding*.

When she looks up, she turns her unreadable gaze on Harris, not Luis. Harris faces away, his hair lit by the sun, putting white flags in as he uncovers each post of "The Cage," working back from the two red flags that mark a corner. Rangy, long-boned, he has straight pale hair that's going to thin. He is, in Luis' view, congenitally and electrically trouble. Luis stands, stretches, takes in the white, ancient shape of an egret in a far cotton field, then turns around to face the long hump of the mound, just as, he imagines, the villagers they study once looked up toward a temple or the houses of the elite. He sees the low rectangle of the Back House and beyond it the white second story, gray roof and brick chimneys of Bishop House, shaded by the bronze tops of the pecan trees. Luis goes back to trenching along a beam where it was superimposed on another, trying to unravel the layers of bygone construction.

Mallory hits something. Metal, which shouldn't be there, but metal scraping metal, she can feel it in her teeth. She brushes away dirt with her gloved hand: pitted metal of a handle leading down to wood—some kind of an old box. Nineteenth or twentieth century? As she would for any artifact, she stays away from its edges, digs to either side. It's about a foot wide, five inches high, ten deep, with the arched handle on top. Then, saying, "Guys," she goes in below with the shovel and gets ready to lift it free.

Luis squats beside her. "Looks like an old tool box," he says. "Or maybe tackle?"

Harris calls, "Treasure?" and heads over.

Luis gets one of the blue tarps. The guys spread it out a couple of yards east of their work area, and Mallory carries over the object on its cushion of dirt and sets it down. Just that motion causes clumps to fall away from the box. It has a simple hasp, no lock.

"Go on, open it," Harris says.

"Should we?" Mallory picks up a long brush and kneels in front of the box.

Luis says, "Whatever it is will belong to Miss Bishop. She came in a while ago—I heard her car."

Harris says, "No reason we can't take a look. Come on, Mal."

With the brush handle, Mallory lifts the hasp, which comes away completely from the wood. "Rotted," Harris says. Mallory levers the lid open and they kneel around the box of silt, dead bugs, and a lot of small dirt-coated objects. "Let it be rubies," Harris says, as Mallory flicks soil away.

Mallory sees the familiar shape of bone ends. Bones that look far too dense to be the porous, trabecular last bits of Mississippian period Indians.

Luis says, "Metacarpals," just as Mallory says, "A hand, or hands. Skeletonized but not ancient."

Harris says, "Oh shit."

Mallory stands. "We need to get Celia Bishop."

Luis is already headed up the slope.

Harris hollers, "Tell her to call the sheriff."

HARRIS ENJOYS WATCHING the arrival of the troops: a county patrol unit, and then the sheriff, a black man with sheriffian girth, with a white deputy. Two state cops; look like the same ones who do the license checks they're always stopping him for on his Harley on Highway 49, or else the state recruits a lot of tall, muscular black men who work out, which is probable. Yes, he notices color. So what? Doesn't mean anything, it's what you can't help doing if you have eyes. Luis up there on the mound is brown, and what of it? He's Mexican, though, okay, born here because his parents were in Texas by then. With black hair cut short so it stands up, that single line of goatee, he looks like a Hispanic hipster, Harris likes to kid him. Mallory is the color of, not honey, more like some honey-vanilla soap, or a candle, there's a layer to her glow. She tells him he should categorize people by some detail like height or age. She's got some silly ideas, being from up north. She doesn't understand how changed things are here, how it's possible to see race and still treat people decently. And being a scientist is about observing everything, not blocking out your noticing to be all politically correct and shit. He's told her that.

Miss Celia Bishop has stood by the box quietly, til the sheriff's arrival. She's probably near sixty, has well-cut chestnut curls, is what his mother would call a handsome woman, which means she's only a little bit overweight and dresses well for it, in black pants and a tan wool jacket. She introduces them to the sheriff, explaining that they're graduate students who she's invited in to do their thesis projects. His investigator takes down their names—Mallory Falco, Luis Perez, Harris Ashbern. But it's Mallory they want to talk to, since she unearthed the remains.

Harris and Luis retreat to the hillside. Harris pulls down green metal chairs from the Back House gallery and finds a level spot among the fallen pecans on the east slope, a catbird seat where they can see the site and anyone coming up Bishop Road. Soon the crime scene unit arrives, and the county coroner, but at least everyone is careful not to tromp any of their flags, respecting their work as if they were an earlier stage of the crime scene crew. Mallory comes up and says they're mostly concerned to make sure no fingerprints got on anything, which of course they didn't. She says she's going to call Professor Martin, which Harris would have done but there's no cell phone signal here. Since Mallory got the Back House, and he and Luis share a shack, it seems like Mallory has the rank—or at least the house access. She throws him out in the middle of the night so Miss Celia won't think he's moved in.

Only vehicles with high clearance can get beyond where the paved drive stops at the parking area occupied by Miss Celia's Honda, Luis' pickup, and Mallory's Mini Cooper. They have to swing around on a track west of the mound, past the guys' shack where Harris' bike is under the lean-to, to drive out into the field. He walks around front and sees they're lined up along Bishop Road: many levels of officialdom and some that look like gawkers. Even the little yellow airplane that sprays the fields is swooping over like a dragonfly. The old black guy who lives in the shack right by the road a bit east of the main house drives up in his blue V-8 Dodge truck, sees his place to pull in is blocked, goes on by, turns around, comes back, parks on the other side a little past his place and gets out. He has kind of a thick body, in jeans, a brown ball cap, and a buff bomber jacket. He takes one look at the scene and goes inside his place. Home at three-thirty, Harris thinks; the guy probably works some kind of carpentry.

Harris cruises back around and sees Mallory and Miss Celia have brought out glasses of iced tea on trays. There's a general break. His glass, tall with indents and bubbles, is like one of his mother's. Tea's good. Just after four, an ambulance-style vehicle shows up from the Northern office of the state crime lab. Mallory says they'll take the bones to the main lab in Jackson, to the bio-science section.

Not too long after, the sheriff tells Miss Celia they'll be back tomorrow with cadaver dogs; no unit is available today. Everybody should stay clear of the taped-off area.

"We won't touch anything," she says. "You really think there's something more?"

"Have to look," he says. "Maybe her hands are all that's here. Don't know."

"They can tell it was a woman?" Mallory asks.

"Doc says yes, from the hand size. Says the bones are some amount of decades old, but nobody can tell more til they get to the lab."

And in procession the officials depart, the alertness unravels. Harris could use a drink.

LUIS HAS WALKED all the way to the oxbow lake they call Old River because it used to be the Mississippi before the river changed course long ago and left this curve of water. He's been roving in the evenings til he knows the landscape. Dead cypresses stand out in the water like pickets guarding the little bay, the boat ramp with its sign:

Public Fishing

No Firearms

Lying on the natural levee, he watches the sky grow dark, til the bugs' whine fills his ears and the moon is rising. He starts back, though he doesn't want to return to the shack where he'll just spend another night waiting for Harris to stumble in from being with Mallory, the slap of the door, the complaining springs of his cot, his curse, cough, groan, snore.

In August, they were here with a dozen students for the field school, sampling and assessing the site, and the three of them laid claim to projects for their theses. After doing construction May to July with his father in Biloxi, he had money, but when he asked Mallory out for dinner at Madidi, she said no, it would be a bad idea to get involved when they were going to work together. So when they came out here last week, what does she do but hook up with Harris the second night, riding into town with him on his bike and taking him into her bed.

Fine, she just said that to put him off politely, because he asked politely. He never can speak with the careless confidence he needs. There's always a hesitation, a gap between thought and words as his mind tries to find language, tossed between the Spanish of his parents, the English of school and books. So, often, he doesn't speak, or speaks too formally. And usually silence is fine with him. Except there are feelings that want out, but maybe these are feelings that have no words in any language.

He nears the area of their excavation—the crime scene, he thinks, but then it doesn't seem like the crime scene is where you'd bury the hands, so this is probably the un-crime scene—and cuts around. Harris' bike is still gone. He hears a sound—crow? train whistle?—and follows it to the shack by the road. This is a solid house compared to theirs: painted dark green, with curtains at the lit-up windows. The old man sits on the porch. He's not playing a tune, just making sounds with the harmonica, wheeze and wail, til he sees Luis watching and says, "How you doing?" The squared shape of his white beard shows by the light of a candle in a jar.

They have a nodding acquaintance, from early mornings when Luis is up drinking coffee outside and the man goes off in his truck. Luis introduces himself, and the man says he's Bill Mc-something. "Mc-Eye?"

"Mc K-I-E. Probably supposed to be McKay or McGee, but it got changed somewhere back before my grandpa."

Luis nods. He's having to concentrate to catch words; the old man has a Southern accent and something more, a slur, and his voice is low.

"Had to stop working out back, right? Tomorrow, too?"

"Tomorrow they're bringing dogs."

"I heard that, in town. Heard they found some bones in a box."

Luis tells what he knows: the bones of a woman's hands. Long dead, but not so long they're not of interest to the authorities.

"Lots of bones," McKie says, "in Mississippi. But you know that. Some rise right out of the ground when it rains, those Indian bones, chips and bits. I worked all around here, driving a grader, leveling, turned plenty of them up: no choice when you want to plant the land."

Luis notices McKie has on a tie, looks like a green tie with a dark blue shirt, dress pants. "Were you going out?"

"Planned to, but then I didn't feel like it. Thinking about those bones. Have a seat," he says.

Luis settles beside him on a rattan chair with seat cushions. "This is much nicer than where we're camping," he says.

"I fixed this one up after I bought it. Helped clean out yours for Miss Bishop before you got here, but it needs a lot of work. They're old, go back to the tenant farming days. You know people pay to stay in shacks like this, over at Hopson Plantation. Italians and Japanese show up and beg to."

"Why?"

"Because of the blues."

The bike comes up Bishop Road with two figures on it, runs by them and turns in. Luis can hear some discussion—Harris wheedling?—and then Harris walks her up to the Back House.

He's aware of them without turning, without trying.

"You got it bad," says McKie.

Luis can say nothing to this, but it seems he doesn't have to. "Told her?"

"Oh no, no," he says. "No. It's awkward enough. I don't get women," he says, and hears the ambiguity in that: so true.

McKie goes into a riff on the harmonica, some fundamental blues. "Women need to know where you stand," he says. "That's a lesson I learned." He gets up, goes into the house, and comes back with something that he hands to Luis: a cold metal bar.

"What's this?" He turns it, feels the holes.

"That's a harp. You know, the Mississippi Saxophone. I got lots of 'em laying around. Take a shot. Blow."

Luis produces a chord and then inhales it.

McKie rumbles something like a laugh. And he starts to play and talk, and Luis, who is feeling unmoored anyway, looks at the moon and lets it roll over him. He doesn't get all the words but he catches the story, like a half-remembered song:

Once McKie loved a woman—met her round here when she was just a girl. He came from Mound Bayou, found work here, everything was getting mechanized and he was always good with driving. Used to make up music out in the middle of the fields, had the turn of the wheels in it. She was a noticeable girl: tall and sassy. A memorable girl. Then he met her again in Memphis when McKie was trying to break into music up there. She remembered him, too. She was involved in the movement. They were organizing sit-ins in Tennessee and she got trained to stand it, being insulted, arrested. Then she came down here Mississippi, which was harder. Sometimes he played Clarksdale juke joints, saw her. But it got nasty, scary here—this would be in 1964, Freedom Summer, you heard of that? Registering people to vote. There was White Knights of the KKK around and just terror. They talked about getting away. He wanted to go to Chicago,

where there were opportunities in music, and he asked her to go
along, but he played it cool when he did it, you know, take it or
leave it. And she said she couldn't leave the movement, but then
one time she said, yes, she wanted to go. So it was set up he'd
pick her up—he had a car, she didn't—one evening, was to get
her outside the bus station and because he was sometimes unre-
liable she said if he didn't show up she'd catch a bus. Was a Saturday, there was a fish fry, he'd been talking and joking with
people, and he arrived just a few minutes late and she wasn't there.
Bus station guy couldn't say much. Maybe there'd been a woman
waiting. Maybe not. Maybe she got on a bus. Maybe just left.
Only a few minutes late, nothing really. He called her mother
who lived up outside of Memphis. She'd told her mother she was
going to Vicksburg, so he went there, but nobody'd seen her and
maybe Vicksburg was just what she told her mother when she
was going off with him. Then somebody said she'd been seen in
Chicago and he thought okay, maybe she went looking for me,
and he went there, picked up playing, but there was no sign of
her. Any place he went, to New Orleans, to New York, to Paris—
can you believe he made it all the way to Paris and to Germany
too?—anywhere he saw somebody from the floating world of
Mississippi, he asked them, where's Veneece? Rumors here and
there, but nothing real. But there were a whole lot of other
women and they're kind when you're lonely, when you can play.
Then styles changed, changed real bad by the 70s unless you were
a star, unless you were a legend. He was back in Chicago, drove
buses there, Illinois and Wisconsin—was married there for a
while, drank too much, but later sobered up. Then things started
up here with the blues, and he came on home. He can teach driving lessons, pick up work sometimes on equipment, and do some
playing too. He gets the Social Security now, but he likes to work.
Mr. Bishop—that's Scott Bishop—gave him some work, and
helped him buy this place. "This isn't the one Veneece grew up

in—that was out in the fields, one of the old shacks Mr. Bishop
knocked down once the agribusiness came in. You'd hardly believe
how it used to be round here, all the work done with mules,
needed two for a wagon, four for a plow. I can make the harmonica sound like mule: See? You try it."

Luis laughs and lifts the harmonica in his hands and blows:
still the same flat chord but it sounds the way he feels.

"Carry it around," McKie says. "Get to know it."

"I couldn't take it."

"That one I don't use. It's fine."

There's the bang of a door up on the mound, and Harris
stomps down to their shack, slams that door too.

"See that?" McKie says. "It's working already."

Luis stands up and thanks him, wanting to go now he'll have
Harris under his eye.

McKie says, "I remember her cleaning her white gloves—gals
wore white gloves then, to go to church in—cleaned them off
with bread crumbs: rolled the soft bread along so it picked up
any little dirt that got on the fingertips."

Luis is filled with a question he can't think of any way to
express.

As he walks along the road, he looks up and sees Celia Bishop
standing in an ivory robe on the porch above the elaborate portico. The house's square whiteness floats above the brick founda-
tion, like the phantom of a temple that was here six hundred years
ago. Over the treetops hangs the huge moon, nearly full, marked
with the pale blue features of a woman looking to her left. The
scene swims through his dreams.

AFTER SHE SHOWERS AND DRESSES, Mallory strips the
bed. The sheets are half off anyway, and they smell too much like
sex and Harris. She grabs her towels, while she's at it, and carries
everything to the washer in the other room, and crams it in.

She fills the kettle, puts it on the little stove. Through the window above the sink she can see, out past the screened porch, the area where men in uniforms stand drinking coffee. Better to get to work, if they can't excavate today. Those bones have told her: time to get serious. She arranges her notes beside her laptop on the kitchen table. She will concentrate away her irritation at herself. It was a mistake to sleep with Harris. Maybe not the first time, but the second—that's when he started to think he had rights. And all this after she'd turned down Luis, who was cute and seemed smart, because she knew it was better to be all business. She could kick herself.

There's a knock on the door and a "Mallory?" It's Celia—as she has told Mallory to call her, although Harris says "Miss Celia" is proper. Celia says, "Phone in there's driving me nuts. And I'd like to look for something in the pantry here, if you don't mind."

"I'm just making tea. Can I give you some?"

"Thank you." Celia throws open the louvered doors to the right of the laundry area. The shelves in there are full of boxes; Mallory has peeked. "This is stuff of my mother's. She lived out here after Daddy died and Scott got married, right through her last illness five years ago."

"So that's why it's a whole little apartment." The kettle whistles. Mallory pours water over teabags in the old brown pot. She sets out blue flowered mugs: all this was here when she arrived, fixed up by Celia.

"This structure's old—see those cypress beams? It was a summer kitchen for my grandparents when they first moved here, before World War I. After they knocked down the farmhouse to build the main house, they used this for laundry; has its own well." She pulls a box out and kneels in front of it, riffling through while she talks. "They did this over as an apartment for my father after he got shot up at Guadalcanal and brought home his bride. Then Scott was born, and I came along, and we all lived in the main house. My grandparents moved to town. This was a laundry and storage. I'd play out here, read." She turns and pulls out another carton, pushes back her hair as she leans over it.

"What are you looking for?"

"The sheriff's people asked me if there's any record of who all lived around here, on Bishop land, at different times. I don't know if there is. When I got here in June the house was a mess. I cleaned, cleaned, cleaned, but I didn't see old business records. So I thought maybe there's something out here."

Mallory pours the tea. "I'm out of milk. I should go into town and pick up some groceries later."

"I'm fine with sugar," Celia says, and stands up, adds some. Mallory can see a hint of silver along her temple where her hair has grown in since the last coloring. The zinnia print of her blouse is over-bright, and Mallory realizes she's never seen Celia without lipstick.

Mallory wraps her hands around her mug and looks at her screen, which has gone to sleep. It seems rude to wake it up now. "Who's been calling?"

"Everybody." Celia sips, shakes her head. "It's going to be in the Clarksdale paper this afternoon, what they found, with a picture of the box, but everyone seems to have heard already. A reporter who called shared the nasty speculation that somebody chopped off a woman's hands but let her go. Said that's what they still do to thieves in some countries."

"Oh, horrible," says Mallory. Though of course she has heard of this. And the Indians slashed hamstrings to keep captives from running off; remains showed it. Human history was cruel, but that was easier to think about at a distance.

"Yes, well," says Celia, "most seem to think it was murder and the body was cut up. The reporter said the North Mississippi authorities have no record of a corpse without hands. They're looking at lists of missing women from the 50s and 60s, where they could try a DNA match to relatives, so I presume the bones look to be that old. Which puts it in what was an ugly time around here, one reason everybody's so damn interested."

"They can tell the age more precisely with Carbon-14 dating."

Celia says, "I know. I was a biology teacher, thirty-five years. I taught over in North Carolina, Asheville. Took my retirement last spring. Never thought I'd be back here." She sits on the floor with a new box. "Cookbooks," she says. "I should look through these. Lots of old ones from churches and here's mother's Women's Club. Hmm."

Mallory sneaks a finger out and brushes her touch pad and the screen comes back. She opens the database where she tracks each day's work and starts entering figures from yesterday.

HARRIS HOSES DOWN HIS BIKE. The hose has a leak in it at the handle—he found it among the old crap under the lean-to. Their so-called shack is really a cabin, you can see daylight through the boards, and the roof, as he said to Luis last night, is mainly rust. No surprise, really, Mississippi is the apotheosis of rust—anything left outside oxidates and stays forever, like something in mythology: girl running from a lusty god becomes an old Ford with no tires.

The dog officers are expected, and he has his eye out for Professor Martin. This research is Martin's baby. In midsummer he came out to set up for the field school, and made them his research assistants when Miss Celia said she'd be willing to house them for a stint in the fall. They're on their honor to behave well and not blow the project.

Martin had them work on methodology and record keeping at the start of the semester, and then sent them off. Wanted them making progress before the cold set in. Then they'd write their thesis proposals, do presentations to his undergrads, and grade his papers and finals. It was a feudal structure, the university, just like this place in its day: big house, little house, shacks. Harris last night argued this to Mallory, that they were the tenant farmers of academia, but she told him he was full of it—they're in it for hope of getting somewhere, not trapped.

Last night—what a disaster. She said she wanted hot food and to get away from there, so he took her for spaghetti at the Rest Haven, but she just picked at it. Then they went around Clarksdale on the Harley and found there was a band at Ground Zero, but when they got there she didn't want to go in, said she needed fresh air. They parked outside and stood around listening to the thrum. He talked to a couple of guys about bikes, one with an Indian Scout from 1941, restored, magnificent. Meantime she wandered around reading the writing on the walls. The place was completely inscribed; started inside with autographs of blues guys, but then everybody else added a name, a date, even outside on the chippy paint. She'd pointed out where it said, high on a window, "If the world didn't suck, we'd fall off." All the more reason to have fun while you can, but she'd wanted none of him last night.

Professor Martin's Isuzu pickup full of tools pulls up, and Harris strolls down to greet him. The others never seem to get it, but he is ambitious.

"NOW HERE'S SOMETHING," Celia says. "In with every greeting card she ever got."

Mallory glances over and sees the mottled cover of a composition book.

"Looks like Mother started to write down some history. Names: Cecil Scott Bishop married Lila Barber, Bee Branch, Arkansas. Then C.S. Junior, that's Daddy, married Mother, Mary Earl Powell, of Chattanooga, daughter of Robert and Evelyn Powell. My mother felt the Powells were better than the Bishops because they came from Virginia originally. Whatever originally means. Then here's Scott, Cecil S. the third, and I'm Celia

Savannah. But then it goes off into things she's copied, recipes and ways to get out stains." Celia flips ahead. "Okay, here's some of the black tenants but she doesn't tell you who was where. Family named Easterday, that's before my time. Here's Wince and Luzie Cole, whose real name was Louisiana, she notes. That seems to be the point, odd names. 'Her daughter is Venice and the son is Roosevelt.' My mother thought all this was hilarious, I'm ashamed to say. She liked to laugh at people naming a kid Moonpie."

"Venice is a pretty name," says Mallory.

"I remember her. I was a little tomboy running around and she was probably fifteen and full-grown and graceful. I remember her striding along. I think I had my first crush on her."

Mallory looks at Celia in sudden speculation, and Celia grins. "Come on, you're not shocked."

Mallory, thinking how little that goes on in the Back House must get by Celia, shrugs.

"I learned early enough I didn't belong here. Neither did a girl like—now, see, I remember, they didn't pronounce it Venice, they shifted it to southern, Veneece. I have the impression she was bright, and what education was she going to get here in the 50s? They moved away. My mother has here: 'Mother of Luzie, Venus, question, Slave?' Luzie's mother could have been born in slavery, certainly. Next page, pink applesauce. Well, I'll put this book aside." She is back in the closet.

Mallory says, "It's very kind of you to let us excavate on your land."

"I always thought it should be looked at. The pity is that there were other mounds out here, but they were leveled. It's just because structures were built on this one that it remains. My grandfather kept relics that would come up when they plowed, but bones, nobody cared. The land was too valuable, that famous fertile soil of the Delta. My father used to joke that Choctaw bone meal was part of the secret." Celia sighs. "When I was a little girl

I adored my father. He was tall and certain and he smelled of cigarettes. You never get over that."

Mallory thinks about her father, who took her to a thousand soccer practices, standing anxiously on the sidelines, trying his best to make her a strong girl. And she should be strong, show some drive. She asks, "Are there any very old textiles in the house? That's what interests me most. I'm not really a bones type, I'm finding out. After I get my master's, I want to get on a research grant for excavation of a plantation up north, study how they grew flax, spun, wove."

"Up north of here?"

"No, in *the* north. They've discovered there were huge plantations with slaves in Massachusetts, New York in the 1700s. They were called manor houses, landed estates, but they were plantations. I grew up not far from where one was in Connecticut, eight thousand acres.

Celia says, "Well, I don't know that there's any really old cloth here. I remember a coverlet, but I think Scott's wife went off with it when they split up."

"Scott, that's your brother?"

"Big brother. I always thought he'd leave. He talked about it, into college, but he wound up coming back, working, staying on even when he'd leased the fields out. I can't say we were close growing up: he was five years older and in tenth grade he got shipped off to military school in Tennessee. He and my father fought. I remember Daddy busted up some records Scott had. He called it 'jungle music.'"

"Rock and roll?"

"I think it would have been rhythm and blues. There's a good-size collection of blues records in the house, now. The ones Daddy smashed would probably be of value."

"I'm not sure how much I like the blues," Mallory says. "All those guys lamenting."

Celia says, "I always think it's about survival. Look what I got through. And the women's blues is a whole different thing. The women were the first stars. Bessie Smith. Ida Cox. You know her 'Wild Women Don't Have the Blues'? 'You never get nothing by being an angel child, you better change your ways and get real wild.'" She sounds surprisingly raunchy. And then she laughs at Mallory's expression. "You need to listen to some Big Mama Thornton and Memphis Minnie."

She sets down her mug and rummages through another box, humming "Wild Women." "Everybody's counting on the blues to revive tourism in the Delta, but once people come, there's other history to be known. I'm thinking this could become some kind of archaeology study center later on. I might want to spend part of the year on the Gulf Coast somewhere, and maybe there could be some kind of exhibit here if it were all arranged right."

"That would be fantastic. I'm sure there's some way to set that up with the University. You should talk to Professor Martin."

"Can't do it yet, of course. There's my brother."

"I'm sorry?" Mallory says. "I thought he'd passed away."

"Oh no, he's in a nursing care facility. I visit a couple times a week. He's got heart trouble and other things. When he got in bad shape, I thought why keep fighting out the Scopes trial all over again with these students who have been raised to deny evidence as an article of faith? And my partner, Ellen, died two years back, of breast cancer. I had my time in so I took retirement and came home."

Celia carries her mug over to the sink and rinses it, looking out the window. "I don't think those dogs are getting anything. Well," she says, "I'm keeping you from your work. I'll just carry these cookbooks into the house." She hoists her carton and goes out.

Mallory saves her work, moves her laundry to the dryer, then decides she's hungry and should really get some food.

THE DOGS, PEARL AND LEVI, went for the dirt where the box was found, but when the men dug it out deeper, under Professor Martin's watchful eye, there was nothing of significance below. And the dogs sniffed around but weren't much interested in anyplace else. The team packs up cheerfully. Elimination of a possibility is as much a fact as finding anything, and being out with Pearl and Levi on a fine October day is a pleasure.

Martin discusses the possibility of training cadaver dogs to find thousand year old bones. The sheriff's investigator says the paper's going to have a picture of the box, in case anybody might know anything, although that box is pretty much typical. People just threw them together, put on the hardware. After calling into the office, he says, "It'll be possible to go back to excavation tomorrow, if it doesn't rain, which it might. Of course, if you turn up anything else, we'll want to know."

Luis sees Mallory's car scoot away. Harris is sucking up to Martin, showing him the Cage and spouting his theory that it was for animals or captives. Town strikes Luis as a good idea.

OVER IN JACKSON, the bones are laid out, pieces of a puzzle, photographed and noted. The bones of the upper right extremity are all there, and an inch of the radius and ulna, to where they were chopped. The upper left extremity was severed across the wrist. Part of the proximal row, scaphoid and lunate, are present, but the triquetrum and pisiform are missing.

Lab tech Josslyn Pulliam slices off a quarter gram of bone. It will be crushed, the DNA extracted and copied. She will isolate the mtDNA, the matrilineal ring around the nucleus. With fluorescent dyes to pick up the repetitions of G, C, A, and T, she'll look for the identifying pattern of the mitochondria, a line she'll find goes back to Africa.

In CLARKSDALE, Mallory orders a cookie and a double espresso at Miss Del's General Store, and while she's waiting the older gentleman who lives in the little front house at the Bishop place comes in to buy some seed for mustard greens, curly top. The guy behind the counter measures it into a little paper bag and they talk about how it's going to rain tomorrow and that's the time for throwing down seed, good soaking rain.

Mallory takes her espresso outside to drink while looking at the plants for sale, thinking maybe she should buy something to brighten up the Back House. Luis comes by—he was over at the library using the wireless to check email—and they stroll down to Cathead where she buys four CDs of women singing the blues, and he asks the owner about harmonicas, and they look at all the folk art, which is this strange combination of creepy and hilarious, not unlike the Mexican Day of the Dead stuff, as Luis points out. Then Luis takes her for Southern tamales and while they eat them in his truck he tells her about how the recipe passed in the cotton fields from Mexican workers to blacks—though it's definitely Mississippian to serve tamales with crackers and Tabasco. He says these have way more cayenne than any his mother would make, but they're good. Mallory finds hers delicious, beef tamales, aching with spice.

HARRIS IS STUCK in Miss Celia's living room with her and Professor Martin, the two of them chatting away, nibbling cheese straws and spiced toasted pecans, drinking white wine. She calls him Greg, he calls her Celia. Harris gathers that she got a letter he'd written her brother asking about excavation and invited him out, last summer. Harris asks if he might have something else and Miss Celia tells him to help himself at the liquor cabinet, an old oak icebox with a lot of hardware that needs polishing. She says she doesn't know what-all her brother kept in there. Well, plenty.

Harris puts a few fingers of Old Granddad in a highball glass and asks her does she know there's a couple Mason jars of homemade whiskey in there?

"My brother's," she says. "I'm sure it was family tradition to have a supplier. You know Muddy Waters sold moonshine in the area, in my grandfather's day."

Shelves on either side of the fireplace are filled with books and artifacts. Greg Martin picks up and admires a frog effigy bowl. "Did this come from out back?" he says.

"I assume so," she says. "It's been here as long as I can remember."

Harris wanders back towards the liquor cabinet. He notices a speaker above it, up near the ceiling, and turns in a circle til he's spotted four of them, and the stereo set-up, which is on shelves by the piano, in the front corner of the room. Above the piano hangs a portrait of a boy already gangly at nine or ten, and a bright-eyed little girl in a red dress, his arm around her protectively, her face alight. Harris crouches and pours himself more bourbon.

Martin has another piece in his hands, a teapot with an up-thrust spout. "You know they thought these were imitations of French teapots made after the French came through here, but carbon dating shows they're older. Some think they were fertility symbols."

Celia snorts with laughter. Maybe she's had too much wine. "Sorry, it just seems basically female, a teapot."

Harris counts the Mason jars in the cupboard. Lots of vodka in here too: several bottles started and not finished, trendy stuff.

Where are Mallory and Luis, that's what Harris wants to know.

THEY'RE AT OLD RIVER—Luis drove, and they walked over the levee and down by the water. "I'd like to take a canoe out there," he says. "Do you know the Arkansas state line is out in the middle? Once they established it, they left it, even when the river abandoned this water."

She sits back on her elbows. "It's peaceful."

He pulls out the harmonica. "I'm supposed to practice," he says. He breathes out his chord and breathes it back in.

"That sounds awful," she says.

"That's right," he says, "but it helps me. Mallory, when I asked you out this summer, I liked you, but I didn't know you."

"You still don't know me," she says.

"True," he says, "but I like you more."

"Why do you guys always make things so complicated?" She leans over to kiss him, and laughs. "I'm getting lessons in being wild," she says.

"Mallory," he says, "I don't think you need any lessons in being wild."

"Yes, I do," she says. "Hey, did you know Celia's gay?"

"No." He is touching her knee with his.

"She had a crush on a black girl named Venice, just for starters."

The moon is coming up behind a lot of rippled clouds, and bugs are dancing around her hair. He waves them off and says, "We have to go back to town to get your car anyway. Let's go hear some music and dance." Then, as he opens the door of his truck, "Did you say Venice?"

JAM NIGHT AT GROUND ZERO. Bill McKie wears a maroon hat, pink shirt, red tie, dusty pink pants, two-tone shoes. He's got three harmonicas stuck in his belt and he's blowing away on a fourth.

Mallory and Luis see him, and wave. They have some beer and proceed to dance it off, sweating. When they go outside for some air, she shows Luis the line about the world sucking,

"It doesn't suck," he says. "Just pulls you close."

WHAT HE NEEDS TO DO, Harris decides, is show Mallory how messed up he is without her and then get her to help him to reform. He sits by the steps to the Back House in one of the metal chairs. He has the jar he took from the liquor cabinet: fine aged mash. Miss Celia is never going to miss it. He has offered himself up to be reformed before. It's one of his best lines. And maybe she can really do it. Fix me, that's what he'll say. Hell, you liked me til yesterday. Fix me.

Celia sits in the living room reading her mother's notes, a catalog of the mundane. So many ways to prepare yams. The address for the headmaster of the school they sent Scott to. A list of presents she got for her aunts at Christmas 1959. A recipe for a pudding that uses shoe peg corn. Garden tips. She pages forward. She can find nothing about the times when things got really dark here, about 1964, the summer when her mother took her away because things were burning and she was afraid out here in the country. Scott was home from Ole Miss, working for Daddy, who asked him repeatedly if he'd seen James Meredith there, which Scott denied. She and her mother visited relatives in Chattanooga, then went up to Asheville, and Hot Springs, following the mountains.

When they got back, Celia was busy understanding who she was and trying to keep it hidden at the same time, planning her escape to boarding school, her father willing to send her because he feared integration. She'd seen daylight and she ran for it. Scott did so poorly at Ole Miss that year, they decided he should come home and work. Celia looks up at the portrait: she and Scott smile away, full of the confidence of 1953. Her grandmother made that red dress with the hand smocking. Scott wears a white shirt with a dark blue tie, his crew cut carefully rendered. "What am I to do?" she says. But there's no answer, just the artifacts of a lost world.

"Fish me," Harris says, as Mallory crosses the lawn.

"Oh my God," she says to Luis, who is walking behind her a step or two. He has decided not to push it, to take it easy, they've had so much fun, although if she wants to be wild, so be it.

"What are you doing with her? You bastard." Harris lurches up from his chair, focuses on Luis, and takes a swing, easily ducked.

Oh, how much Luis wants to hit him. He grabs him by the arms and tries to turn him away, but Harris is taller and off balance, and the two of them fall hard.

Mallory is saying, "Get out of here, Harris," but Luis, sprawled on top of him, doesn't feel him breathing. Luis pushes himself up, frightened. Then Harris groans and pukes on the steps.

Celia is there suddenly, in her robe. She turns Harris so he's throwing up into the grass. "Get me some water," she says. Luis goes inside the Back House kitchen, finds a galvanized pail under the sink, and fills it nearly full. When he runs out, Celia's got Harris over where there are some bushes, and she's holding his head. Mallory stands a few yards away, looking up into the pecan branches shaking in the wind, casting down nuts. A front is coming through.

"Fish me," Harris moans.

Celia says, mopping his face, "Those were perfectly good cheese straws, but they're not enough if you're going to do really heavy drinking."

Luis takes the bucket and dumps half over Harris' head and chest, then sluices off the steps.

Bill McKie comes up still in his music togs, hat and all. "Got a problem here?"

"A little youthful overindulgence," says Celia.

"You going to be okay?" Luis asks. Harris just looks at him.

McKie spots something in the dark, goes and picks up a Mason jar. "He got into your brother's stuff," he says.

"Let's get him inside and cleaned up." Celia leads Harris into the house, with Bill on his other side.

Mallory clears her throat. "Well, see you tomorrow."

"I had a lot of fun," says Luis. She blows him a kiss and goes in. He stands in the garden til he sees her light go off. He hesitates at the back door of the house, but what has he got to say that'll make any difference?

CELIA PUTS FRESH SHEETS on the bed in the back bedroom. She's done it over in pale green for friends she hopes will visit this winter. She left the shelves filled with books and rocks and shells, on either side of the window that looks over the low roof of the Back House towards the fields.

Bill comes out of the bathroom with Harris' clothes rolled up in a towel. "I told him not to drown in there."

"If you'll get him into bed, I'll bring up some iced tea, get him rehydrated." Celia tucks in the last corner and stands. "When I was a girl, this was Scott's room."

Bill says, "I'd like to talk to you about your brother."

"I've been thinking, too," says Celia.

THE MAN IS A RUIN AT SIXTY-FIVE. Heart mainly, acute coronary syndrome, but kidneys, veins, legs, lungs—what isn't wrong with him? He's on oxygen, his breath a cold whistle up his nose when he puts the cannula in, though sometimes it sits around his neck, because too much oxygen gives him reflux. From the blood thinners, his skin is translucent and in places broken. You can see the purple bruises where IVs were put into the backs of his hands when he was in hospital care in the summer, though right now he's back on the residential side, in his own room. His nose is lopsided where a skin cancer was cut away.

In June when she'd reported on cleaning up the house he got irritated, so Celia stopped telling him about anything going on there, stuck to general news in town, not that he responds. He'll leaf through a *Sports Illustrated* she's brought him or listen to a small radio he has, on earphones, all through her visit. Usually after a little while she goes down the hall and talks to the nursing staff, wanting to be sure they know somebody cares about him.

This morning, he is sitting in a wheelchair, looking out the window at the rain. Celia lays the newspaper on his lap. "Grim Find by Archaeologists" is the headline, below the picture of the box. He looks at her, looks down, reads, frowning. "What're archaeologists doing there?"

She says, "I invited them. Scott, we have to talk."

He puts the cannula in his nostrils, breathes. Mouth clamped shut.

Celia says, "There's someone else to see you," and leaves the room. When she comes back in with Bill McKie, Scott clasps his hand. Bill pulls over the guest chair for Celia but she gestures him into it and sits on the bed.

Celia says, "Bill thinks those were the hands of Veneece Cole."

Scott clears his throat, nods. To Bill he says, "I told her to get out of town." He breathes. "She was going with you."

Bill says, "What happened? I need to know."

"I told her to get gone. Daddy's friends were all talking about the activists. Had lists of what he called the agitative." He says, "Sister, could I have a glass of water?"

Celia goes and fills a Dixie cup in the little bathroom, hands it to him, and he drinks, then speaks with more voice.

"She rode around with them. She knew where black folks lived, way off the road. People they might register." He coughs. "I saw her one morning near the courthouse. Going to stand in support of some who were registering. She could get arrested too. Just for being there. Get sent to Parchman. I told her she was on a list and ought to get away.

"We fooled around when we were younger." He says to Bill, "Just kid stuff. Then they moved; everybody was going to the cities for work. Daddy'd caught on, saw me looking at her. Said I should go down to Miss Nelly's in Natchez to become a man.

Fought with him a lot til I got shipped off—that was Mom's idea. Military school, where they taught me to shut up and fit in." He breathes a while. "When James Meredith came into the dining hall at Ole Miss, we banged our silverware. That's what you did.

"I attended a dance that evening at the country club. Had a black band playing for the white people. Still no blacks allowed in there, right? Shit. I got home and Daddy was out in the Back House. He had her hands." He shakes his head. "In a bucket. There was blood. No body. He'd been with his group, at a meeting, out east of Clarksdale, and on the way home he saw her walking. He offered her a ride, and she got in, but then he must have said something because she tried to jump back out and he shoved her head against the dashboard, knocked her out. That was his Olds Super 88, hard dashboard."

Bill says, "She was going to the bus station. I was meeting her there."

"Yes, she had a small suitcase with her, but I don't know if she had a chance to tell him where she was going. With her knocked out he drove home and found that she was dead. He hadn't intended to, he insisted."

"What did he intend?" asks Celia.

"Said they all said she was his responsibility, cause she grew up out here. Said he thought he'd scare her, but here she was, dead. He had to get rid of the body and best he could think was to put it in the water, weighted down. But he was worried she'd come up. Bodies kept coming back up. That was something they'd learned. He knew she'd been arrested, her fingerprints would be on file. I don't know that you could get fingerprints off a body that'd been in the water, but that's what he said. So he took a hatchet, a bucket, went down by Old River, drug her over to a swampy part, chopped off her hands. He went into the water with her and he weighted her down with some chains, a tire iron, not sure what all. He got back just before I got there. He was going to dissolve the hands in lye, at least enough to get the skin off. Mom had lye out there, for hominy.

"Celia, you wouldn't have recognized him. He was soaking wet, shaking. Said he was sick, that carrying all the weight had ripped up where he was gut-shot in the war. Said he'd killed Japs, but he didn't mean to do this. And he wasn't going to be caught for it. He was as big a coward as I've always been." Scott breathes, looking at the ceiling.

"So he went along when I told him I'd take care of it. The box was one I had around, kept old stuff in it, coins, fossils, arrowheads. I put the hands in. They were drained out, gray looking. I knew it was a burial ground out back, so I thought that would be the right place. Put the box down deep, made sure the dirt was packed back in, laid the grass back across. Made sure no animals dug it up. If you weren't looking, you could never tell the spot.

"Daddy, the day after, burned up her suitcase and her pocketbook in a fire with a lot of brush. Asked me where her hands were, he wanted to burn them too, but I told him they were long gone. Later I drove over the whole area back of the mound with a big mower, and the rains settled it all down. Made me nervous to be away though. Couldn't concentrate at school. Had to drink to sleep. I felt better being at home and watching over her.

"Sometimes I thought, if her body surfaced and they were investigating, I would dig up the box and turn him in, but it didn't and I don't know that I'd ever have had the guts. My own father, you know. No matter what.

"And then he died. And just I lived with it. I tried to be a decent man, but I've got my demons. Married for a while, but she said I was hard to talk to. When there's something you can never say—"

He says to Celia, "Never could talk to you, either. Just tried to keep Mom off your back when she got real religious. Tried to help people. Quit that country club and drank at home. Worked so I could give a helping hand where I could. I came to feel I wasn't watching over her so much as she was watching over me."

He takes out the cannula, coughs. "Man," he says to Bill, "you know I'm sorry."

Bill says, "Okay, I know. Everything counts." He lays his palm on the back of Scott's hand, where it's bruised.

"The body never came up, but the box did. Who would have thought that? What happens now?"

Bill says, "She had a brother, might be alive, would want to know."

Scott nods.

Celia says, "We'll talk to the sheriff. I guess he'll come see you and take a statement, for starters."

Scott says, "Tell him to hurry up. I won't last long." And he smiles. "My stupid heart."

SHIT FIRE, Harris feels awful. He's in a real bed, though, in a room with a smell of pine cleaner. After careful consideration he rolls over and sees there's a wastebasket beside the bed, in case he has to hurl. It makes him laugh. He checks out the bruises down his right side. Luis must have kicked his ass. He can't find his clothes, but when he tiptoes downstairs with a towel around him, he finds them clean and dry on the dining room table. He dresses fast. When he checks the big clock in the hall, it's nearly eleven. He opens the front door and stands in the portico, breathing in the cool rain that's drenching the Delta.

Out near the road, he sees Luis bent over talking to Mallory, who's in her car headed out. What did he say to her last night? He remembers thinking he was in bad need of reform. Too right.

Mallory tells Luis she's going back to school, might as well get some work done. They're not going to do a thing here in this downpour. Luis says he laid out tarps when he got up early this morning, but he has to agree, it'll take at least a few days for their site to dry, even if the weather clears tonight. He leans towards her through the car window, his dark hair full of rain.

She explains she's not sure whether the Kitchen is going to be considered compromised by all the messing they did with it yesterday, perhaps a bad choice for a thesis. "Here comes Harris. Let's let things settle down," she says. "I'll see you at school."

She kisses him convincingly, pops a CD into the player and goes off listening to Memphis Minnie's "Me and My Chauffeur Blues."

Luis turns and sees Harris making his way down to him with his shirt draped over his head. He braces.

"Hey," says Harris. "Pax."

Luis says, "You swung at me."

"Listen," says Harris. "When you lose a woman, it's easier to blame the other man."

"Okay," says Luis.

"'The past is over. Let the dead bury the dead.' Know who said that?"

Luis shakes his head.

"Jefferson Davis. Too bad nobody listened. Takes a man who really lost to give that advice, I guess."

Somebody hollers Luis' name. Bill McKie is standing out by his house, in a long slicker. He beckons them over. Luis looks at Harris.

"Already wet," says Harris. "Let's go."

They dash and reach McKie's porch. He's standing on a patch of turned-up ground beside it, scattering seeds. "Best time to plant greens," he says. "Celia has business in town. She'll be a while. I'm cooking some red beans and rice. Got plenty. Come on in."

They follow him into a room rich with the smell of sausage. In the dimness, they turn in wonder. Silvered boards of cypress are papered with a hundred notices and posters in deep and gaudy hues. On some, Luis spots the younger face of Bill McKie.

"This one here's Bill Big Broonzy," says McKie, "and that's Sonny Boy Williamson II. You can visit his grave in Tutwiler, not far from here. People leave harmonicas there for him. You boys ready now to learn about the blues?"

Crossroads Bargain

Charlaine Harris

IT WAS HOT AS THE SIX SHADES OF HELL, even in the middle of the night. The moon was a full orange globe that hung frighteningly close to the flat Delta earth. All around the locusts sang.

A black man walked down the middle of the dirt road by himself in the night. He blessed the moon, which gave him enough light to avoid the worst ruts baked in the dusty soil. He'd been playing at a jook joint outside Clarksdale, and his hands and soul were tired. His guitar case thumped softly against his right leg as he walked. Sweat stained his clothes and his shoes were broken and worn.

Two more miles and he'd be home.

He didn't have the money to travel far to play. Most of his singing was done in the ramshackle jook joints of the Delta. When he could afford it, he caught a train to some of the nearby towns, but even then he had a far piece to walk. The joints were out in the fields. He figured he could eat twice what he did and still not grow fat because he walked so much. He hoped some day to have the opportunity to test that idea.

It was easier to wear his hat than to carry it, though its broad brim was a hindrance at night.

As he walked, Ernest Washington wrote a song in his head. Though he was tired, he still felt the power of the music, the songs the small crowd had enjoyed so much. Ernest Washington, who was called Partner in the joints, glanced up at the radiant moon. It made him think of the woman who'd danced right in front of him, a well-rounded woman with a beautiful bottom and a glow to her complexion, an undertone of orange as if she was a pumpkin pie right out of the oven, sweet and spicy. Her boyfriend was Isaiah Cleveland, though, and no matter how many looks her dark eyes had cast Partner's way, he'd taken care not to look back. Isaiah Cleveland lived down the road from Partner, and Partner knew for a fact that Isaiah had blacked a few eyes that rested on his woman for too long a stare. Partner had no desire to have his own face punched. However, the pumpkin pie woman was worthy of a song, and Partner had fixed a few lines in his head.

Partner was so absorbed in his composition that it took him a while to realize he wasn't alone on the road. Another man walked at the same pace. Even the glow of the moon didn't show Partner clearly what the man looked like. He seemed to be a hole in the night, absorbing all the light and giving back none. He was tall, taller than Partner, who was not a large man. The stranger wore a suit like Partner, and a white shirt like Partner, and, like Partner, a hat.

But the big man's steps were silent.

"Who are you?" Partner asked, though he was almost too frightened to speak.

"I'm the man gone save your life," said his new companion, in a deep voice as resonant as the bass fiddle Partner had once seen played by the backup band for a gospel singer.

"Save me from what?" Partner clutched his guitar case a little more firmly.

"Listen! The truck's coming," the man said. "You better hide. These men mean mischief."

As if he'd taken earmuffs off, Partner heard a truck turning down the road he'd taken. Two bright cones of the headlights cut across the fields. Any minute they'd spot him, and he could hear the yelling from the truck's passengers. The truck swerved and bounced across the ruts. By the way it veered, Partner could tell the driver was drunk. This was exactly the situation that got black men killed. Partner had feared it all his life.

Moving quick as a rabbit, Partner dashed into the cotton, down one of the rows. It had been hoed recently, making a clear aisle, but the stalks of the mature cotton grabbed at his clothes. Partner moved like the devil was after him. As far as he was concerned, that was the situation. The all-important guitar case banged his leg violently as he ran, and he feared the noise it made, though maybe over the truck engine and the hollering the men would not hear it.

Jesus, protect me from harm, he prayed. He felt the man who'd warned him had nothing to do with Jesus.

A tree stood where four fields converged, and Partner ran toward it with single-minded purpose. Just as the headlights swept the place where he'd left the road, he got to the tree, a big live oak, and hid behind it. His guitar case didn't match the profile of the tree, and he shoved it up into the lowest branches and prayed he hadn't damaged it. He'd saved and saved to buy it from Sears.

"Stop drivin'! I see me some tracks!" a white man yelled.

Partner's heart constricted. Partner recognized the voice. It belonged to Jimmy Bradley, the son of the cotton gin owner. Jimmy Bradley was a bad man, a drinker and abuser, and he'd raped Mary Emma Johnson, his mother's maid. The fact that Jimmy Bradley's father had beaten his son after he'd found out didn't help Mary Emma. She was so shamed she'd only told Partner's wife Bessie, her best friend, when Bessie had been offered the job Mary Emma had vacated.

The truck halted, and the sound of its idling motor made Partner feel faint. The blues man thought his own heart might stop, right along with the drone of the crickets and locusts.

"I ain't driving out in my daddy's cotton," said another voice, carrying clearly in the night. This voice didn't sound quite as drunk as Jimmy Bradley's, and Partner thought it might belong to Theron Dale, a planter's son. "We ain't hurting anyone tonight, Jimmy, and we ain't driving out into the fields. We're moving on. Let's go visit the cathouse behind Moses' jook."

And quick as that, Jimmy Bradley was diverted and Partner's life was safe … at least that was what he hoped. The truck lurched off, and when it was far away and he was sure it would not turn back, that this was not some sadistic trick, Partner sagged against the tree in profound relief. A tear trickled down each cheek.

"What you cryin' for, man?" the bass voice said.

Partner smiled, though he knew that it would be invisible to his companion. "I'm cryin' cause I'm alive," he said. The voice had come from above him, and he looked up to see the dark man sitting in the branches of the live oak. In fact, he perched right beside the guitar case and he gripped the handle.

"You pass me my guitar, please?" Partner said, unable to keep the alarm out of his voice.

"Maybe," said the dark man.

"I'm grateful you told me they was comin'," Partner said, very carefully. He was trying to think his way through the problem presented by the unexpected company he was keeping. "And I appreciate your helpin' me. But I would sure like to have my guitar back."

"I know you would," said the other, with imperturbable gravity. "You play in the jooks?"

"Yes sir, I sure do. I played at Moses Coldwater's place tonight."

"They pay you for that?"

Partner thought of the coins in his pocket. "A little," he said. "Just a little."

"Will you give it to me?"

Partner closed his eyes. He'd been planning on turning the money over to his wife, who was sick of his being gone all the time. The money, which they needed, would have helped reconcile Bessie to his frequent absences. "Yes, I will," he said, loathing himself for his quick capitulation. But this man had alerted him to danger, and Partner realized he owed a debt.

"What else do you have?" the deep voice asked from the branches.

"All I got is me, my wife Bessie, and my guitar," Partner said.

"Then we gots something to talk about," his companion rumbled, and with a leap descended from the tree. The big man landed lightly on his feet with Partner's guitar held by the handle on the case.

Partner made an involuntary gesture toward the guitar, but the man suddenly seemed larger than ever, as if he'd puffed up like a snake. Partner's hand fell back to his side.

"Let's keep walking," the man said, and they went back to the road.

The stranger seemed to glide between the rows of cotton until he reached the rutted track. Partner stumbled and sweated behind him. The sound of the motor had retreated to a safe distance, and Partner could just see the taillights across the fields.

The two turned again to the east, Partner plodding behind the man. He tried to think of a good side to this strange night. The playing had gone well, better than ever. He had a deep longing to try his luck in Chicago, but after tonight's scare, Partner didn't have the courage to imagine he'd ever make it that far. He should forget Chicago, and concentrate on being grateful that he hadn't gotten lynched or dragged behind the truck. Just being alive was a sweet relief. And since they were walking in the general direction of the house he shared with Bessie, he'd be home soon in her familiar presence. He respected her for the hard worker and fine cook she was. On this particular night, he longed for her more than he had in many previous months.

But before he could reach home, he had to pass through the crossroads.

Everyone knew what happened at crossroads—especially one like this, one with graves around it. Partner didn't know anyone who remembered who was buried here, or why the graveyard was located out in the middle of nothing, but there were twelve headstones marking the earth. Theron Dale's father had left the headstones standing and instructed one of his hands to clean away the weeds once or twice a year, which most men would not have done, in Partner's estimation.

Partner began to shake as he realized he was no longer alone with the big man. A ragged woman sat on one of the tombstones. She was a white woman, but like no white woman he'd ever seen. Her dark hair was loose and long and tangled, and her dress was ripped and torn. Though her flesh shone through, Partner was not the least bit interested in seeing her body. In fact, he averted his eyes. He knew what happened to black men who looked at white women, though he was sure this was not a regular white woman.

"May," the big black man said. He halted, so Partner did, too, though he couldn't suppress a shudder. "You out tonight?"

"Yes, Baron," she answered, in a voice that was somehow sharp and also cracked. "Me and Baby." Baby stepped out of the high weeds, and Partner gasped in fear. Baby was a huge wolf. Folks didn't see wolves much any more, though alligators might still be found in the bayous, and every now and then he'd heard a pain'ter scream in the night.

The strange white woman and the ominous black man—Baron, she'd called him—didn't look at Partner when he made a strangled sound of fear, but Partner figured they'd stop him right quick if he tried to run.

"This man plays the blues," Baron said.

"I heared him across the fields," May said. She had a heavy accent, and was for sure some kind of foreigner. Her skeletal hand caressed the head of the wolf, whose eyes glowed when they looked at Partner. Those eyes were orange, a warm color, and yet to Partner they seemed cold and calculating, as if the wolf was wondering how a black man would taste. "What are you going to do with him?" she asked.

"I'm going to change his life," Baron said. "I've started already."

"Those men were supposed to kill him," May said casually. "Why did you change everything?"

"His voice would be gone," Baron said. "My people don't have enough voices. I got to let him live."

"But you changed more than *his* fate," she said, and for the first time there was some fire in her voice. "Jimmy Bradley was bound to kill a man tonight. Theron won't be able to stop him. The drink changes Jimmy Bradley. He's one of mine."

Baron shrugged. "It don't have to be this man who dies, this man has a gift. Jimmy can kill someone else."

She looked to the east, where the truck had gone. "Yes, he can," she said, and her voice was distant, as if she wasn't seeing the night-dark fields, but something entirely different. "Partner Washington, do you want to keep your life?"

Partner's choices had always been simple, he realized, now that he was faced with a more complex problem. On the other hand, what could be simpler than choosing to die or choosing to live?

"Ma'am, you sayin' someone else gone be killed?" he asked. "That Jimmy Bradley, he gone kill someone tonight?" He couldn't believe he was daring to address her, but there was no other way to find out what she was offering.

"Yes, that's what I'm saying." Her accent was heavy, but he understood her clearly.

"Bessie?" he asked timidly.

After a moment, during which she again seemed to be looking through time instead of the night, the ragged white woman shook her head. "No," she said. "Not Bessie."

Reassured, Partner felt a surge of pride that his life was worth saving to this huge black man she called Baron—that his guitar playing and singing made him worthy of being saved, and he dreamed again of singing to men and women who knew something, men and women in big cities, not the rough farmhands and their ignorant women who'd listened to him tonight. That rush of pride made up Partner's mind for him. "I want my life saved," he said, his voice stronger.

The two people and the wolf looked at him steadily for what seemed to be a very long time.

"Well, then, it's a bargain," the ragged woman said, and across the moonlit fields came a terrible scream followed by the sound of laughter. She rose from the headstone and the wolf pressed his head against her legs, visible through the rips in her skirt. She came closer to Partner, her eyes black holes in the pallor of her face. "You may see the bad side of it before long, but again, you may not," she told Partner. She turned to the big man. "Baron, good night to you, and happy hunting."

The baron grinned at her. "And to you also, May," he said, and he bowed in a courtly way. "I'm much obliged."

"I know you are," she said over her shoulder, as she went into the fields, carrying her own darkness with her. The wolf at her side looked over his shoulder, too, his orange eyes taking in Partner for one last malignant moment.

Baron faced Partner and extended the guitar case. "You take this, man," he said. "You go home tonight, but tomorrow you leave for Chicago."

"How will I get there?" Partner took the guitar with a rush of relief to have it back in his hand. "I got no money."

Baron reached into his black coat and handed Partner more money than the blues man had made in six months. Some of this, of course, was Partner's own pay from the jook, and Partner spared a second to wonder how much of it was from some other poor man's pocket.

"Will I go with you?" Partner asked, putting the money away.

Baron made a sound that was almost a laugh. "I don't think you'd like the way I travel," he said. "You better catch you a train in Tunica."

"What do I do now?"

"Keep walkin' home." The Baron, as May had done, vanished into the tall cotton.

For a long time, Partner Washington stood at the crossroads, wondering if he'd lost his mind, wondering if he'd been dreaming, wondering if he'd been cursed by some witch woman. He knew down deep that the Baron and May were something other than human, though they'd been wearing human-looking bodies. When his knees stopped shaking, Partner began walking. He'd covered perhaps a mile when he found Isaiah Cleveland and his pumpkin pie woman lying by the side of the road covered in blood. Isaiah wouldn't be blacking any more eyes, and no one would look at his glowing woman with anything but revulsion and pity.

Partner understood what he'd done and regret lanced the bubble of pride that encased him.

But there was nothing he could do now, he told himself. They were already dead and there was no bringing them back to life. Partner was horrified, but he was even more relieved to be alive, and no amount of guilt could change that relief to self-loathing.

Partner didn't want anyone showing up at his door the next morning, either, so when he resumed his trek homeward he dragged the guitar case behind him to erase his tracks. When his muscles refused to do that any longer, he shuffled his feet. After half a mile, he left the road and picked his way through the fields very carefully, determined not to leave a clear path to his door.

Bessie deserved better than that.

His wife woke up when he came in the door.

"You do good tonight?" she mumbled.

"Yeah, they loved it," he said, his voice as hushed as hers. "I made some money. I got to go work in the mornin', I'll leave it on the table."

"Oh, good," she said, already drifting off into sleep.

Since he knew he would be leaving her in the morning, he could only be thankful they didn't have children. Partner was afraid that he would have abandoned children even as he was planning to abandon Bessie. She was a good woman who deserved better treatment, and he knew it; but he'd been offered a temptation he couldn't resist.

He slept a little in the bed beside her, rolling down easily into the dip in the middle he'd shared with her for five years. But mostly Partner fluttered in and out of consciousness as he thought about what he had to do the next day, and the craving to be heard throbbed in his blood, warring with his guilt over his wife. Once, when he woke, he heard the rain falling, and he knew his tracks were washed away. He slept a little better after that.

The sun rose on a clear, hot day. Partner washed his face, put back on his only suit, and left some money on the bare plank table while Bessie still slept. He passed out his front door for the last time and walked to Tunica, the Sears guitar once again banging against his leg. He turned his face away from the south, where the bodies of Isaiah and his woman were surely still laying by the side of the road, and where the live oak surely still stood in the middle of the fields. He wondered, with a shudder, where the Baron and May and the wolf were. He figured no one could see them in daylight, and he wondered how they'd come to be the way they were, and how they'd appeared to him.

But in his excitement, he didn't wonder too long.

He had enough money for the train trip to Chicago, and enough to support himself for a month after he got there. He spent that time walking around the city, at first aghast and amazed. But then the fever gripped him again, and he found the blues clubs. He showed up at one or the other with his guitar every night, until his face became known. He stuck around after hours to play with the musicians who didn't want to go home. When they'd seen his worth, he got a chance to play on a stage.

After three years, Partner Washington became one of the greatest blues men in Chicago. He played every night, and women showed up at his door with smiles on their faces, ready to party. None of them were as good as Bessie, but he tried not to think about her, and after a while he succeeded very well. He still had nightmares about Isaiah and the pumpkin pie woman, but after a year or two, the awful memories faded.

From time to time, in some dive where the cigarette smoke hung thick in the air and the people were packed in like cotton in the boll, Partner would glimpse a pair of eyes in the crowd. He never stopped playing when he saw those gleaming eyes—nothing would make him do that—but he forced himself to look down at the floor so his gaze wouldn't mesh with those eyes, either. He was afraid if he met that gaze full-on, something awful would happen to him…and he'd have a flash of two bodies, torn and bloody by the side of the road. He met some other black people who practiced a curious religion he'd never heard of and began to understand a little more about the Baron.

After a few years of playing around Chicago. Partner began travelling. He went to the big cities, and to the smaller cities, wherever there was a jook joint that would pay him. The pay got as good as it would get for a black blues man; enough to keep

Partner in clothes and smokes and women, and the occasional evening of good eating and bad drinking … though Partner was never a big drinker, after he realized he saw those shining eyes more often if he was hitting the bottle.

Once, in Cincinnati, he glimpsed the Baron on the other side of the street. The tall dark man, his top hat set at a rakish angle, was talking to a skinny boy no more than eighteen. The boy carried a clarinet case, and he looked hungry … as hungry as Partner had once been.

But the Baron didn't look Partner's way, and Partner sure didn't call out to him.

A week after that, while Partner was standing on the sidewalk in front of his hotel in New York City talking to a drummer everyone called the Greek, he caught a flutter of white out of the corner of his eye. Partner swiveled to get a better look, while the Greek made a curious sign with his hand. If he'd really glimpsed May, she'd whisked around the corner. He was relieved she hadn't spoken to him. He didn't know if she was a madwoman or a goddess, and he didn't want to get close enough to find out.

"What's that you did with your hand?" he asked the Greek.

"Sign against evil," the olive-skinned drummer said. "My mama taught me."

Partner almost asked the Greek what he had seen, but then, as if they'd agreed out loud, he and the drummer turned and went into the hotel.

The next night as Partner poured out his soul on the tiny stage of a dive in Harlem, he thought he saw May's wolf tracking close to the walls. Partner shut his eyes and played on.

He couldn't stop himself from realizing that they were getting bolder.

From that time on, he saw the frightening figures frequently.

He began to play and sing with his eyes shut. Instead of "Partner," he was called "Shutter." About a year after he became known as Shutter Washington, he had an unexpected conversation with two white men.

Most often, conversations with white men led to no good consequences. Now in his late thirties, Partner was adept in keeping to his world, and his world was black. Some white people, like the Greek, loved the blues; but Partner seldom spoke to those fans impressed enough to try to get to know him. As "Shutter," he didn't even have to see them.

These two white men wouldn't go away without being seen, though. They stayed in the club after it emptied, and when Shutter was packing away his guitar (one much finer than the Sears instrument), he felt them approach like wild dogs sniffing around something tasty and easy to kill.

They introduced themselves as Jim and Nathan Lowe and said they owned a record company. Shutter nodded heavily. He'd heard of them. They'd recorded Screamin' Odessa and James Gray, two other long-time blues performers and acquaintances of Shutter's.

"I know who you are," Shutter said. "You gentlemen want a drink?" He figured he might as well settle in, because this was a conversation that was going to take place sooner rather than later. This was the talk he'd been waiting for. Something in him jumped and wriggled with delight, but something else warned that he'd be damned if he'd show these men any hint of pleasure or excitement.

Both the Lowes agreed to a drink, and when they were sipping the whiskey he brought from the bar, Shutter said, "You want to talk to me, talk."

"We want to record you," Nathan said. "We think you're a big influence on the blues, and we think you deserve to be recognized."

Shutter felt the corners of his mouth turn down, as if he was considering what they were saying. "What you offering?" he asked, and after an hour of discussion the deal was hammered out.

No one he'd met in his travels knew who Shutter really was. They'd never known him as Ernest, or even Partner. They'd never known he worked in the fields once upon a time. After the white men left, there was no one Shutter could think of who would really appreciate the enormity of what he'd just been offered.

Of course, no one knew that he'd sacrificed the lives of two other people to get this chance, either.

Shutter made his record. He got to see the appreciation, the excitement, on the faces of the other musicians, on the faces of the men who worked in the recording studio. He got to work on his songs and make them sound good, and those songs would ensure he was remembered forever. He knew it, just as surely as he knew his run of luck would wind down soon.

Three weeks after his recording sessions, Shutter was walking home from a jook at three in the morning. He had his guitar with him, as he always did, and he almost dropped it when a tall man stepped out of an alley as Shutter passed.

Shutter jumped with fright, but then his startled eyes told him that despite the top hat, this was not the same man he'd talked to in the fields. This man had a broader face, was altogether bigger.

"What you want?" he asked. Tension made his voice hard and even.

"You know what I want," the big man said. "It's time to pay the bill for my services."

"You didn't talk about a bill when I last saw you, but you're not the same man either," Shutter said. He put the guitar down carefully in case he had to fight. He tried to pull his knife out of his pocket without the big man noticing.

"No point in that, no point whatsoever," the man with the top hat said, and then he smiled, flashing a row of white and even teeth. "Or I should say, your knife got a point, but not you. You think you can hurt me?"

"No," Shutter said. His hand fell away from his pocket, and he accepted his defeat before the fight had even begun. "What do I have to do, Baron?"

"I got to pass this hat along," the man said. "You get to be me, you lucky son of a bitch."

"And what will happen to you?" Shutter asked, trying to understand.

"I get to leave for good," the Baron said. "We lesser ones, we get tired. Not enough people love us, fear us, feed us. We got to recruit."

"What about the raggedy woman, May?" Shutter asked.

"What about me?" a female voice asked. She stepped out of the shadows at the end of the alley. The clothes were the same, or almost—torn and bloody, ripped and shredded—but the body wearing them was rounder and browner than the last May. Her streaming hair was golden chestnut in the light from the street lamp, and her fingers were curled into the fur of a…God almighty, a bear.

"Why have you changed?" Shutter asked.

"We the lesser ones," the Baron said. "We've only got enough spirit left to pass from one body to the other."

Shutter said, "All right, then. Let's get on with it." He moved his guitar case to the mouth of the alley.

The Baron reached out his hand, and extracted Shutter's heart. Shutter's face went slack, and he fell to the pavement. The Baron crouched over Shutter's open mouth, and a white wisp passed from the Baron's lips into the dying man's mouth. Then somehow, they changed places. The tall, round-faced body lay on the pavement, empty and spent.

May watched, smiling a little, as the new Baron stood. Of course, now he was a bit shorter, his face narrower, and his body thinner. But the suit still fit and the top hat looked just as jaunty. The new Baron said, "Well, Miss May, I got to find a man and give him a warning." And May replied, "There's a singer on down the street waiting for me to give her that one big chance."

The two nodded to each other and went on their ways.

After a time, the big body was picked up by a group of drunks and deposited on the corner, to be removed the next day. Police didn't come to this area.

Shutter Washington's guitar was found the next morning by a little boy who'd gotten up early to shine the shoes of men on their way to work. He hid the guitar so no one else would get it, and he ran on to his station, but he thought about his discovery all day. When he returned home, he pulled the guitar case from the back of the closet under the tenement stairs, and he carried it up to the roof. Once he was sure he was alone, he opened the case and gasped at the beauty of the instrument inside. With hands that shook from excitement, he pulled the guitar out and held it as he'd seen others do. It dwarfed him, but it didn't scare him, and by and by, he strummed a chord.

And then another.

He glanced up, because he thought he saw a flash of movement out of the corner of his eye, a flash of white. But then he bent his head again to the instrument.

IT WAS NEARLY DAWN before the underfed cop finally escorted me to the station's interview room, where the lieutenant in
charge was trying to sort out what had happened. I didn't hold
the long wait against him. I've been an insurance investigator for
five years, and the first thing I learned on the job was that everybody lies. As many people as the cops had had to question before
me, they must have already been up to their eyeballs in evasion,
confusion, and pure out invention. Besides, it had given me more
time to figure out what I wanted to tell him.

"Ms. Grace Monroe?" the lieutenant asked, checking a
notepad covered with some personal form of hieroglyphics.

I nodded.

"I'm Lieutenant Johnson. I'd like to ask you some questions.
Have you been advised of your rights?"

"Yes, sir."

"Good." He turned a page on his pad and wrote my name.
"What can you tell me about the shooting?"

"It was after Buddy finished his set. I went backstage to see
him, and then we both came out and sat at Akers' table."

"Mr. Kendricks was there as well?"

"That's right."

"And you knew all three men?"

"I'd seen Akers and Kendricks twice before, and had spoken to Akers, but tonight was the first time I spoke to Kendricks. I suppose you'd call them acquaintances."

"And Mr. Bartholomew?"

"Oh, I've known Buddy Bartholomew for over ten years. He was married to my sister, Brandy."

Since he didn't add anything to his notes, I figured he already knew that. "Then what happened?" he asked me.

"Akers offered Buddy a drink and sent Kendricks up to the bar to get it."

Johnson still wasn't writing, so I knew I still hadn't told him anything he hadn't already found out.

I went on. "Akers told Buddy what a good job he'd done, that it was the best he'd ever heard him play. Buddy said it was because of Akers, and then he came out with the gun."

"You hadn't seen the gun before then?"

"No, sir. Buddy had a towel in his hand, the one he'd used during the show to wipe his face down. The gun was under the towel."

"Then what?"

"Buddy aimed the gun at Akers, and some woman must have seen it, because there was a scream. Akers just went still, and I grabbed Buddy's hand and tried to point it away. Then the gun went off."

"Just once?"

"No, sir. It went off twice."

Still no notes.

"Do you have any idea why your brother-in-law would want to shoot Akers?"

"Yes, sir, I do."

"Beg pardon?"

"I know exactly why Buddy wanted to hurt Phillip Akers."

TWO WEEKS EARLIER

The blues club was smoke-fogged and not nearly well enough air-conditioned for early May in the Delta. Though nobody was on the platform that passed for a stage, the place was already crowded, over half of the people gobbling down sausage sandwiches that were dripping with grease.

There was a battered wooden door to the right of the stage, and I knocked on it under the hand-printed sign that said PRIVATE. A minute later, a harassed-looking older woman stuck her head out. "The bathroom is around back," she said, already closing the door.

"I need to see Buddy." She looked me up and down, making me wonder if he was getting popular enough to attract blues groupies. "Could you tell him his sister-in-law Grace is here?" That must have convinced her that I wasn't there for a pre-show blow job, because she stepped back to let me in.

"Down that way," she said, nodding toward the last of three doors off of the narrow hall. I passed the busy, clattering kitchen and a paper-strewn office before getting to the combination storage and dressing room.

Buddy Bartholomew, a wiry man with sandy hair that needed a trim, was concentrating so hard on tuning his guitar that he didn't notice me until I cleared my throat a second time. Then he jerked up, blinking, as if he'd been far away. "Is it time already?" He blinked again. "Grace?"

"Hi, Buddy."

He put the guitar down long enough to give me a hug. "This is a surprise!"

"I don't see why. I've been leaving messages for the last two weeks. Did your phone get cut off again?" It wouldn't have been the first time—though it looked as if Buddy had drawn a good crowd this time, there'd been plenty of nights where his take had barely covered gas money.

"No, I've been meaning to call you back. Just got busy."

"Busy?" I gave him a look. My messages had stressed that it was urgent. "What about Brandy? Is she so damned busy she can't pick up a phone?"

"I guess. I mean … I don't know."

"Where is she anyway? She wasn't at your apartment, which is why I tracked you down here." I didn't have to tell him how much of a pain that had been, first to figure out which hole-in-the-wall joint he was playing at, and then to find the place. "Is she here?"

"No." He swallowed visibly. "The fact is, I don't know where she is, Grace. Brandy left me."

Now it was my turn to blink. "Are you shitting me?"

"I wish to God I was. I came back from an overnight gig and found a note on the kitchen counter. I haven't seen or heard from her since."

"When did she go?"

"About a month ago."

"Jesus! When were you planning to tell Mama and me?"

He shrugged. "I figured she'd tell you herself. Haven't y'all heard from her?"

"Would I be here if we'd heard from her?" I rubbed my eyes, which were red and sore from lack of sleep. "I can't believe you didn't call."

"I thought she'd come back! I've been praying for her to come back. I can't imagine why she'd up and leave like that."

I sighed. I knew damned well why Brandy left. She thought she'd married a big-time musician, not realizing how hard it was for a man to make a living playing the blues, one of the few occupations on earth where being white was a liability. Instead of him supporting her, she'd had to support him, and she hadn't been happy about it.

"Didn't she leave a forwarding address, or phone number? Anything?"

He shook his head.

"Have you even tried to find her?" I asked.

"Her note said not to."

So naturally, he hadn't bothered. "Look, Buddy, I've got to find Brandy."

"She'll come back, I know she will."

"I can't wait. Didn't you listen to my messages?"

"What's wrong?"

"It's Mama. She's …" I swallowed. "She hasn't got much time left."

That led to the usual questions, which meant I had to repeat all the hateful phrases: lung cancer, fourth stage, hadn't responded to chemo. Then of course Buddy had to tell me how he'd heard about somebody in way worse health than Mama who'd beaten the Big C and lived for another ten years. I know he meant well—Buddy always meant well—but I didn't have time for good intentions. So when he said, "If there's anything I can do, just name it," I quickly said, "You can help me find Brandy."

"But I don't know where to look."

"Didn't you call her friends? What about her job?"

"I think she quit her job."

"Don't you know for sure?"

"Grace, I work nights and sleep days. How am I supposed to call people?" A light seemed to go off in his head. "Wait, you're a detective. I bet you could find her a lot faster than I could."

"I'm an insurance investigator, Buddy. Unless you think Brandy is pretending to have back problems or faking a hearing loss, I've got nothing."

"It's all the same thing, isn't it? Investigating is investigating."

I sighed and rubbed my eyes again. Technically, I'm a private investigator—I've got the license—but all I'd ever done was claims work, not missing person searches. But I was on leave to tend to Mama, and I couldn't very well bully Buddy into finding his wife if he didn't want to. "Fine, I'll see what I can do, but I need names and phone numbers for her friends, and her job, and anything else you can think of. And I want to go through your apartment to see if she left anything."

"You got it. You want to call tomorrow? After lunch, because I sleep late."

"Buddy, Mama's in a bad way. I need you to tell me what you know right now."

"But I go on in a few minutes."

"Then we don't have time to mess around." I dug into my pocketbook and found a notepad, then pulled over a stack of beer crates to lean on. "Let's get going."

A quarter of an hour later, I had all the names I could wring out of him. The visit to his and Brandy's apartment could wait, since he didn't have a spare set of keys to give me, but at least I had a place to start the next day without having to wait for him to wake up.

"What about Brandy's note?" I asked. "What exactly did she say?"

"You can read it for yourself." He pulled out his wallet and unfolded a piece of cheap stationery before handing it to me. I couldn't imagine why he'd carried it around with him as if it were a love note instead of a Dear John letter—maybe it was like a sore tooth that you just couldn't help running your tongue over, even when it hurt.

The note was classic Brandy—short, self-centered, and thoughtlessly cruel.

Buddy,

I'm sorry, but I've had it. This isn't what I signed up for, and it's time for me to go. I wish you luck, but I want more out of life than working all day and hanging around in some lousy bar every night. Don't come looking for me--I'll be fine.

Brandy

I handed it back to him, and he carefully refolded it and put it back in his wallet. Then the woman who'd let me in the back stuck her head in to say, "Two minutes, Buddy."

"Thanks, Lorna." He absently reached for his guitar.

"Your boyfriend is here tonight," she said with a snicker and disappeared again.

I raised one eyebrow, and Buddy looked embarrassed. "It's not like that. There's this guy who comes to a lot of my shows. Always sits in front, always buys me a beer afterward. Big blues fan—you wouldn't believe how much he knows about the music. He's given me a lot of good advice, too. He says he'll help me get a recording contract when I get good enough."

"Is that right?" I said, remembering the other times Buddy had claimed this man or that was going to propel him to the big time. At least this one paid for the beer. We started walking toward the door. "I'll call you tomorrow."

"You're not sticking around for the show?"

"I've got other things on my mind right now."

"The music might make you feel better. You know what they say. The blues ain't nothing but a good man or a good woman feeling bad."

"Not tonight, Buddy."

"Another time, then. You give my best to your mama."

I said I would, and as he stepped toward the stage, I slipped through the crowd, which had grown even larger while I was backstage. The last time I'd come to one of Buddy's shows, back when he and Brandy had first married, he hadn't drawn even a quarter of that many people. Maybe he really was improving.

I thought I spotted his big fan sitting at a table right in front of the stage. He was chunky, with suspiciously dark hair for a man his age and a sweating mug of beer in front of him. There was a tall, lean man with him who looked as bored as the first man looked expectant.

Buddy wasted no time chatting up the audience, just tore into "It Serves Me Right to Suffer," as I left. As much as I agreed with his choice of song, I was in no mood to listen to him. I may have grown up in the Delta, but that didn't mean I wanted to hear a man whining about how he'd lost his job, his dog, and his woman, in that order. I'd become a blues fan just as soon as they wrote me a song about having to track down my idiot sister so my dying mother could say goodbye.

The next morning, I drove to Memphis, more than a little ashamed at how relieved I was to get out of the house. Mama and I lived in Senatobia, a town small enough that people know when there's illness in the family, and some of the ladies from our church were taking turns staying with her. That meant I didn't have to be there every minute, but I felt like I should be unless I had a good excuse. The look in Mama's eyes when I told her I was going out to look for Brandy was as good an excuse as I was going to get.

My first stop was the moving company where Brandy worked. I'd decided not to mention Brandy was my sister, at least not right away. I had my PI card and my business cards from the agency, and I thought people might be more willing to talk to somebody official, or at least semi-official. If that didn't work, I'd tell the truth. Hell, I'd cry if I thought it would help.

As it was, the boss was perfectly willing to tell me that Brandy had quit about the same time she left Buddy. She'd taken her final paycheck right then and hadn't left a forwarding address, so he had nothing for me but complaints about her leaving with no notice. It could have been a total waste of time, but one thing I've learned as an investigator is that every office has a gossip queen, somebody who knows everything about everybody, and who likes to tell what she knows.

I had a hunch that the moving company's reigning queen was an older lady in elastic-waist pants and a flowered top who answered the phones. The whole time I was talking to her boss, she had her mouth squeezed shut, as if she was trying to hold in what she was thinking. It was nearly noon, so before I left, I made a point of asking her if there was some place nearby where I could get a bite to eat. She directed me to a lunch counter just across the street, and I went in, ordered, and watched for her.

Sure enough, I hadn't even started on my club sandwich when she came in, and I asked her to join me. Her name was Ethel, and she couldn't wait to start dishing the dirt on my sister.

"That girl never really cared about the job," she said between bites of her chef salad. "She was always watching the clock, coming in a little late, leaving a little early. And expecting somebody else to make up for it." From the indignant look on her face, I suspected "somebody else" was usually Ethel.

"Did she talk about her personal life?"

"Lord, did she! How her husband was such a good musician and she was only working until he got discovered and signed a fat recording contract." Ethel rolled her eyes. "The bloom came off that rose mighty quick. I don't know if he's any good or not, but I do know how hard it is to make a living playing the kind of places she was talking about. I told her he ought to go on *American Idol*—that's the way to start a music career. But all he wanted to play was the blues, and that won't get you the votes on *American Idol*."

"Do you think that affected their marriage?"

"How could it not? She thought he was going to make her rich, but they were barely scraping by."

"With her working a job she didn't like." For a moment, I almost felt sorry for my sister.

"I suppose I shouldn't have been surprised about what she did next, but I wasn't raised to expect that kind of behavior from a married woman."

It sounded as if Ethel was implying more than just a faltering marriage. "Do you think she was seeing somebody else?"

"I don't know for sure, but I do know she suddenly quit complaining about her husband and started looking a whole lot happier. She showed up to work in new clothes—expensive outfits, too—and when I asked where she got the money, she laughed and said she'd gotten lucky at one of the casinos in Tunica." Ethel raised her eyebrows significantly. "It seems to me that 'getting lucky' doesn't always mean a slot machine jackpot."

I wished I'd been shocked. "Do you think Brandy left her husband for this other man?"

"I wouldn't be surprised."

"Did she ever mention his name? Or drop a hint about where she'd be living?"

"No," Ethel said with obvious regret. "I was out sick the day she quit, so I didn't even get to tell her goodbye."

I was fairly sure Ethel was sorrier about missing a chance to ask questions than she was about an opportunity for a fond farewell. "Do you know which casino she went to?" If Brandy really had won big money, there'd be records.

"She didn't say."

I asked a few more questions, but Ethel didn't have anything else I could use, so I thanked her for her time and gave her my cell phone number, in case she remembered anything else. I paid for her lunch while I was at it—she seemed to expect it, and I figured that was what a real detective would do.

Brandy and Buddy had an apartment on the edge of Memphis, close to the highway so Buddy could get to the blues clubs that were sprinkled all over the Delta. He'd said he'd be awake by one, but there was no answer when I knocked at his door. I decided I'd cross off some of the names he'd given me, people in the apartment building Brandy had been friends with.

Unfortunately, Brandy hadn't been close to either the stay-at-home mother of twin toddlers or the part-time church secretary, and neither had any idea where she'd gone.

At least the twins' mother had seen Brandy loading up her car and had spoken to her before she drove off, reassuring me that my sister had left on her own steam. I'd never known Buddy to be violent, so I hadn't really thought he'd had anything to do with her disappearance, but even insurance investigators know that the obvious suspect is always the husband.

"Was Brandy by herself?" I asked.

"No, she had somebody helping her."

"Was it a man or a woman?"

"Um, a man."

"Did you know him?"

"No, and Brandy didn't introduce us. He kept carrying things out to the car while I was talking to her."

"What did he look like?"

"Tall, nice-looking, dark hair." She grinned. "He had a great butt—I saw him bending over to fit stuff in the trunk."

He sounded just like the type of man Brandy liked, assuming that he had money to spend on her. "Did you get the sense that the two of them were more than friends?"

She looked uncomfortable with the thought, but nodded. "Nothing blatant, but yeah, that's what it looked like. She was smiling at him a lot, that way. You know what I mean?"

It had been a long time since I'd smiled at anybody that way myself, but I did know what she meant. "But she didn't mention his name?"

"Not to me, but when he said they needed to get going, she said, 'Okay, Duke.'" One twin tugged at her leg, and the woman excused herself.

I went back to Buddy's door and knocked harder. After a while, he opened the door, his eyes so bleary from lack of sleep that he looked like a mole. As he stumbled back into the dim apartment, I couldn't help noticing that he didn't have much of a butt at all.

"How's your mama?" he asked.

"About the same," I said, not wanting to get into the details of the numerous times she'd woken up during the night, moaning with pain. Her doctor wasn't willing to give her decent meds—he kept saying he didn't want her addicted, as if it mattered that a dying woman was a morphine addict. What was she going to do? Start knocking off convenience stores to supply her habit when she couldn't even make it to the bathroom by herself?

"What about Brandy? Did you find her?"

"Not yet. She did quit her job—you were right about that—but she didn't tell anybody where she was going." I hesitated, then decided I wasn't ready to accuse my sister of adultery until I was sure. "Are you okay with my looking around?"

"Sure. I've got to hit the shower."

He stumbled off, and I started snooping. I wished I could say I felt bad about looking through their drawers, but if I hadn't been nosy, I'd never have become an investigator in the first place. The problem was there wasn't a whole lot to find, just clutter and junk, and nothing of Brandy's—no letters or pictures, none of her bills, and the only item of her clothing was a pair of panties so worn out that they weren't fit to wear. I threw those out.

After a while, Buddy scooted past with wet hair and a towel wrapped round his waist and shut himself up in the bedroom, so I took a look in the bathroom. More nothing, unless you wanted to count the mildew. As I was going out, I saw something hanging on the back of the door. It was a cheap, dark blue nylon fanny pack with a big-busted queen of hearts grinning on it—I recognized it from the Lucky Lady casino in Tunica. I unzipped it and found half a pack of cigarettes and a partially used book of matches, also from the Lucky Lady.

I carried it with me to the kitchen, where a now-dressed Buddy was watching a coffee cup spin around in the microwave. "Is this yours?" I asked him.

He shook his head. "I guess Brandy left it."

"Was she doing a lot of gambling?"

"You know we don't have the money for her to do much. Didn't, I mean. Maybe that's why she left. Do you think that's why, Grace?"

Of course that was why, that and realizing she hadn't married the man she'd fooled herself into thinking Buddy was. But I couldn't tell him that—he wasn't a bad man, really. "I don't know, Buddy. People change. They decide they want different things. It happens all the time."

"I guess."

The microwave went off, and he reached inside to get his coffee. "You want something to drink?"

"No, thanks," I said. "I've got to get going."

"About your mama ... You told her about Brandy leaving?"

"Last night." I'd hated it, too, and afterward Mama had gone back and forth between worry for her perennially prodigal daughter and anger at her for not keeping in touch. She'd been so agitated that it had been no surprise that she'd had such a rough night.

Buddy said, "I was thinking I'd go visit her after I get something to eat, maybe take her some flowers. Do you think she'd like that, with me and Brandy having problems?"

"I'm sure she would, Buddy."

"Maybe I'll take my guitar and play her some music."

"That'd be real nice. Just don't sing the blues—I think she's got enough troubles of her own."

He nodded, and I let myself out.

The next step was to talk to some of Brandy's girlfriends, and for that I went to the drive-through at McDonald's to get a Diet Coke, then pulled into the back corner of the parking lot to make phone calls. Buddy had told me the night before that he'd spoken to a couple of them himself, and that they'd said they didn't know where Brandy was, but it couldn't hurt to talk to them again. They might have lied to him out of loyalty to Brandy, but with Mama's illness as a spur, I thought they'd tell me the truth. Unfortunately, the truth was that nobody had seen or talked to Brandy since she left Buddy, and nobody knew where she was.

Her two best friends were happily married with kids, and had tired of Brandy's complaints a while back. Her single friends had gotten sick of footing the bill for her to party with them, and since she didn't have the money to pay her own way, they'd drifted apart, too. There were some wives and girlfriends of other bluesmen that Brandy had met when accompanying Buddy to his shows, but none of them were close enough for her to confide in them. At least one actively disliked her.

The last one was the only one who'd say flat out that she thought Brandy was fooling around on Buddy—my sister had been dropping hints for a couple of months before she took off. Some of the others dodged the issue, or admitted it was possible when I asked them, but nobody knew who Brandy had been seeing.

Two hours later, I had nothing but an empty McDonald's cup and a sore ear. I thought back over what I'd heard, and all I had left was the Lucky Lady casino. It wasn't much of a lead, but I had a friend who worked there. I might have gotten what I needed over the phone, but I do better in person. That's what I told myself, anyway. Had I been more honest, I'd have admitted that I just didn't want to go home—early evening seemed to be Mama's worst time, when she was restless and out of sorts. Maybe it was because she was tired or because that's when her meds wore off, but I think it was because she wanted to be busy fixing a big dinner and she just wasn't able. Any more than I was able to watch her like that. So I kept lying to myself for the hour or so it took me to drive to Tunica.

The Lucky Lady isn't the biggest of the casinos that have taken over Tunica, but the parking lot is probably still bigger than some of the towns where Buddy went to perform. I let a valet handle the parking. He was good enough that he almost concealed his disdain when he had to climb into my ten-year-old Honda, so I gave him a tip that was almost generous.

The casino was filled with day-trippers and junket gamblers who fly in from all over the southeast to take advantage of mid-week price breaks. I was years younger than most of them, but it was my lack of a fanny pack that really made me stand out. I hadn't realized they were part of the gambler's lifestyle, but it made sense. It was a lot more relaxing to blow a day feeding quarters into a slot machine when you didn't have to worry about keeping up with a pocketbook.

The Mississippi Delta has a love-hate relationship with the casinos. We love the money they bring in, the jobs they provide, and even the cheap buffets; but hate the crazy traffic, drain on our infrastructure, and undesirable elements that seem to come along with gambling. The money wins, of course.

Quite a few of the people I'd grown up with had gone to work for the casinos, including my friend Leland. Though he did taxes on the side, including for Mama and me, his real job was in the accounting office of the Lucky Lady. I found a teller that didn't have a line and asked if she'd let Leland know I was there. A few minutes later, he popped out to give me a hug.

"Please tell me you're here for the buffet and not to gamble," he said. "If I could show you the money people throw away every day, you'd never so much as put a quarter in a slot machine again. But the buffet is damned good."

"I'm not here for either. I'm looking for somebody."

"A case to do with the Lucky Lady?" he asked guardedly. He might not approve of gambling, but he did approve of keeping his job.

"I don't think so. Not directly, anyway. Have you got a minute?"

He looked at his watch. "Not right now, but I'll be off the clock in half an hour. Why don't you go get a beer, and then let me introduce you to the buffet? My treat!"

"Something to eat might not be bad," I admitted.

He sent me to the quieter of the casino's two bars, the one that played music videos instead of sports. I found a table and ordered a beer. I was halfway through it when I saw a familiar-looking man sitting by himself, watching Beyonce dancing on a TV screen. After a minute, I remembered where I'd seen him. It was Buddy's fan from the blues club.

I idly wondered if the man knew my sister. Come to think of it, if he was a regular at Buddy's shows, he almost certainly had met her and might have noticed if she'd been flirting with any-body in particular. It stood to reason that Brandy had met her new flame at one of the clubs—if she'd met him at her old job, Ethel would have known about it. I picked up what was left of my beer and went over to the man's table.

"Not exactly the blues, is it?" I said to him.

"I beg your pardon?" he said.

"I saw you at Buddy Bartholomew's show last night, and he told me that you really know the blues."

"Ah, another blues fan!" he said happily, and pulled out a chair. "Please, won't you join me?"

"Thank you," I said, sitting down. "I'm Grace Monroe."

"Phillip Akers. I don't believe I've seen you at any of Buddy's shows before."

"Do you go to a lot of blues shows?"

"As many as I can," he said. "I went to my first while I was living in Chicago and was immediately captivated. The blues speak to me in a way no other music ever has. Such power, such raw emotion." He actually sighed. "I cannot tell you how many hours I've spent listening to musicians like Junior Wells and John Lee Hooker. I'm afraid I'm a living reminder that 'fan' is short for 'fanatic.'"

"There are worse things to be addicted to."

"I was so pleased to have an opportunity to move to the Delta and hear even more musicians. Particularly Buddy. I first saw him at an open mike night, and even then his talent was prodigious. I sensed that he had the potential to be great, and I'm pleased to see how far he's come. I don't feel he's reached his peak yet, but I believe he shall."

"He did sound pretty good last night," I said, even though I hadn't heard more than a few bars. "But to tell you the truth, I'm not a huge blues fan. Buddy is my brother-in-law."

"I didn't realize he had a brother."

"He doesn't. I'm his wife's sister."

"Really? Brandy's sister?" He looked at me more closely, and I thought I knew what he was thinking. Brandy was pretty and petite, almost dainty. I am not.

"Do you know Brandy?" I asked.

"We've spoken a few times. I haven't seen her recently."

"She and Buddy have split up."

"What a shame."

"In fact, that's why I wanted to talk to you."

He lifted one eyebrow.

"I'm trying to track Brandy down. Our mother is very ill."

"I'm sorry to hear that."

"Thank you. The thing is, Brandy hasn't always gotten along with my mother and me, and we haven't been in touch. We don't even know where she's living. I need to find her before—" My voice caught.

"I wish I could help you, but the last time I saw Brandy was at a show at least a month ago. I've never seen her outside the clubs."

I was a touch embarrassed to bring up the next question, but it was for Mama. "I've been told that Brandy was seeing another man. I don't suppose you ever noticed her with anyone, did you?"

He shook his head. "Surely she wouldn't have taken up with another man right in front of her husband."

Obviously he didn't know Brandy all that well. Just then I saw Leland standing by the entrance, looking in my direction. "It looks like my dinner date is here, so I should go. Thank you for your time."

"I wish I'd been able to assist you more."

I left him at his table, and as soon as I got to Leland, he pulled me aside. "Since when do you know Phil Akers?"

"I just met him. Why?"

"Don't you know who he is?"

"Should I?"

He lowered his voice. "Word is, he's the real owner of this place. He had to put together a corporation to sign the paperwork because he's not exactly the kind of man the powers that be want running a casino."

"Why not?"

He lowered his voice even further. "I hear he's connected."

"Connected? As in …"

"As in *connected*."

"In Tunica?"

"Where there's gambling, there's money, and where there's money, there are people with connections."

"I guess you're right. I just never pictured Tony Soprano in Mississippi."

A few minutes later, Leland and I were sitting in a corner of the Country Time Buffet, the most casual of the casino's five restaurants. We both had plates of fried chicken, biscuits, green beans, and corn on the cob, with iced tea and blueberry cobbler on the side, though Buddy had filled his plate considerably higher than I had mine.

"Where do you put all that food?" I asked him. He was as skinny as a rail and had been ever since I'd known him.

"I work it off! You think it's easy lugging buckets of quarters around?"

While we ate, we gossiped about mutual friends and our families, and Leland expressed sympathy for my mother's condition. He knew all about it, of course—his mother went to our church. It wasn't until we'd finished the last bites of cobbler that Leland said, "What can I do you for?"

"I'm trying to find Brandy," I said. "She left Buddy about a month ago, and nobody's heard from her since."

"You think something's happened to her?"

"There's no telling. You know Brandy."

He nodded. Everybody in our circle knew Brandy.

"I hear she started doing some shopping she shouldn't have been able to afford, and she told a woman at her job that she'd gotten lucky at a casino. Since she had a Lucky Lady fanny pack, I thought she might have done her winning here. Don't you keep records of big winners?"

"Absolutely—when the pot is fat enough, the IRS comes running for their cut right away. The thing is, I'm usually the one that helps winners with their paperwork, and I'd have remembered if Brandy had shown up."

"Couldn't it have happened when you weren't on duty?"

"Maybe, but they always make a big deal and take pictures when a good-looking woman is involved, and I haven't seen any pictures of Brandy on the bulletin board."

"Damn." Either she'd lied about the win, or it hadn't been as big as she'd pretended. Or maybe she'd been at an entirely different casino. At least I'd gotten a good dinner out of it.

Except Leland was saying, "What does that fanny pack look like? Is it like that one?" He pointed to a woman rolling past in an electric wheelchair wearing a black nylon fanny pack with the casino's trademark on it.

"Brandy's is blue."

"Close enough. They come in all colors. We give them to people when they join the Player's Club, and to join you have to fill out an application with your address and phone number."

"Brandy had that pack before she left Buddy—the application would have her old address."

"Maybe, but if she's a loyal customer, she'd want to keep getting her comps and coupons in the mail, so she'd have changed her address in our records."

"It's worth a try, if you don't mind checking."

Leland went back to his office while I went back to the bar. Akers was long gone, which was probably just as well. If he really was in charge, Leland might not want him knowing he was digging up information on guests. I ordered beers for both of us and even considered picking up a six-pack to take home to Mama. She wasn't supposed to drink with all her meds, but she sure did love a cold beer. What harm could it do anyway?

I was still trying to decide when Leland slid into the other side of the booth. "Bingo!" Then he looked around in mock alarm. "Better not say that too loud—people will want to play that, too."

"What did you get?"

"Brandy's new address." He handed me a printout of a Memphis address and phone number.

"Leland, I could kiss you."

"What's stopping you?"

"The fact that your girlfriend would beat the crap out of me."

He grinned and took a big swallow out of his beer. "I guess you really get into this detective stuff."

"It's okay, usually paperwork, really." Seeing that he looked disappointed, I figured the least I could do was tell a few funny stories about the crazy claims people made to try to cheat insurance companies—from the woman who pretended she'd lost her hearing until the fire alarm went off behind her to the man who hired somebody to key his car so he could get it repainted for free. But we didn't talk long. He had his girlfriend to see, and I was hoping to find Brandy right away.

I pulled out my cell phone when I got outside, but there was no answer at Brandy's new number and no answering machine. I got another disdainful valet to retrieve my car, and while I waited, made up my mind about what to do next. By rights, I should have gone home to check on Mama, but I knew she'd want me to find Brandy sooner rather than later. Besides, I didn't mind being away from the house a little while longer.

It wasn't that I didn't want to be with Mama, but I hated feeling so damned useless, not able to make her feel better. And though I'd rather have had my nails pulled out with pliers than tell her, it was the smell that really got to me. I didn't know if it was something chemical from the endless progression of pills, the difficulty of getting Mama really clean with a sponge bath, or the cancer itself stinking up the air. Maybe it was all three. Whatever it was, I didn't think I'd ever be totally free of it.

So I decided to go to Brandy's new address. If nothing else, I'd be able to leave her a note.

According to the information Leland had given me, Brandy was still in Memphis, but when I got to her new apartment building, I could see she'd moved up a few steps. The building she'd lived in with Buddy had been built in the seventies to look modern, while this place had been built twenty years later and designed to look old. It was obviously much more expensive.

When I rang the bell, I was buzzed in right away, as if Brandy were expecting me, but from the look on her face when I stepped out of the elevator, I could tell I wasn't the one she was waiting for. She was dressed in a skirt that was too short for a woman her age, and a silky top that showed far too much cleavage.

"Grace! What are you doing here?"

"It's good to see you, too," I said, and I admit I sounded peevish.

"I mean, I wasn't sure you'd gotten my change of address card—I hadn't heard from you."

Change of address card? Right. "Can I come in?"

"Um, sure. For a little while."

Brandy's apartment was filled with new furniture, all straight out of a box so that it matched and showed no character whatsoever.

"Are you going out?" I said.

"Sure am. I've got a date." She held up a hand as if to forestall some comment from me. "You know Buddy and I are separated, right?"

"I know you up and left him."

"Well I had good reasons."

I could have argued with her, but the fact was, I didn't give a crap. "Brandy, your relationship with Buddy or whoever it is you're seeing is no concern of mine. I'm here about Mama."

She slid down on the shiny, faux leather sofa. "What about Mama?"

I sat next to her. "She's bad off. It's cancer. You need to come home right away."

"You don't mean tonight?"

"I mean right this minute. She's dying, Brandy. I don't know how much longer she's got."

"What did the doctor say?"

"He's giving her another month. Maybe less."

"Damned doctors! If we had money, he wouldn't give up on her."

"You really think I'd let him give up on Mama? There's nothing anybody can do. She didn't want to admit she was sick, and by the time she finally got checked out, it was too late for chemo or radiation to do her any good. We've been trying to get a hold of you, but I just found out yesterday that you and Buddy had split up and it took me all day to find you." I was trying to keep the anger out of my voice, but I don't imagine I did too well.

"How was I supposed to know?"

"Well, you might have—" I stopped myself. There was no point. "Let's just head on over to the house. Mama can't wait to see you."

Brandy didn't get up. "Does she look bad?"

The fact was, Mama's illness had been so overwhelming that I was already forgetting what she'd looked like when she was healthy. "She looks pretty rough."

"I hate to see her when she's so sick. I don't want to remember her that way."

I wanted to tell her that I'd have given a lot not to have those memories myself, but I clamped down on my temper. "It's not about you, Brandy. Mama wants to say goodbye."

Brandy started crying, and I tried to comfort her, but I've never been a nurturing person and had to settle for looking around until I found a box of tissues to hand her. Eventually she quieted down enough to talk.

"I can't deal with this tonight, Grace. I've got plans, and—I'll be over there first thing in the morning. No, even better—I'll make a batch of my egg salad and bring it for lunch. Mama loves my egg salad."

"I don't know if she can even keep it down."

"I'm sure she can—it'll make her feel so much better. You just wait and see."

"Then come on over tonight. You visit with Mama, and I'll go to the store and get what you need for the egg salad. You can make it over there just as easy as here."

Brandy looked at the clock. "No, not tonight. I'll come to-morrow. I swear."

"I'm sure your date will understand if you have to cancel."

"It's not that," she insisted. "I just need some time to process it all."

I didn't want to leave without her, but short of picking her up and carrying her, there wasn't anything else I could do. In fairness to my sister, it would have been a shock for me to show up unexpectedly, even without such bad news. Brandy wasn't always the fastest on her feet, so maybe it was best to give her a night to come to terms with Mama's condition. "Tomorrow morning? You promise? I don't want to get Mama's hopes up if you're not coming."

"Tomorrow at lunch. I swear."

"All right, Brandy. I'm counting on you to show up."

"I said I'd be there," she snapped.

"Fine. I'll see you tomorrow at lunchtime."

"By one at the latest," she said, and walked me to the door. We hugged briefly, and I got back into the elevator.

As I stepped into the building's lobby, a tall man in tight jeans was ringing a doorbell. I wasn't sure, but I thought it was Brandy's. He got buzzed in before I could get a good look at him, but as he walked to the elevator, I noticed that he had a nice butt. I wondered if he was Brandy's mysterious boyfriend Duke. I also wondered where I'd seen him before—he looked familiar.

Mama was asleep when I got home. Buddy had been true to his word and come by to play for her earlier, and Mrs. Pembroke, the church lady on duty, said Mama had dozed off during "How Great Thou Art." After checking with Mrs. Pembroke about which meds were due when, I walked her out to her car and locked up for the night. I settled down in the old recliner in Mama's room where I'd been sleeping in case she needed me overnight, happy to have dodged explanations about Brandy until the next day.

The phone rang at three in the morning, and in my sleep-fogged state, my first instinct was to go to Mama, thinking she was calling for me, but she wasn't even stirring. I grabbed the cordless phone and took it out into the hall to talk without disturbing her.

Maybe fifteen minutes later, I was back and I automatically checked Mama again before sitting in my chair. This time I didn't sleep. I don't think I so much as closed my eyes. Instead I spent the next few hours wondering how I was going to tell Mama that Brandy was dead.

I was tempted to make up a lie, but Mama would have seen right through that, so I had to tell her the truth. Brandy had died in a head-on collision with an eighteen-wheeler. When I asked about Brandy's boyfriend, the police told me she'd been alone in the car.

I expected Mama to take it hard, but all she said was that God must have taken Brandy so there'd be somebody to meet her in heaven. She died almost exactly twenty-four hours later.

As much as it hurt for them to go so close together, I realized a few days later it was a blessing it had happened that way. That was when the police called again, this time to let me know the lab results had come back, proving that Brandy was high on cocaine when she died.

Buddy came to their joint funeral and played "How Great Thou Art" again. It was the prettiest thing I'd ever heard.

About a week after I buried my mother and my sister, I found some things in Brandy's apartment I thought Buddy might want: pictures of the two of them and a couple of cassette tapes of him playing music. I could have mailed it all, but with Mama gone and the church ladies moved on to other needy families, the empty house was getting to me. Even listening to the blues would be better than trying to turn the TV up loud enough to drown out the silence. So I called around until I found out where Buddy was playing and drove over.

Though this place was considerably bigger than the last bar I'd met Buddy at, it was even more crowded. I was glad for Buddy's success, but I couldn't help thinking that if Brandy had hung on just a little longer, maybe she could have quit her job to bask in his reflected glory. Instead she'd died alone, and her precious boyfriend hadn't even cared about her enough to show up at the funeral.

As I tried to make my way backstage, I saw Buddy's fan, Akers, sitting front and center again, with the same companion as before. After what Leland had told me about him, I guessed that the younger man was his bodyguard.

I'd just gotten to Akers' table when the house lights dimmed, and the stage lights went on. That meant I'd have to stay until the first set was over if I wanted to talk to Buddy. I looked around for an empty table, but the place was packed solid, and I started toward the edge of the room as Buddy stepped onto the stage, resigned to leaning against the wall for the next hour.

Then Akers waved me over to his table, which had the only empty chairs in view. I could barely hear him over the applause for Buddy, saying, "Please, join us."

I smiled and nodded gratefully. I didn't know if he was connected or not, but it couldn't hurt to share his table. He introduced the man with him, but honestly I couldn't hear his name or even see him clearly in the dim light, and I didn't think he'd heard my name either.

A minute later, Buddy started playing, and none of us paid any attention to one another anyway.

I suppose the reason I'd never cared for the blues was because it all sounded like whining to me, and Mama had never let me get away with whining. But Mama was gone, and Brandy was gone, and this time, it felt as if Buddy was playing for me and me alone. I don't think I so much as moved during his whole set, other than to clap as hard as I could after each song.

Buddy started by picking out "The Sky is Crying" on his electric guitar, then went straight into "Where Did You Sleep Last Night." It didn't take a psychologist to realize why he'd chosen those two. I didn't recognize the next few songs, which were more up tempo. Then he switched to an acoustic guitar for "Trouble Soon Be Over," and the nearly wordless musical moan of "Dark Was the Night." Sweat poured down his face, despite the towel he used to wipe himself, and he hunched protectively over whichever guitar he was playing. He finished up with "Lonesome Valley," and though I don't cry in public, I came damned close as Buddy sang about a mother and a sister following their solitary paths toward death.

The few times I glanced away from Buddy, I saw that Akers was as hypnotized as I was. His eyes were shining, either with pure pleasure or unshed tears, or maybe both.

When Buddy finished the set, Akers stood to applaud, and Buddy grinned as if he'd won the lottery. Then he saw me, and looked pleased that I'd come. He mouthed, "Give me ten minutes," before going backstage.

The house lights came back up, and the crowd surged toward the bar. Akers must have given prior instructions, because his bodyguard immediately got up to join the line waiting for service.

"That was incredible," Akers said. "I was certain Buddy had it in him, and tonight's performance proves it."

I remembered how Buddy had described the blues to me. "I guess he's mourning Brandy the best way he can."

"Oh, yes. His wife's accident. Your sister. Forgive me. Please accept my condolences for your loss."

"Thank you."

The bodyguard returned with a pitcher of beer and mugs, and poured a round for us. Akers was lost in his thoughts, humming one of the songs Buddy had sung. Just to make conversation, I asked the younger man, "Are you a blues fan, too?"

He shook his head. "Me, I like something to dance to. All that whining gets on my nerves."

Though I'd thought the same thing myself, I felt contrary enough to defend Buddy's music. "It's not whining. The blues are nothing but a good man feeling bad."

"Yeah? I'd rather make a bad woman feel good." He grinned, and I guess it was supposed to be roguish, but to me it looked like nothing so much as an alligator's leer.

I blinked and suddenly realized why the man I'd seen at Brandy's place had looked familiar. "I'm sorry, I don't think I caught your name.

"Kendricks," he said. "Duke Kendricks."

I'm fairly sure I thanked Akers for the seat and the beer before standing up and making my way backstage, but the next thing I really remember was telling Buddy why Brandy had left him.

Buddy held his guitar as he listened to me, and he pressed his fingers so tightly against the metal strings that he drew blood, but he didn't say a word until I was finished. All he said then was, "I'll be right back."

He was gone for a couple of minutes, and I realized after the fact that he must have known there was a gun in the club's office. At the time, all I noticed when he got back was that he'd draped a towel over one hand. Without speaking, we went into the club and walked to Akers' table, with Buddy ignoring the people slapping his back in congratulation.

Akers beamed at him. "My boy, my boy. You've surpassed yourself. You must be parched." He saw the beer pitcher was empty and said, "Duke, get Buddy something to drink."

"Yes, sir," Duke said and pushed his way back toward the bar.

Buddy and I sat down, and Akers said, "I feel privileged to have been here tonight, and I like to think that my advice and support has helped you, at least in a small way."

"Oh, you've been a big help. You always said I needed a little seasoning and the rest would come. So you made sure I got what I needed."

"I beg your pardon?"

"The blues are a good man feeling bad, right? I don't know that I'm a good man, but I'm hurting, Mr. Akers. Brandy left me, and now she's dead, and I'm playing better than I've ever played in my life. That's exactly what you wanted, isn't it?"

I'd expected Akers to deny it, but he said, "She wasn't worthy of you, Buddy. You always had it in you to be great, and she was holding you back. Now that I've cleared the way for you, the world can hear your music, just as I have."

"You want to hear music?" Buddy said. "Listen to this."

That's when I saw the gun in his hand.

PRESENT

"You know the rest."

"Wait a minute," Lieutenant Johnson said. "If Kendricks was having an affair with Bartholomew's wife, why didn't Bartholomew go after Kendricks?"

"Kendricks only slept with Brandy because Akers told him to." I could see Johnson still didn't get it. "Akers wanted to discover a new blues legend and decided Buddy needed to feel the blues so he could play them better. So he got Kendricks to seduce Brandy." Knowing my sister, it probably hadn't been difficult. "He must have taken her out to the casino and shown her a big time. Probably supplied the nose candy, too.

"Only Buddy didn't even notice his wife was screwing around on him, so Kendricks got Brandy to leave him. I don't know if they meant for Brandy to die, but it's a hell of a coincidence that she picked the night I spoke to Akers to drive while high. I know Kendricks was at her place that night, and she was planning to go out with him. How did she end up driving around alone if he didn't set it up?" I shrugged. "Whatever they intended, Brandy died, and all Akers cared about was Buddy's music."

"And that's why Bartholomew went after Akers?"

I nodded. "I tried to get the gun away from him, but it went off."

"Twice?"

"That's right. Then Buddy dropped the gun. Kendricks tried to tackle Buddy, but some of the men from the club grabbed him. Then you police got there, and the ambulance. I don't know what else I can tell you."

Finally Johnson consulted his notes. "One thing confuses me. Kendricks may have been across the room when Bartholomew pulled out the gun, but like you said, somebody screamed, so he looked over. According to him, Buddy aimed the gun at his own forehead. He was planning to commit suicide, not murder."

I tried not to change position or my tone of voice. "It would take an awfully self-centered man to kill himself right in public that way."

"It seems to me that it takes a self-centered man to be so focused on his music that he didn't realize his wife was that unhappy."

I didn't respond.

Johnson said, "Kendricks told me that it was you who pushed the gun toward Akers, and that Buddy was trying to get the gun away from you when it went off the second time, not the other way around."

"What does Buddy say?"

"He says he doesn't mind doing the time—he said that a lot of good bluesmen have done a stretch or two behind bars."

"That sounds like Buddy." He'd probably milk any jail time he got for the rest of his career.

"He also said Akers got what was coming to him."

"I think he's right about that. Don't you?"

Johnson tried to stare me down, but I had no problem meeting his eyes, and finally he relented. "I guess I do. As for what Kendricks saw ..."

"I'm not a cop, but the first thing any investigator learns is that people lie."

"Oh yeah, people lie all the time," he said wryly. "Funny thing, a gun going off twice in a crowded place like that, and nobody got hit. Both bullets went straight down into the floor."

"I guess we were lucky."

"I don't know if Akers feels that way. The doctor tells me he might not ever get his hearing back, what with one shot going off so close to his right ear and the other one next to his left ear."

"It must have hurt, too. After the shots, Akers grabbed his head and started screaming, and when he realized he couldn't hear himself, he screamed even louder."

"Didn't you mention that you've investigated claims about hearing loss?"

"I might have. I've had a couple of cases like that. Most people don't realize how fragile hearing can be."

"Is that right?"

"Even if Akers' hearing does come back, he'll probably never hear as well as he did before. I doubt he'll ever be able to enjoy music the same way."

I may not know much about the blues, but I do know how to make a man feel bad.

14 Kidd Diamond
Daniel Martine

WHEN THE BLUES COME OVER YOU they can smack you down like a bitch slap from a tidal wave, or they can creep under your skin like a nasty chigger laying its larvae. Both conspire to break you down, and both eventually will make you bleed. I guess that's what the Blues is all about ... making us bleed. If that's the case, and I believe it is, down to the unfathomable, murky depths of my sinner's soul, then at the age of sixty-two, I'm about bled white.

Kidd Diamond is my name. Playing and living the Blues has always been my game, but not my only pursuit. And yes, that's the real name given to me at birth by a woman who was no mother and who abandoned me at age ten as cavalierly as she disposed of the many used condoms I saw carelessly strewn about on the floor next to her bed nearly every morning. Addled by drugs, wasting away and spent as only a twenty-something year old heroin-addicted hooker can be, Sadie Diamond went to the store one dreary Clarksdale morning to get some cigarettes and a pint bottle of Ten High to start her day. She never came back. You could say that was the day I received my first bitch slap from the Blues. The first of many.

And now, all these years later, here I am, back in the Delta, sitting in a dark, lonely hotel room listening to an apocalyptic thunderstorm raging outside and drinking steadily from a bottle of Maker's Mark, trying desperately to get drunk while waiting for a knock on the door I know is coming. I was finally back home in Clarksdale, Mississippi, staying at the infamous Riverside Hotel less than a mile from where Robert Johnson had allegedly made his pact with the devil at the crossroads of Highways 61 and 49. What the hell was I doing here? Why had I come back to the town of my birth? Why indeed? Well, that's what you're here to find out, I expect. It's the Blues we're talking about, after all.

Years of despair, self-recrimination and self-loathing, even through all my successes, had precluded me from coming home. Perhaps it was that very despair that made me the artist I had become, and still was, in the eyes of my loyal fans. They were my cocoon, my insulation against the guilt that had driven me from my childhood home of Clarksdale.

And yet, here I sat, trying desperately to get drunk, waiting for destiny to knock on my door, almost paralyzed by a sense of foreboding, a familiar dread that had followed me for decades. The trepidation was so palpable it crawled under my skin. Like damn chiggers.

To my horror, I realized what it was. For the first time in decades, I sensed my mother's presence. The sensation felt real, and unbearably sad.

I stared at my favorite guitar, reliving some of the glory days on the road playing my sweet, petite "Diamond Lil." In between bouts of rampant melancholia and still feeling my mother's presence, I watched Lil, illuminated by an occasional flash of lightning, as she lay peaceably in the plush confines of an open guitar case on the bed. My baby was a 1966 hollow-body Rickenbacker 335 model with two pickups, a vibrato bar I manipulated as expertly as a pimp does his whores, and a fingerboard that fit me like I was born to it.

Discontinued as a model in 1978, making her all the more precious to me, Lil was all dressed up, ready to thrill, in Fireglow yellow to red hues. She was a damn sight prettier than most of the women I'd slept with in my time and a hell of a lot more forgiving. I'd played many guitars throughout my career, but I always came home to Diamond Lil. No other guitar so profoundly personified the bonding and love I felt when playing the blues. She was as familiar to me as a former lover's body, where every crevice, contour and secret lay exposed and revealed under my loving, heated stroking. And there were secrets. Just at that moment, however, she looked more like a body in repose in a coffin. A body I recognized. It was Sadie Diamond, my mother, the woman who abandoned me like a junkyard dog.

That thought struck terror in my heart and I looked down the barrel of the shot glass in my trembling hands. I swallowed the whiskey, savoring its comforting heat as it scalded a path to the pit of my stomach. When I looked up again, Lil was no longer visible in the guitar case. Instead, a specter stared back at me from the case, now a coffin. It was, indeed, my mother. Her eyes bored into me, and instead of the drug and alcohol glaze I remember, they were filled with a despondency so unexpected it brought tears to my eyes.

Shocked into breathlessness, I dropped the shot glass on the floor and broke out in a cold, clammy sweat—the kind that plasters your shirt to the skin and sends a jolt of icy, incomprehensible fear surging from deep in your gut all the way up your throat to the ends of your hair follicles, causing them to feel as if they were on fire. Fire and ice, the twin demons of true fear, like Blues on steroids. I was freezing and burning all at once as the specter that seemed to be my mother stared at me, unmoving. Unsmiling.

I fought to avert my eyes from what I suspected was a demon from Hell. Finally I tore my gaze away. Shaking my head fiercely to make the apparition dissipate, I reached for the half empty Maker's Mark. If I couldn't shake this thing off, I reasoned, maybe I could drink it away. I had no more than poured another shot when the specter began to sing.

That's right, I said "sing." I was struck by a long buried memory of my mother's arms and the warmth of her body as she rocked me and sang. Beneath the words was the sound of her softly lilting voice, insistent. "Kidd … Kidd … Judgment is due. I'm—"

But the melody line and the timbre of the voice changed, and I thought … not this song, which I knew as intimately as my own social security number. It was a lyric any Blues lover would recognize, an ancient lament writ modern in the pain-wracked, soul-searing lexicon familiar to former slaves and bluesmen of the post-bellum South.

"I got to keep moving, I got to keep moving
Blues falling down like hail, blues falling down like hail
Mmm, blues falling down like hail, blues falling down like hail
And the day keeps on remindin' me, there's a hellhound on my trail
Hellhound on my trail, hellhound on my trail."

"Hellhound On My Trail" was the name of the lament, an original Robert Johnson composition. I was chilled to the marrow to hear Sadie's voice wailing in the distinctive, plaintive yet sinister style that was the hallmark of Johnson's vocals. That the lyrics' sentiments so completely matched my current mood and situation mattered not at all. I only wanted it to end.

Now. And forever.

I was hearing my personal history, all the pain, the anger, the sorrow and all those opportunities and people I'd lost in this lifetime and would never get back contained in this one song. And yet, when it ended, no matter how it ended, I understood that my life, as it had been, would also be at an end.

I was caught in a place no man should find himself and I had no choice. I was right where I was supposed to be with my fate signed, sealed and ready to be delivered with C.O.D. branded on my soul. My hellhound had tracked me down to this hotel room in Clarksdale. Setting the stage for … for what? I didn't know for sure, but in my life up to now, I'd always been a betting man, come hell or high water.

This time I was laying odds I wasn't about to hit a gut-shot straight on the river. Whatever hand was coming my way, it would be what I deserved. No more, no less.

A thunderous knock shook the door. The room was icy cold, and Sadie was gone.

The knock came again. Here he was at last, the devil come to claim his due.

A jagged bolt of electric blue lightning lit the sky so close to the window it initiated a flash-bulb burst inside my room. The next flash, staggered after a peal of thunder that sounded as if it had exploded on the pavement just across the street, again lit up the room. This time I caught the tableau in the Windex-streaked mirror of an old beat-up, worn pinewood bureau set against the far wall.

I barely recognized the desolate face that returned my stare, eerily back-lit in the vaporous glow of a bluish-gray haze. Every time lightning flashed, the same scene appeared in the mirror. Time all but stopped. I was the sole subject of this morbid, other-worldly photographic exercise, and I had become hypnotized by the lightning. I even fancied I heard an audience somewhere in the ether applauding me wildly after ripping off a long-forgotten, blazing guitar solo.

The knock came again.

Not thunderous, as before, but a typical, ordinary knock. The very ordinariness of the lightly insistent rapping brought me back to reality, a sinking, icy feeling gripping my bowels. The fucker was here.

I had a vision of me on my knees, begging for my eternal life from the likes of Beelzebub—and broke out into laughter. I couldn't help it, that visual was too rife with absurdity. Can you imagine it? Me, Kidd Diamond, master fornicator, liar and thief, bastard child of a two-bit hooker, and ... worse, asking the Devil for a break. It was beyond absurdity. It was fucking ridiculous.

The knocking became more insistent as I sank to the floor huffing and coughing with breathy laughter.

A voice I recognized, a nether-worldly voice that dripped with the malevolence and finality of impending doom, lasered through my consciousness. The self-mocking laughter died in my constricted throat.

He was here, come to claim me as his rightful, legal possession. At that moment I realized with a gut-wrenching pang of regret and Johnny-come-lately remorse, I did not want to belong to Satan for all eternity. No matter what blood promises I'd made to him so many years ago when I was just a scruffy, poor, orphaned young black man from the Delta with my only meaningful possession a stolen 1966 hollow-body Red Rickenbacker 335 guitar strapped across my back.

"Kidd," the voice of doom said through the door.

I rose up from the floor, my heart pounding the Anvil Chorus. He knew I was in the room.

"Kidd, open up. It's your old friend Nick Belial. Remember me?"

I couldn't help it. Whether it was a leftover reaction from my laughing jag or from pure terror, or more likely both, I had to suppress a giggle. I'd thought about this moment a hundred times a day for over forty years. Of course I remembered who in hell he was.

I found my voice. "Hey, Nick. Hang on, I'll be right there."

I got myself together and hurried to the bureau mirror to check my frazzled appearance.

I gave a passing thought to uttering a prayer for deliverance, yet, I had no reason to believe God was in a mood to grant the likes of me anything more than outright scorn. Maybe He'd even laugh his ass off at my impertinence. I was the worst kind of sinner. And totally in line with my hard-shell Southern Baptist upraising, I figured God to be a vengeful, wrathful being. The God of hellfire and eternal damnation, the very phrase with which my long-dead, preachy, pushy Grandmama, Miz Lorna Mae Diamond, would harangue her daughter, Sadie. I naturally figured the Man was full of contempt and righteous anger for the moral bottom feeders of this worst of all possible worlds.

I didn't look to Him for any favors.

I was deliberating on this thought when the door busted wide open, as if a great wind had unhinged it. A crackling, overpowering blast of hot air swept into the room, rousting a pile of newspapers and music magazines from the desk to the floor. My guitar case snapped shut like a river turtle's jaws, and every drawer in that ancient pinewood bureau burst forth from its berth and clattered noisily, my clothes and underwear tumbling out and blowing every which way. The curtains on the windows violently flapped up into a horizontal position as the windows slammed shut. The gust blew me backwards onto the bed where I fell over my guitar case, which jammed painfully into my ribs.

Nick's rather dramatic entrance was punctuated by a tympanic peal of rolling thunder in a *basso profundo* register. He stood, silhouetted in the frame of the ruined doorjamb, backlit by an accompanying phosphorescent burst of red-tinged lightning that crashed behind him in the hallway.

"Well, well. Kidd Diamond. Long time, no see, partner. How's it hangin'?"

Not a very original greeting, but then again, the Devil was a knockoff of an angel. I didn't expect originality from a counterfeit.

Once my heart stopped pounding and my breathing dropped back to normal, I looked him over. He'd radically changed his appearance in the four decades since last I'd seen him.

Our first meeting he'd been dressed as primly as a preacher. Young I may have been at the time, but I was not a complete fool. I knew him for who and what he was, not who he professed to be in his Southern Baptist clerical garb and sporting a head of fried, lye-straightened hair of the period you could only get in a "conk parlor."

Of course, I was green and dumb enough to cut a deal with the devil.

The second time we met, the meeting that sealed the deal, he'd been dressed more like I expected the devil to look—a flashy black pimp in an ankle-length white fur coat and garish purple felt pork pie hat with a green feather stuck in it and perched jauntily on a fluffy, well-picked Afro.

I guess Nick thought that type of inner-city persona would appeal to my sense of blackness. In fact, I hated that shuck-and-jive shit that most of my seventies friends and acquaintances would lay on me. But Nick dazzled me with visions of the success I could be if I signed what he euphemistically called his "deal memo." It sure as hell was a contract, and one I signed with my own blood.

One thing you could say for Nick, devil or not, he kept up with what was fashionable. He was as tall as I remembered, somewhere around six feet nine or ten. Lean, but muscular. His huge head, shaved bald, sported the patented Air Jordan look. Heavy gold hoop earrings hung on his lobes, and on his chin was a hip, up-to-the-minute style of goatee known as the "Johnny Boy."

Nick looked dapper in an exquisitely tailored dark, pinstriped single-breasted suit with high Edwardian lapels. Underneath, an immaculate white shirt was set off by a thickly knotted silver silk tie that matched the pinstripes on his suit. A pair of ruby cufflinks tied it all together.

His shoes were actually a pair of black Spanish-looking designer boots of soft, pliable leather. I was afraid to speculate on the source of that skin.

"What do you think, Kidd? I look good, don't I?"

My first thought was that Nick looked like the epítome of a successful modern day NBA basketball player. And he did look pretty damned good. For a demon from hell.

Nick performed a slow pirouette so I could admire his sartorial splendor. When he turned his back I noticed a tattoo on his head just above his neckline. **GOD IS DEAD!**

Nick finished his mini-runway exhibition with a flourish and a deep bow. He looked at me expectantly, a shit-eating Cheshire grin as big as Toledo on his face. Okay, I decided, I'll play your cat and mouse game, you bastard.

"You're looking natty dread, Nick. Real GQ! Nice moves, too. The Memphis Grizzlies oughta sign you up. They could use a power forward with your, uh, charisma and game."

Nick belly-laughed deep and hard, which made me nervous.

"Nah! I'm a Lakers fan. You know what everybody is saying … Showtime is back! Ko-babay is the shit! Man, I love L.A. My kind of town."

"College football is more my thing, Nick. You know how it is down South. Following the SEC is like going to church. Only, we eat more barbecue while we're doing it."

"I hear you, Kidd. Right up my alley. Nothing like a good barbecue. Well, you gonna invite me in or do I have to stir up some more shit?"

It was then I noticed that nothing in the room was out of place. Everything was just like it was before he blew in. Except for one small detail. My ribs still hurt.

"Hey! *Mi casa, su casa.*" I feigned casualness, though I don't think Nick bought that act for a second.

I sat down next to Lil as Nick sashayed in and shut the door behind him. I opened the guitar case and looked her over to make sure Lil hadn't been damaged in the maelstrom of Nick's patented "Shock and Awe" entrance. She looked just fine. I shut the case and mulled my options. There didn't seem to be many.

Suddenly icy, insistent fingers traced ripples down my neck, and I again became aware of another presence in the room. And I didn't mean Nick. It was weird and eerie, yet oddly, it felt safe, reassuring. The feeling kept getting stronger. Unfortunately, Nick's bombastic presence didn't give me the opportunity to further explore the sensation. Whatever "it" was.

"Well, Kidd, this ain't exactly the Ritz Carlton, is it? Last I checked, you're still a viable, classic act that people pay good money to see. What's the deal with staying in a dump like this?"

"My reasons aren't exactly in your line of work. Trust me, you wouldn't give three shits and a giggle for why I'm back in Clarksdale."

"Don't count on it, Kidd. You might be surprised."

Nick's response was cryptic, and worrisome, but I had no time to suss it out. At the moment, I had all I could handle agonizing over the impending disposition of my immortal soul.

God knew I was a mostly unrepentant sinner, but I was silently praying my ass off, hoping that His mighty hand would reach down from the heavens into that hotel room and pluck the Devil out by his Johnny-boy and deposit him directly back into hell.

In short, I was looking for a sign, any kind of sign, that I would be let off the hook. Like it was a bad dream, or a waking nightmare.

All I could think was that I was well and truly fucked! I'd come into the world alone, and now it appeared to be a mortal lock I was going out the same way. With nary a witness or a loved one present to preside over my imminent, untimely demise.

"You're lonely, aren't you Kidd?" Nick asked in the tone of a therapist. "You were born lonely, son. Not even your mama wanted you. Three bad marriages, countless women, and none of them wanted you either, did they?"

From the corner of the room came something that sounded like a softly moaning sigh. It didn't seem like Nick had heard it, but I sure as hell did. This scene was getting weirder by the minute.

"I'm my own in-house expert on lonely," I said. "So what?"

"Think on it, Kidd," the devil commanded.

And I did.

Night after interminable night, during every tour, in hotel rooms all over the world, post-gig depression would set in and trigger bouts of insomnia. I'd always known I was destined and doomed to lead a life of crushing solitude.

Just as regularly, I was drunk and/or coked out of my head, often in the company of a parade of star-fucking bimbos of all colors, creeds and nationalities who thought it'd be hip to score a notch on their garter belts with a raucous-voiced, guitar-sling-ing, heavy-hung, bluesman. Go back to the roots, kind of, if you get my meaning. But after the hellish childhood I'd lived with Sadie, and then being abandoned by her when I was ten years old, I didn't trust women any further than my next loveless, inevitable assignation in yet another hotel room in some podunk town.

I knew what loneliness was. Or so I thought. But I also knew, deep down in my gut, that a lifetime of guilt was the engine of my despair. And that despair fueled my playing, cost me my family life, drove me to drink and drugs, and made me a lying, cheating fornicator of the first rank.

Nick watched me closely. The merest wisp of a sardonic smile creased his rugged, redbone features. He enjoyed my discomfiture and probably was already reveling in the fact that I would soon be just another faded inkblot in his ledger of damned souls.

I'd survived abandonment, near starvation and drug addiction to rise to stardom. I was going down fighting. That's all there was to it. Regrettably, I could foresee no obvious path to victory over the devil. I was in way over my head. Yet, I couldn't help speculating there was something more going on underneath the surface here. It struck me that he was being extra vigilant with me, and it nagged at me like a persistent toothache. Nick had me dead to rights, and we both knew it. What was he worried about?

"I've been meaning to stop by long before this, Kidd. But you know how it is. One thing and then another. And next thing you know, it's what ... forty some years later?" Nick winked. "Truth is, I've been pretty busy lately. Business is booming!"

"Yeah," I replied, a slight edge to my voice he instantly picked up on. "This day and age it must be easy pickings for you."

Nick nodded, affably enough. "I've never underestimated man's greed. Or his need to be the best at something. Just like you, Kidd. Remember?"

Ok, we were getting down to the nut-cutting. Nick was making his play. I had to do something, anything, to delay the inevitable. So, I countered with a confident rejoinder of my own.

"I was always the best. Even before I met you, Nick. And you know it."

"You're still the best, Kidd, and you've got the hardware, rep and money to back up that claim. And you can thank me."

Nick's smugness was really getting to me, but I saw an opening. So, I went for it. "You just admitted I was the best, then and now. So, how do I know you were actually responsible for any of my success? Can you prove it, Nick? Maybe it was just a matter of time before I hit it big. Maybe I never really needed you."

Nick gave me a quizzical look. My breath caught in my throat. Hope, however slight, flared in my breast like a flickering candle.

"You're the best. No argument from me. But that's hardly the issue, is it, Kidd? You signed on the dotted line. And now you're mine."

That persistent nagging doubt mushroomed into full-fledged suspicion. Nick was toying with me. But not like a cat that plays with a hapless mouse before the kill. This was different. Like the devil knew something about me I didn't know he knew. And he was only waiting to spring the trap shut.

Why?

I made a snap decision to go diversionary until I could figure out Nick's game. "I bet you didn't know that practically every Southern black bluesman and woman of note stayed here at the Riverside at one time or another. It's like a shrine to the Blues. People come from all over the world to stay here. Hell, this room was John Lee Hooker's favorite. He was a mean-ass, wild motherfucker. Man, I'll never forget the first time I opened a gig for him."

I could see I hadn't exactly thrown Nick off stride with my new tactics. He knew I was up to something, though he was unsure of what shape the ploy would take.

I continued, "About a mile and a half right down the road, that's where Robert Johnson made his pact with you. Isn't that right?"

Nick's eyes narrowed and flashed, registering barely discernible annoyance. I'd touched some kind of nerve when I mentioned Robert Johnson's name, so I hit it again. "You know, I never asked you about Johnson back when we first met. I always meant to but never quite got around to it. You know, what with one thing and another."

Damn, did Nick flinch when I paraphrased his line? Things were definitely looking up.

"So, I wanted to ask whether or not you actually did that whole crossroads thing with Johnson. You know, the famous 'Hellhounds On My Trail' shtick."

Nick said nothing, but I swear one of his red eyes twitched.

"Legend has it you met him at midnight at the junction of Highways 61 and 49," I went on. "You did your thing, and then he went off and did his and became an enduring legend, et cetera. Is that true? I ask because I want to know if I'm the only motherfucker dumb enough to go for your deal?"

"Are you jivin' me, Diamond? Because, if you are, you're way out of your league, boy."

Nick's voice was even and low key. I would have felt better if he'd lost his cool. I had the nasty sensation thin ice was cracking beneath me. I was twisting the dragon's tail, but I had nothing to lose. "Instead of the crossroads, you came to my hotel room in L.A. Right after the Grammys that year. Remember?"

Nick sounded bored. "What's your point, Diamond? Stalling won't work. You know what I'm here for, so let's get to it." He reached inside his suit coat and brought out a folded, red leather packet sealed with black wax. His gaze never left mine as he tossed the packet onto the bed where it landed next to my guitar case.

"You like to gamble, don't you, Kidd?" Nick didn't wait for an answer. His fleshy, wet red lips slit into a feral smile. "I've got a pair of aces in the pocket, boy, and another one on the river." He nodded at the packet on the bed. "Read it and weep. It's all there, signed and sealed in your own blood."

My ass was most decidedly in serious jeopardy of frying for all eternity. I pressed. "The question still stands. Am I the only bluesman who went for your bullshit? I think I deserve to know that before we complete our business."

"Well, Diamond, you seem to be hell-bent on this line of inquiry." Nick took a seat, supremely confident. "I guess if I was in your shoes I'd do the exact same thing. But that's none of your business. It's strictly on a need-to-know basis. And you don't need to know."

"I want an answer." I was really pushing the envelope.

Nick creeped me out with that nasty grin of his. "What makes you think you have a choice in the matter, Diamond? You gave that up long ago. Today is the last day of the rest of your life. Get used to it. Now read the damn contract, sign it and let's get this shit over with."

"What's the rush? You going to a fire?" As bad a fix as I was in, I was heartened to know I could still crack wise with the Devil. For all the good it would do. "Besides, I don't believe you, Nick. I think you won't answer me because it would invalidate our 'deal'—which I still don't think is legal, in any case, because there's no real proof you did what you say you did on behalf of my career."

I stood up and paced about the room. It was surreal. Here I was debating with the Devil in Clarksdale, Mississippi, in an effort to keep my soul from going to everlasting hell. The only thing missing was a studio audience.

The crazy thing about this whole mess was that I never really believed in God until I did my deal with the Devil. I figured if there was a Satan, or one of his acolytes, who could make my dreams of being a star and music legend come true, then, by rights (and what little I had gleaned from my Grandmama's unrelenting efforts to read Scripture to me) there had to be Satan's opposite … God. But even after closing the "deal" with Nick, I'd never believed anything substantive would happen in my then-moribund chosen occupation.

I didn't think Nick was for real, not at the time. I was grasping at straws when I drunkenly called on the Devil. That early in my career I was playing brilliant, if unappreciated, lead guitar while backing up a has-been blues legend. We'd spent years knocking around on the "chitlin' circuit" until our partnership revitalized his all but flat-lined career. He was being given a lifetime honor on the Grammys while I was stuck, once more, playing in the background with zero recognition for years of stellar work.

I had the right stuff all right, but no one seemed to recognize that except me and a few of my friends. It was maddening to know I was just an adjunct to someone else's success. Just another guitar-slinger from the Delta with outsized dreams, while all around me other people enjoyed the fruits of their labors.

When Nick promised me the world—recognition of my talents compared with the likes of Jimi, B.B., Stevie Ray, T Bone, John Lee, and Muddy—and he held out a contract to sign, in my own blood, I did it; even though I never quite believed Nick could affect my career in any meaningful way. But, I thought, what the hell, I'd cast my soul to Satan long before that so what could be the harm in taking a shot that Nick was the Devil. I had everything to gain if he was for real, and very little to lose, either way.

Within a week of signing the contract, I was offered a festival gig in Europe by a respected promoter who'd heard a tape of me playing my own, older material. To this day, I have no idea where he got a hold of it, but I never figured Nick as the responsible party. It's hard to explain rationally, but my burgeoning success just didn't feel like it had the Devil's imprint all over it.

Events began moving my career like a runaway train. I all but forgot, for a time, about Nick, the contract, and what it represented in the distant future. I was firmly planted in the here and now and enjoying my long-awaited success.

While in Europe, in an unprecedented fit of creativity that astounded me, I wrote an album's worth of new material that I recorded in Paris with some hot French cats who played Delta blues better than most of the guys I knew back home. The album came out three months later to international acclaim, and I went back to America, a bona fide blues guitar hero. I was heralded as the natural-born successor to B.B. and the reincarnation of Hendrix, with my potent mix of psychedelic Delta blues. I had a crossover hit on early FM album rock radio in the mid-seventies. When that record sold a couple million units it was Katy-bar-the-door.

That was then, this is now. My stature as an elder statesman in the worldwide blues community, my financial success, my accomplishments were no more than dust. I squared myself up and stood toe to toe with Nick.

"All right, Nick, let's get down to business."

"Well, well, Kidd, that's the spirit. That's what I'm talkin' about. About fuckin' time, too. I've got things to do and people to tempt." Nick winked at me. "Let's get this show on the road. Now, if you'll just read this and sign on the dotted line ..."

As Nick stood up to retrieve the packet from the bed where it still lay, I stopped him cold with my next words.

"I'm not signing shit, Nick. Not until I get some answers."

Nick couldn't have looked more surprised if Jesus Christ had invited him out for a male-bonding night of bowling and beer. He got real quiet. I had to strain to hear his next words. And they sent a ghastly chill up my spine.

"Diamond, I warned you about fucking with me. Don't push me, boy. You'll regret it."

"What are you gonna do? Threaten me with hellfire and damnation? I'm already there. What else can you do to me?"

"You really don't want to ask me that question. Once we get to our final destination, I can put you in situations not even Dante imagined in his worst nightmares. And he knew what he was writing about, because I gave him an extended, up-close-and-personal glimpse of hell."

"Do your worst, Nick, but I'm going to get my answer. Or I won't sign that damn contract closure. Now, do you want to shadowbox like this or are we going to resolve this issue?"

Nick said nothing. I took that as a sign to continue.

"Ok, all bullshit aside. Here's what I think. You were never able to entice Robert Johnson to sell his soul to you. He had premonitions he was destined to live a short, brutish life. He didn't see the sense of dealing with the likes of you. I'm guessing, of course, but I'll lay odds I'm right."

"Like I said, Diamond, you don't need to know."

"I know this, Nick. I talked to several guys over the years who knew Johnson. Guys like his cousin Tommy Johnson and Johnny Shines, both of whom owed their careers to him. And Pinetop Perkins and Honeyboy Edwards, who are still alive and perhaps the last living bluesmen who actually knew and played with Robert Johnson. None of them ever believed the legend. It was good PR for bluesmen everywhere, and for you too, Nick. It served your purposes when you dealt with lesser lights, didn't it? Guys who bought into the lie … into the legend. I mean, when you really get down to it, I'm a derivative of the original, real McCoy. Oh, I'm a damn spectacular derivative, but I'm not the gen-u-wine article like those guys were. Especially, Robert Johnson."

I had Nick's full and rapt attention. I kept talking, hoping against hope I was making some headway toward a resolution that didn't feature me playing "Melancholy Baby" on a cheap Sears & Roebuck electric guitar in front of an audience of miscreants, sinners and perpetual drunks in Hell until the next Big Bang happened.

"Oh sure, maybe you were capable of doing a few things to kick-start someone's career, but if they hadn't possessed God-given talent, you couldn't have done shit. Chops like that are sacrosanct and out of your league. You're not the Big Boss Man."

Damn! I could see I'd scored heavy on that exchange. Nick's eyes burned with silent enmity, but he was listening to every word.

The room was deathly still now.

"So, what I guess I'm saying is, while you're a very nasty customer with a prodigious amount, but narrow scope, of power, without the public perception of you as 'evil personified,' you're nothing. Less than dogshit. A fucking sham. A plug-ugly conjurer who picks on the weak and the oppressed. Isn't that right, Nick?"

I'd just played the most dangerous ghetto game of the dozens ever with the Devil. I had a sense of what he was going to say, and I was ready for it. *If* he rose to take the bait. If he didn't, I was all out of options. Plus, there was the "river" card he was holding. Nick had made damn sure I knew about that.

"You trying to play the dozens with me, boy? That's your plan?" Nick laughed with real mirth. "I've squared off with hundreds of thousands of losers like you, Diamond. Most of them smarter. But no one, I mean no one, has ever played the dozens with me and won."

Nick settled into a belly laugh, and the result shook the walls. Could I have miscalculated? He seemed so cocksure. Well, all I could do now was wait for the hammer to come down.

"Hey, how about this, Mr. Kidd Diamond."

Oh shit! Here it comes, I thought. The *coup de gráce.*

"Your mother wears army boots!"

Another roar of laughter from Nick had the room shaking with tremors. He was really enjoying this.

"Fuck you, Nick," I replied quietly.

"That's it? Fuck you, Nick. That's all you got? You can't crack no better than that?"

I shrugged my shoulders.

"All right, little man, here be the big smackdown. You ready?"

Nick didn't wait for an answer. There really was no reason to. It was his game now, and he knew it. I could only hope the throw-down would go my way, a slim hope at best.

"It was never about whether or not I could advance your career, Diamond. In fact, I couldn't. You're right about that. You had the talent and the drive. It was only a matter of time. You were just too impatient. And you're right about the whole Robert Johnson thing, too. Don't ever underestimate the value of good public relations. You know what they say in Hollywood—bad pub is better than no pub at all."

Oh shit! My arteries froze at his words.

"Here's the real skinny, Diamond. I know you killed your own mama, boy. Murdered her in cold blood. If that ain't enough to consign you to hell, regardless of our deal, then chew on this. Through my … intercession, let's call it, the cops never figured out who did the dirty deed. Don't look now, Kidd, but that's you wriggling on my hook. How does it feel?"

Game. Set. Match. Nick didn't need style points to get over. His shit-eating grin said it all. He had the genuine goods on me. I was finished.

"And guess what, numb nuts, it gets worse."

I stared at Nick, slack-mouthed with horror. How could it possibly get worse then being consigned to hell for all eternity.

"Murder has got no statute of limitations in the good ole U.S. of A. So, what's going to happen is, if you don't sign, I'm gonna leave here without you, Kidd. Shortly after that the local gendarmes will stop by for an unfriendly visit. It appears that new evidence has come to light connecting you with the murder of your mother. But don't worry, I'll be back for you, after you've spent the rest of your natural days inside Parchman Farm waiting for the needle. Count on it. And when that day comes, it's my face you'll be seeing, not 'Big Boss Man.' You'll be living hell on earth and then you'll come home to me. Hell is truly for the damned, boy, and you surely are. You remember how it happened, don't you? Yes, you can't go a day without thinking about it."

To prove his point, I found myself back at the age of fourteen.

I'd tracked my mother to Memphis where she was living with another man, a blues guitarist, as it happened, who doubled as a drug dealer. An apropos choice for my mother.

I'd been on my own, nearly dying more than once, for four long years.

I'd hitchhiked up Highway 61 to Memphis and spent the better part of two weeks looking for Sadie. I slept in hallways and on the street, stealing food when I could and begging for money when the opportunity arose, all the while eluding cops, kiddie pimps and pedophiles. I finally found Sadie in a flophouse just off Beale Street toward the old Mississippi river docks. I followed her for two days, learning her movements and checking out the guy she was staying with. One time she took me by surprise as I rounded a corner following her. She must have forgotten something because she'd turned back toward home and bumped right into me. She stared at me for a full five seconds, then hastily excused herself past me. I couldn't tell if she recognized me or not. It didn't matter.

Whatever doubts I had about killing her evaporated.

One Saturday night I followed Sadie and her bluesman as they hit Beale Street for a night of drinking and carousing. Her man played on a blues bill at what's now called the New Daisy, an old movie theatre repurposed into a nightclub. By the time they got to the flophouse they were both falling-down drunk. I followed them discreetly into the building and up the stairs. The hall lights had long been broken or just plain didn't work, so it was pretty dark. They never saw me. Sadie's lover fumbled for the key to the door, but it dropped out of his hands to the floor and in trying to pick it up he accidentally kicked it under the door and into the room.

Drunk as he was and cursing a blue streak, he put his shoulder to the door a couple of times until it splintered off the hinges. They both laughed like hyenas and stumbled into the room and fell onto the bed. They didn't bother to shut the door. It wasn't long before they were loudly drunk-fucking. I squeezed in and crept up to the bed. I'd scrounged up a brick and had it in my hand ready to use. I was accustomed to seeing my mother fuck strange men, so I was able to keep my wits about me.

I slammed the brick against the man's bobbing head with all my strength. He huffed in pain and anger, so I did it again three more times in rapid succession until he collapsed on my mother, flopping like a hooked flounder. Sadie tried to focus her eyes on me, and she had the oddest expression on her face.

"Kidd, is that you?"

Hearing Sadie's voice infuriated me and brought back, in living color, all the old resentments and abuse she'd visited on me. Something primal snapped and I lunged toward her. I hefted the brick to hit her when I tripped over the man's pants on the floor. I fell and landed on a gun carelessly stuffed in his pants pocket. Grabbing it, I stood and faced my mother. She'd sobered up sufficiently to understand it was her own flesh and blood who was about to shoot her sorry ass. She tried to lift the man's dead weight off her naked body in a belated effort to save herself.

"Kidd. Wait. Don't shoot—"

Unthinking and unfeeling, I aimed the pistol at my mother's heaving breasts and promptly shot her at point-blank range. A starburst of blood sprouted above her left tit. The gun recoiled and seemed to bite me like a snake. I howled in pain and dropped the weapon. I glared at Sadie one last time. Astonishingly, her eyes were anything but accusatory. Rather, she looked resigned, almost peaceful. She reached out feebly to me with her right hand and tried to speak. Confused and frightened, I ran out the door as fast as I could, but not before swiping the man's guitar case on my way out. I never looked back, and that was that. Justice was done.

The guitar I'd stolen? It was a 1966 hollow-body Red Rickenbacker 335.

"Reliving past deeds is one of my specialties, Kidd. You like?" Nick asked.

I didn't answer Nick straightaway, because the room had abruptly begun to get cold. It was doubly weird, because ever since Nick had crashed my room, the heat had been palpable, and several times I thought to open a window or turn on the air-conditioning. There was no question that the room was cooling down rapidly.

Nick seemed as perplexed as I at the change in room temperature. He began to look alarmed.

"What's going on?" he asked.

"I don't have a fucking clue."

In point of fact, I suspected. The feeling that another presence was in the room had grown considerably stronger. Someone, or something, had joined us. The question was … what? Or, who?

I didn't have long to wait for an answer.

A chilly white mist seeped through the walls, and a soft keening cry became recognizable. My name. It kept repeating my name, along with this phrase.

"Kidd, Kidd. It's all raht, Kidd. I'm here now."

The voice galvanized Nick into action. "Son of a bitch! This isn't happening." He turned his attention to me and pointed at the packet. "Sign it now or suffer the consequences!" Flames arced from his finger tip to Diamond Lil. She began to smoke.

"Don't you sign nothin', Kidd." The voice came again, and in the blink of an eye, my mother stood before me. She was beautiful in death in a way she'd never been in life.

I was stunned at her sudden, unexpected appearance. And Nick, well, Nick's smile had an edge to it that boded no good.

At first the apparition floated, staring intensely at me. Nick kept his distance still as a stone. He made no move to intercede. For all I knew, he was incapable. As for the apparition, I had no idea what to say. This was the ghost of my mother. A woman I'd murdered.

Then the apparition addressed me.

"Kidd, I ain't got much time. You gotta listen to me, son. I know you hate me, and you got every raht to, God hisself knows, but what I got to say may be yo' sal-vation." She nodded at Nick as she said this.

I was spellbound.

Nick strode over to Sadie wearing that ghastly grin. When he spoke, his voice was thunderous. "What thinkest thou to accomplish by thy presence? Begone, shade. Thou hast no power here on earth. Begone from mine sight and returnst from whence thee came."

Sadie held her ground. "Belial, you be a liar and a thief, an' phony as a three dollah bill. You got no power over me the way I am now."

I could hardly believe what was happening. Sadie's next words punched a hole in my heart. And she spoke them with a sly smile of her own.

"Belial, you know why I come—to ask fo' giveness from Kidd for my sins a'ginst him. Fo' leavin' him to face the cruel world wit'out love."

"What about his sins against you?" Nick was back in battle mode.

"Ain't none." Sadie's eyes burrowed into my skull. "What do you say, son?"

For the briefest of moments, I felt like a ten-year-old child again. But could I trust this Sadie? This ghost? She must have seen the uncertainty in my eyes. I croaked, "What do you want Sadie?"

"Like you, Kidd, I'm seekin' redempshun' fo' my sins. We can help each other."

Nick saw an opening and swooped in for the kill.

"Kidd, remember what she did to you. She left you high and dry when you were only ten. A poor, defenseless little kid. And for what? To score another lousy dime bag or another bottle of cheap hooch? Fuck another loser who was gonna pimp her out anyway?"

Nick scored a direct hit. I took it right on the chin. He rocked me and I was reeling from the blow. I looked imploringly at Sadie. "Mom?"

Nick was in double barrel mode, blasting away. "Yeah, what about that … *Mom?*" he sneered. "Some fucking mother you were. And poor old *sonny boy* doesn't know the half of it, does he, Sadie?"

"What are you talking about, Nick?" The rekindled hope I'd felt at Sadie's initial appearance, however slight, faded. Sadie said nothing.

Quick as a snake Nick palmed a rolled-up document from his suit coat pocket. He unfurled it like a scroll. It was obviously a list of some sort, and it was distressingly long, nearly reaching the floor. "Sadie was a busy, busy girl."

Nick scanned over the list quickly.

"A girl after my own heart. Hmmm … you may not remember this one, Kidd, but let's see. The Christmas you were five Sadie stumbled into some money and bought a tree with all the trimmings, and even a couple of presents for you. A real holiday first. But her 'significant other' decided he needed to score some holiday cheer, and *poof,* that was the end of your Christmas. What really made that event memorable was the sumptuous meal she fixed for her 'man.' You, she locked in the closet so they could eat in peace. With you screaming and starving in the background. You remember that, Kidd?"

I hadn't until Nick reminded me. My spirits hit rock bottom.

"Here's my favorite of all your mother's peccadilloes." His breath reeked of sulfur. "Tell him, Sadie … tell him his street value to a little-boy-loving chickenhawk. Was it a lousy five hundred dollars?"

"I don't remember her doing that," I defended her.

"Because a mediocre bluesman dangled a bottle of cheap booze and a couple hundred dollars in her face and she forgot all about you and headed to Memphis." He nailed my coffin shut.

I couldn't look Sadie in the face. I remembered her abuse, and I killed her in an act of revenge. I was Nick's chattel for all eternity.

Sadie spoke softly. "Another half-truth from Satan's lyin' lips."

I perked up, if only a little.

"I left with that man 'cause I couldn't be no real mama to you, son, and I drew the line at sellin' my own flesh an' blood. I was weak, Kidd. I admit it. I done terr'ble thangs to my own mind an' body. So, I left you. I figgered you'd be safer alone, or wit' someone else 'sides me. I didn't trust myself."

"And I don't trust you." The memories Nick had served up left me desolate. "We're both lost, Sadie. At least, I am."

"You got that right, partner." Nick was in high spirits now.

"Mebbe not, son. I ask you ag'in. Can you forgive me?"

Sadie's guileless, tender gaze melted my heart, as well as my resolve to hate her. I was tired of despising my mother, tired of the self-loathing, of the intense pain and sorrow I felt for all the lost opportunities of my benighted life. I decided then and there to let go of all of it, and rolled the dice.

Nick sensed a sea-change. "Kidd, you're not buying that line of shit, are you? Come on, this is Sadie fucking Diamond we're talking about here. She wanted to sell your little black ass to kiddie sex freaks."

For some reason, he'd lost the power to ignite my ire. "You know, Nick, I've fucked up my life so many times I can't even begin to count them all. So has Sadie. So has everyone who's ever drawn breath. I'm going to partake of a little forgiveness, and maybe get some." I held Sadie's eyes. "I forgive you ... Mama. Can you forgive me?"

The look she gave me was worth all the blues licks I'd ever invented or stolen, and then some.

"Oh, for fuck's sake. Kidd, you're a sap. Always have been. Always will be. Now, I'm out of patience. Read this thing and sign on the dotted line and let's get this fucking show on the road. I'm a busy man." Nick held out the contract to me.

"No, Kidd! You ain't got to read or sign that evil thang. He can't make you. He ain't got that power." Sadie's form became more solid, more real, and the scent of jasmine, her favorite flower, filled the room. She faced Nick, a knowing smile creasing her pale lips. "You wanna know why, devil? 'Cause Kidd didn't kill me. You got no claim on his soul."

With that stunning revelation, the contract turned into ice in Nick's overheated hand and crumbled to the floor in pieces.

"But I did—"

"No, you was a scared, fo'teen-year-old boy who nevah had held a gun. You shot me in my shouldah, thass all. I didn't blame you for shootin' me, Kidd. I deserved it. I just wanted to talk to you … ask you to fo'give me. But you lit out so fast. I tried to follow you. I din't get no farther than the alley behind our buildin'. That's where the po'lice found me. I nevah tole them who done it. They took me to the Med. And that was the end of it." Sadie paused to let that sink in. "You fo'gave me, Kidd, but it ain't proper I got to fo'give you. Now, I can be released from this bondage o' neither death nor life. We have redempted each other."

I was rendered speechless, but only for a moment. "Does that mean it's all over?"

"It's all over, Kidd. You're free now."

I whooped and hollered and danced around the apparition of my mother like a crazy man. That lasted all of ten seconds.

Nick shot us both down. "Not so fast, pardner. Remember the river card? Perhaps, you should ask Sadie when and how she actually died."

The cold, cruel finger of fate jabbed me in the gut. "What are you talking about, Nick?"

Nick didn't answer. The nasty little smirk on his face said it all. My nuts were still in the fire.

"Mom, what's he talking about?"

"I bled to death in that alley, Kidd. I nevah made it to the hospital alive."

Nick chimed in, "Which means you *were* responsible for her death, Diamond. And that makes you still mine."

With a flourish, Nick whipped out another contract from the recesses of his suit coat. He placed it carefully in my hand. It burned to the touch.

So close to salvation, and now I stood on the precipice of the Devil's inferno. "What's with a new contract? I never signed two. You can't do this."

"I just did. Clue him in, Sadie." Nick leaned against the wall, smugness oozing from every pore.

"In the spirit world, Kidd, murdah don't get no pass, either. Just like in real life."

"True," Nick chortled. "You kill someone up here, whether you meant to or not, and a contract is auto-generated in my neck of the woods with your name written in the victim's blood. All legal and binding, Diamond. Even the Big Boss Man doesn't interfere. Makes my job real easy. Gotta love it, don't you?"

Nick unsheathed a ruby-studded dagger hidden in his clothes. It gleamed in the gathering dawn, a ray of light from the rising sun reflecting red fire off the hilt.

"What say we draw a little ink from you, Diamond. Time to rock and roll."

Sadie's eyes became cold, flashing like icy blue fire. "Belial, you won't put one finger on my son. You won't draw one drop o' blood."

Amused, Nick answered back. "And why is that, slut?"

"'Cause he still wasn't responsible for my death. I been waitin' to see what you had up yo' sleeve." Nick was skeptical, but listening hard. "I let myself bleed out in that alley. I wasn't fit to live. If I'd a stayed where I was, I woulda got to the Med in time to live. 'Cause the po-lice found my man and thought I done it. Two hours later they found me … lyin' in that filthy alley. Nearly bled out. They asked me, but I told them nuthin'. I never made it to the Med." Sadie paused. "You lose, Devil. Git you gone from here an' leave my son alone."

The new contract crumbled to ashes in my hand.

Nick was a practical demon and knew when he was licked.

"I'm rarely outfoxed, only a handful of times in twenty millennia. And I get jacked by a two-bit dead hooker and a guitar-slinging fool." Nick shook his head in wonderment. His red eyes flashed fire at me. "You're one of the lucky ones, boy. You actually got a second chance. Don't fuck it up, or you'll see me again."

Ignoring the apparition of my mother, Nick dissipated in a flash of smoke, flame and raucous laughter. "Don't take any wooden nickels, Kidd." And then he was gone.

I turned back to the apparition. "What happens now … Mama?"

Sadie began to fade, but a real mother's loving smile lingered to the last.

"You live life the best way you can, Son. You hear me?" And then she was gone.

I lay down on the bed, cradling Lil. Was this all a dream, or had it really happened?

My ribs throbbed. And while it hurt, the pain served to remind me that I'd received a gift. If only in my heart.

I had finally come home.

15 Run Don't Run
Mary Saums

THE REPLAY'S ALWAYS THE SAME. An old man, skinny dude, hugs the corner of a building ahead. He steps from darkness into the low light of a closed store's window. He carries a brown bag. His tweed hat and suit jacket shine from wear. His stiff shuffle does not hurry, does not lag.

His eyes lie. They're good at it. At his age, it comes natural. They stare straight ahead, do not blink. They pretend not to see me, that everything is fine, that there's no hurry, that he sees nothing. I understood this part but not the whole lie, hidden well by a master but so obvious to me now.

Traffic stills in the memory of it as his soft footsteps fade in the distance behind me. A long beat of thicker quiet hangs in the night, a hesitation, just before a click, ahead and to my left. I see an arm in slow motion coming out straight from behind a car, the swivel to point and squeeze, the barrel flash, the hit like a grizzly knocking me down and sitting on my chest, suffocating, pressing me into asphalt like it was water, great claws ripping into my heart, drowning me, pushing a lost memory to the surface. Then cold, then darkness. I thought I was gone.

I came back gradually to lights and sounds. Not the light of heaven or songs of angels welcoming me to my reward. Painful fluorescents overhead stung my eyes. Sirens and ambulance shrieks. Yelling, car horns, garbage trucks. Chicago.

Louder and closer was the fool yammering of my partner, Detective George Ehrman, talking about the good food in the cafeteria, for Christ sakes, about how he'd been at the hospital every minute he wasn't on duty. At this, my eyes adjusted enough to see that the nurse standing on the other side of my bed was white. She came into focus as she leaned closer. Young, pretty. Her expression, eyes widening, lips tightening with patience, confirmed what George said, that he'd been a constant annoyance.

My mouth must have twitched. She smiled back at me and said, "You're at Saint Joseph, Mr. Crosby. You're going to be fine. Rest."

Even then, as early as that, the plan was in my head. Every word George spoke, going on about how lucky I was, how the bullet grazed a rib, nothing else, about the time he got shot and his life passed before his eyes. All of it made things clearer, more sure in my mind.

"Like a reel of film," he said. "Everybody I ever knew, special days, days when nothing happened, all 3-D and in color, the whole thing. You know the weird part? This feeling, like God was telling me everything was all right. No fire and brimstone over not going to confession. I'd had a good life. No regrets. I was ready to go. Anything like that happen to you?"

I managed to croak out a few words. "No, man. Nothing like that."

He talked nonstop. I pushed my thoughts away for later. I convinced him to go home, that I was fine.

The hospital noises in the hall became more familiar and more hushed. I slept hard and woke up in the dark. The nurse came in to change the IV bag. Then I was left alone in the quiet to consider.

When I thought I was about to die, there was no movie. No feeling that it was all good, that I could go into the great beyond happy. George had no regrets. Regrets were about all I had. They hit me as I lay in that hospital bed like a second bullet. The force slapped my insides awake, like my soul had been in hibernation. I saw the whole of my life in one strange scene from thirteen years earlier.

I was eighteen, just out of high school, with a bus ticket out of Mississippi in my pocket. I had cousins living in Chicago who said they could get me a job and I could stay with them until I was on my feet. I told my father the night before I was going to leave. He didn't have much to say.

The next morning before I went to the station, I walked down to the riverbank to tell him good-bye. He hung out there every day with a bunch of other old sots who pretended to fish. I stood next to him a while, neither of us saying anything, just watching the corks bob in the water, before he told his buddies.

"My boy here is leaving," he said. He put his hand on my shoulder. A couple of the fishermen turned and said, "That right?" and, "Whereabouts you going?"

I said, "Chicago," and while some made friendly comments, one old man turned toward me in his ratty lawn chair and fixed me with a hard stare.

"Lots of dust up there. Lots of wind. And a whole lotta concrete." He moved his fishing pole to his left hand and reached down with his right. His fingers dug into the ground and came up with a ball of red and black sod. "It's a cold, cold place." He looked up and held his hand out toward me. "This is who you are, young son. Don't forget."

Crazy old drunk, I thought. And I did forget. The city's excitement pulled me in from the minute I stepped off the bus.

Two years later, I was a rookie in the police department. Got married but it didn't last. I loved my job. Thought it would be enough. It wasn't. Earlier brushes with death in the line of duty had not deterred me. This time, I realized I was not immortal. Even my love of the city was about gone. As I lay in the hospital, that bony fist of dirt, the pungent smell of fish and the river and the past kept rising up before me.

The day I was released from the hospital, George waited outside the exit doors when the attendant rolled my wheelchair to the curb. A good breeze from the lake pushed us along to his car. Jackhammers in the parking lot made it hard to hear each other. We drove past a construction site where the high keen of cutting metal sliced through the air. I looked up to rusted trestles. The El screeched by me one last time.

A DIFFERENT METAL-ON-METAL SCRATCHING twanged in the breeze and blew into my car on the way to the river. It was the healing kind, a sweet sound that made me grin as I drove through the countryside. It moved and slid around, sorrowful and jubilant, went through my chest and wrapped around me like it was part of the sunlight, or maybe the midday heat was making it wave up out of the fields before it floated down and out over the Pearl River.

I'd settled into small town life again. I took a sandwich every day for lunch and drove out past Jester Dupree's land to hear him playing slide on one of his guitars he made from scraps. Neither he nor his house could be seen from the main road. It made no difference. His improvisations carried for miles here where the terrain was flat. The locals could picture him easily. Didn't need to see him to know he was sitting under his tree, didn't need to see the big hands, gnarled from old age and six or seven decades of farm work, that somehow became young again when he played.

That particular day, six years after I left Chicago, he wasn't in top form. He kept starting and stopping and missing notes. The tunes sounded like he was aggravated with himself or that his mind was on something else. Didn't matter to me. His playing eased the job I had to do. After I had my lunch, I'd be on my way down the road to serve a warrant.

I'd joined the sheriff's department when I came back to Mississippi, still in Allmon County where I was raised. Now I lived in Solley, the county seat. A few years later when the old sheriff died, I filled in and then got the job in the next election.

When the music stopped, I sat a little longer at the picnic table in the shade. I picked up my trash, got in the patrol car and drove east about a mile to a rental house on the water.

I wasn't looking forward to confronting the man I came to see. As much as I hated the thought, Terrell Long was here in Mississippi because of me.

I knew Terrell in Chicago. Not friends. I busted him for peddling dope a dozen or more times from a juvvy on up. He was the kind of kid who lied every time he opened his mouth. Was known to cheat people who helped him. Fought and argued for no reason.

In spite of these things, Terrell had a certain charm that made me want to believe he had potential. He was still a screw-up, still had a mean streak when he got drunk, but he was one who might make something of himself one day, legally, if he could just get his shit together and grow up.

I hadn't given him a thought in years when he showed up in Solley at my office. There he was, in the middle of August, wearing a yellow polyester shirt and yellow plaid pants and sweating like a hog. I watched him through the window, stretching out of the car, looking as out of place as an alien from Mars. He appraised the surrounding buildings with a disapproving eye before doing a city strut down the sidewalk and into the building.

He leaned into the frame of my office door, fanned himself with a thin-brimmed summer hat, smiling like he'd hit the lottery.

"Well, well. Sheriff. How bout that." He was a man now, probably twenty-seven if I figured right, but still looked like an undernourished kid.

"Terrell. You're a long way from home."

"On vacation. Actually, I'm on my way to New Orleans. Got a new place down there. Thought I'd take a side trip to see your domain." He looked around the walls, nodding. "Nice. Looks like you're staying. Hard to believe."

"How did you know I was here?"

"Oh, you know me. I always keep up with people."

We walked outside together. He wiped a handkerchief across his brow and put his hat on. He said he had gone straight. I didn't ask for specifics. I tried to ignore the hint of worry in the back of my mind. I wished him luck.

When I saw him walking downtown two days later, I knew he hadn't changed. Can't say I was altogether surprised. He said he liked it here, enough to maybe buy a place nearby. Said he decided to stay in town a while to check things out.

The next day, I got a phone call from my ex-partner, George, in Chicago.

"Let me guess," I said before he told me his reason for calling. "Terrell Long is in trouble and you think he might be headed my way."

A pause. "You've seen him."

"Yep."

"It's worse than that. He's playing Little Eddie."

I spun my chair around, put my legs up on the desk, leaned back and rubbed my eyes. Little Eddie Burton, son of Big Eddie and heir to his drug, numbers and prostitution empire, got his MBA and joined the family business, one that grew considerably as Little Eddie was given more control. This wasn't totally due to his business skills. He showed early talent in areas usually reserved for the old man's lieutenants. He got a quick reputation for being as ruthless and intimidating as the best of them. He was linked to a dozen or more murders in the Chicago area. We never got a conviction on him. Too slick.

I had a hard time believing George. "How is this possible? Terrell's never been anything but small-time."

"All I know for sure," George said, "is Little Eddie's pissed enough to come for Terrell himself. The word inside is that he and two of his goons left this morning. They know he's there. So be careful, my friend."

"Yeah. Thanks, George."

After I hung up, I wished I had asked how they knew he was in town. Had Terrell called Little Eddie from here? More likely, Terrell got drunk and talked too much about his plans before he left.

I tried to warn him. I drove out to the rental house where he was staying. He wasn't there. I went back after work, and again around nine that night. I stopped in at the local clubs and asked around.

When he wasn't at Brace's, the last one, I thought, hoped he'd left town already. He might be in New Orleans by now. With any luck, Little Eddie and his boys might skip Solley altogether. I sat at the bar and ordered a beer.

"That's right. Sit down and relax," Charlie Brace said. "They're gonna start the next set in a minute." Charlie always hired good musicians on the weekends. He used to be a band-leader himself in the old days, booking gigs and playing bass in jazz and blues bands around the South. He sure had some stories.

He told me a little about the band there that night, pointed to the stage and said, "You see the drummer? His great-grand-daddy gave me my first job. He was a strange bird. Always had the best working for him though. Said he never hired a man just because he was a good player, but he had to walk right, too. Wouldn't decide on him until after the audition and had time to watch him walk away. It's true. I saw him do it many a time."

"You mean, like, to see if they were drunks?"

Charlie shook his head. "I don't think so. He never would say what he was looking for. Just said he could see who they were. He was a smart guy. Had big crowds everywhere we went. Smart, but a little strange. Eccentric, I guess you'd say."

I stayed until the band finished their last number. Early next morning, I had a meeting at the courthouse and didn't get back to my office until about ten o'clock. A woman was inside waiting on me. She had a black eye and bruises on her arms. She filed a report claiming Terrell Long was the man who hit her. I made a few calls before getting the warrant, but I believed her. This was the business I dreaded, what brought me out past Jester's land that day, to bring Terrell to jail.

This time, his car was parked in the drive. I glanced inside it, saw nothing unusual, on the way to the porch. The screen door was closed but the wooden one stood open. Through the screen, I saw an overturned chair in the front room.

I knocked and called his name. Nothing. I stepped inside, saw a broken vase on the floor, walked through, checking rooms, all trashed. In the kitchen, red splatters, surely blood, dotted the sink and counter.

I went out the back door, circled and came back to his car. That's when I noticed the tracks of a heavier, wider vehicle. It pulled in and backed out after Terrell came home. From over the fields, I heard Jester's guitar again, the tune moving in a disjointed raggedy way, like he was distracted again.

Or somebody was with him.

Jester had seen a lot in his years but he was still a shy man. People made him nervous. He could play at Brace's with the other old-timers, but that was because he got lost in their company and what they played. One-on-one, he messed up.

I ran to my vehicle and got the dispatcher on the line as I drove. A few minutes later, I turned onto the dirt drive to Jester's house. About a half-mile up, I passed a windbreak of a double row of pines set into an upward slope. Just beyond that, his house came into view. My heart sank upon seeing a new four-wheel drive SUV, parked in the grass and pointed outward toward the main road, as if for a quick getaway.

The one-story farmhouse had a tin roof and wide front porch. Makeshift tables scattered around the side yard held all sorts of machine parts, with lawn mowers and other household appliances in various states of repair. Behind them, the barn and sheds looked as weathered as if they'd stood there a hundred years.

Jester looked about that old himself. He wore overalls and a t-shirt like he always did. He sat in a cane-back chair in his usual spot, in the front yard under an oak that gave a wide ring of shade. Next to him, he'd set up a work table full of small tools, wire and bits of metal. A bucket of ice, a spit can and a smooth-coated mutt sat nearby on the ground. A primitive replica of a National guitar leaned against the table.

It was a work of art. Not just the homemade guitar, the whole picture. The lines of history in Jester's face alone told their own story. The surroundings told another, of contrasts between the peace of an old man and his home and the threat leaning toward him, a well-groomed man in fine clothes, smiling, all innocence. I watched him as I approached, watched him set the wire cutters he held down on the table and then turn his palms upward as if he had nothing to hide.

"Afternoon, Sheriff," Jester said. I crossed to him, shook his hand. Little Eddie either didn't recognize me or pretended he didn't. His smile dimmed a fraction when I held my hand out to him as well, but he took it. Two broad-backed henchmen walked toward us from the side yard. They looked like feds out of their element, wearing jackets on a hot day out in the sticks of Mississippi. After a look from their boss, they smiled like gargoyles and stepped farther away from the shorter, slimmer guy with a bloodied lip who walked between them.

"Sorry to interrupt while you have company," I said.

"They're not company," Jester said. "Strangers. Real estate people."

Little Eddie and his gargoyles grinned wider.

"I didn't realize you were thinking about selling," I said. Through this exchange, Terrell's expression brightened more and more. He knew I knew Little Eddie. Which made me Terrell's savior. From what mess he'd made, I wasn't certain, but I could make a fair guess.

"I'm not. They just think they can outfox an old man and take his land for nothing like I ain't got any sense."

"Whoa, now, Mr. Dupree," Little Eddie said. "That is not the case. I'm here to do the opposite. I like your place for myself, not for resale or making money off you. I got plenty of money. What I want is for you to afford to live wherever you want in luxury. An old brother such as yourself deserves that after all you've been through. Think about it. If you could live anywhere, anywhere at all, where would you go?"

Jester looked up into the oak branches. "I used to want to live in the mountains. There was a TV show about Colorado. I went out there. It was beautiful, in its own way. I rode all over. But it was empty. Like a shell. Pretty colors. No soul. My place suits me better. Good fishing right here. Ain't that right, Sheriff?" He picked up his guitar again and started plinking around.

"Pretty good," I said.

Little Eddie tried another tack. "Some people go around the country to fish, to find the best spots. You could have a fine new home near one of them with all new furniture and fancy appliances, and still have enough to travel. Wouldn't you like that?"

Jester didn't look up from his playing when he spoke. "Why don't you buy that place with fancy stuff for yourself instead of here if it's so much better?"

Little Eddie laughed and shook his head while he tried to think of an answer. "I guess I'm looking for some soul, too. All I'm asking is that you think about it."

We turned at the sound of a car coming up the drive. One of my deputies.

"Folks," I said, "everything's okay. Mr. Dupree, I stopped by to see if you'd seen Mr. Long here." I took out my warrant and waved it at Terrell. I motioned for him to walk toward me. "I need him to come down to the station to ask him some questions."

Terrell came forward with an unsteady gait, like he'd hurt his legs, but smiled as if nothing in the world was wrong. Little Eddie's smile disappeared. His eyes moved, assessing the yard, as he considered his next move. Jester rose slowly from his chair.

"Sheriff, while you're at it, these boys need arresting, too, all of them, now that you got help." He said it in a calm way. His voice cracked only once. He stood as straight as his crooked frame allowed. "I lied a while ago. This one here," he said with a nod at Little Eddie, "said they'd hurt me if I didn't sell. They been beating up that young man. He's as bad as the rest. They been talking mean and nasty, talking about how they know where my granddaughter lives, like they'll hurt her if I don't sell them my place here. They think I don't know why. They want to set up a drug stop, come in with boats and such at my cove. That young one wants to run it for them. Said they'd cut off my fingers where I couldn't play no more if I didn't do what they want." His voice cracked again as he rubbed his hands, looked at the table where the wire cutters lay.

A hush fell over the yard. Seconds passed with only the sound of the deputy car coming closer. Jester had spoken too soon.

Terrell changed. Sweat beaded on his face. His eyes looked wild, like he was on the verge of panic.

Little Eddie faked dismay, walked backward toward his men, called the old man crazy. Jester stepped away from the tree, closer to him. His dog rose and followed, not blinking, not taking his eyes off Little Eddie. The car stopped. The deputy got out, shut the door and walked toward us.

It was not Jester's fault. He lived in his own world, came from a place and a time when no bad guy would dare harm an officer of the law. I doubt it ever crossed his mind that these men would do anything other than what I instructed them to do. But even down here, Little Eddie and his boys were still in their own world, one with no such rules. The family business and keeping it healthy rated higher than the lives of a two-bit hustler and a few hicks, even hicks wearing badges.

Terrell stole a look behind him just as Little Eddie whispered an order. His goons reached under their jackets, came out with guns. One turned about face and dropped the deputy with one shot.

The other aimed at me and fired as Terrell rushed me from the side. We both went to the ground, my bullet in his back.

Another shot rang out and then a short barrage from two, maybe three guns as I rolled Terrell off me. The first shot had missed Jester due to the dog's intervention. That bullet and the rest went into the dog.

I pulled my sidearm and yelled, "Drop 'em now."

They didn't hear me. At the same time, Jester screamed and threw himself, arms out, toward the nearest gunman. The other one turned my way, raised to shoot, but I got him first, a split second before his friend shot Jester between the eyes. I yelled again and shot the killer, saw a movement to my right, swiveled and had no time to think. Little Eddie's arm was extended, gun pointed at me. I shot him in the belly. He groaned and crumpled.

He died in the hospital. The others didn't get that far.

It takes forever for things like this to be over, but we got through it. Other than myself, the only survivor was the deputy. He sells insurance now. Everybody else went back to Chicago in boxes.

A low-ranking punk in Little Eddie's organization testified that Terrell worked on small jobs for them. An opportunity to steal over seven hundred thousand dollars from a drug transaction accidentally came Terrell's way and he took it. He ran, but thought better of it once he got to Solley. Like Jester said, he got the idea of setting up his own kingdom there by the river. He thought he could talk Little Eddie into moving him into upper management. He didn't know Little Eddie like I did.

Jester and the way he played can't ever be replaced. It was himself that he pressed out in twangs and steel bends, a shy man with sad stories, using the only language that goes straight from heart to heart. The sound was like an extra dimension over the land and riverbanks, a part of the scenery. I still hear it faintly, and it makes me wonder if what he played still echoes off the trees and plowed fields and laps in at the water's edge again and again, or if the whisper of it has always been here, and that Jester only magnified it.

I think of these things now as I watch the measured walk of folks in this town, something I never noticed before. Usually it's the older people, men and women, who move to a blues soundtrack. They know the horrors of the world but they keep on moving through it.

That old skinny dude in Chicago, the night I got shot, he felt a similar thing. The clamor of city life, bouncing off concrete and pummeling in the wind, gave him a different groove in his walk, harder and more stiff than those of us down here. That's the

Chicago style. Harsher tones, a faster clip on top of the beat. Less give, less soul.

He saw what was fixing to happen to me that night. His city survivor instincts kicked in automatically and though he gave no sign, I knew from his eyes that the calm he displayed was a lie. Inside, he felt the push and the pull, the need to hurry away from trouble, the equal need to stay slow, not draw attention, to delay what trouble might be ahead.

It comes natural after a while, always will, so long as the world is looking for a man to hurt or to blame, to shoot in the back if he runs, to knife up close if he stays. All we can do is keep going, pour out the sorrow in measures, by the river, in the fields, on the street, in dark clubs; not too fast, not too slow.

16 The Sugar Cure
Carolyn Haines

THEY SAY THE MISSISSIPPI HEAT IN AUGUST is the
match that lights the fuse of violent men. Used to be, when I was
young, my mother would recline on her bed, naked, dribbling
cold water over herself. She said such heat made a woman turn to
the Devil. She'd drip a rag in a bowl of ice water, hold it over herself, and squeeze, laughing at the chill bumps that danced across
her pale skin.

"Lord, Nilla, it's a shame to sweat like this with no pleasure
attached."

Pleasure was the quest for my mama. She set quite a store by
having it. And she taught me the hard coin it could earn. I guess
you could say my mama educated me in the lessons of survival.
That's what she sent me out the door with when I married Dale
Walters and became the wife of a captain at Parchman State Penitentiary.

It was a hot mid-August day and the sun had cleared the end
of the long, empty horizon when I walked through the dew-
soaked grass to the small barn. Dale had eaten his breakfast and left
for work. Rusty Bellow, one of the inmate trustees, was cleaning

up the kitchen, and I was free to ride. Free. An interesting word in the world where I lived.

One of the inmates would have groomed and saddled for me, but I liked doing it myself. Running the brush over Piper's white-speckled coat, I tried to tamp down the panic. I was surrounded by men, many of whom had acted either in stupidity or desperation—or perhaps been in the wrong place at the wrong time. Now they hoed the cotton or chopped the trees, sweating in the state-owned fields to atone for their crimes, perceived or real.

Piper snuffled and pushed against my shoulder as I put the saddle on her back. "Easy there," I whispered. "We'll get goin' soon enough."

After I mounted, we walked out of the barnyard and down the dirt road that ran straight and true as a plumb line. I never left in a hurry, never wanted anyone to suspect my desperate need to run as hard as I could. I'd taken up riding after I married Dale. Looking back at the house, freshly painted white with zinnias and marigolds blooming around the front porch, I felt a stab of panic. Though it had been rat infested when I moved in, it was the finest house I'd ever lived in. Not nearly as big or lavish as the warden's house, but the hardwood floors were waxed to a high gloss. The porches were tightly screened and safe from the hordes of mosquitoes, so that at night I could slip from bed when I couldn't breathe. I'd sit in an old rocker and listen to the moths beating against the screen mesh. Sometimes I thought it was my heart trying to break out of my chest.

Today the air was hot and heavy. Once the house was behind us, I let Piper gallop. On either side of us the fields stretched out forever, green and profitable. This was rich man's land, fertile, bathed by the Mississippi River before the levees were built to hold back the floodwaters.

Far in the distance I saw a work crew wearing the black and white ring-arounds tending the cotton. The long line, maybe a hundred men, labored over the land like single-minded insects. The men chopped in unison, backs bent to the hoe. A captain on horse-back, shotgun resting on the pommel of his saddle, watched with the help of several trustee shooters—convicts given guns and the job of guarding other prisoners. It was a system with a lot of flaws.

I turned west, headed to the fields behind Camp Nine, won-dering if the men dreamed of escape. There weren't fences at Parchman. Wire wasn't needed to keep a prisoner inside. The long stretches of open land left no place to hide.

The old oak that was being chopped down held an attach-ment for me. Last winter I'd ridden there often, letting Piper graze beneath the branches while I perched on a limb, sometimes read-ing, sometimes dreaming of any life but the one I had. When Dale told me the tree was going to be removed, I wondered if it was because I'd shown some partiality to it. But that wasn't a ques-tion I could ask, and if I did, there would be no answer.

When I could see the branches reaching into the sky on the flat horizon, I heard the work crew, axes biting into that old oak tree that had been the only shade in the back field near Camp Nine. The tree was going down, another few rows of cotton going in. It was the way of the Farm, as the state prison was known. Amos Sample called the beat, helping the men work in unison.

The convicts' axes rang in the heat. Chomp. "No more, my Lord." Chomp. "No more, my Lord." Chomp. "Lord, I'll never turn back no more." Chomp.

Amos Sample had a clear baritone. I'd heard talk about him, and though I'd convinced myself that my mare needed a gallop, it was really an excuse to find this Amos Sample and take a look. He was a bluesman, a Negro with some education and a taste for fine things. To hear my husband tell it, Amos Sample was a man who'd gotten above himself, which was the thing that got him put in Parchman in the first place.

Before I married, I'd bought one of his records. The man had a voice that walked right down my body to the place I didn't let no one touch. Now I was fixin' to see him. I'd heard he was six foot five and fit. That it had taken five deputies with weighted blackjacks to bring him down, and he'd seriously injured two of them. Within the week he was tried, sentenced, and put on the farm for twenty years.

There was other talk about Amos Sample. Whispers that faded away whenever I entered the room. I caught the gist of them, though. While I worked to make Dale think I was as thick and bland as the white gravy he sopped his biscuits in, I knew things.

Some of the talk involved women, of course. The other, though, was what interested me. Amos Sample walked on the dark side, or that was the gossip, and it had planted a seed inside my head that was nudgin' into life.

I slowed Piper while I tried to see which captain was workin' the crew. With some, I could draw closer. Others were trouble I didn't care to court. Being pleasant to some of the men resulted in false stories to Dale. I'd learned to keep a good distance between the prison employees and myself.

Piper's ears moved forward and back, listening to the men and reading my mood. We ambled down the road, dust rising from her hooves. She seemed to walk in rhythm to the singing. Pic Davison was the captain in charge, and I took a breath. Pic minded his own business and didn't feel a need to curry favor with Dale by making up tales about me. I let Piper continue forward until we drew abreast of him as he sat his horse, gun angled to the ground.

"Mornin', Mrs. Walters."

"Mornin' to you, Pic." I focused on the tree. Bits of wood flew from the axes as the men worked. In less than an hour the tree would be down. The urge to cry nearly overcame me, but I beat it back. Amos Sample worked the ax as he sang out the beat.

"Sad to see something that grand die." Pic's words reflected my thinking.

"Yes, it is." My opinion on such things, I'd learned, was like a gnat in my husband's eye.

"You'd best enjoy your ride before the sun gets up much higher." Pic glanced at me and I looked away from the men working. "August at noon ain't kind to no one."

"Yes, I thought I'd ride down toward that little branch then head home to make some lunch for Dale."

"He tells us what a good cook you are. Says he won't have no trustees cookin' when you make everything just the way he likes it."

I nodded. "That's my job, now isn't it?" I closed my legs on Piper's side and she walked forward. "Have a good day, Pic."

"It won't be a good day til November when this heat breaks."

I didn't answer as I rode past the tree. Up close, I could see that it shuddered with each blow of the axes. Amos Sample caught my eye but he never missed a word or a lick with his ax. But he'd seen me, and I'd seen him. It was a start.

THE SUMMER HEAT finally passed off. Standing at the open kitchen window I washed my cup and saucer and enjoyed the cool air. Dale sat at the kitchen table finishing the breakfast I'd cooked. I blocked out the sounds of his eating and focused on the view out the window. I could see the barn and my horse, with her head out of her stall waiting for me. She had a little buck in her as the mornings came in brisk, and I saw the first frost covered the fields, a sure sign it was hog killin' weather.

My first year on The Farm, Dale volunteered me to help make the cures for the pork. One was a vinegar brine and the other was a sugar cure, Dale's favorite. After that slaughter day with the hogs squealin' and screamin', I can't eat pork and the smell of cookin' sugar makes me sick. It didn't stop Dale, who gobbled down a quarter pound of bacon at each sittin'. He said there was no help for it, the first cold snap was the time of year when pigs died.

It was also the season when my plan took root and began to sprout.

"Nilla, I'm sending some of the boys over this morning. Buster's gonna cook a couple of hogs. You'll do the side dishes. Cotton's in and we're gonna have a little shindig."

"Yes, Dale." Obedience lingered in the curve of my lips.

"Tell Luther where to set up the tables. Around back, near where Buster digs the pit. Get Luleen to bring six or seven wash-tubs from the laundry. Warden said I could use what I needed." He grinned. "Says he and the missus are stoppin' by. I'm gonna make a run into town, get some beer to put on ice."

I nodded. In the two years of my marriage, I'd learned to let Dale tell me how he wanted things done. Didn't matter that I'd suggested the party and nourished the thought for the past eight weeks. Next he'd bring up the entertainment.

"Some of the boys gone play and sing." He caught my hand as I walked by and pulled me roughly into his lap. "You think you might dance with me to some Ne-gra music?"

I hated the way he pronounced Ne-gra, like the high class white folks. I kissed him full on the lips. "I'd dance to seventy-six trombones if you asked me, Dale."

He frowned. "Where do you get the stuff you come up with, Nilla? Maybe you ought to keep outta them books or turn off that radio you love."

Before that idea took root in his head, I kissed him again, wig-gling a little on his lap. For all intents and purposes, my mama sold me to Dale, but she didn't send me out without some weapons. At eighteen, I could look like a vixen or a child. What-ever it took to keep Dale on the smile side of life.

He pushed me off his lap and stood. "I told Luleen to come

on over. I want these floors scrubbed to a shine. They bringin'
some a them red-like mums for the flowerbeds. Festive. That's
what I want. See to it."

"I'll take care of it."

"Stay here and be sure they work. You know if you turn your
back, they'll—"

"I'll make sure. I know exactly how you taught me."

He patted my ass as I walked by. "Might pick out a dress for
you in town."

"Thank you, Dale. You're so good to me."

He scooted back from the table, belched, and then he was
gone to devil the inmates who shared my prison.

Luleen showed up fifteen minutes later, and I helped her unload the galvanized washtubs that weighed at least twenty pounds
each. We set them up near the place Dale had marked off for the
two pits Buster would dig. He'd burn oak logs down to a bed of
hot coals. The hogs would roast for the whole next day til they
could be pulled from the bone with the gentlest touch.

"What got Mr. Dale in a mood for a party?" Luleen asked as
she took her bucket of hot sudsy water and a brush and settled
onto her knees in the hallway.

"He took a notion. I think it was that bluesman, Amos somethin'. Dale's been talkin' about him since he came here. Says he's
the best caller he's ever seen. Dale wants to hear him sing, I
guess." My face fell into innocence. "I hear the church doors slam
shut whenever Amos Sample walks by. They say he consorts with
the Devil."

Luleen cut me a look, and for a minute I thought she'd caught
on to my manipulation. "Mr. Dale never struck me as someone
who'd like Ne-gra music." She said the word like Dale did.

"Dale's a mystery to me. He seems truly caught up in that
bluesman's reputation. Must be he's just tryin' to put a chill in
me on dark nights, but he says he's seen a tall stranger standin'

outside the camp where Amos Samples is. Says the man has a long butcher knife that catches the moonlight. When they go out to check, ain't no one there. No footprints or nothin'."

She dropped her brush in the bucket of water. "Mr. Dale's not tellin' you that kind of foolishness. Where you hearin' that talk?"

Fighting the panic, I tried for nonchalance. "I don't recall who told me."

"Talk like that gone get someone kilt." She went to work, and I went to the kitchen window to watch Buster and the three men with him begin to set up for the party. There was work for me to do, but I allowed myself a moment to gather my nerve and imagine what would come next.

FULL MOON. Harvest moon. The light gilded the cotton fields, softening the thousands of acres into a strange beauty that belied the harshness of the harvest. The white bolls were picked and gone, leaving the dead plants, which would be chopped under in a matter of days.

Parchman prison stretched out in all directions, a place where anything except justice could take root and grow.

Dale lit some torches and stuck them around to illuminate the backyard. The smell of cooking meat permeated everything, a sickly sweet odor. Dale shared a family resemblance with the two hogs. Small eyes, flat nose. All he needed was an apple.

He'd been drinkin' since noon, when he'd come to supervise Buster as he basted the hogs. Dale wouldn't hit Buster because he worked in the big house for the warden. He was a favorite of Warden and Mrs. Langford. What Buster didn't catch, I would get later. That was the way it fell out with Dale. Somebody had a good time, then somebody paid.

I'd made up my mind it wasn't going to be me.

Wearing the new yellow dress Dale bought me, I made sure the tea was in good supply. While the men drank beer and whiskey, it wasn't seemly for the women. I'd made tea for us, ice cold and sweet with fresh lemons floating. My mama used to let me sip her whiskey, but Dale put a stop to that. No man wanted a woman with a vice. Wasn't enough room in most marriages for two partners with that kind of trouble.

I put the last garnishes on the big pan of potato salad I'd made just the way Dale liked it. Lots of mustard and tiny cubes of bread and butter pickles. The kitchen was unbearably stuffy, and I wiped the sweat from my brow on my arm. My hair had been set in pale blond ringlets, the way Dale liked it, but the kitchen heat had worked me over even before the first guest arrived. I carried the pan out to the picnic table and the cooler temperatures of the yard.

As I took a breather, the guests began to arrive. Most everyone worked at Parchman; some lived on the grounds like me and Dale. Others were day workers or somehow connected with the buying and selling of the many goods produced on the prison grounds. Parchman was a state institution that turned a profit.

"I like that dress." Dale came up behind me. His hands circled my bare arms and squeezed, hard. Something about bruises made him happy.

"Thank you, Dale." I'd learned quickly the important lines for the role I played—thank you, yes, yes and thank you. The dress was awful. The bright yellow made my white skin look sallow and my hair garish.

The band struck up then. Mizelle moved the bottle neck along the guitar strings, makin' a guttural sound that made me close my eyes. Dale lost his focus on me and walked up to the temporary stage he'd had built. "Don't play none a that dirty music," he told Mizelle. "There are ladies here."

"Yes sir, Mr. Dale." Mizelle knew his role, too. He was doing hard time for trespassing.

"Get on with it. Play somethin' frisky. My wife wants to dance."

Amos Sample watched the exchange, but his gaze drifted to me. I looked back, using everything in my power to tell him what I needed him to know.

Still looking at me, he started to sing. A popular war tune. Sweet and sentimental. Not what I'd expected at all. Dale grabbed my wrist and pulled me to the dance floor. He crushed me against him and let his hands wander along my waist and down on my ass. I tried not to stiffen, but I saw Betty Havard, another wife, bite her lip as she watched. She knew where this night was headed, or at least she thought she did.

"You need to wear long sleeves when you ride that horse," Dale said as he danced me close. "I don't want your arms all splotched with sun."

"Yes, Dale. I'll do that."

"And gloves."

"Yes, Dale." He was sweating hard, and the feel of it, pressed into my skin, made me want to scream.

"That Ne-gra bluesman is watchin' you." His thumb dug into the small of my back with such force that I lost my footing. Only his grip held me up.

"I've heard things about that man." My voice was breathy because of the pain he inflicted. "I've heard he traffics with a tall black man carrying a sharp knife." He lessened the pressure of his thumb and I tightened my grip around his neck. "Don't let him look at me."

"Lookin' at you could come at a high price for him."

I kissed his neck. "Who cares about a Ne-gra convict. He'll spend the rest of his days choppin' and waitin' to die, and you won't let nothin' bad happen to me."

Dale's chest rumbled with a laugh. "You sound like you was born to the role of bein' my wife."

"My mama always said I was a quick learner. And you taught me good." I caught his ear lobe in my teeth but applied no pressure. Over Dale's shoulder, I made eye contact with Amos Sample. Help me. I let him read it plain on my face.

Amos Sample broke into a frisky number that allowed me to escape Dale's embrace and dance on my own. Others joined us, crowding to get up and move to the raw power of Amos Sample's voice. I never looked at him again, but I could feel him lookin' at me, calculatin' what it might be that I wanted from him.

Toward the end, Amos held the audience transfixed. Too tired or too drunk to dance more, Dale had fallen into a chair, his legs sprawled wide and spittle strung between his lips. My feet throbbed. Dale had stomped all over them, demonstrating his oafishness on the dance floor, again and again.

"Let me help you clean up," Betty offered. Together we carried in the leftovers. Luleen stacked a tray with meat, potato salad, beans, rolls and some pies. I wanted the prisoners to eat, and Dale wouldn't let them in front of the guests. They'd take the food back with them and Dale would never know.

I walked out with the tray and handed it to the guard who rode in the back of the truck to watch the prisoners. Amos Sample sat on the tailgate.

"Luleen made that sweet potato pie special for the singer," I whispered to the guard. "She's got a crush, I think." I thought my knees might buckle, but I locked them and stood my ground.

He took the tray, looking it over in the moonlight. He didn't say anything as the truck pulled out of the yard.

Once the prisoners were gone, I sent Luleen on her way. Dale had fallen asleep in the chair. I stood at the kitchen window, looking out at him.

"Can you get him in?" Betty asked.

Anyway I went about it, I was going to get hurt. I could take it with or without an audience. "I can manage."

She patted my back and went to find her husband, Verl. He'd wandered down to the barn with Pic and a couple of other prison employees. I went outside, gathered up the rest of the party detritus and doused the torches. The coals in the fire pits smoldered red beneath a thick coat of ash, but they were safely contained. Once my eyes adjusted to the darkness, I walked over to Dale. It was now or never. I let myself see what I had to.

In the thin moonlight, something moved at the edge of the cotton field. The figure was darker than night, more shadow than real, except for the glint of moonlight on a long silver blade.

My scream cut the silence, shrill and blood-curdling. I shook Dale, hard, screaming for all I was worth. "Get up! Get Up! There's a man with a knife!"

Verl, Pic and two other men came running from the barn with Betty in tow. Dale fell to the ground, cursing me.

"Mrs. Walters, what is it?" Pic caught my shoulders, trying to grasp the meaning of my terrified screams.

"I saw a man in the field," I managed. "He had a knife. He was watchin' me and Dale."

Pic and two others ran toward the field, calling to each other as they fanned out, searching. Verl helped Dale to his feet.

"Crazy bitch!" Dale's fist connected with my cheek and I spun backward into a table.

"Stop it!" Verl grabbed Dale from behind. The two men tumbled to the ground, scuffling. Dale was no match for Verl, who was far more sober. Betty grabbed a pitcher of iced tea and dumped it on Dale's head. He came up sputtering and cursing her until Verl slugged him hard enough to stun him.

"Jesus," Betty said.

Pic and the other two men returned from the cotton field. "I didn't see anyone," he said. "Tomorrow I'll come and check for tracks."

"Thank you, Pic." I didn't look at anyone. My face throbbed.

"Let's get 'im in the house," Verl said.

They lifted Dale and half dragged him inside, his boots scarring the waxed polish of the floor. Without asking, they put him on the sofa.

"You want to come home with us?" Betty asked. "It ain't safe out here alone with some man watchin' your place."

We both knew it wasn't a strange man she feared would harm me, but I couldn't leave. Not this night. "I'll be fine," I said.

"I'll be back at daybreak," Pic said. "We'll find the tracks and run down whoever was out there watchin' you."

They left, but I heard Betty tell her husband that Dale would one day kill me. They didn't know the half of it.

I filled a dishcloth with ice and held it to my cheek while I sat on the front porch and listened to the silence. The first frost had hushed the crickets and frogs. At dawn, birds would call each other, but now there was no sound. The night had grown chill, and while the moon was round and full and the stars were bright, they cast no warmth.

I wondered if my mama was still alive and where she might be. Dale hadn't allowed me to write her, and if she wrote me, he destroyed the letters. I was his. Period. He approved my moment-to-moment activities. After tonight, if he remembered what had occurred, he would stop my friendship with Betty.

The ice soothed my face, finally numbing it. I went to the kitchen and looked out the window to the cotton fields. If I squinted hard, I could see a shadowy figure holding a knife. I left the doors unlocked before I went to bed.

THE NEXT MORNING I'd barely had time to dress when Pic arrived with the Warden. They took note of my bruised cheek and black eye, but they said nothing. Dale still snored on the sofa, and they got him up and moving in the breaking day. They spread out from the backyard, working the field behind the house, looking for the prints I knew they'd never find. With the Warden there, I was safe from Dale's abuse. He didn't dare step out of line. I was left in peace to tidy up the house.

An hour later they returned, puzzled and worried.

"Mrs. Walters, we didn't find a single track," Pic said. Dale glowered in the background.

I folded the dish towel I held and put it on the drainboard. "I can't explain that," I said, "but I saw him, as clearly as I'm seein' you right now." I described again the apparition with the long, silver blade in his hand.

"There's been talk about one of the prisoners," the Warden said. "Maybe you heard some of that. Maybe that stirred up your imagination."

I shook my head. "Dale don't allow such talk in the house, and he can tell you I don't talk to anyone. I don't know nothin' about gossip and talk, I'm just tellin' you what I saw."

"She wasn't drinkin'," Dale said. "My wife don't drink."

The Warden nodded. "Well, if you see anything else, you tell us. We'll get to the bottom of this."

They left and took Dale with them. I hoped one of them would hose him off before they sent him home. He stank.

I saddled Piper and set out for the backfields where the old oak had once stood. A work crew was still chopping the tree into firewood. They'd left it for several months, harvesting the cotton instead. Now it was time to lay up a store of wood for heating and cooking.

I missed the branches of the tree on the bare horizon, but when I was close enough to hear the powerful voice of Amos Sample and the work song of the prisoners, I slowed. Pic wasn't in charge of this crew and I dared not get too close.

Amos Sample must have heard the beat of my horse's hooves, because he looked up. There was the tiniest nod of his head, just that. Nothing more. But it was enough.

THANKSGIVING CAME, as it does each year, a time when many prisoners were furloughed home for family gatherings. The Warden allowed this favor for some prisoners who worked hard and gave no trouble. Those who had a family to go to. Some of the prison employees, too, made visits off the penitentiary grounds to places where life had a different rhythm. Dale had no truck with his family, and I had no idea where my mama might be. We stayed at the prison. I cooked and he ate.

I'd made his favorites and loaded his plate three times. He celebrated the day with a bottle of corn hooch made by one of the prisoners. It was his Thanksgiving tradition. I made sure that when he passed out, he was sitting on the front porch.

Dusk finally fell and I went to the barn and saddled Piper. I took her apples and carrots, and I wept against her mane before I led her to the front yard and tied her to a tree. Dale snored, slumped sideways in his chair. He was always meaner when he drank.

Easing past him, I went upstairs and put on my riding clothes and one of his big shirts. In the kitchen I pulled on my rubber cleaning gloves and retrieved the carving knife I'd washed so carefully. When I stepped onto the porch, I gave myself no time to think. I walked up behind him, grabbed his greasy hair, laid his neck bare and slid the sharp blade across in a slashing motion that cut so deep I felt the bones of his spine.

When I pushed him to the porch, he tried to crawl. The noise he made reminded me of the pigs he killed. He'd told me that a clean cut across the throat was humane. I wondered if he felt that way now.

He made it to the steps before he collapsed. Blood seeped from the porch onto the steps, dribbling from one to the other like a slow, red waterfall. I dropped the knife, removed his shirt and the gloves, bundled them up, and ran to get on Piper.

Instead of going to the prison for help, I rode toward the old oak tree that had been my source of comfort. Night had fallen, a dark, overcast sky hid everything. Piper knew the road and I let her have her head. She galloped with joy, and I prayed I had secured her freedom as well as mine.

When I got to the tree, my heart fell. No one was there. A cry of fear and desperation tore from my throat.

Amos Sample stepped away from the trunk. "I got your note baked in the crust of that pie. I couldn't have made it, except lots of trustees went home for Thanksgiving."

I wanted to weep with relief, but there was no time. I dismounted and handed him Piper's reins. "Ride north," I told him. "Go fast. I killed my husband and you're gonna get the blame. They'll know you got out of the camp, and they'll say you did it."

"And you?" he asked.

"No need to worry for me," I said. "I'll be in Memphis in two weeks. Take care of my horse."

He mounted and set out across the fields as if Satan clung to his coat tails.

I buried Dale's shirt and gloves in the soft dirt near the tree. I dug deep in the soil that was already loosened, deeper than any plow would cut for cotton. Then I climbed into the branches of the dead tree and jumped, meeting the ground with my body.

When I'd reclaimed my breath, I got up and started walking to the prison. Blood seeped from my wounds and I limped. It all made for a better story.

I SAT IN THE SUN on my freshly scrubbed front steps. The funeral was over, and the prisoners had packed my belongings and moved them out to the front yard. In a while, one of the prison trucks would come to pick me and my things up. The Warden had been kind and considerate, but the house I lived in belonged to someone who worked at the prison. I had to go.

It was Pic who showed up in the truck. He tipped back his hat and studied me as the men loaded the four suitcases. At his signal, I climbed in the passenger seat. The truck eased away from the house, going slow, like I used to do when I rode Piper. I didn't want to but I couldn't stop myself from looking back. It was the nicest house I'd ever lived in.

"We found your horse," Pic said.

"Is she hurt?"

"No, she's in good shape. A family in Cleveland said a black man left her with them. He caught a train north. Looks like Amos Sample got away."

The dirt road led out of the prison, past the gate where a man with a shotgun waved Pic through. The cotton followed us, flanking us on both sides, the rows of dead stalks ready to be plowed under. No matter. This was free cotton. Even the air was sweeter.

I reached over and flipped on the radio, tuning in to the channel where I'd first heard Amos Sample sing. Through the static and scratch, the wail of a blues guitar came through and then the haunted voice of Skip James. The words spoke to me in a way that only the blues could do.

"If I ever get off this killin' floor,
I'll never get down like this no more
No-no, no-no, I'll never get down this low no more."

I clicked off the radio. "Do you think Amos Sample killed Dale?" I asked Pic.

"Funny thing," he said. "We found the horse tracks from your house across the field, but we never found any footprints for the man you said was with Amos Sample."

"No footprints?" I let him see my fear. "The man didn't leave no footprints?"

"None we could find."

"How'd he manage that?"

Pic drove for a ways before he answered. "No human bein' can travel without leaving prints."

But that was where he was wrong. Once the wind blew the dust across the Delta, no trace of me would ever be found.

DEL HAD PASSED the last chance to exit the Parkway when the fog started rolling in. He noticed the tendrils creeping down out of the sumac just as the Explorer began to chew its way around a tightly banked hairpin. In the next moment, as the heavy vehicle dropped its nose along the steep double yellow and started down, everything blanked out, just that quick. He swore softly, tapping the brakes, his fingers suddenly tight on the wheel. There'd been a time when he might have remembered what was coming next— could have handled it blind—but it had been too long since he'd driven this road. All he could do was hold on and hope. He might be left of center, poised for a head-on—or maybe he was a foot away from jumping the rail and a plunge to the center of the earth, hard to tell.

With that thought formed, the wall of white vanished as suddenly as it came. The gray asphalt rose abruptly in front of him, twisting to the right, and he leaned hard into the wheel, gassing the Explorer into the turn and up the rise. The fog was nothing but runners again on higher ground. He blinked and shook his head, realizing he'd been drifting toward sleep when he piled into that last turn. Should have taken the Cottrell exit. Ten miles longer to angle eastward toward that hamlet in the valley, then the state road back west along the river and a steady climb towards the cabin, but at least those roads were straight.

Now he was stuck on the high spine of the Blue Ridge, nothing but twists and turns and pockets of fog for forty miles. An hour in good weather, but torturous with fog. There was an overlook not far up ahead. He could turn around there, head back to the exit, do the smart thing, he told himself. And laughed. Since when?

The Labrador stirred on the seat beside him, lifting its head off its paws. Something funny was worth waking up for, evidently. Sailing off the side of a mountain, now that you could sleep through. Del smiled. He'd like to come back as a dog.

He saw the sign for the overlook then, and knew it was two relatively uneventful miles. "Pit stop coming up, Sonny. What do you think of that?" Whatever he thought, the dog wasn't saying. Sonny yawned, then put its chin back on its paws.

Del glanced at the radio, but that was no good here. He'd lost the last FM station when he passed Boone. AM was nothing but static and lunatic preachers at this hour. He might have called Ginny but it was too late for that too. He'd lost coverage on his cell phone an hour ago. Just as well. He might get to talking and change his mind.

He noted the flare of the asphalt for the turnout ahead and slowed, easing the Explorer off the Parkway and onto the graveled lot. Had it been daylight, there would be quite a vista out ahead of him, he thought. A sheer drop-off at the edge of the parking area, and the sweeping valley stretched out for miles below, the shadow of blue hump-backed mountains running endless at the horizon. But he would have needed to leave Miami in the middle of the night to make it for any of that, though. Right now there was only a sheet of darkness in the distance and, below, a shelf of fog glowing vaguely in the light of a half moon.

He switched off the engine and got down from the Explorer, then went to open the passenger door for the dog. Sonny took his time stepping down to the mats, then made a nimble move to the gravel. The dog went snuffling off in the darkness while Del walked to the rail and unzipped, relieving himself into the pillow of mist below. "So easy for you guys," Elizabeth had often grumbled. About the only thing she envied, he thought. That self-certainty was just one of the things he'd loved about her.

He was zipping up when he heard a commotion in the brush at the edge of the turnout: an odd bellow followed quickly by Sonny's *I-mean-business* bark. Del turned in time to see a dark shape crash out of the bushes, lumbering across the turnout with Sonny hot on its tail. At first Del thought it was a bear cub, but as it sped past him, panting, nails raking the gravel, he realized it was a raccoon, a huge one, as big as he'd ever seen.

"Sonny!" he called, as the dog sped past, but it was a waste of breath. The raccoon hit the top of the rail at the edge of the overlook in full stride and launched itself out into the mist without hesitation. Sonny's feet cleared the rail by a foot.

"Shit," Del muttered as his dog disappeared. He held his breath, then heard the snapping of limbs and a clattering of stones from below. A pair of urgent barks came soon afterward, then more clattering and crashing, dampened now through the shroud of fog.

"Sonny!" he tried again, but it was useless. The chase would go on until the 'coon turned and gave the dog what for, or found a tree to climb. Nothing to do now but wait.

Del stood at the rail until the sounds from below had dimmed almost entirely. His own damned fault, he found himself thinking. If he kept a Pekinese this wouldn't have happened.

He turned away from the rail with a sigh and moved toward the truck. There was a chill in the air, he noted. No surprise for September up this high. He climbed into the Explorer and sat a moment. If Elizabeth had been here, she would have reminded him why cats were better. Too bad she wasn't.

He reached to turn on the key. He'd run the heater for a moment and let the parking lights burn. The dog wouldn't need a light to find his way back, but still it seemed the right thing to do.

He turned on the lights and reached to ease the seat back a notch when he noticed the music, so faint at first that it might have been drifting down the mountain outside. But it was coming from the radio, he realized, the singer's voice thin and nasally, accompanied only by an acoustic guitar and a hiss of static that was part of the recording, not the broadcast. *"Yonder come Miss Rosie, piece of paper in her hand,"* intoned the singer, *"She come to see the gov'ner, wants to free her man ..."*

No wonder he nearly mistook the source of the music, he thought as the chorus kicked in. This was no digitally enhanced version of the old classic, no enthusiastic cover by some latter day bluesman. Except for the certainty in the voice and the clarity of the tone, this could have been coming from the stoop of a porch overlooking a cotton field or the steps of a trailer house sitting crooked up a narrow ravine. *"Let the Midnight Special, shine her light on me ... Let the Midnight Special shine her everlovin' light on me."*

Del hadn't heard the song in a while, and he'd never heard it sung quite so bare bones as this. Elizabeth was more partial to pop, but she'd indulge his interest in rhythm and blues at times. The last time they'd gone to New Orleans, he'd managed to coax her out to Tipitina's twice.

The song had concluded now, and Del noticed the thickness at the back of his throat. Just the cool air he told himself, reaching to see if he might dial the station in a bit clearer. Sonny had done him something of a favor, he supposed, stopping them at the only spot in these mountains where he might have heard such a thing. And where was the signal bouncing in from, he wondered? Up from Boone, some college station DJ who'd discovered where Eric Clapton got his ideas from, maybe; or maybe all the way over from the coast, where there were these little pockets that time had still not touched, music-wise.

He was squinting at the display, trying to make out the frequency before he went fiddling with the dial, when he heard the announcer's voice cut clearly through the night air and his hand stopped. "… that's just one of the five records you'll receive from Randy's Record Shop on the .45 Special this week, and all for only three dollars. When you call the number, tell 'em the Hoss Man sent you."

The voice faded away as an advertisement for Philip Morris cigarettes took over, and Del stared dumbly at the glowing display of the Explorer's radio. There was no mistaking what he'd just heard—it just took him a few moments to make sense of it. He'd listened to that DJ hundreds of nights in his youth, a white man named Bill "Hoss" Allen who sounded black and spun down-home R&B on a station out of Nashville, Tennessee. It was music so raw that it made Elvis Presley seem tame—the Hoss Man and his cohorts, Gene Nobles and John R., also white, favored the rough hewn rendition of "Blue Suede Shoes" issued by Carl Perkins, for instance, and in fact rarely played Presley on their late-night shows. Del had stayed up to all hours, listening to artists whose names alone were a promise: Muddy Waters, Lightning Hopkins, Howling Wolf. Compared to what most of his schoolmates in his benighted rural town were listening to, Del—ever the enthusiast—felt like he had tapped into the planet Pluto.

But that was long, long ago, and the Hoss Man and John R. and Gene Nobles had all been dead for years. Del had seen a squib about the DJ's and their offbeat station and its "cult following" in the *New York Times* in fact, a dozen years or so ago, when the Hoss Man, the last surviving member of the group, had passed away. WLAC, he recalled then. "The voice of Nashville Life and Casualty." But what was the Hoss Man doing on the air a few decades after his last broadcast? One of those stations that filled up the dead air of late night with recordings of old time radio, he guessed. Like those he had heard featuring reruns of Jack Benny and The Shadow.

He was leaning closer to the display, happy to take note of a station astute enough to replay the Hoss Man and John R. and their offer of five singles for three dollars or a hundred baby chicks delivered C.O.D. to your doorstep, when a knock came at the window of the Explorer.

"What the hell?" Del blurted, whirling at the sound.

The silhouette of a figure in a hooded sweatshirt loomed outside the driver's window, the shadowed face no more than a foot from his own. "This your dog, man?" Del heard panic in the voice and then, behind it, the low threatening rumble that was Sonny's characteristic form of address to unfamiliar males, especially those approaching in the dead of night.

Del yanked the door open quickly, his relief at Sonny's reappearance tempered by the need to get the dog calmed down before the guy in the sweatshirt did something stupid. "Sonny!" Del commanded, and the dog's growling dropped a notch in volume.

"It's all right," he said, turning to the figure beside him. "Long as I'm out here, he won't bother you."

"He already got me," Del heard. It was a young man's voice, he realized—a bit of a tremble there, and also some resentment.

"He bit you?"

The kid pulled back the hood of his sweatshirt with one hand and held up his sleeve for Del to see. "Messed me *up,* man."

Del saw a flap of fabric dancing as the kid thrust his hand forward. Sonny's growl was suddenly menacing again. Del thought a moment. "He break the skin?" he asked.

There was a pause. "Naw, man. He could've though. Look at my shirt."

Del fought the urge to tell the kid Sonny hadn't misbehaved so badly. He'd been trained to bring back game the same way he found it. Del had never hunted Sonny, but the breeder he'd bought him from was a legend in the business. Del snapped his fingers and Sonny sat back on his haunches, quiet now.

"Where'd this happen, anyway?" Del asked.

The kid pointed vaguely over his shoulder. "Just around the bend. I was walking the shoulder and your dog just came up at me. Good thing I put my arm up. He was going for my throat."

Del nodded as if he were agreeing. A kid is walking along a road on a dark night, he sees a big dog growling, coming his way, who could blame him for being scared?

Del reached into his pocket. "I'm sorry," he said. "I'll pay you for your sweatshirt."

"Naw, man. That's okay." The kid looked off to the north. "Maybe you could give me a lift, though."

Del pursed his lips. "I'm going north," he said.

"So am I."

Del stared at him in the dim light. "I thought you were headed toward Cottrell."

The kid shook his head. "I'm hitchin' north," he insisted. "But there ain't been a car going that way for two hours now. I figured I'd hike on back to Cottrell and try that route."

Del glanced at the Explorer. He had the cargo hold full, and a few boxes on the back seat as well. But Sonny could manage on the boxes for the short distance they had left. He felt he owed the kid something. And maybe the company would keep him awake.

"I'm only going about forty miles," he told the kid.

A shrug. "Better'n walking to Cottrell," the kid said.

"Okay," Del said. "I'll have to move the dog's things out of the front."

He motioned to Sonny who stood with a meaningful glance at the kid. "He's all right now," he assured the kid. "You must have scared him, that's all."

The kid made a sound that might have been meant as a laugh but came out more like a snort. "He scared the shit out of me, I'll tell you that much."

Del nodded, leading the way around the Explorer. He opened the passenger's door and leaned in to pull Sonny's rug off the seat. An old hooked rug that Elizabeth had brought home from a second-hand store one day. "If you're going to let that dog ride in the front seat …" Before they'd left Miami, Del had tucked one edge in snug between the cushions and the center console so it wouldn't slide, and sure enough the fabric caught on something as he was pulling. He might have reached to see what it was, but he didn't feel comfortable bent over that way, his back exposed to a stranger, and so he caught the rug with both hands and jerked it free.

"Go ahead," he turned to the kid. "Get in."

The kid looked at him, then at the dog, and climbed up into the passenger's seat. Del opened the rear door and surveyed his cargo. He moved a box of books onto the floorboards, and squeezed a bag of undone laundry into the crowded cargo hold. That looked like enough room for the dog, he thought. They weren't going that far.

"Looks like you're movin'," he heard the kid say from the front seat.

"For a while, anyway," Del said as he worked to tuck the rug so it wouldn't slide.

"I didn't think you were from these parts."

Del glanced over his shoulder. "Why's that?"

"Florida plates is one thing," the kid said. "Plus you just don't sound like it."

"I been away a long time," Del said. "I met my wife in Florida, and ..."

He broke off when he heard a faint, familiar snapping sound and realized the kid was stepping down from the passenger's seat. That was wrong, Del thought. But he wasn't sure exactly why until he turned from fooling with the boxes and the rug to see the kid facing him and the glint of steel between them in the soft moonlight.

"How come you got a gun?" the kid said neutrally. He'd un-snapped the holster of the .38 Del kept tucked beneath the passenger seat—that was the thing the rug had caught on, he realized—and held it easily at stomach level. If the kid had seemed nervous earlier, he was now entirely at ease. Born to train a handgun on someone, Del thought.

Del glanced down at the pistol, then at the kid's shadowed face. "I'm from Miami," he said evenly. "They give them out down there."

The kid nodded. "I bet they do." He nodded at Sonny, who was back on his haunches now, staring at Del. "I saw how you talk to that dog," he said. "You keep your hands still, or I'll put one in you. Him and me'll finish up by ourselves."

"There's nothing to worry about," Del said. "I don't want trouble."

"Nobody does," the kid said. "You not a cop, are you."

It was a statement, not a question. "I build houses," Del said.

The kid made the sound that approximated laughter. "People try to steal your houses from you? That why you pack?"

Del shrugged, careful to keep his hands still. "You'd be surprised what they steal when a house is under construction. Appliances. Air-conditioning units. Sometimes the copper wire right out of the walls. You go out checking things at night, you have to be careful."

"I wouldn't be surprised at nothing nobody steals," the kid said, a trace of bitterness in his voice.

Del broke the momentary silence. "You come out of Guilford by any chance?" There was a work farm outside of Asheville, about fifty miles south of where they stood. If you got away from the dogs and into the hills, you could find your way up the Appalachian Trail, just a late-season camper on a stroll.

"Doesn't really matter where I come from, does it?" the kid said.

Del supposed that it didn't. And cursed his luck. He'd left Miami for his old home, a quiet place where he could try and get his feet under him again with Elizabeth gone. Ginny was sweet, and it had been more than a year since his wife's death, but if anything, the pain had only grown.

"You want the truck, just take it," Del said, finally. "Just take it and go where you're going."

"I expect I will," the kid said.

"You want my money …" Del said, shrugging.

"I told you, keep your hands still," the kid said. "That's all you have to worry about."

There was a pause then, and the slightest rustling of a breeze. "You don't want to do anything stupid," he told the kid.

"That's right," the kid said. "Leave you here to tell who took your truck, that would be stupid."

He raised his chin and lowered it, as if he'd made his decision. Del made his as well. What good was all this talk? If he was going to die, he'd do it headed in the right direction.

He saw the kid's hand start up, felt himself lean forward … and then the night was split by an ungodly Tarzan call, a yodel out of Hollywood by way of a long-dead Nashville DJ. Del had heard it played on the station a thousand times in his youth, and never understood why Gene Nobles found it so funny.

The kid turned, momentarily distracted. And that was all it took for the dog to spring forward and fasten on his arm. In nearly the same instant Del had closed the gap too.

They stumbled together through the gravel, the kid back-pedaling, cursing, trying to pull his arm free. Sonny growled as if he were gargling blood. Del drove himself forward like a linebacker on his last rush, groping in the darkness for the glinting pistol.

The kid slammed into the side of the Explorer with a grunt. Del felt his fingers close briefly on steel, then slip away. His feet were sliding in gravel as slick as marbles, and he was going down.

There was a blast hot at his cheek, then, and a stinging at his forehead as he fell. He landed face down, his chin bouncing hard, his palms digging into sharp gravel. He lay stunned, wondering if he was dying already or simply waiting for the one he'd never hear. But there was only silence from above him, and then, a strange rattling sigh as something heavy dropped into the gravel and a body slid awkwardly down the Explorer's side.

Del forced himself to his knees, his palms stinging, his head throbbing from the proximity of the blast. The kid lay face up in the dim glow of the kickboard lights, his eyes sightless. There was a dimpled hole beneath his chin, a flap open at the top of his skull, oozing dark into the gravel. Beside him, Sonny lay motionless.

Del scrabbled toward the dog, sweeping the fallen pistol out of the way as he went on hands and knees. He saw blood at Sonny's muzzle, a dark furrow in the pale fur at his ear ... and then the dog's eyes fluttered.

He had water in the console, Del thought. Shirts in the laundry bag for bandages. He was pulling himself up by the running board when he heard a whimper, felt the Labrador's tongue lapping at his forehead, its breath hot at his cheek. Del sensed something give in his chest, and he turned to bury his face in the fur at the dog's thick shoulder for what seemed like a long time, until the night had swallowed the moon, until the radio had faded to a soft buzz of static. Finally he rose and went looking for his phone.

"Unusual that your call went through up here," the young ranger told Del. "Probably had something to do with the fog." He waved at the early morning mist that had risen around them.

"You'd have come along sooner or later," Del said. When he found his cell phone, he was sure that he'd have to drive back to Cottrell for help, but there'd been service after all. "Anyway, everything was over by the time I called." He sipped at the coffee the ranger had shared from his thermos. Sonny sat eagerly nearby as if it were just another morning, as if they might be about to set out for a hike.

At the entrance to the turnout, while a trooper kept a watchful eye for traffic, the EMS van turned out onto the Parkway toward Cottrell, its cargo loaded, flashers rolling, sirens quiet. When the van had departed, the trooper raised the yellow crime scene tape again. "You're lucky, you know," the ranger said. "That boy hurt a few people on his way out of Guilford."

"I *am* lucky," Del said.

"I never did hear that radio station you were telling me about, either," the ranger said, shaking his head. "Course I could've missed it. I'm more into the country and western myself."

Del nodded. "That doesn't make you a bad person," he said. The ranger glanced up, uncertain, then ducked into his truck when a call came on his radio.

Del looked out toward the highway, past the investigators still busy at the Explorer, past the yellow tape where the trooper stood guard. He was thinking about that last night at Tipitina's, with Elizabeth. They were dancing, her cheek pressed warm on his, Professor Longhair at the piano, and—uncharacteristically—having slowed the boogie-woogie way, way down: "*Ain't no food upon the table, and no pork up in the pan. But you better not complain, boy, you get in trouble with the man.*"

As the Professor implored the Midnight Special in his own inimitable way, Del heard a rumble gathering out on the Parkway, and gradually the lights and bulk of a northbound Greyhound took shape in the mist. It was an old one, Del saw, rounded at all the corners, and laboring with the hill. "TOUR," it said, in the slot above the windshield where the destination city was usually displayed. There was an old black man in a slouch hat and suspenders at the wheel, wearing dark glasses despite the gloom. He smiled as the bus rolled past the turnout and pointed a finger Del's way. Del lifted a hand as the bus rolled by and disappeared into the mist. All the while, the trooper stood at the roadside with his arms folded, as if he hadn't seen a thing.

MR. MCBRIDE ran his upholstery shop in the old ice house on Lee Street, a few blocks off the square in downtown Clanton. To haul the sofas and chairs back and forth he used a white Ford cargo van with "McBride Upholstery" stenciled in thick black letters above a phone number and the address on Lee. The van, always clean and never in a hurry, was a common sight in Clanton, and Mr. McBride was fairly well-known because he was the only upholsterer in town. He rarely lent his van to anyone, thought the requests were more frequent than he would have liked. His usual response was a polite, "No, I have some deliveries."

He said yes to Leon Graney, though, and did so for two reasons. First, the circumstances surrounding the request were quite unusual, and, second, Leon's boss at the lamp factory was Mr. McBride's third cousin. Small-town relationships being what they are, Leon Graney arrived at the upholstery shop as scheduled at four o'clock on a hot Wednesday afternoon in late July.

Most of Ford County was listening to the radio, and it was widely known that things were not going well for the Graney family.

Mr. McBride walked with Leon to the van, handed over the key, and said, "You take care of it now."

Leon took the key and said, "I'm much obliged."

"I filled up the tank. Should be plenty to get you there and back."

"How much do I owe?"

Mr. McBride shook his head and spat on the gravel beside the van. "Nothing. It's on me. Just bring it back with a full tank."

"I'd feel better if I could pay something," Leon protested.

"No."

"Well, thank you, then."

"I need it back by noon tomorrow."

"It'll be here. Mind if I leave my truck?" Leon nodded to an old Japanese pickup wedged between two cars across the lot.

"That'll be fine."

Leon opened the door and got inside the van. He started the engine, adjusted the seat and the mirrors. Mr. McBride walked to the driver's door, lit an unfiltered cigarette, and watched Leon. "You know, some folks don't like this," he said.

"Thank you, but most folks around here don't care," Leon replied. He was preoccupied and not in the mood for small talk.

"Me, I think it's wrong."

"Thank you. I'll be back before noon," Leon said softly, then backed away and disappeared down the street. He settled into the seat, tested the brakes, slowly gunned the engine to check the power. Twenty minutes later he was far from Clanton, and deep in the hills of northern Ford County.

Out from the settlement of Pleasant Ridge, the road became gravel, the homes smaller and farther apart. Leon turned into a short driveway that stopped at a boxlike house with weeds at the doors and an asphalt shingle roof in need of replacement. It was the Graney home, the place he'd been raised along with his brothers, the only constant in their sad and chaotic lives. A jerry-rigged plywood ramp ran to the side door so that his mother, Inez Graney, could come and go in her wheelchair.

By the time Leon turned off the engine, the side door was open and Inez was rolling out and onto the ramp. Behind her was the hulking mass of her middle son, Butch, who still lived with his mother because he'd never lived anywhere else, at least not in the free world. Sixteen of his forty-six years had been behind bars, and he looked the part of the career criminal—long ponytail, studs in his ears, all manner of facial hair, massive biceps, and a collection of cheap tattoos a prison artist had sold him for cigarettes. In spite of his past, Butch handled his mother and her wheelchair with great tenderness and care, speaking softly to her as they negotiated the ramp.

Leon watched and waited, then walked to the rear of the van and opened its double doors. He and Butch gently lifted their mother up and sat her inside the van. Butch pushed her forward to the console that separated the two bucket seats bolted into the floor. Leon latched the wheelchair into place with strips of packing twine someone at McBride's had left in the van, and when Inez was secure, her boys got settled in their seats. The journey began. Within minutes they were back on the asphalt and headed for a long night.

Inez was seventy-two, a mother of three, grandmother of at least four, a lonely old woman in failing health who couldn't remember her last bit of good luck. Though she'd considered herself single for almost thirty years, she was not, at least to her knowledge, officially divorced from the miserable creature who'd practically raped her when she was seventeen, married her when she was eighteen, fathered her three boys, then mercifully disappeared from the face of the earth. When she prayed on occasion, she never failed to toss in an earnest request that Ernie be kept away from her, be kept wherever his miserable life had taken him, if in fact his life had not already ended in some painful manner, which was really what she dreamed of but didn't have the audacity to ask of the Lord. Ernie was still blamed for everything—for her bad health and poverty, her reduced status in life, her seclusion, her lack of friends, the scorn of her own family. But her harshest condemnation of Ernie was for his despicable treatment of his three sons. Abandoning them was far more merciful than beating them.

By the time they reached the highway, all three needed a cigarette. "Reckon McBride'll mind if we smoke?" Butch said. At three packs a day he was always reaching for a pocket.

"Somebody's been smokin' in here," Inez said. "Smells like a tar pit. Is the air conditioner on, Leon?"

"Yes, but you can't tell it if the windows are down."

With little concern for Mr. McBride's preferences on smoking in his van, they were soon puffing away with the windows down, the warm wind rushing in and swirling about. Once inside the van, the wind had no exit, no other windows, no vents, nothing to let it out, so it roared back toward the front and engulfed the three Graneys, who were staring at the road, smoking intently, seemingly oblivious to everything as the van moved along the county road. Butch and Leon casually flicked their ashes out of the windows. Inez gently tapped hers into her cupped left hand.

"How much did McBride charge you?" Butch asked from the passenger's seat.

Leon shook his head. "Nothing. Even filled up the tank. Said he didn't agree with this. Claimed a lot of folks don't like it."

"I'm not sure I believe that."

"I don't."

When the three cigarettes were finished, Leon and Butch rolled up their windows and fiddled with the air conditioner and the vents. Hot air shot out and minutes passed before the heat was broken. All three were sweating.

"You okay back there?" Leon asked, glancing over his shoulder and smiling at his mother.

"I'm fine. Thank you. Does the air conditioner work?"

"Yes, it's gettin' cooler now."

"I can't feel a thang."

"You wanna stop for a soda or something?"

"No. Let's hurry along."

"I'd like a beer," Butch said, and, as if this was expected, Leon immediately shook his head in the negative and Inez shot forth with an emphatic, "No."

"There'll be no drinking," she said, and the issue was laid to rest. When Ernie abandoned the family years earlier, he'd taken nothing but his shotgun, a few clothes, and all the liquor from his private supply. He'd been a violent drunk, and his boys still carried the scars, emotional and physical. Leon, the oldest, had felt more of the brutality than his younger brothers, and as a small boy equated alcohol with the horrors of an abusive father. He had never taken a drink, though with time had found his own vices. Butch, on the other hand, had drunk heavily since his early teens, though he'd never been tempted to sneak alcohol into his mother's home. Raymond, the youngest, had chosen to follow the example of Butch rather than of Leon.

To shift away from such an unpleasant topic, Leon asked his mother about the latest news from a friend down the road, an old spinster who'd been dying of cancer for years. Inez, as always, perked up when discussing the ailments and treatments of neighbors, and herself as well. The air conditioner finally broke through, and the thick humidity inside the van began to subside. When he stopped sweating, Butch reached for his pocket, fished out a cigarette, lit it, then cracked the window. The temperature rose immediately. Soon all three were smoking, and the windows went lower and lower until the air was again thick with heat and nicotine.

When they finished, Inez said to Leon, "Raymond called two hours ago."

This was no surprise. Raymond had been making calls, collect, for days now, and not only to his mother. Leon's phone was ringing so often that his (third) wife refused to answer it. Others around town were also declining to accept charges.

"What'd he say?" Leon asked, but only because he had to reply. He knew exactly what Raymond had said, maybe not verbatim, but certainly in general.

"Said thangs are lookin' real good, said he'd probably have to fire the team of lawyers he has now so he can hire another team of lawyers. You know Raymond. He's tellin' the lawyers what to do and they're just fallin' all over themselves."

Without turning his head, Butch cut his eyes at Leon, and Leon returned the glance. Nothing was said because words were not necessary.

"Said his new team comes from a firm in Chicago with a thousand lawyers. Can you imagine? A thousand lawyers workin' for Raymond. And he's tellin' 'em what to do."

Another glance between driver and right-side passenger. Inez had cataracts, and her peripheral vision had declined. If she had seen the looks being passed between her two oldest, she would not be pleased.

"Said they've just discovered some new evidence that shoulda been produced at trial but wasn't because the cops and the prosecutors covered it up, and with this new evidence Raymond feels real good about gettin' a new trial back here in Clanton, though he's not sure he wants it here so he might move it somewhere else. He's thinkin' about somewhere in the Delta because the Delta juries have more blacks and he says that blacks are more sympathetic in cases like this. What do you thank about that, Leon?"

"There are definitely more blacks in the Delta," Leon said. Butch grunted and mumbled, but his words weren't clear.

"Said he don't trust anyone in Ford County, especially the law and the judges. God knows they've never given us a break."

Leon and Butch nodded in silent agreement. Both had been chewed up by the law in Ford County, Butch much more so than Leon. And though they had pled guilty to their crimes in negotiated deals, they'd always believed they were persecuted simply because they were Graneys.

"Don't know if I can stand another trial, though," she said, and her words trailed off.

Leon wanted to say that Raymond's chances of getting a new trial were worse than slim, and that he'd been making noise about a new trial for over a decade. Butch wanted to say pretty much the same thing, but he would've added that he was sick of Raymond's jailhouse bullshit about lawyers and trials and new evidence and that it was past time for the boy to stop blaming everybody else and take his medicine like a man.

But neither said a word.

"Said the both of you ain't sent him his stipends for last month," she said. "That true?"

Five miles passed before another word was spoken.

"Y'all hear me up there?" Inez said. "Raymond says y'all ain't mailed in his stipends for the month of June, and now it's already July. Y'all forget about it?"

Leon went first, and unloaded. "Forget about it? How can we forget about it? That's all he talks about. I get a letter every day, sometimes two, not that I read 'em all, but every letter mentions the stipend. 'Thanks for the money, bro.' 'Don't forget the money, Leon, I'm counting on you, big brother.' 'Gotta have the money to pay the lawyers, you know how much those bloodsuckers can charge.' 'Ain't seen the stipend this month, bro.'"

"What the hell is a stipend?" Butch shot from the right side, his voice suddenly edgy.

"A regular or fixed payment, according to Webster's," Leon said.

"It's just money, right?"

"Right."

"So why can't he just say something like, 'Send me the damned money?' Or, 'Where's the damned money?' Why does he have to use the fancy words?"

"We've had this conversation a thousand times," Inez said.

"Well, you sent him a dictionary," Leon said to Butch.

"That was ten years ago, at least. And he begged me for it."

"Well, he's still got it, still wearing it out looking for words we ain't seen before."

"I often wonder if his lawyers can keep up with his vocabulary," Butch mused.

"Y'all're tryin' to change the subject up there," Inez said. "Why didn't you send him his stipends last month?"

"I thought I did," Butch said without conviction.

"I don't believe that," she said.

"The check's in the mail," Leon said.

"I don't believe that either. We all agreed to send him a hundred dollars each, every month, twelve months a year. It's the least we can do. I know it's hard, especially on me, livin' on Social Security and all. But you boys have jobs and the least you can do is squeeze out a hundred dollars each for your little brother so he can buy decent food and pay his lawyers."

"Do we have to go through this again?" Leon asked.

"I hear it every day," Butch said. "If I don't hear from Raymond, on the phone or through the mail, then I hear it from Momma."

"Is that a complaint?" she asked. "Got a problem with your livin' arrangements? Stayin' in my house for free, and yet you want to complain?"

"Come on," Leon said.

"Who'll take care of you?" Butch offered in his defense.

"Knock it off, you two. This gets so old."

All three took a deep breath, then began reaching for the cigarettes. After a long, quiet smoke, they settled in for another round. Inez got things started with a pleasant, "Me, I never miss a month. And, if you'll recall, I never missed a month when the both of you was locked up at Parchman."

Leon grunted, slapped the wheel, and said angrily, "Momma, that was twenty-five years ago. Why bring it up now? I ain't had so much as a speedin' ticket since I got paroled." Butch, whose life in crime had been much more colorful than Leon's, and who was still on parole, said nothing.

"I never missed a month," she said.

"Come on."

"And sometimes it was two hundred dollars a month 'cause I had two of you there at one time, as I recall. Guess I was lucky I never had all three behind bars. Couldn't've paid my light bill."

"I thought those lawyers worked for free," Butch said in an effort to deflect attention from himself and hopefully direct it toward a target outside the family.

"They do," Leon said. "It's called pro bono work, and all lawyers are supposed to do some of it. As far as I know, these big firms who come in on cases like this don't expect to get paid."

"Then what's Raymond doin' with three hundred dollars a month if he ain't payin' his lawyers?"

"We've had this conversation," Inez said.

"I'm sure he spends a fortune on pens, paper, envelopes and postage," Leon said. "He claims he writes ten letters a day. Hell, that's over a hundred dollars a month right there."

"Plus he's written eight novels," Butch added quickly, "Or is it nine, Momma? I can't remember."

"Nine."

"Nine novels, several volumes of poetry, bunch of short stories, hundreds of songs. Just think of all the paper he goes through," Butch said.

"Are you pokin' fun at Raymond?" she asked.

"Never."

"He sold a short story once," she said.

"Of course he did. What was the magazine? *Hot Rodder*? Paid him forty bucks for a story about a man who stole a thousand hubcaps. They say you write what you know."

"How many stories have you sold?" she asked.

"None, because I haven't written any, and the reason I haven't written any is because I realize that I don't have the talent to write. If my little brother would also realize that he has no artistic talents whatsoever, then he could save some money and hundreds of people would not be subjected to his nonsense."

"That's very cruel."

"No, Momma, it's very honest. And if you'd been honest with him a long time ago, then maybe he would've stopped writing. But no. You read his books and his poetry and his short stories and told him the stuff was great. So he wrote more, with longer words, longer sentences, longer paragraphs, and got to the point to where now we can hardly understand a damned thang he writes."

"So it's all my fault?"

"Not a hundred percent, no."

"He writes for therapy."

"I've been there. I don't see how writin' helps any."

"He says it helps."

"Are these books handwritten or typed up?" Leon asked, interrupting.

"Typed," Butch said.

"Who types 'em?"

"He has to pay some guy over in the law library," Inez said. "A dollar a page, and one of the books was over eight hundred pages. I read it, though, ever' word."

"Did you understand ever' word?" Butch asked.

"Most of 'em. A dictionary helps. Lord, I don't know where that boy finds those words."

"And Raymond sent these books up to New York to get published, right?" Leon asked, pressing on.

"Yes, and they sent 'em right back," she said. "I guess they couldn't understand all his words either."

"You'd think those people in New York would understand what he's sayin'," Leon said.

"No one understands what he's sayin'," Butch said. "That's the problem with Raymond the novelist, and Raymond the poet, and Raymond the political prisoner, and Raymond the songwriter, and Raymond the lawyer. No person in his right mind could possibly have any idea what Raymond says when he starts writin'."

"So, if I understand this correctly," Leon said, "a large portion of Raymond's overhead has been spent to finance his literary career. Paper, postage, typing, copying, shipping to New York and back. That right, Momma?"

"I guess."

"And it's doubtful if his stipends have actually gone to pay his lawyers," Leon said.

"Very doubtful," Butch said. "And don't forget his music career. He spends money on guitar strings and sheet music. Plus, they now allow the prisoners to rent tapes. That's how Raymond became a blues singer. He listened to B.B. King and Muddy Waters, and, according to Raymond, he now entertains his colleagues on death row, with late-night sessions of the blues."

"Oh, I know. He's told me about it in his letters."

"He always had a good voice," Inez said.

"I never heard 'im sang," Leon said.

"Me neither," Butch added.

They were on the bypass around Oxford, two hours away from Parchman. The upholstery van seemed to run best at sixty miles an hour; anything faster and the front tires shook a bit. There was no hurry. West of Oxford the hills began to flatten; the Delta was not far away. Inez recognized a little white country church off to the right, next to a cemetery, and it occurred to her that the church had not changed in all the many years she had made this journey to the state penitentiary. She asked herself how many other women in Ford County had made as many of these trips, but she knew the answer. Leon had started the tradition many years earlier with a thirty-month incarceration, and back then the rules allowed her to visit on the first Sunday of each month. Sometimes Butch drove her and sometimes she paid a neighbor's son, but she never missed a visitation and she always took peanut butter fudge and extra toothpaste. Six months after Leon was paroled, he was driving her so she could visit Butch. Then it was Butch and Raymond, but in different units with different rules.

Then Raymond killed the deputy, and they locked him down on death row, which has its own rules.

With practice, most unpleasant tasks become bearable, and Inez Graney had learned to look forward to the visits. Her sons had been condemned by the rest of the county, but their mother would never abandon them. She was there when they were born and she was there when they were beaten. She had suffered through their court appearances and parole hearings, and she had told anyone who would listen that they were good boys who'd been abused by the man she'd chosen to marry. All of it was her fault. If she'd married a decent man, her children might have had normal lives.

"Reckon that woman'll be there?" Leon asked.

"Lord, Lord," Inez groaned.

"Why would she miss the show?" Butch said. "I'm sure she'll be around somewhere."

"Lord, Lord."

That woman was Tallulah, a fruitcake who'd entered their lives a few years earlier and managed to make a bad situation much worse. Through one of the abolitionist groups, she'd made contact with Raymond, who responded in typical fashion with a lengthy letter filled with claims of innocence and maltreatment and the usual drivel about his budding literary and music careers. He sent her some poems, love sonnets, and she became obsessed with him. They met in the visitation room at death row and, through a thick metal screen window, fell in love. Raymond sang a few blues tunes, and Tallulah was swept away. There was talk of a marriage, but those plans were put on hold until Tallulah's then-current husband was executed by the State of Georgia. After a brief period of mourning, she traveled to Parchman for a bizarre ceremony recognized by no identifiable state law or religious doctrine. Anyway, Raymond was in love, and, thus inspired, his prodigious letter writing reached new heights. The family was forewarned that Tallulah was anxious to visit Ford County and see her new in-laws. She indeed arrived, but, when they refused to acknowledge her, she instead paid a visit to the *Ford County Times* where she shared her rambling thoughts, her insights into the plight of poor Raymond Graney, and her promises that new evidence would clear him in the death of the deputy. She also announced that she was pregnant with Raymond's child, a result of several conjugal visits now available to death row inmates.

Tallulah made the front page, photo and all, but the reporter had been wise enough to check with Parchman. Conjugal visits were not allowed for the inmates, especially those on death row.

And there was no official record of a marriage. Undaunted, Tallulah continued to wave Raymond's flag, and even went so far as to haul several of his bulky manuscripts to New York, where they were again rejected by publishers with little vision. With time she faded away, though Inez, Leon, and Butch lived with the horror that another Graney might soon be born, somewhere. In spite of the rules regarding conjugal visits, they knew Raymond.

After two years, Raymond informed the family that he and Tallulah would be seeking a divorce and, to properly obtain one, he needed $500. This touched off another nasty episode of bickering and name-calling, and the money was raised only after he threatened suicide, and not for the first time. Not long after the checks had been mailed, Raymond wrote with the great news that he and Tallulah had reconciled. He did not offer to return the money to Inez, Butch, and Leon, though all three suggested that he do so. Raymond declined on the grounds that his new team of lawyers needed the money to hire experts and investigators.

What irked Leon and Butch was their brother's sense of entitlement, as though they, the family, owed him the money because of his persecution. In the early days of his imprisonment, both Leon and Butch had reminded Raymond that he had not sent along the first penny when they were behind bars and he was not. This had led to another nasty episode that Inez had been forced to mediate.

She sat bent and unmoving in her wheelchair, with a large canvas bag in her lap. As the thoughts of Tallulah began to fade, she opened the bag and withdrew a letter from Raymond, his latest. She opened the envelope, plain and white with his swirling cursive writing all over the front, and unfolded two sheets of yellow tablet paper.

Dearest Mother:

It is becoming increasingly obvious and apparent that the cumbersome and unwieldy yes even lethargic machinations of our inequitable and dishonorable yes even corrupt judicial system have inevitably and irrevocably trained their loathsome and despicable eyes upon me.

Inez took a breath, then read the first sentence again. Most of the words looked familiar. After years of reading with a letter in one hand and a dictionary in the other, she was amazed at how much her vocabulary had expanded.

Butch glanced back, saw the letter, shook his head, but said nothing.

However, the State of Mississippi will once again be thwarted and stymied and left in thorough and consummate degradation in its resolution to extract blood from Raymond T. Graney. For I have procured and retained the services of a young lawyer with astonishing skills, an extraordinary advocate judiciously chosen by me from the innumerable legions of barristers quite literally throwing themselves at my feet.

Another pause, another quick rereading. Inez was barely hanging on.

Not surprisingly, a lawyer of such exquisite and superlative yes even singular proficiencies and dexterities cannot labor and effectively advocate on my behalf without appropriate recompense.

"What's recompense?" she asked.

"Spell it," Butch said.

She spelled it slowly, and the three pondered the word. This exercise in language skills had become as routine as talking about the weather.

"How's it used?" Butch asked, so she read the sentence.

"Money," Butch said, and Leon quickly agreed. Raymond's mysterious words often had something to do with money.

"Let me guess. He's got a new lawyer and needs some extra money to pay him."

Inez ignored him and kept reading.

It is with great reluctance even trepidation that I desperately beseech you and implore you to procure the quite reasonable sum of $1500 which will forthrightly find application in my defense and undoubtedly extricate me and emancipate me and otherwise save my ass. Come on, Momma, now is the hour for the family to join hands and metaphorically circle the wagons. Your reluctance yes even your recalcitrance will be deemed pernicious neglect.

"What's recalcitrance?" she asked.

"Spell it," Leon said. She spelled "recalcitrance," then "pernicious," and after a halfhearted debate it was obvious that none of the three had a clue.

One final note before I move on to more pressing correspondence—Butch and Leon have again neglected my stipends. Their latest perfidies concern the month of June, and it's already halfway through July. Please torment, harass, vex, heckle, and badger those two blockheads until they honor their commitments to my defense fund.

Love, as always, from your dearest and favorite son,

Raymond

Each letter sent to a death row inmate was read by someone in the mail room at Parchman, and each outgoing letter was likewise scrutinized. Inez had often pitied the poor soul assigned to read Raymond's missives. They never failed to tire Inez, primarily because they required work. She was afraid she would miss something important.

The letters drained her. The lyrics put her to sleep. The novels produced migraines. The poetry could not be penetrated.

She wrote back twice a week, without fail, because if she neglected her youngest by even a day or so, she could expect a torrent of abuse, a four-pager or maybe a five-pager with blistering language that contained words often not found in a dictionary. And even the slightest delay in mailing in her stipend would cause unpleasant collect phone calls.

Of the three, Raymond had been the best student, though none had finished high school. Leon had been the better athlete, Butch the better musician, but little Raymond got the brains. And he made it all the way to the eleventh grade before he got caught with a stolen motorcycle and spent sixty days in a juvenile facility. He was sixteen, five years younger than Butch and ten younger than Leon, and already the Graney boys were developing the reputation as skillful car thieves. Raymond joined the family business and forgot about school.

"So how much does he want this time?" Butch asked.

"Fifteen hundred, for a new lawyer. Said you two ain't sent his stipends for the last month."

"Drop it, Momma," Leon said harshly, and for a long time nothing else was said.

When the first car theft ring was broken, Leon took the fall and did his time at Parchman. Upon his release, he married his second wife and managed to go straight. Butch and Raymond made no effort at going straight; in fact, they expanded their activities. They fenced stolen guns and appliances, dabbled in the marijuana trade, ran moonshine, and of course stole cars and sold them to various chop shops in north Mississippi. Butch got busted when he stole an 18-wheeler that was supposed to be full of Sony televisions but in fact was a load of chain link fencing. Televisions are easy to move on the black market. Chain link proved far more difficult. In the course of events the sheriff raided Butch's hiding place and found the contraband, useless as it was. He pleaded to eighteen months, his first stint at Parchman. Raymond avoided indictment and lived to steal again. He stuck to his first love—cars and pickups—and prospered nicely, though all profits were wasted on booze, gambling, and an astounding string of bad women.

From the beginning of their careers as thieves, the Graney boys were hounded by an obnoxious deputy named Coy Childers. Coy suspected them in every misdemeanor and felony in Ford County. He watched them, followed them, threatened them, harassed them, and at various times arrested them for good cause and for no cause whatsoever. All three had been beaten by Coy in the depths of the Ford County jail. They had complained bitterly to the sheriff, Coy's boss, but no one listens to the whining of known criminals. And the Graneys became quite well-known.

For revenge, Raymond stole Coy's patrol car and sold it to a chop shop in Memphis. He kept the police radio and mailed it back to Coy in an unmarked parcel. Raymond was arrested and would've been beaten but for the intervention of his court-appointed lawyer. There was no proof at all, nothing to link him to the crime except some well-founded suspicion. Two months later, after Raymond had been released, Coy bought his wife a new Chevrolet Impala. Raymond promptly stole it from a church parking lot during Wednesday night prayer meeting and sold it to a chop shop near Tupelo. By then, Coy was openly vowing to kill Raymond Graney.

There were no witnesses to the actual killing, or at least none who would come forward. It happened late on a Friday night, on a gravel road not far from a double-wide trailer Raymond was sharing with his latest girlfriend. The prosecution's theory was that Coy had parked his car and was approaching quietly on foot, alone, with the plan to confront Raymond and perhaps even arrest him. Coy was found after sunrise by some deer hunters. He'd been shot twice in the forehead by a high-powered rifle, and he was positioned in a slight dip in the gravel road, which allowed a large amount of blood to accumulate around his body. The crime scene photos caused two jurors to vomit.

Raymond and his girl claimed to be away at a honky-tonk, but evidently they'd been the only customers because no other alibi witnesses could be found. Ballistics traced the bullets to a stolen rifle fenced through one of Raymond's longtime underworld associates, and though there was no proof that Raymond had ever owned, stolen, borrowed, or possessed the rifle, the suspicion was enough. The prosecutor convinced the jury that Raymond had motive—he hated Coy, and he was, after all, a convicted felon; he had opportunity—Coy was found near Raymond's trailer, and there was no neighbors within miles; and he had the means—the alleged murder weapon was waved around the courtroom, complete with an army-issue scope that may have allowed the killer to see through the darkness, though there was no evidence the scope was actually attached to the rifle when it was used to kill Coy.

Raymond's alibi was weak. His girlfriend, too, had a criminal record and made a lousy witness. His court-appointed defense lawyer subpoenaed three people who were supposed to testify that they had heard Coy vow to kill Raymond Graney. All three faltered under the pressure of sitting in the witness chair and being glared at by the sheriff and at least ten of his uniformed deputies. It was a questionable defense strategy to begin with. If Raymond believed Coy was coming to kill him, then did he, Raymond, act in self-defense? Was Raymond admitting to the crime? No, he was not. He insisted he knew nothing about it and was dancing in a bar when someone else took care of Coy.

In spite of the overwhelming public pressure to convict Raymond, the jury stayed out for two days before finally doing so.

A year later, the feds broke up a methamphetamine ring, and in the aftermath of a dozen hasty plea bargains it was learned that Deputy Coy Childers had been heavily involved in the drug distribution syndicate. Two other murders, very similar in details, had taken place over in Marshall County, sixty miles away. Coy's stellar reputation among the locals was badly tarnished. The gossip began to fester about who really killed him, though Raymond remained the favorite suspect.

Raymond's conviction and death sentence were unanimously affirmed by the state's supreme court. More appeals led to more affirmations, and now, eleven years later, the case was winding down.

West of Batesville, the hills finally yielded to the flatlands, and the highway cut through fields thick with mid-summer cotton and soybeans. Farmers on their green John Deeres poked along the highway as if it had been built for tractors and not automobiles. But the Graneys were in no hurry. The van moved on, past an idle cotton gin, abandoned shotgun shacks, new double-wide trailers with satellite dishes and big trucks parked at the doors, and an occasional fine home set back to keep the traffic away from the landowners. At the town of Marks, Leon turned south, and they moved deeper into the Delta.

"I reckon Charlene'll be there," Inez said.

"Most certainly," Leon said.

"She wouldn't miss it for anything," Butch said.

Charlene was Coy's widow, a long-suffering woman who had embraced the martyrdom of her husband with unusual enthusiasm. Over the years she'd joined every victims' group she could find, state and national. She threatened lawsuits against the newspaper and anybody else who questioned Coy's integrity. She had written long letters to the editor demanding speedier justice for Raymond Graney. And she had missed not one court hearing along the way, even traveling as far as New Orleans when the federal Fifth Circuit Court of Appeals had the case.

"She's been prayin' for this day," Leon said.

"Well, she better keep prayin', 'cause Raymond said it ain't gonna happen," Inez said. "He promised me his lawyers are much better than the State's lawyers and that they're filin' papers by the truckload."

Leon glanced at Butch, who made eye contact, then gazed at the cotton fields. They passed through the farm settlements of Vance, Tutweiler, and Rome as the sun was finally fading. Dusk brought the swarms of insects that hit the hood and windshield. They smoked with the windows down, and said little. The approach to Parchman always subdued the Graneys—Butch and Leon for obvious reasons, and Inez because it reminded her of her shortcomings as a mother.

Parchman was an infamous prison, but it was also a farm, a plantation, that sprawled over eighteen thousand acres of rich, black soil that had produced cotton and profits for the state for decades until the federal courts got involved and pretty much abolished slave labor. In another lawsuit, another federal court ended the segregated conditions. More litigation had made life slightly better, though violence was worse.

For Leon, thirty months there turned him away from crime, and that was what the law-abiding citizens demanded of a prison. For Butch, his first sentence proved that he could survive another, and no car or truck was safe in Ford County.

Highway 3 ran straight and flat, and there was little traffic. It was almost dark when the van passed the small green highway sign that simply said, PARCHMAN. Ahead there were lights, activity; something unusual happening. To the right were the white stone front gates of the prison, and across the highway in a gravel lot a circus was underway. Death penalty protestors were busy. Some knelt in a circle and prayed. Some walked a tight formation with handmade posters supporting Ray Graney. Another group sang a hymn. Another knelt around a priest and held candles. Farther down the highway, a smaller group chanted pro-death slogans and tossed insults at the supporters of Graney. Uniformed deputies kept the peace. Television news crews were busy recording it all.

Leon stopped at the guard house, which was crawling with prison guards and anxious security personnel. A guard with a clipboard stepped to the driver's door and said, "Your name?"

"Graney, family of Mr. Raymond Graney. Leon, Butch, and our mother, Inez."

The guard wrote nothing, took a step back, managed to say, "Wait a minute," then left them. Three guards stood directly in front of the van, at a barricade across the entry road.

"He's gone to get Fitch," Butch said. "Wanna bet?"

"No," Leon replied.

Fitch was an assistant warden of some variety, a career prison employee whose dead-end job was brightened only by an escape or an execution. In cowboy boots, fake Stetson, and with a large pistol on his hip, he swaggered around Parchman as if he owned it. Fitch had outlasted a dozen wardens and had survived that many lawsuits. As he approached the van, he said loudly, "Well, well, the Graney boys're back where they belong. Here for a little furniture repair, boys? We have an old electric chair y'all can reupholster." He laughed at his own humor and there was more laughter behind him.

"Evenin', Mr. Fitch," Leon said. "We have our mother with us."

"Evenin', ma'am," Fitch said as he glanced inside the van. Inez did not respond.

"Where'd you get this van?" Fitch asked.

"We borrowed it," Leon answered. Butch stared straight ahead and refused to look at Fitch.

"Borrowed, my ass. When's the last time you boys borrowed anything? I'm sure Mr. McBride is lookin' for his van right now. Might give him a call."

"You do that, Fitch," Leon said.

"It's Mr. Fitch to you."

"Whatever you say."

Fitch unloaded a mouthful of spit. He nodded ahead as if he and he alone controlled the details. "I reckon you boys know where you're goin'," he said. "God knows you been here enough. Follow that car back to max security. They'll do the search there." He waved at the guards at the barricade. An opening was created, and they left Fitch without another word. For a few minutes they followed an unmarked car filled with armed men. They passed one unit after another, each entirely separate, each encircled by chain link topped with razor wire. Butch gazed at the unit where he'd surrendered several years of his life. In a well-lit open area, the "playground," as they called it, he saw the inevitable basketball game with shirtless men drenched in sweat, always one hard foul away from another mindless brawl. He saw the calmer ones sitting on picnic tables, waiting for the ten p.m. bed check, waiting for the heat to break because the barracks air units seldom worked, especially in July.

As usual, Leon glanced at his old unit, but did not dwell on his time there. After so many years, he'd been able to tuck away the emotional scars of physical abuse. The inmate population was eighty percent black, and Parchman was one of the few places in Mississippi where the whites did not make the rules.

The maximum security unit was a 1950s-style flat-roofed building, one level, red brick, much like countless elementary schools built back then. It, too, was wrapped in chain link and razor wire and watched by guards lounging in towers, though on this night everyone in uniform was awake and excited. Leon parked where he was directed, then he and Butch were thoroughly searched by a small battalion of unsmiling guards. Inez was lifted out, rolled to a makeshift checkpoint, and carefully inspected by two female guards. They were escorted inside the building, through a series of heavy doors, past more guards, and finally to a small room they had never seen before. The visitors' room was elsewhere. Two guards stayed with them as they settled in. The room had a sofa, two folding chairs, a row of ancient file cabinets, and the look of an office that belonged to some trifling bureaucrat who'd been chased away for the night.

The two prison guards weighed at least two hundred and fifty pounds each, had twenty-four-inch necks, and the obligatory shaved heads. After five awkward minutes in the room with the family, Butch had had enough. He took a few steps, and challenged them with a bold, "What, exactly, are you two doing in here?"

"Following orders," one said.

"Whose orders?"

"The warden's."

"Do you realize how stupid you look? Here we are, the family of the condemned man, waiting to spend a few minutes with our brother, in this tiny shithole of a room, with no windows, cinder-block walls, only one door, and you're standing here guarding us as if we're dangerous. Do you realize how stupid this is?"

Both necks seemed to expand. Both faces turned scarlet. Had Butch been an inmate he would have been beaten, but he wasn't. He was a citizen, a former convict, who hated every cop, trooper, guard, agent, and security type he'd ever seen. Every man in a uniform was his enemy.

"Sir, please sit down," one said coolly.

"In case you idiots don't realize it, you can guard this room from the other side of that door just as easily as you can from this side. I swear. It's true. I know you probably haven't been trained enough to realize this, but if you just walked through the door and parked your big asses on the other side, then ever'thang would still be secure and we'd have some privacy. We could talk to our little brother without worryin' about you clowns eavesdroppin'."

"You better knock it off, pal."

"Go ahead, just step through the door, close it, stare at it, guard it. I know you boys can handle it. I know you can keep us safe in here."

Of course the guards didn't move, and Butch eventually sat in a folding chair close to his mother. After a thirty-minute wait that seemed to last forever, the warden entered with his entourage and introduced himself. "The execution is still planned for one minute after midnight," he said officially, as if he were discussing a routine meeting with his staff. "We've been told not to expect a last-minute call from the Governor's office." There was no hint of compassion.

Inez placed both hands over her face and began crying softly.

He continued, "The lawyers are busy with all the last-minute stuff they always do, but our lawyers tell us a reprieve is unlikely."

Leon and Butch stared at the floor.

"We relax the rules a little for these events. You're free to stay in here as long as you like, and we'll bring in Raymond shortly. I'm sorry it's come down to this. If I can do anything, just let me know."

"Get those two jackasses outta here," Butch said, pointing to the guards. "We'd like some privacy."

The warden hesitated, looked around the room, then said, "No problem." He left and took the guards with him. Fifteen minutes later, the door opened again, and Raymond bounced in with a big smile and went straight for his mother. After a long hug and a few tears, he bear-hugged his brothers and told them things were moving in their favor. They pulled the chairs close to the sofa and sat in a small huddle, with Raymond clutching his mother's hands.

"We got these sumbitches on the run," he said, still smiling, the picture of confidence. "My lawyers are filin' a truckload of habeas corpus petitions as we speak, and they're quite certain the U.S. Supreme Court will grant certiorari within the hour."

"What does that mean?" Inez asked.

"Means the Supreme Court will agree to hear the case, and it's an automatic delay. Means we'll probably get a new trial in Ford County, though I'm not sure I want it there."

He was wearing prison whites, no socks, and a pair of cheap rubber sandals. And it was clear that Raymond was packing on the pounds. His cheeks were round and puffy. A spare tire hung over his belt. They hadn't seen him in almost six weeks, and his weight gain was noticeable. As usual, he prattled on about matters they did not understand and did not believe, at least as far as Butch and Leon were concerned. Raymond had been born with a vivid imagination, a quick tongue, and an innate inability to tell the truth.

The boy could lie.

"Got two dozen lawyers scramblin' right now," he said. "State can't keep up with 'em."

"When do you hear somethin' from the court?" Inez asked.

"Any minute now. I got federal judges in Jackson, in New Orleans, and in Washington sittin' by, just ready to kick the state's ass."

After eleven years of having his ass thoroughly kicked by the state, it was difficult to believe that Raymond had now, at this late hour, managed to turn the tide. Leon and Butch nodded gravely, as if they bought this and believed that the inevitable was not about to happen. They had known for many years that their little brother had ambushed Coy and practically blown his head off with a stolen rifle. Raymond had told Butch years earlier, long after he'd landed on death row, that he'd been so stoned he could hardly remember the killing.

"Plus we got some big-shot lawyers in Jackson puttin' pressure on the governor, just in case the Supreme Court chickens out again," he said.

All three nodded, but no one mentioned the comments from the warden.

"You got my last letter, Momma? The one about the new lawyer?"

"Sure did. Read it drivin' over here," she said, nodding.

"I'd like to hire him as soon as we get an order for the new trial. He's from Mobile, and he is one bad boy, lemme tell you. But we can talk about him later."

"Sure, son."

"Thank you. Look, Momma, I know this is hard, but you gotta have faith in me and my lawyers. I been runnin' my own defense for a year now, bossin' the lawyers around 'cause that's what you gotta do these days, and thangs're gonna work out, Momma. Trust me."

"I do, I do."

Raymond jumped to his feet and thrust his arms high above, stretching with his eyes closed. "I'm into yoga now, did I tell y'all about it?"

All three nodded. His letter had been loaded with the details of his latest fascination. Over the years the family had suffered through Raymond's breathless accounts of his conversion to Buddhism, then Isalm, then Hinduism, and his discoveries of meditation, kung fu, aerobics, weight lifting, fasting, and of course his quest to become a poet, novelist, singer, and musician. Little had been spared in his letters home.

Whatever the current passion, it was obvious that the fasting and aerobics had been abandoned. Raymond was so fat his britches strained in the seat.

"Did you bring the brownies?" he asked his mother. He loved her pecan brownies.

"No, honey, I'm sorry. I've been so tore up over this."

"You always bring the brownies."

"I'm sorry."

Just like Raymond. Berating his mother over nothing just hours before his final walk.

"Well, don't forget them again."

"I won't, honey."

"And another thang. Tallulah is supposed to be here any minute. She'd love to meet y'all because y'all have always rejected her. She's part of the family regardless of what y'all thank. As a favor at this unfortunate moment in my life, I ask that y'all accept her and be nice."

Leon and Butch could not respond, but Inez managed to say, "Yes, dear."

"When I get outta this damned place we're movin' to Hawaii and havin' ten kids. No way I'm stayin' in Mississippi, not after all this. So she'll be part of the family from now on."

For the first time Leon glanced at his watch with the thought that relief was just over two hours away. Butch was thinking, too, but his thoughts were far different. The idea of choking Raymond to death before the state could kill him posed an interesting dilemma.

Raymond suddenly stood and said, "Well, look, I gotta go meet with the lawyers. I'll be back in half an hour." He walked to the door, opened it, then thrust out his arms for the handcuffs. The door closed, and Inez said, "I guess thangs're okay."

"Look, Momma, we'd best listen to the warden," Leon said.

"Raymond's kiddin' himself," Butch added. She started crying again.

The chaplain was a Catholic priest, Father Leland, and he quietly introduced himself to the family. They asked him to have a seat.

"I'm deeply sorry about this," he said somberly. "It's the worst part of my job."

Catholics were rare in Ford County, and the Graneys certainly didn't know any. They looked suspiciously at the white collar around his neck.

"I've tried to talk to Raymond," Father Leland continued. "But he has little interest in the Christian faith. Said he hadn't been to church since he was a little boy."

"I shoulda took him more," Inez said, lamenting.

"In fact, he claims to be an atheist."

"Lord, Lord."

Of course, the three Graneys had known for some time that Raymond had renounced all religious beliefs and had proclaimed that there was no God. This, too, they had read about in excruciating detail in his lengthy letters.

"We're not church people," Leon admitted.

"I'll be praying for you."

"Raymond stole the deputy's wife's new car outta the church parking lot," Butch said. "Did he tell you that?"

"No. We've talked a lot lately, and he's told me many stories. But not that one."

"Thank you, sir, for bein' so nice to Raymond," Inez said.

"I'll be with him until the end."

"So, they're really gonna do it?" she asked.

"It'll take a miracle to stop things now."

"Lord, help us," she said.

"Let's pray," Father Leland said. He closed his eyes, folded his hands together, and began: "Dear Heavenly Father, please look down upon us at this hour and let your Holy Spirit enter this place and give us peace. Give strength and wisdom to the lawyers and judges who are laboring diligently at this moment. Give courage to Raymond as he makes his preparations." Father Leland paused for a second and barely opened his left eye. All three Graneys were staring at him as if he had two heads. Rattled, he closed his eye and wrapped things up quickly with: "And, Father, grant grace and forgiveness to the officials and the people of Mississippi, for they know not what they're doing. Amen."

He said good-bye, and they waited a few minutes before Raymond returned. He had his guitar, and as soon as he settled into the sofa he strummed a few chords. He closed his eyes and began to hum, then he sang:

I got time to see you baby
I got time to come on by
I got time to stay forever
'Cause I got no time to die.

"It's an old tune by Mudcat Malone," he explained. "One of my favorites."

I got time to see you smilin'
I got time to see you cry
I got time to hold you, baby
'Cause I got no time to die.

The song was unlike any they'd heard before. Butch had once picked the banjo in a bluegrass band, but had given up music many years earlier. He had no voice whatsoever, a family trait shared by his younger brother. Raymond crooned in a guttural lurch, an affected attempt to sound like a black blues singer, apparently one in severe distress.

I got time to be yo' daddy
I got time to be yo' guy
I got time to be yo' lover
'Cause I got no time to die.

When the words stopped, he kept strumming and did a passable job of playing a tune. Butch, though, couldn't help but think that after eleven years of practice in his cell, his guitar playing was rudimentary.

"That's so nice," Inez said.

"Thanks, Momma. Here's one from Little Bennie Burke, probably the greatest of all. He's from Indianola, you know?" They did not know. Like most white hill folks, they knew nothing about the blues and cared even less.

Raymond's face contorted again. He hit the strings harder.

I packed my bags on Monday
Tuesday said so long
Wednesday saw my baby
Thursday she was gone
Got paid this Friday mornin'
Mad said I's all right
Told him he could shove it
I'm walkin' out tonight.

Leon glanced at his watch. It was almost eleven p.m., just over an hour to go. He wasn't sure he could listen to the blues for another hour, but he resigned himself. The singing unnerved Butch as well, but he managed to sit with his eyes closed, as if soothed by the words and music.

I'm tired of pickin' cotton
I'm tired of shootin' dice
I'm tired of gettin' hassled
I'm tired of tryin' to be nice
I'm tired of workin' for nothin'
I'm tired of havin' to fight
Everything's behind me now
I'm walkin' out tonight.

Raymond forgot the words but continued with his humming. When he finally stopped, he sat with his eyes closed for a minute or so, as if the music had transported him to another world, to a much more pleasant place.

"What time is it, bro?" he asked Leon.

"Eleven straight up."

"I gotta go check with the lawyers. They're expectin' a ruling right about now."

He placed his guitar in a corner, then knocked on the door and stepped through it. The guards handcuffed him and led him away. Within minutes a crew from the kitchen arrived with armed escort. Hurriedly, they unfolded a square card table and covered it with a rather large amount of food. The smells were immediately thick in the room, and Leon and Butch were weak with hunger. They had not eaten since noon. Inez was too distraught to think about food, though she did examine the spread. Fried catfish, French fried potatoes, hushpuppies, cole slaw, all in the center of the table. To the right was a mammoth cheeseburger, with another order of fries and one of onion rings. To the left was a medium-sized pizza with pepperoni and hot, bubbling cheese. Directly in front of the catfish was a huge slice of what appeared to be lemon pie, and next to it was a dessert plate covered with chocolate cake. A bowl of vanilla ice cream was wedged along the edge of the table.

As the three Graneys gawked at the food, one of the guards said, "For the last meal, he gets anything he wants."

"Lord, Lord," Inez said, and began crying again.

When they were alone, Butch and Leon tried to ignore the food, which they could almost touch, but the aromas were overwhelming. Catfish battered and fried in corn oil. Fried onion rings. Pepperoni. The air in the small room was thick with the competing yet delicious smells.

The feast could easily accommodate four people.

At 11:15, Raymond made a noisy entry. He was griping at the guards and complaining incoherently about his lawyers. When he saw the food, he forgot about his problems and his family and took the only seat at the table. Using primarily his fingers, he crammed in a few loads of fries and onion rings and began talking. "Fifth Circuit just turned us down, the idiots. Our habeas petition was beautiful, wrote it myself. We're on the way to Washington, to the Supreme Court. Got a whole law firm up there ready to attack. Thangs look good." He managed to deftly shove food into his mouth, and chew it, while talking. Inez stared at her feet and wiped tears. Butch and Leon appeared to listen patiently while studying the tiled floor.

"Y'all seen Tallulah?" Raymond asked, still chomping after a gulp of iced tea.

"No," Leon said.

"Bitch. She just wants the book rights to my life story. That's all. But it ain't gonna happen. I'm leavin' all literary rights with the three of y'all. What about that?"

"Nice," said Leon.

"Great," said Butch.

The final chapter of his life was now close at hand. Raymond had already written his autobiography—two hundred pages—and it had been rejected by every publisher in America.

He chomped away, wreaking havoc with the catfish, burger, and pizza in no particular order. His fork and fingers moved around the table, often headed in different directions, poking, stabbing, grabbing, and shoveling food into his mouth as fast as he could swallow it. A starving hog at a trough would have made less noise. Inez had never spent much time with table manners, and her boys had learned all the bad habits. Eleven years on death row had taken Raymond to new depths of crude behavior.

Leon's third wife, though, had been properly raised. He snapped ten minutes into the last meal. "Do you have to smack like that?" he barked.

"Damn, son, you're makin' more noise than a horse eatin' corn," Butch piled on instantly.

Raymond froze, glared at both of his brothers, and for a few long tense seconds the situation could've gone either way. It could've erupted into a classic Graney brawl with lots of cursing and personal insults. Over the years, there had been several ugly spats in the visitors' room at death row, all painful, all memorable. But Raymond, to his credit, took a softer approach.

"It's my last meal," he said. "And my own family's bitchin' at me."

"I'm not," Inez said.

"Thank you, Momma."

Leon held his hands wide in surrender and said, "I'm sorry. We're all a little tense."

"Tense?" Raymond said. "You think you're tense?"

"I'm sorry, Ray."

"Me too," Butch said, but only because it was expected.

"You want a hushpuppy?" Ray said, offering one to Butch.

A few minutes earlier the last meal had been an irresistible feast. Now, though, after Raymond's frenzied assault, the table was in ruins. In spite of this, Butch was craving some fries and a hushpuppy, but he declined. There was something eerily wrong with nibbling off the edges of a man's last meal. "No, thanks," he said.

After catching his breath, Raymond plowed ahead, albeit at a slower and quieter pace. He finished off the lemon pie and chocolate cake, with ice cream, belched, and laughed about it, then said, "Ain't my last meal, I can promise you that."

There was a knock on the door, and a guard stepped in and said, "Mr. Tanner would like to see you."

"Send him in," Raymond said. "My chief lawyer," he announced proudly to his family.

Mr. Tanner was a slight, balding young man in a faded navy jacket, old khakis, and even older tennis shoes. He wore no tie.

He carried a thick stack of papers. His face was gaunt and pale and he looked as if he needed a long rest. Raymond quickly introduced him to his family, but Mr. Tanner showed no interest in meeting new people at that moment.

"The Supreme Court just turned us down," he announced gravely to Raymond.

Raymond swallowed hard and the room was silent.

"What about the governor?" Leon asked. "And all those lawyers down there talkin' to him?"

Tanner shot a blank look at Raymond, who said, "I fired them."

"What about all those lawyers in Washington?" Butch asked.

"I fired them too."

"What about that big firm from Chicago?" Leon asked.

"I fired them too."

Tanner looked back and forth among the Graneys.

"Seems like a bad time to be firin' your lawyers," Leon said.

"What lawyers?" Tanner asked. "I'm the only lawyer working on this case."

"You're fired too," Raymond said, and violently slapped his glass of tea off the card table, sending ice and liquid splashing against a wall. "Go ahead and kill me!" he screamed. "I don't care anymore."

No one breathed for a few seconds, then the door opened suddenly and the warden was back, with his entourage. "It's time, Raymond," he said, somewhat impatiently. "The appeals are over and the governor's gone to bed."

There was a long, heavy pause as the finality sank in. Inez was crying. Leon was staring blankly at the wall where the tea and ice were sliding to the floor. Butch was looking forlornly at the last two hushpuppies. Tanner appeared ready to faint.

Raymond cleared his throat and said, "I'd like to see that Catholic guy. We need to pray."

"I'll get him," the warden said. "You can have one last moment with your family, then it's time to go."

The warden left with his assistants. Tanner quickly followed them.

Raymond's shoulders slumped and his face was pale. All defiance and bravado vanished. He walked slowly to his mother, fell to his knees in front of her, and put his head in her lap. She rubbed it, wiped her eyes, and kept saying, "Lord, Lord."

"I'm so sorry, Momma," Raymond mumbled. "I'm so sorry."

They cried together for a moment while Leon and Butch stood silently by. Father Leland entered the room, and Raymond slowly stood. His eyes were wet and red and his voice was soft and weak. "I guess it's over," he said to the priest, who nodded sadly and patted his shoulder.

"I'll be with you in the isolation room, Raymond," he said. "We'll have a final prayer, if you wish."

"Probably not a bad idea."

The door opened again and the warden was back. He addressed the Graneys and Father Leland. "Please listen to me," he said. "This is my fourth execution, and I've learned a few things. One is that it is a bad idea for the mother to witness the execution. I strongly suggest, Mrs. Graney, that you remain here, in this room, for the next hour or so, until it's over. We have a nurse who will sit with you, and she has a sedative that I recommend. Please." He looked at Leon and Butch and pleaded with his eyes. Both got the message.

"I'll be there til the end," Inez said, then wailed so loudly that even the warden had a flash of goose bumps.

Butch stepped next to her and stroked her shoulder.

"You need to stay here, Momma," Leon said. Inez wailed again.

"She'll stay," Leon said to the warden. "Just get her that pill."

Raymond hugged both of his brothers, and for the first time ever he said that he loved them, an act that was difficult even at that awful moment. He kissed his mother on the cheek and said good-bye.

"Be a man," Butch said with clenched teeth and wet eyes, and they embraced for the final time.

They led him away, and the nurse entered the room. She handed Inez a pill and a cup of water, and within minutes she was slumped in her wheelchair. The nurse sat beside her, and said, "I'm very sorry," to Butch and Leon.

At 12:15 the door opened and a guard said, "Come with me." The brothers were led from the room, into the hallway that was packed with guards and officials and many other curious onlookers lucky enough to gain access, and then back through the front entrance. Outside, the air was heavy and the heat had not broken. They quickly lit cigarettes as they walked along a narrow sidewalk next to the west wing of maximum security unit, past the open windows covered with thick black bars, and as they moved casually to the death room, they could hear the other condemned men banging their cell doors, yelling in protest, all making whatever noise they could in a last-minute farewell to one of their own.

Butch and Leon smoked furiously and wanted to yell something of their own, something in support of the inmates. But neither said a word. They turned a corner and saw a small, flat redbrick building with guards and others milling around its door. There was an ambulance beside it. Their escort led them through a side door to a cramped witness room, and upon entering, they saw faces they expected, but had no interest in seeing. Sheriff Walls was there because the law required it. The prosecutor was there, by choice. Charlene, Coy's long-suffering widow, sat next to the sheriff. She was joined by two hefty young gals who were no doubt her daughters. The victims' side of the witness room was separated by a wall of plexiglass that allowed them to glare at the condemned man's family but prevented them from speaking, or cursing. Butch and Leon sat in plastic chairs. Strangers shuffled in behind them, and when everyone was in place, the door was closed. The witness room was packed and hot.

They stared at nothing. The windows before them were shielded by black curtains so that they could not see the sinister preparations underway on the other side. There were sounds, indistinguishable movements. Suddenly, the curtains were yanked open and they were looking at the death room, twelve feet by fifteen, with a freshly painted concrete floor. In the center of it was the gas chamber, an octagon-shaped silver cylinder with windows of its own to allow proper witnessing and verification of death.

And, there was Raymond, strapped to a chair inside the gas chamber, his head secured with some hideous brace that forced him to look ahead and prevented him from seeing the witnesses. At that moment he seemed to be looking up as the warden spoke to him. The prison attorney was present, as were some guards and of course the executioner and his assistant. All went about their tasks, whatever they were supposed to be doing, with grim determined looks, as if they were bothered by this ritual. In fact, all were volunteers, except for the warden and the attorney.

A small speaker hung from a nail in the witness room and conveyed the final sounds.

The attorney stepped close to the chamber door and said, "Raymond, by law I'm required to read your death warrant." He lifted a sheet of paper and continued: "Pursuant to a verdict of guilty and a sentence of death returned against you in the Circuit Court of Ford County, you are hereby sentenced to death by lethal gas in the gas chamber of the Mississippi State Penitentiary at Parchman. May God have mercy on your soul." He stepped away and lifted a telephone from its receiver on the wall. He listened, then said, "No stays."

The warden said, "Any reason why this execution should not go forward?"

"No," said the attorney.

"Any last words, Raymond?"

Raymond's voice was barely audible, but in the perfect stillness of the witness room he was heard: "I am sorry for what I did. I ask the forgiveness of the family of Coy Childers. I have been forgiven by my Lord. Let's get this over with."

The guards left the death room, leaving the warden and the attorney, who shuffled backward as far from Raymond as possible. The executioner stepped forward and closed the narrow chamber door. His assistant checked the seals around it. When the chamber was ready, they glanced around the death room—a quick inspection. No problems. The executioner disappeared into a small closet, the chemical room, where he controlled his valves.

Long seconds passed. The witnesses gawked in horror and fascination and held their breaths. Raymond held his, too, but not for long.

The executioner placed a plastic container of sulphuric acid into a tube that ran from the chemical room to a bowl in the bottom of the chamber, just under the chair that Raymond now occupied. He pulled a lever to release the canister. A clicking sound occurred, and most of those watching flinched. Raymond flinched too. His fingers clutched the arms of the chair. His spine stiffened. Seconds passed, then the sulphuric acid mixed with a collection of cyanide pellets already in the bowl, and the lethal steam began rising. When Raymond finally exhaled, when he could no longer hold his breath, he sucked in as much poison as possible to speed things along. His entire body reacted instantly with jolts and gyrations. His shoulders jumped back. His chin and forehead fought mightily against the leather head brace. His hands, arms, and legs shook violently as the steam rose and grew thicker.

His body reacted and fought for a minute or so, then the cyanide took control. The convulsions slowed. His head became still. His fingers loosened their death grip on the arms of the chair. The air continued to thicken as Raymond's breathing slowed, then stopped. Some final twitching, a jolt in his chest muscles, a vibration in his hands, and finally it was over.

He was pronounced dead at 12:31 a.m. The black curtains were closed, and the witnesses hustled from the room. Outside, Butch and Leon leaned on a corner of the redbrick building and smoked a cigarette.

Inside the death room, a vent above the chamber was opened, and the gas escaped into the sticky air over Parchman. Fifteen minutes later, guards with gloves unshackled Raymond and wrestled his body out of the chamber. His clothing was cut off, to be burned. His corpse was hosed off with cold water, then dried with kitchen towels, reclothed in prison whites, and laid inside a cheap pine coffin.

Leon and Butch sat with their mother and waited for the warden. Inez was still sedated, but she clearly understood what had taken place in the last few minutes. Her head was buried in her hands and she cried softly, mumbling occasionally. A guard entered and asked for the keys to Mr. McBride's van. An hour dragged by.

The warden, fresh from his press announcement, finally entered the room. He offered some sappy condolences, managed to look sad and sympathetic, then asked Leon to sign some forms. He explained that Raymond left almost $1000 in his prison account, and a check would be sent within a week. He said the van was loaded with the coffin and four boxes of Raymond's belongings—his guitar, clothing, books, correspondence, legal materials, and manuscripts. They were free to go.

The coffin was moved to one side so Inez could be rolled through the back of the van, and when she touched it she broke down again. Leon and Butch rearranged the boxes, secured the wheelchair, then moved the coffin again. When everything was in its place, they followed a car full of guards back to the front of the prison, through the entrance, and when they turned onto Highway 3 they drove past the last of the protestors. The television crews were gone. Leon and Butch lit cigarettes, but Inez was too emotional to smoke. No one spoke for miles as they hurried through the cotton and soybean fields. Near the town of Marks, Leon spotted an all-night convenience store. He bought a soda for Butch and tall coffees for his mother and himself.

When the Delta yielded to the hill country, they felt better.

"What did he say last?" Inez asked, her tongue thick.

"He apologized," Butch said. "Asked Charlene for forgiveness."

"So she watched it?"

"Oh yes. You didn't think she'd miss it."

"I should've seen it."

"No, Momma," Leon said. "You can be thankful for the rest of your days that you didn't witness the execution. Your last memory of Raymond was a long hug and a nice farewell. Please don't think you missed anything."

"It was horrible," Butch said.

"I should've seen it."

In the town of Batesville they passed a fast-food place that advertised chicken biscuits and twenty-four-hour service. Leon turned around. "I could use the ladies'," Inez said. There were no other customers inside at 3:15 in the morning. Butch rolled his mother to a table near the front, and they ate in silence. The van with Raymond's coffin was less than thirty feet away.

Inez managed a few bites, then lost her appetite. Butch and Leon ate like refugees.

They entered Ford County just after 5 a.m., still very dark, the roads empty. They drove to Pleasant Ridge in the north end of the county, to a small Pentecostal church where they parked in the gravel lot, and waited. At the first hint of sunlight, they heard an engine start somewhere in the distance.

"Wait here," Leon said to Butch, then left the van and disappeared. Behind the church there was a cemetery, and at the far end of it a backhoe had just begun digging the grave. The backhoe was owned by a cousin's boss. At 6:30, several men from the church arrived and went to the grave site. Leon drove the van down a dirt trail and stopped near the backhoe, which had finished its digging and was now just waiting. The men pulled the coffin from the van. Butch and Leon gently placed their mother's wheelchair on the ground, and pushed her as they followed the coffin.

They lowered it with ropes, and when it settled onto the four-by-four studs at the bottom, they withdrew the ropes. The preacher read a short verse of Scripture, then said a prayer. Leon and Butch shoveled some dirt onto the coffin, then thanked the men for their assistance.

As they drove away, the backhoe was refilling the grave.

The house was empty—no concerned neighbors waiting, no relatives there to mourn. They unloaded Inez and rolled her into the house and into her bedroom. She was soon fast asleep. The four boxes were placed in a storage shed, where their contents would weather and fade along with the memories of Raymond.

It was decided that Butch would stay home that day to care for Inez, and to ward off the reporters. There had been many calls in the past week, and someone was bound to show up with a camera. He worked at a sawmill and his boss would understand.

Leon drove to Clanton and stopped on the edge of town to fill up with gas. At 8 a.m. sharp he pulled into the lot at McBride Upholstery and returned the van. An employee explained that Mr. McBride wasn't in yet, was probably still at the coffee shop, and usually got to work around 9. Leon handed over the keys, thanked the employee, and left.

He drove to the lamp factory east of town, and punched the clock at 8:30, as always.

19 What His Hands Had Been Waiting For
Tom Franklin and Beth Ann Fennelly

July, 1927

They left the dead looters in the house and were striding toward their horses, Ham Johnson reloading his .30-30, when they heard what sounded like a cat.

"Ain't no cat," said Ingersoll.

"Naw." Ham clicked a cartridge into the port of his rifle. He clicked in another.

They followed the squawling past the house's slanted silhouette—the owners smart enough to leave the doors and windows open, which had let the flood waters swirl through. Behind the house, a shade tree, now like something dipped in batter halfway up. Snagged in the top branches, a coop filled with dead chickens.

Anyway, Ingersoll was right about it not being a cat. It was a baby.

The men stared. A bushel basket on a low branch held the red-faced thing. In the mud, beneath the basket, a shred of blanket it'd kicked away.

"Mother of God," Ingersoll said.

"Wasn't nothing of God about this one's mother," Ham said. He raised his right arm, aiming his shotgun at the door of the house, and closed one eye. "She was the one. Got-damn it. When she heard us coming she must've up and left this one here and hid herself in the house."

Ingersoll considered the baby. It wore a gnarl of diaper and was impossible to name boy or girl. It was bald. Red from crying and he realized they'd been yelling above its noise.

"You better off," Ham told it. "Take a chance with the current elements. Maybe a gang of coyote'll take you in. Isn't that what happened to you, Ingersoll? Band of coyotes found you in the tundra and raised you as their own?"

Ham shoved the silver tray they'd taken from the looters into his saddlebag. A white man just over six feet tall with a red face and bright red hair he kept cut short, Ham wore mutton chops (also red) he called burnsides, and a belly nutria derby that he was slightly vain about and endeavored to keep clean. Ingersoll's hat was bigger and more practical, a black Stetson Dakota.

"Ain't no coyotes this far south," he said.

"Is too," Ham said. He kicked his leg to flap his boot sole down—the leather wet so long it'd rotted—and fitted his boot into his stirrup and swung onto his saddle.

"It's wild dogs a plenty, Ham. But it ain't no coyotes."

Ingersoll was looking beyond the house, studying the inland sea of dried and drying mud where cotton plants had once been, the horizon unrelenting brown, flat and cracking like so much poorly thrown pottery. Twice he had seen arms of the dead reaching out of it.

The levees had ruptured back in April, and even here, twenty-five miles southeast of the Mounds Landing crevasse, the waves had surged six feet. Thunderous breakers of coffee-colored froth had flattened near every tree and building, then just wiped them all away, like something out of Revelation. Ingersoll recalled the buried road to Yazoo City, a bloated mare and in front of its muzzle a bloated Bible as if the horse were verifying the events of the end time when they befell him.

"Tell Junior goodbye," Ham said.

"What you mean?"

"I mean it's somebody'll come along sooner or later and get this damn baby's what I mean. We got to skedaddle." He looked over his shoulder at the basket, now swaying in the breeze. "What's that lullaby? 'When the bow breaks, the cradle will fall, and down will come baby, cradle and all.'"

"Ham—"

"C'mon," Ham said. "Let's get to New Orleans, spend some of this looter loot. I got me a mind for a foreign girl. Russian if we can find one. Get a steak and lay some pipe. Then buy me a new pair of boots."

"I can't leave no baby, Ham."

"Well we ain't bringing it, Ing."

The foul wind from the east moaned through the leaning mule barn.

"Adios, Junior," Ham said, and gigged his sorrel with his heels. *"Vaya con dios."*

Ingersoll stared down at the kicking baby like maybe he'd had a baby himself long ago. And a wife.

But he hadn't. He was twenty-seven years old. He had no living family anywhere. He'd never even touched a baby.

"Ah, hell," he said and looked at the pewter sky, which gave a chuckle of thunder.

WILD DOGS FOLLOWING. Or coyotes if you asked Ham. Ingersoll rode a quarter-mile behind his partner and figured the big man wouldn't hear the thing fussing in his arms. It smelled like piss and flung its fists out and kicked. As he rode it was the beating and kicking that impressed Ingersoll. Little dickens had some fight.

In an hour the baby had lulled to a hiccupping sleep and Ingersoll let the horse follow the deeply-etched tracks Ham's sorrel was carving. Ingersoll had learned to trust Ham's lead after Ham had spotted and dispatched two of the saboteurs back in Marked Tree, Arkansas. Their next orders, sent via telegram by Coolidge's men, had brought them to the Old Moore plantation near Greenville, Mississippi, where they were told to monitor local Negroes, some growing seditious, planning to head North, put the lapping Mississippi far behind them. But the landowners— and the officials the landowners elected—couldn't allow the Negros to leave.Who would pick the cotton then?

But the cotton hadn't mattered. They were perhaps a dozen miles from Mounds Landing, searching for runaway Negroes, when that levee had burst. As if from the sky they heard it, heard the terrible roar, like a twister first but then an earthquake, it seemed, coming from beneath the horses. "Go," Ham had yelled. They spurred their mounts to a gallop and within minutes, the floodtide was upon them, washing trees and bodies past, brown water splashing over the horses' hooves first, then quickly over their withers to the riders' legs and then the horses were careening and swimming and the men fighting to stay on, the land gone behind them, there passing in the current a church steeple, there a wagon still hitched to a pair of kicking mules, there a school house desk.

Now Ingersoll's horse gave a lurch. He grasped the baby, which startled it awake, its arms flying outward, and set it to crying. The horse's back legs had sunk, stuck again. Ingersoll would have to dismount and wrench its hooves free. But what to do with the baby?

"Ham?"

He heard a horseshoe clip a rock behind him and lowered his head and shook it.

"I told you about that damn baby," Ham Johnson shouted at his back. "Look where your instincts are."

"It's my decision," Ingersoll called over his shoulder. "I'll ditch it first people we find."

Ham skidded to a stop beside Ingersoll's horse, wiggling its rump and straining its neck and rolling its eyes in panic. Ingersoll slid off clutching the squalling baby. It was horribly red in the face and its tears left tracks in its coat of dust.

"I think it's hungry," Ingersoll said.

Ham leaned and spat. "So am I." He spurred his horse, which threw beads of mud on Ingersoll's neck as it trotted away.

Ingersoll looked before him, behind. His own feet were heavy with mud and he saw nothing to do but set his upended Stetson in the mud and place the wailing baby ass-first in its crown. When he saw it wouldn't topple out he stood behind the horse, talking to it, and grounded his feet and squatted and with both hands around the horse's fetlock yanked it free, the mud yielding with an anguished and greedy slurp.

IT WAS A LONG AFTERNOON that they traveled south across the birdless crackled brown mudscape without ever arriving at its edge. At four it rained and woke the baby but they kept riding. They passed through the rain and through a spell of cool, the air dotted with mosquitoes, before it got hot again. Twice Ingersoll's horse jumped the bloated bodies of goats, his mount so weary and jaded it hardly broke stride. They crossed a patch where strange arcs and teeth of stone pressed through the mud that Ham said must have been a cemetery. As they rode, Ingersoll switched the baby from sore arm crook to sore arm crook, grateful that his horse had fidelity, hardly needed guiding at all.

As they pushed south, Ingersoll held his drinking pouch—he'd mixed sugar and water—for the baby to suck on. He'd also peered in its swaddle and seen its tiny knob, cleaned its backside with a rag dipped in puddle water and rigged his kerchief to make a new diaper.

They dismounted at the top of a small hill with a swift swollen creek below, a butter churn bobbing against speckled rocks. Ham hobbled the horses, keeping them close and saddled. Ingersoll took off his Stetson and frowned at the rotten smudges on his fingers but lowered the baby in it anyway, extending its arms along the brim. Ham had arranged a few twigs and branches and soon had a fire sputtering, its pops and sparks and orbiting moths a fascination for the baby, who pointed a crooked finger.

They chewed beef jerky and drank water from their canteens and rolled out their bedrolls. Ham unstoppered his pouch of mescal and pushed out his feet like he did when he was fixing to elaborate. His boots, caked in mud, were twice their regular size. Ingersoll reached into his saddlebag and lifted out his taterbug mandolin, a bowl-backed beauty of maple and mahogany, now warped a few degrees because of the rain. They'd found it washed ashore in a hussar trunk that Ham opened by shooting off the lock. Ingersoll, by tuning it a step and a half below standard, could play all the blues keys on it.

He laid down a few licks and the baby turned its attention to watch Ingersoll with its bright blue eyes. Ingersoll began to pick out a little ballad he'd made up.

"Tell this youngun your real name, Ham."

His partner swigged from his pouch. "Nobody knows it, living ner dead."

Ingersoll always enjoyed the next question for the contradictory answers it provoked. "And tell him how you come to be called Ham."

Ham took another pull. "You know how babies have that good smell, that sweet smell to their heads? Well, when I was a baby, my head gave off the perfume of ham."

"Oh, yeah?" Ingersoll played two bar fills and saw that the baby's eyelids were heavy, its head bobbing towards sleep.

"Yeah. Smelled like ham, like real good roast ham. People around me always getting hungry. It was my breath, something from inside. Over the years"—he took another swig, and Ingersoll laid down a blues lick—"over the years, I learned to stand downwind of folks. Naturally, as I grew I lost that sweet ham smell some, but it's still there if you get close, whore-close. In fact, had there been this flood back then, I'd likely have been the first one cannibalized. 'Ham Johnson' they'd say, shaking their heads. 'Damn but he made a fine breakfast.'" Ham leaned to pass the mescal. "Nobody would of ever thought he'd a been a genuine war hero and confiscated by the military government itself to pursue saboteurs of levees—"

"Dynamite-wielding saboteurs," Ingersoll added, taking a drink.

"Dynamite-wielding saboteurs of such a low stripe," Ham said, "that they're willing to set their charges wherever the highest bidder says." He started talking about how one group of saboteurs, posing as government engineers, had taken money from a village on the east side of the river and then blown the west side, flooding a village over there in order to keep theirs dry.

Ingersoll handed the tequila back and laid down a turnaround in E, just showing off now. He'd gotten his first guitar at ten, and holding it felt like somebody had attached a missing piece to his body. By fourteen he was making a living, a little gambling on the side, playing blues up in Clarksdale. But in 1916, he left for the Great War, put down his guitar for a U.S. Government-issue Mossberg 50-caliber rifle. He'd taken to it the same way, either-handed and cool-headed and pitch-perfect and fingers as nimble as air.

Finally Ham belched and tapped his chest and aimed the neck of his pouch at the baby in the Stetson.

"Sleeping like a gotdamn baby," he said.

Ingersoll went to his saddlebag, put his taterbug back and removed his spare dungaree shirt. He tucked it around the baby, whose breathing seemed shallow. "We need to get some milk fore long. Tomorrow."

Ham sighed. He pulled his legs in and stood. "You want first watch?"

Ingersoll slipped his thumb into the baby's hand and felt his fingers close around it. He waggled his thumb and admired the baby's fierce grip. "Yeah."

"Well, I'll turn in."

"All right."

Soon he was asleep and Ingersoll sat holding the hatful of baby in his lap. When the fire cracked out an ember that lay fizzing in the mud, the baby opened its eyes. It began to fuss and so he lifted it out and held it against his shoulder and started rocking, singing the one about the Corps men sandbagging the levee: "I work on the levee, mama, both night and day. I works so hard to keep the water away, he sang. It's a mean old levee, cause me to weep and moan. Gotta leave my baby, and my happy home."

THE FIRST HOMESTEAD they came to the next morning was deserted—aback their horses, through the busted door, they saw standing water and a rat swimming in a lazy circle. Ingersoll was anxious. During the night he'd dreamed about riding up a grassy hill crowned with a sweet olive tree and finding tethered to it a massively uddered milk cow, and he admitted now to himself that he didn't give a damn about finding the saboteurs unless they were running a dairy. The baby had been feasted upon in the night by mosquitoes and bore the bites stoically. It didn't cry and felt hot. Riding, Ingersoll kept touching its head.

The next place they came upon seemed as deserted as the first. It was a stone building with slotted windows. Essentially a small fort, bearded along its bottom in green mold. Nothing moved.

But Ham said, "Wait."

Ingersoll shifted the baby behind him and raised his sixteen gauge toward the windows.

Ham was already off his horse and standing against the wall with rifle ready. He spun and kicked in the log door. Ingersoll was on the ground using his horse for cover. He'd put the baby behind him and it was starting to fuss.

"Come on in," Ham called to him.

Ingersoll blocked the baby with his body as he sidewindered up. He trailed his single-barrel in the room and followed his partner's gaze to four people crouched in the corner. They were thin, white, dressed in rags. Three were men and one, behind them, a stringy-haired woman. The room smelled like piss. There wasn't a stick of furniture. Only a big washpot and the remains of a fire in a dugout fireplace. They weren't saboteurs, or even looters, but Ham eyed them warily. The baby was crying in a raspy way.

Then the girl stepped forward. "Can I hold it?"

She was skinny but her breasts were enormous under her tattered housedress. They were wet at the nipples.

"What the hell?" Ham glanced at Ingersoll.

"Here." Ingersoll offered her the baby.

She took it and turned her back to them and the baby's squall muffled for a second and then ceased, replaced by wet sucking sounds. She stood, rocking from side to side.

"Oh." Ham grinned and lowered his weapon.

"You can put yours away, too, son," one of the men said to Ingersoll. "We ain't got no guns. All we got is sticks."

Another of the men raised his, a pathetic cane.

Ingersoll slid his shotgun into his boot holster.

"What's your all's story?" Ham asked the oldest-looking of the men, though in truth you couldn't tell how old (or how young) any of them were.

"Our story?" The man looked around. He flung out his arms. "Here it is. Me." He pointed. "Him. Him. Her. This place that used to be a farm. Forty days and nights of rain, no goddamn ark. Near six days spent on the roof with a bellowing coon dog till we ate it. Then suddenly appear a baby and two maniacs with guns. That's our story."

"What happened to her youngun?" Ingersoll asked, nodding to the girl.

She stiffened and looked at him over her shoulder.

"It died," one of the men said.

"How."

He looked down.

"The way babies die," the oldest man said. "In the middle of the night."

"Y'all been sucking her milk?" Ham asked.

The old man met his gaze. "It's worse sins than that when you're starving."

Ingersoll and Ham exchanged a glance.

"I expect it is," Ham said.

Ingersoll looked at the girl. She just rocked with her eyes closed as the baby's hand climbed her neck and hooked a finger in her lip.

"Who're y'all?" another of the men asked.

"We ain't nobody you need to worry about," Ham said.

"Is anybody coming to help us down here? Is anybody sending food?"

Ingersoll shook his head. "Just to the camps in Greenville. Y'all should head over there. They're giving tents and food and seventy-five cents a day to levee repairers."

"We ain't leaving," the old man said.

"Suit yourself," Ham told him. "But the next party through might not be so kind as we are."

It was decided they'd leave the baby with the girl. They also left matches, sugar, lard and jerked beef, which the men fell upon instantly.

"Don't eat too fast," Ham said. "You'll produce it right back."

The girl didn't want any. Ingersoll studied her and she smiled and revealed a row of small, even teeth.

"What's your name?" he asked.

"Dixie Clay."

"You okay, Dixie Clay?"

She didn't answer.

"She's fine," the younger man said.

"Let's skedaddle," Ham said to Ingersoll. He touched the brim of his derby with his rifle barrel and turned for the door.

Ingersoll watched the girl. For a moment she seemed to lean in his direction, her eyes intensified at him, until the young man stepped in front of her.

"Thank you for your kindness," he said.

"I'll be back," Ingersoll said. "To check on that baby."

HE WAS QUIET as they walked their horses side by side, though Ham kept trying to provoke him.

"I read water poured through the Mounds Landing crevasse harder than Niagara. Did you know that?"

"No."

"True. Three-quarters mile crevasse, and near three hundred levee workers swept clean away right then and there. Unless newspapers lie."

"Some do."

"Could be our saboteurs made that breach," Ham said.

Ingersoll didn't answer. He kept seeing the girl's eyes and how tightly she held the baby to her chest.

It was growing dark and Ham said this looked like a good spot to camp, didn't it, pretty dry. They dismounted and Ham sat on his roll and tugged at his boots, which slurped free. He peeled down his socks and sat looking at his toes, wrinkled and mushroomed.

Ingersoll took off his hat and set it on the ground beside him. How empty it seemed. Ham produced two cans of beans and his opener as Ingersoll turned the pegs, played a lick, tuned it again.

Then he put it down and looked up into the night. "I'm tired of never seeing no stars," he said.

"Just be glad it ain't raining. You gone play?"

"Not right now."

Ham set the cans of beans in the fire to warm and they'd just begun to bubble at the top when he sat alert and laid his hand on his .30-30. Ingersoll had heard it too, dried mud crunching, and they rolled away from the fire on their bellies, aiming into the dark.

"Don't shoot. I got the baby."

"Oh for Christ sake." Ham spat into the dark.

Dixie Clay stepped forward into the firelight. She was clutching the baby, and she was bleeding across the forehead some.

"We nearly blew your fool head off," Ham said, pushing to his feet. "And for making me spill my mescal, you'd a deserved it."

Dixie Clay looked at Ingersoll, rising himself.

"You okay?" he asked.

"Yeah."

"They following you?"

"No. I don't think so."

"They will," Ham said.

"The baby," she said, "the baby wasn't safe there. With them."

Ingersoll looked at Ham, who didn't meet his eyes and sat down before the fire. He commenced to scraping mud from his book with a stick.

Ingersoll waited for her to say more, but she didn't. "They eat your baby?" he asked at last.

She lowered her head.

"Girl? I asked you a question. If you don't answer I'm gone send you right back to 'em."

"Yeah."

"Yeah?"

"Yeah. They eat her. She was dead already and they said we had to or they'd starve."

"But they won't eat this one," Ham said. "They got food now. We gave 'em some."

She hugged the baby higher on her chest. It was still wrapped in Ingersoll's shirt.

"Well?" Ham demanded.

She was looking at Ingersoll. "Something's wrong with them. Something went wrong."

Ham resumed scraping mud from his boot heel.

"Sit down," Ingersoll said to the girl, and pointed to his roll. She sank onto it still holding the baby. It gave an enormous yawn. Its color was better.

He opened his pack and offered her an apple.

"No, thank you."

But he tossed it anyway and she caught it with one hand without disturbing the baby.

"Eat it, girl. Otherwise you and this little one both gonna die and all for nothing."

She took a bite and chewed and looked at the baby in her arms and looked back up. "What's gonna happen to us?"

Ingersoll wondered the same thing.

WHEN INGERSOLL WOKE the next morning, Ham had already put coffee on and was pissing into a mud puddle fifty yards off. Ingersoll looked across the ashen coals where he'd lain out his bedding for the girl. She'd slept with the baby nestled against her, and in the dawn light he saw where some of her blood had crusted on the baby's cheek. For the first time he wondered what its name was.

Ingersoll rose quietly and stretched and filled their tin cups with coffee and went to where Ham was loading the saddlebag.

"Obliged," Ham said.

They stood together facing the lip of sun pushing itself over the flat brown world, glazing the mud puddles like copper ingots.

Ham sipped his coffee and studied his partner. "What the hell are you about to do?"

"I don't know."

"Yes you do."

"I can't leave 'em."

"Yes you can."

"No I can't, Ham."

"You've connected 'em and saved that damn baby's life. At some point you just have to do your job. Our job."

Ingersoll stood silent, watching the sunrise.

"Shit," Ham said. He flung his coffee into the mud.

"Just tell 'em I'm dead. When you get back."

Ham sighed. "That won't even be no lie," he said. "It's what you call a self-fulfilling prophecy. If the looters don't get you, or the saboteurs, ole Coolidge will. You done seen too much."

"Just do what you have to."

"I will, Ing. Got damn it."

They shook hands and looked for a long moment into one another's eyes. Ingersoll couldn't see a thing in Ham's and wondered what Ham saw in his own. For the first time it occurred to Ingersoll that if Ham killed him now he'd merely be doing his job. But instead Ham nodded and turned away and Ingersoll turned too with his coffee and went to nudge the coals.

The girl's face had relaxed from its fear and he watched her sleep. She was pretty under the dirt and the blood, freckles on her up-turned nose and brown hair that she could probably fix nice if she wanted. The baby was sleeping too, its mouth slack around her nipple, a trace of watery milk on its tongue. He stood and turned to gaze across the cracked leather earth to where Ham was cinching the girth on his horse.

"Last chance," Ham called. He kicked the flap of his boot sole down and swung into the saddle, grinning. "Russian girls can smoke a cigarette with they virginias. They let you do 'em up the chute if you pay 'em five more dollars."

"Naw," Ingersoll said, grinning too, and raised his hand, and Ham raised his back and then turned and rode away, the sorrel kicking up arcs of mud behind him.

When Dixie Clay woke he doctored her head a little while she licked her thumb and rubbed some of the dirt and dried blood from the baby's cheeks. He told her about Ham leaving and then turned his attention to heating another can of beans so she could nurse. He sang as he stirred, a tune of nonsense, swimming with bowlegged women, the words not making sense but neither were his feelings.

THEY WERE ABACK HIS HORSE, the girl before him on the saddle, holding the baby, and they were headed west. The sun was out and the earth drier, trees on the horizon. Dixie Clay said she was two months shy of eighteen. One of them back there had been her husband.

"Which one?"

"The one with the different colored eyes."

"What was his name?"

She paused. "I'll say it just this one more time. But don't never ask me again, okay?"

"Okay."

"Jesse Swan Holliver." She brushed away a mosquito from the baby's forehead. Then she turned her head to look up at him. "I'm better off now."

A little while later, facing forward in the saddle, she said it again. "I'm better off now."

He rode on, thinking, as she slept within the cage his arms made. He remembered killing the looters in the house in Leland. Killing the baby's mother. She'd had a gold-plated forty-five caliber pistol and she was fixing to shoot him. Instead he shot her. Now in his imagination he shot her again. He shot her and then the man she'd been with and the one before him and the saboteurs in Marked Tree and the Krauts on the Flemish Coast and all the way back through his life of murder and mandolining. He probably should have shot Dixie Clay's husband and the other two, and might come to regret not doing so. But it was not yet noon and already he'd carried them fifteen miles farther west from the river and closer to land where you could see some stars. Even the horse seemed spry, its head high and pace quickening despite the heavier load.

The girl nodded in the saddle as she slept. He thought about the Memphis Minnie song, "Going to Chicago, Sorry but I can't take you." He sang it softly to himself and Dixie Clay opened her eyes.

"You gone leave me?" She sat up and turned to look into his face.

He could smell her sour sleep breath, his chest warm from where her back had rested.

"It don't look like it," he said.

She reached to where his hand lay over the pommel and wove her fingers through his. He wondered if she noticed how calloused he was. He wondered was it too late to unlearn being good at certain things with your hands. He wondered about the tiny half-moon scar on her lip that shone white when she smiled as she was doing now. He had time to find out.

He looked into her lap where she held the baby, his eyelids jerking in sleep, but his breath was easy, his lungs puffing, and

Ingersoll knew they were tiny bellows that would play the rest of his days.

"He's dreaming," she said.

"Yeah," he said, "he must be."

Suzanne Hudson

Suzanne Hudson won an international prize for short fiction in a contest whose judges included Kurt Vonnegut, Jr. and Toni Morrison. Then she withdrew from the publishing world. Over twenty years later, however, a short story collection, *Opposable Thumbs*, was published and was a finalist for the John Gardner Fiction Book Award. She has since had short stories in *Stories from the Blue Moon Café*, volumes I, II, and IV; *The Alumni Grill*; *Climbing Mt. Cheaha*; *A Kudzu Christmas*; *Christmas Stories From the South's Best Writers*; and *A State of Laughter*. Her first novel, *In a Temple of Trees*, and her second novel, *In the Dark of the Moon*, have both been released in paperback. Her current book is a genre-bent fictional nonfiction one, *Second Sluthood: A Manifesto for the Postmenopausal, Pre-Senilic Matriarch* by Ruby Pearl Saffire. She lives at the Waterhole Branch Art Project near Fairhope, Alabama, with author Joe Formichella.

> *Opposable Thumbs*
> *In a Temple of Trees*
> *In the Dark of the Moon*
> *Second Sluthood: A Manifesto for the Postmenopausal, Pre-senilic Matriarch*

David Sheffield

David Sheffield is a Mississippi writer whose credits include *Saturday Night Live* and the screenplays for *Coming to America* and *The Nutty Professor*. He and his wife, Cynthia Ward Walker, live on a farm in Ovett, Mississippi, where they keep four horses, three dogs, and each other company.

Ace Atkins

Ace Atkins, a former journalist, has written eight novels. His writing career began at twenty-eight, when *Crossroad Blues*, the first of four Nick Travers novels, was published. In 2001, he earned a Pulitzer Prize nomination for his investigation into a 1950s murder that inspired his 2006 novel, *White Shadow*. In 2008, he published *Wicked City*, also based on a true story from the 50s and set in the author's native Alabama. His latest book, *Infamous*, was published in 2010. He lives outside Oxford, Mississippi.

> | | |
> |---|---|
> | *Crossroad Blues* | *Wicked City* |
> | *Leavin' Trunk Blues* | *Devil's Garden* |
> | *Dark End of the Street* | *Infamous* |
> | *Dirty South* | *New Orleans Noid* |
> | *White Shadow* | *In the Wake of Katrina* |

Alice Jackson

Alice Jackson is a veteran journalist who has reported on crime, politics and public corruption for newspapers, television and magazines, including *Time*, *People* and the *New York Times*. During the 1990s, her investigative reporting of questionable land deals and government bond issues led to the indictment and prosecution of a prominent Mississippi politician and resulted in the return of millions of dollars from off-shore bank accounts to taxpayer coffers. During more than 30 years of news assignments, she traveled her adopted state from the Mississippi Delta to the Mississippi Gulf Coast. She resided on the shores of the Mississippi Sound, near the coastal arts community of Ocean Springs, until Hurricane Katrina destroyed her home in 2005. "Cuttin' Heads" is her fiction debut.

Bill Fitzhugh

Bill Fitzhugh is the award-winning author of eight satiric crime novels. The New York Times called him "a strange and deadly amalgam of screenwriter and comic novelist. His facility and wit, and his taste for the perverse, put him in a league with Carl Hiaasen and Elmore Leonard." Warner Brothers and Universal Studios bought the film rights to his novels *Pest Control* and *Cross Dressing*, respectively. *Pest Control* was produced as a radio series in Germany by Deutschland Radio and as a stage musical by Open at The Top Theatre Company at the NoHo Arts Center in Los Angeles. Reviewing *Highway 61 Resurfaced, Time Magazine* said, "Fitzhugh's dialogue is as cool as a pitcher of iced tea, and his characters are just over the top, like a Carl Hiaasen cast plucked from the Everglades and planted, as Dylan would put it, out on Highway 61." His novels have been translated into German, Japanese, Italian, and Spanish. Fitzhugh also writes, produces, and hosts a show on Sirius-XM's Deep Tracks channel called "Fitzhugh's All Hand Mixed Vinyl." He is a member of the Southern California Chapter of Mystery Writers of America. He lives in Los Angeles with his wife, two dogs, and a cat named Crusty Boogers.

Pest Control	*Heart Seizure*
The Organ Grinders	*Radio Activity*
Cross Dressing	*Highway 61 Resurfaced*
Fender Benders	*The Adventures of Slim and Howdy*

James Lee Burke

James Lee Burke is the recipient of the 2009 Mystery Writers of American Grand Master Award and he has also been honored with two Edgar Awards for Best Crime Novel of the Year. He grew up on the Louisiana-Texas coast and has worked as a pipeliner, land surveyor, social worker, newspaper reporter, U.S. Forest service employee and university professor. He wrote and published his first novel, *Half of Paradise*, by the age of twenty-three. He's published twenty-eight novels and two short story collections. He also managed to go thirteen years during the middle of his career without publishing a novel in hardback. During that period, his novel *The Lost Get-Back Boogie* received over 100 editorial rejections. Later, after it was published with Louisiana State University

Press, it was nominated for a Pulitzer Prize. He is both a Breadloaf and Guggenheim fellow and has been a recipient of an NEA grant. Three of his novels have been adapted as motion pictures. He and his wife, Pearl, have four children and divide their time between Missoula, Montana, and New Iberia, Louisiana.

Half of Paradise	*Cimarron Rose*
To the Bright and Shining Sun	*Sunset Limited*
Lay Down My Sword and Sheild	*Heartwood*
Two for Texas	*Purple Cain Road*
The Convict and Other Stories	*Bitterroot*
The Lost Get Back Boogie	*Jolie Blon's Bounce*
The Neon Rain	*White Doves at Morning*
Heaven's Prisoners	*Last Car to Elysian Fields*
Black Cherry Blues	*In the Moon of Red Ponies*
A Morning for Flamingos	*Crusader's Cross*
A Stained White Radiance	*Pegasus Descending*
In the Electric Mist with	*Jesus Out to Sea*
Confederate Dead	*The Tin Roof Blowdown*
Dixie City Jam	*Swan Peak*
Burning Angel	*Rain Gods*
Cadillac Jukebox	

Dean James

Dean James is a seventh-generation Mississippi long transplanted to Texas. He grew up on a farm near Grenada, often visited relatives living in the Delta, and earned two degrees from Delta State University. He has published numerous mystery short stories and has co-authored a number of award-winning works of mystery non-fiction. Writing under his own name and two pseudonyms—Jimmie Ruth Evans and Honor Hartman— he has published fourteen mystery novels. He currently works as a librarian in the Texas Medical Center and likes to spend time thinking of interesting ways to kill people.

Cruel as the Grave	*The Dick Francis Companion*
Closer than the Bones	*The Robert B. Parker Companion*
Posted to Death	As Jimmie Ruth Evans:
Faked to Death	*Flamingo Fatale*
Decorated to Death	*Murder Over Easy*
Baked to Death	*Best Served Cold*
Death Dines In	*Bring Your Own Poison*
Death by Dissertation	*Leftover Dead*
By a Woman's Hand: A Guide to	As Honor Hartman:
Mystery Fiction by Women	*On the Slam*
Killer Books: A Reader's Guide to	*The Unkindest Cut*
Exploring the Popular World of	
Mystery and Suspense	

Nathan Singer

Nathan Singer is a novelist, playwright, musician, and experimental performing artist from Cincinnati, Ohio. He is the author of the critically acclaimed novels *A Prayer for Dawn*, *Chasing the Wolf*, and *In the Light of You*, as well as numerous plays including the stage adaption of *Chasing the Wolf*. His work has appeared in several anthologies such as 2007's *Expletive Deleted*. He teaches writing at Northern Kentucky University and the University of Cincinnati and is currently at work on a multitude of new projects.

A Prayer for Dawn
Chasing the Wolf
In the Light of You

Suzann Ellingsworth

Suzann Ellingsworth is an insatiable history buff fascinated by hoboes, tramps, the Dillinger era, and its music. Suzann memorized the lyrics to Cab Calloway's recordings of "Minnie the Moocher" and "St. James Infirmary" by second grade, though then, as now, she can't carry a tune in a tow sack. Suzann's father often said he drove bootleg whiskey across Mississippi during Prohibition. Since his car's speedometer seldom topped 35 m.p.h., Suzann was highly skeptical of that claim, and will forever wish she'd questioned him further when she had the chance. The story, "Songbyrd Dead at 23," is dedicated to the memory of the South's (probably) slowest bootlegger: Howard A. Rodgers.

Redemption Trail
Deliverance Drive
Colorado Reverie
Pure Justice
Klondike Fever
Trinity Strike
East of Peculiar
South of Sanity
North of Clever
West of Bliss
A Lady Never Trifles With Thieves
In Hot Pursuit
Ahead of the Game
Deadly Housewives

Once a Thief
Halfway to Half Way
Let Sleeping Dogs Lie
Nellie Cashman: Prospector and Trailblazer
Shady Ladies: Nineteen Surprising and Rebellious American Women
The Toast Always Lands Jelly-Side Down: And Other Tales of Suburban Life
I Have Everything I Had Twenty Years Ago, Except Now It's All Lower

Michael Lister

Michael Lister is a novelist, essayist, and playwright who lives in northwest Florida. A former prison chaplain, Michael is the author of the "Blood" series featuring prison chaplain/detective, John Jordan (*Blood of the Lamb*, *Blood Money*, *The Body and the Blood*, etc.). His second series features Jimmy

"Soldier" Riley, a PI in Panama City during Word War II (www.Flori-daNoir.com). In addition to fiction, Michael writes two columns, River Readings (www.RiverReadings.com), chronicling his search for wisdom and meaning, and Of Font and Film (www.OfFontandFilm.com), reviews of film and fiction. Michael's latest novel, *Double Exposure*, is a literary thriller set in the North Florida pine flats and river swamps along the Apalachicola River. When Michael isn't writing, he teaches college, operates a charity and community theater. His website is www.MichaelLister.com

Power in the Blood	*Double Exposure*
Blood of the Lamb	*Thunder Beach*
Flesh and Blood	*Florida Heat Wave*

Lynne Barrett

Lynne Barrett , Edgar Award winner for best mystery short story, is the au-thor of *The Secret Names of Women* and *The Land of Go*, and co-editor of *Birth: A Literary Companion* and *The James M. Cain Cookbook, Guide to Home Singing, Physical Fitness and Animals (Especially Cats)*. Her stories ap-pear in *One Year to a Writing Life*, *A Hell of A Woman*, *Miami Noir*, *A Dixie Christmas*, and many other anthologies and magazines. For more informa-tion, see www.http://lynne.barrett.googlepages.com . She is grateful for the generous assistance of John Connaway of the Mississippi Department of Archives and History, who is in no way responsible for any inaccuracies or misbehavior by her story's fictional archaeologists.

The Secret Names of Women	*The James M. Cain Cookbook, Guide*
The Land of Go	*to Home Singing, Physical Fitness*
Birth: A Literary Companion	*and Animals (Especially Cats)*

Charlaine Harris

Charlaine Harris was born in Mississippi and lives in southern Arkansas with her husband and daughter and three dogs. Their sons are out of the nest. In her years as a published writer, she's written four series and two stand-alones, plus numerous short stories. Her Sookie Stackhouse books have appeared in twenty different languages and on many best-seller lists. They're also the basis of the number one HBO show *True Blood*, produced by Alan Ball (*Six Feet Under*). An avid reader of genre literature, Charlaine is deeply involved in the life of the small town where she and her family live. You can visit Charlaine online at her website www.charlaineharris.com

Sookie Stackhouse Series

Dead in the Family	*Definitely Dead*
Dead and Gone	*Dead as a Doornail*
From Dead To Worse	*Dead to the World*
All Together Dead	*Club Dead*

Living Dead in Dallas
Dead Until
A Touch of Dead (Sookie short story collection)

Aurora Teagarden Series
Poppy Done to Death
Last Scene Alive
A Fool and His Honey
Dead Over Heels
The Julius House
Three Bedrooms, One Corpse
A Bone to Pick
Real Murders

Lily Bard Shakespeare Series
Shakespeare's Counselor
Shakespeare's Trollop
Shakespeare's Christmas
Shakespeare's Champion
Shakespeare's Landlord

Harper Connelly Series
Grave Secret
An Ice Cold
Grave Surprise
Grave Sight

Non-Series
A Secret Rage
Crimes by Moonlight
Sweet and Deadly
Wolfsbane and Mistletoe
Death's Excellent Vacation
Must Love Hellhounds

Toni L.P. Kelner

Toni L.P. Kelner believes in trying new things, which explains "A Man Feeling Bad," her first private eye story as well as her first noir story. She also believes in multi-tasking. *Who Killed the Pinup Queen?*, her second "Where are they Now?" mystery, was released in January, and *Death's Excellent Vacation*, her third urban fantasy anthology co-edited with Charlaine Harris, is due out in August. Previous work includes nine novels, two anthologies, and numerous short stories. She's won a Romantic Times Career Achievement Award and an Agatha Award, and has been nominated for two other Agathas, four Anthonys, and two Macavity awards. Kelner lives north of Boston with her husband, author Stephen Kelner; two daughters; and two guinea pigs.

Laura Fleming Series
  Down Home Murder
  Dead Ringer
  *Trouble Looking for a Place
    to Happen*
  Country Comes to Town
  Tight as a Tick
  Death of a Damn Yankee
  Mad as the Dickens

Wed and Buried
Where are they Now? Series
  Curse of the Kissing Cousins
  Who Killed the Pinup Queen?
Anthologies
  Many Bloody Returns
  Wolfsbane and Mistletoe
  Death's Excellent Vacation

Daniel Martine

Daniel Martine is an actor, writer, musician and film producer who has worked in the film industry for over twenty years. He has been published in numerous magazines and periodicals. Daniel is a partner and co-founder of Cinema Pacifica Entertainment, Inc. and Cinepac Films, Inc., a Latino-oriented film production company based in Santa Barbara, California. He is currently writing and developing three projects for future feature release for the company. Well traveled, Daniel now resides in Memphis, Tennessee, and travels frequently to Santa Barbara, California.

Mary Saums

Mary Saums worked as a recording engineer in her youth in Muscle Shoals on albums by Bob Dylan, Roy Orbison, Jimmy Buffett and many other fine artists. Her first novel, Midnight Hour, was the first in a mystery series set in Nashville. Her poem "The Blues Reminds Me" was chosen by Nikki Giovanni for a Tennessee Writers Alliance award. The first book in her new series, *Thistle & Twig*, was a finalist for the 2008 SIBA Award for Fiction. Mary currently serves as a national officer of Sisters In Crime and as vice-president of the Southeast chapter of Mystery Writers of America.

Midnight Hour	*The Valley of Jewels*
When the Last Magnolia Weeps	*Thistle & Twig*

Carolyn Haines

Carolyn Haines is a 2009 recipient of the Richard Wright Award for Literary Excellence and will be awarded the 2010 Harper Lee Distinguished Writing Award in May. She is also a past recipient of an Alabama State Arts Council writing fellowship. Her Sarah Booth Delaney mysteries, set in the Mississippi Delta, as well as her darker fiction such as *Penumbra, Touched*, and *Summer of the Redeemers* reflect her great love of and passion for her home state of Mississippi. Born in Lucedale, she was a journalist for ten years before turning to fiction. She is an avid worker for animal rights and lives on a farm with 21 critters—equine, feline and canine—all of them smarter than she is. She is an assistant professor of English and Fiction Coordinator at the University of South Alabama where she teaches the graduate and undergraduate fiction classes. For more information, go to www.carolynhaines.com

Sarah Booth Delaney Mysteries	*Splintered Bones*
Bone Appetit	*Buried Bones*
Greedy Bones	*Them Bones*
Wishbones	
Ham Bones	Novels
Bones to Pick	*Revenant*
Hallowed Bones	*Fever Moon*
Crossed Bones	*Penumbra*

Judas Burning
Touched
Summer of the Redeemers
Summer of Fear

Non-fiction
My Mother's Witness:
 The Peggy Morgan Story

Les Standiford

Les Standiford is the author of fifteen books, including the novels *Spill* and the John Deal series set in the Miami and Key West area and four critically acclaimed works of non-fiction including 2008's *The Man Who Invented Christmas: How Charles Dickens's A Christmas Carol Rescued His Career and Revived Our Holiday Spirits. Last Train to Paradise* was one of the History Channel's Top Ten picks and was read coast to coast by Dick Estell, NPR's "Radio Reader." Booklist called John Deal, Standiford's recurring series character, "the most emotionally centered protagonist in crime fiction today," and the *New York Times* has said of his suspense writing, "each scene is like a little gasp for breath." He edited and contributed to *The Putt at the End of the World* and edited the anthology of crime fiction *Miami Noir*. He also authored one of the chapters in the national best-selling satire, *Naked Came the Manatee* with Dave Barry, Carl Hiaasen and others. He has received the Barnes & Noble Discover Great New Writers Award, the Frank O'Connor Award for Short Fiction, and Fellowships from the National Endowment for the Arts and the National Endowment for the Humanities. A native Ohioan, he is a Professor of English and Director of the Creative Writing Program at Florida International University in Miami, where he lives with his wife Kimberly, a psychotherapist, and their three children, Jeremy, Hannah, and Alexander. Visit Les's website at www.les-standiford.com & his blog: www.grandstandifordstation.blogspot.com

Done Deal
Raw Deal
Deal to Die For
Deal on Ice
Presidential Deal
Black Mountain
Deal with the Dead
Bone Key
Havana Run
Spill
Miami Noir
The Putt at the End of the World
Opening Day
Miami: City of Dreams

The Man Who Invented Christmas:
 How Charles Dickens's A Christ-
 mas Carol Rescued His Career and
 Revived Our Holiday Spirits
Last Train to Paradise: Henry Flagler
 and the Spectacular Rise and Fall
 of the Railroad that Crossed an
 Ocean
Meet You in Hell: Andrew Carnegie,
 Henry Clay Frick, and the Bitter
 Partnership that Changed America
Washington Burning: How a French-
 man's Vision for Our Nation's
 Capital Survived Congress, the
 Founding Fathers, and the Invad-
 ing British Army

John Grisham

John Grisham is the author of twenty-two bestselling novels, many of them dealing with the law. A graduate of the University of Mississippi Law School in Oxford, Mississippi, John was born in Jonesboro, Arkansas, but grew up in Southaven, Mississippi. He was admitted to the State Bar of Mississippi in 1981 and practiced in Southaven until 1990. He was elected to the Mississippi House of Representatives in 1983 and served until 1990. During that time he was vice-chairman of the Committee on Apportionment and Elections. He also served as a member of the State Democratic Executive Committee from 1988 to 1990. Many of his books have been adapted for the screen. His first novel, *A Time to Kill*, was published in 1989, and his latest novel, *The Associate*, was published in 2009.

A Time to Kill	*Skipping Christmas*
The Firm	*The Summons*
The Pelican Brief	*The King of Torts*
The Client	*Bleachers*
The Chamber	*The Last Juror*
The Rainmaker	*The Broker*
The Runaway Jury	*The Innocent Man*
The Partner	*Playing for Pizza*
The Street Lawyer	*The Appeal*
The Testament	*The Associate*
The Brethren	*Ford County*
A Painted House	

Tom Franklin

Tom Franklin, from Dickinson, Alabama, is the author of *Poachers*, a collection of stories, and the novels *Hell at the Breech* and *Smonk*, all published by William Morrow. A 2001 Guggenheim Fellow, his stories have been reprinted in *New Stories from the South*, *Best American Mystery Stories of the Century* and *Best American Noir Stories of the Century*. He teaches at Ole Miss and lives in Oxford, MS, with his wife, poet Beth Ann Fennelly, and their children.

Poachers	*Hell at the Breech*	*Smonk*

Beth Ann Fennelly

Beth Ann Fennelly is an Assoc. Professor at the University of Mississippi. She's published three books of poetry and a book of nonfiction, all with W. W. Norton. She's the recipient of grants and awards from the National Endowment of Arts, the United States Artists, a Pushcart, and a Fulbright to Brazil. Her work has three times been included in *The Best American Poetry* Series.

Open House	*Tender Hooks*
Great with Child: Letters to a Young Mother	
Unmentionables	

Carolyn Haines

Carolyn Haines is a 2009 recipient of the Richard Wright Award for Literary Excellence and will be awarded the 2010 Harper Lee Distinguished Writing Award in May. She is also a past recipient of an Alabama State Arts Council writing fellowship. Her Sarah Booth Delaney mysteries, set in the Mississippi Delta, as well as her darker fiction such as *Penumbra*, *Touched*, and *Summer of the Redeemers* reflect her great love of and passion for her home state of Mississippi. Born in Lucedale, she was a journalist for ten years before turning to fiction. She is an avid worker for animal rights and lives on a farm with 21 critters—equine, feline and canine—all of them smarter than she is. She is an assistant professor of English and Fiction Coordinator at the University of South Alabama where she teaches the graduate and undergraduate fiction classes. For more information, go to www.carolynhaines.com